DISCARD

AT THE COFFEE SHOP OF CURIOSITIES

HEATHER WEBBER

TOR PUBLISHING GROUP
NEW YORK

AT THE COFFEE SHOP OF CURIOSITIES

A Forge Book
Published by Tom Doherty Associates / Tor Publishing Group
120 Broadway
New York, NY 10271

www.tor-forge.com

Forge® is a registered trademark of Macmillan Publishing Group, LLC.

The Library of Congress Cataloging-in-Publication Data
is available upon request.

ISBN 978-1-250-86726-1 (hardcover)
ISBN 978-1-250-86728-5 (ebook)

Our books may be purchased in bulk for promotional, educational, or business use. Please contact your local bookseller or the Macmillan Corporate and Premium Sales Department at 1-800-221-7945, extension 5442, or by email at MacmillanSpecialMarkets@macmillan.com.

First Edition: 2023

Printed in the United States of America

0 9 8 7 6 5 4 3 2 1

*This book is for all those who yearn
to spread their wings and fly.*

AT THE
COFFEE SHOP
OF CURIOSITIES

Ava,

Chin up, buttercup. Everything you've always wanted is only one job interview away. Use your wings to take a chance. Be yourself and it'll all be okay. You'll be happy in Driftwood. xx

HELP WANTED

Patient, energetic, unflappable in-home caretaker wanted for a peculiar, stubborn old man; a spoiled, she-devil cat; and a cluttered, possibly haunted beach house. No experience necessary but preferred skills include strong organizational and housekeeping abilities and an indifference to sharing space with a ghost, chaos, cat hair, dust, birds in the attic - or bats in the belfry as the case may more aptly be. Apply at your own risk on Monday morning, 9 AM, at Magpie's coffee shop in Driftwood, Alabama. Ask for the plum-tuckered Maggie.

CHAPTER 1

AVA

The letter had been sent by a dead man.

There was no doubt in my mind.

Fine. There was a *little* doubt. Okay, a lot of doubt. Buckets of it.

But after thirteen long hours in the car during which I'd thought of very little else, I couldn't come up with anyone else who might have sent the note. Not one single person, other than Alexander Bryant, who'd died exactly a month ago yesterday.

Yesterday also happened to be when a late-summer breeze blew through my apartment's kitchen window and caused an unassuming envelope to fall from the thin stack of this week's mail on the countertop. The letter had drifted steadily downward, soundlessly landing at my feet while I'd been washing dishes.

The strange thing was I didn't remember receiving the letter. I didn't get much mail, so it should've stood out to me. But I had no recollection of the crisp kraft brown paper envelope that had no return address. Or the way my name and address had been hand-printed in neat letters that almost looked machine-produced except for the unevenness of the blue ink. I definitely didn't remember the butterfly stamp in the upper right corner of the envelope, the colorful sticker unmarred by an adjacent postmark too smudged to read.

Now, as I rolled to a stop at a traffic light, waiting to turn left down a road lined with palm trees that swayed in the breeze, I thought it *extremely* odd I'd not noticed the stamp. Usually, all things animal-related captured my attention. But I had to admit that life had been a bit of a blur since Alex had passed away. My mind had been elsewhere, tangled up in a guilty net of what-ifs and should-haves.

"Are you sure this is the best job choice for you?"

My mother's voice drifted through the car's sound system, her concern crisp and clear.

"Only one way to find out," I said, adjusting the volume on the Bluetooth system. Her sharp worried tones made my ears ache.

"Ava," she said on a sigh. "I know you've been a little lost this past month, but this feels rash. You've always worked a computer job from home, now suddenly you're applying to be a *caretaker*?"

I'd told her a little bit about the job I was applying for, but not all. I hadn't told her how the position had come to my attention. Or that the job was in Alabama. Or that I'd driven through the night to get here.

It didn't matter that I was twenty-seven years old—she'd have thrown a fit if she thought for a second I wasn't taking good care of myself.

I almost hadn't answered her call at all, but that would've only sent her into a blind panic. It was better to ease her fears now, get them out of the way.

I didn't want her worrying about me. She'd had a lifetime of that already. It was only in the last couple of years that she could breathe more easily, sleep better, and live a normal life without feeling like she always had to be on alert to keep me safe.

I didn't want to go back to what used to be.

"I think a change of pace will be good for me," I finally said. I swallowed hard. "Get me out of my comfort zone."

It was a gray morning, the sky filled with low-hanging clouds. Leftover rain droplets from a storm that had rolled through in the wee hours of the morning sat fat and sparkly on the edges of my bug-splattered windshield as I glanced at the dashboard clock: 8:38.

I drummed my fingers on the steering wheel, unable to stop thinking about the letter that had set this trip in motion.

Inside the envelope had been a wrinkled piece of paper, folded neatly in thirds. It was a typed help-wanted ad that looked to have been crumpled up at one point then smoothed out. At the top of it, someone had written me a note.

Someone.

Alex?

The short, scribbled message had several of my ex-boyfriend Alexander's earmarks. The cheesy buttercup line? That's exactly something he would say. He had a way of making old-timey phrases sound endearing. Plus, that double *x*? It's how he'd always signed off on his text messages. The handwriting could've been his, that slanting, masculine scrawl, but I didn't know for sure and didn't have anything to compare it to other than a belated birthday card he'd given me back in June. But that had only *xx Alex* handwritten on it. He'd been a nice guy but not overly sentimental and often forgetful—always too focused on the next thing to simply be present, to take notice, to just *be.*

That, honestly, was one of the many reasons I'd broken up with him after only three months of dating. We'd parted the same way we'd started—as friends—and made promises to stay that way. But he'd pushed those boundaries in the weeks after the breakup. And then he was gone.

"All right, Ava," Mom said. "I'll let it go for now. What time is the interview?"

If the letter *had* come from Alex, why? How?

I let out a frustrated huff of air, my breath making a soft whistling sound, as if testing its wings in the unfamiliar humidity. I had a suspicion about a reason, but the *how* baffled me. I supposed it was possible he'd mailed the letter before he passed away. It could've been lost for a month in the mail system, then found and delivered recently. That kind of thing happened all the time. All. The. Time.

But . . .

Why send a letter? As someone who had his phone with him twenty-four/seven, why not just snap a picture of the want ad and text it to me? That seemed more like something Alexander would do. Snail mail was too old-school for him. Plus, why not put a return address on the envelope? Or sign the note? Also, it was only recently that I'd started looking for a new job—I hadn't needed one when he was still here—so how would he have known? It had been only two weeks since I was fired, unable to concentrate on much of anything in the aftermath of Alex's death.

"Ava?" Mom asked. "You still there?"

"I'm here. Just lost in thought."

"I asked what time the interview is," she said.

Without a doubt, the timing of that letter felt all kinds of un-explainable. Was it simply coincidence that the letter had fallen from the stack of mail the *day before* the job interview, giving me just enough time to get to Alabama? Never mind the strange manner in which it had floated to my feet. It was almost as if . . .

I could hardly allow myself to think that it looked like it had been taken out of the stack of mail by invisible hands and placed at my feet. Goose bumps popped up on my arms, and I rubbed them away. Ghosts weren't real. They *weren't*.

Were they?

Shaking my head, I finally settled on the letter being *mysterious*. That was all.

"Ava!"

My head jerked back at her shout. My ears rang. "It's at nine," I said quickly.

"You'll text me after?" she asked.

"I promise."

"All right, since you're so distracted, I'll let you go to concentrate on the road. I love you. Don't forget to text."

"I won't. I love you, too," I said, then disconnected the call and let out a deep breath.

I powered down the windows, letting the wind gust through the car. Immediately I picked up the scent of the sea in the air—a distinct briny smell that I recognized immediately even though I'd only been to the beach one other time in my life, on a family vacation to Florida when I was ten years old. The brief trip had been enough to fall in love with the water.

My blinker ticked steadily, the sound faint, nearly lost in the wind. Only a few miles back, I'd noticed dense fog sitting low along the shoreline. It masked any views of the gulf, but if I concentrated, blocking out the wind, the birdsong, the traffic noise, I could hear waves crashing against the beach, which somehow sounded both melodious and discordant, as if warning of dangerous surf while reminding that beauty could be found in chaos.

I wished I were standing at the water's edge now. I'd dance in the foamy surf. Maybe fling myself in the salty water, let it flow over me, shushing all other noises, wash away all my worries. Over the years, I'd pleaded for a return to the beach, only to be denied again and again, because that one trip had ended in an ambulance ride to the nearest hospital and a vow from my mother that it was the last time we traveled so far from our home in Cincinnati.

I should've returned to the beach after I moved out on my own, but I'd been too fearful to go alone, my mom's worries having become my own at some point.

I glanced at the clock: 8:40.

The red light finally gave way to a green arrow and I closed the windows to silence the noise. As I drove toward Driftwood, my stomach twisted with nerves. My mom was right. This felt rash. Why, after reading that letter, had I decided to throw caution to the wind by hurriedly packing, then jumping into my car to make the long drive to Alabama? All so I could *apply* for the job in the letter?

If there was anything I knew about myself, it was that Ava Laine Harrison didn't throw caution. Or do spontaneity. Or wild-goose chases, which this foray south suddenly felt like. I was used to staying in my comfort zone, surrounded by familiarity. Routine. Quiet.

Especially quiet.

Now here I was racing to Magpie's, a coffeehouse located in a cozy beachside community, so I could be interviewed for a dreadful-sounding job I wasn't sure I even wanted.

I didn't have a good reason why I was here. I only knew that

I *had* to do it. It was a feeling that beat so strongly within me that there was no denying it, even when I wanted nothing more than to turn the car around, head back north.

As I approached a picturesque tree-lined town square, I turned right, carefully navigating the one-way streets. I wanted to inch along, to take in every detail I could of my surroundings, to study every shop. But I kept going, my sights on the coffee-house, painted a pretty blue green, that I could see on the other side of the square. I threw a look at the clock: 8:44.

I made a left turn, then another as I searched for a parking spot and finally found an open space in between two golf carts not far from the coffee shop. I shut off the engine, grabbed my handbag, and jumped out of the car.

Walking as quickly as I could manage, I hurried along the brick sidewalk. However, as I neared Magpie's, my steps slowed. Then stopped. Now that I was here, it felt too early to go inside.

Unfamiliar noises swirled around me like a tornado of musical notes, some low, like the rustling of palm tree fronds, some sharp, like the enthusiastic squawk of a seagull—conflicting but somehow harmonious.

I was grateful for the harmony. It wasn't the norm. Then again, there wasn't much about my life that could be considered ordinary. I was hoping that would change here in Driftwood. After all, that was what the letter had inferred, wasn't it?

Everything you've always wanted is only one job interview away.

All I'd ever wanted—for as long as I could remember—was normalcy. I'd spent so much of my life tucked away, being kept safe and sound, that I didn't know how to be part of a bigger whole. I longed to live someplace where people would treat me the same as everyone else. A place where I was simply Ava and not someone to be pitied or judged blindly.

Being in Driftwood was about as far out of my comfort zone as I could wander, yet as I stood here, my nerves settled, calmed. It gave me hope that coming here hadn't been a big mistake.

So far, the small beachside town seemed perfectly normal.

Magpie's was one of two dozen businesses that comprised three sides of a square, each storefront painted a cheerful pastel color. On the fourth side, seemingly anchoring the town, stood a simple pearly white church topped with a bell tower and cross.

Sitting prettily in the center of the square was an oval green space. On one end of it two women sat on a blanket chatting as two young children kicked a red ball to one another, and on the other side of the lawn, a line dancing class was taking place with ten or so elderly participants.

As I watched the dancers scoot forward, then back, behind me came the sound of scuffling footsteps and the jingle of dog tags. I turned and saw a man and his dog walking along the sidewalk toward the coffee shop.

He was a big guy, broad and tall. The type of guy you'd expect to see with a Labrador, golden retriever, or German shepherd at his side—not a small cream-colored long-haired dachshund. The disparity amused me to no end.

Flashing me a distantly friendly smile, he said, "Good morning" as he used a hook on the storefront to secure the leash.

He had a nice voice, the timbre mellow with a hint of raspy.

With a quick rub of the dog's long, furry ears he said, "I'll be right back, Norman. *Stay.*"

The dog sat.

Norman? For some reason I'd expected the dog to be a girl with a name like Goldilocks or Godiva. He was just so . . . *pretty.* I sent him a silent apology for jumping to conclusions.

The man strode past me and pulled open the shop's wide glass door. Bells tinkled and the scent of freshly ground coffee beans wafted out of the shop, along with the dissonant strains of many voices, the clink of dishes, the whizzing of a grinder.

Using his shoulder to prop the door open, he regarded me with downturned eyes, dark brown with golden flecks. I was taken aback by the heartache I saw in their depths.

With thick eyebrows lifted in question, he said, "You goin' on in?"

I glanced at my watch: 8:49. It was too soon. I wasn't ready. "Not yet, thank you."

With a nod, he stepped into the shop. The door closed slowly behind him, but not before a hollow burst of a woman's laughter floated out, sounding so brittle that it might break. That *she* might break.

As if the dog had heard the woman, too, and was sympathizing, he made a guttural noise, low and staccato. I wouldn't call it a bark. It sounded more like it was half bark, half . . . quack. I immediately termed it a *quabark*. It was adorable. *He* was adorable.

"You're a handsome fellow," I said to him.

He blinked his sweet brown eyes.

Across the street came a burst of children's laughter, and Norman *quabark*ed again, as if wanting to join in the fun. Dozens of people roamed about, walking here, there, everywhere. Bicycles adorned with baskets rolled past, and people pulling wagons loaded with fishing gear headed toward the beach.

"This seems like a nice place to live," I said to Norman.

He tipped his head and I swore it looked like he was nodding. I started to wonder if I was dreaming. This couldn't possibly be real. Any of it. The mysterious letter. The out-of-character road trip. This delightful town, which looked postcard perfect despite gloomy skies. The beautiful, expressive dachshund.

To make sure my imagination hadn't gotten the best of me, I held my breath until I felt fit to explode, then gasped for air. Instead of waking up in my apartment in Cincinnati, I still stood in front of Magpie's, breathing in the salty air caught on a warm, whispering September breeze.

The line dancers grapevined left, then right, in rhythm to a bouncy country song. The little ones giggled as they mimicked— or mocked, I couldn't be sure from this distance—the dancers. A golf cart rolled into an empty parking spot in front of a breakfast diner across the square, its brakes squealing. Norman scratched his ear, making his tags jingle.

All this was absolutely real, or *surreal,* if I was calling it straight. There wasn't anything I could see or hear, near or far, that didn't feel absolutely enchanting. Even the gray clouds were puffed up with charm, edged in pale gold, as if an artist had watercolored their scalloped ridges.

Could I ever possibly fit in around here? Among all this perfection? Little imperfect me, who'd so often been called *weird* or *strange* because some people didn't know how to label something they didn't understand.

As slivers of sunshine poked through the clouds, light spilled across the coffee shop's aqua exterior. The unexpected brightness spotlighted an older woman sitting at a small table on the other side of a large picture window. With furrowed pencil-thin eyebrows lofted high, she peered at me, a hint of surprise in her steady gaze.

I returned the look, simply because I was spellbound by her attire. She wore a form-fitting black sequin gown that accentuated her overly curved spine and a black pillbox hat with a birdcage veil.

I offered the woman a hesitant smile. She responded by puckering her lips as though tasting something sour. Then she lifted her chin, sticking her nose up in the air, and turned her hunched back on me. The sequins on her dress shimmered in solidarity, as if bidding me a not-so-fond farewell, and I couldn't help the spark of hope that flashed through me.

"Perhaps this charming town does have a place for an odd-ball or two."

Norman's tail happily thumped the ground. I took that as complete agreement and suddenly I wanted to be part of this charming town more than anything. I needed to get this job.

I glanced at my watch again: 8:51. Almost time. I put my hand on my stomach in an attempt to settle the nerves that had come sneaking back. I could do this. I *could.*

Taking a moment to scan inwardly, I searched for any dire signs of distress and found none. I let out a breath of relief, wondering for the thousandth time—maybe the millionth—

when I would stop checking and accept that my body was healed.

The truth was that I'd probably never stop.

Self-screening for symptoms—warning signs—had been ingrained into me early. I had been only four years old when my life, my health, had taken a sharp turn on a road that offered no way back to what once was.

Outwardly, there was no hint that I'd ever been anything but healthy, except, perhaps, the dark bags under my eyes that I tried to hide with concealer. Truly, I hadn't slept a whole night through since Alexander had passed away. If I was being completely honest, I hadn't felt well since then, either, my grief and guilt affecting me physically as well as emotionally.

"Give it a little time," my mother had said, "but call a doctor if it gets worse. You don't want to take any chances."

So far time hadn't helped much at all. Yet I hesitated to call a doctor. I didn't really want to go down that dreaded road again.

Lost in my thoughts, I jumped in surprise when the door to the shop flew open and a beautiful older woman with long black hair ran out like her feet were on fire. She quickly disappeared around the corner, her hurried steps pounding against the sidewalk.

A moment later Norman's companion came out of the shop, carrying an iced coffee in a plastic cup and a paper dish full of whipped cream that he placed in front of the dog. Norman immediately set about lapping it up. The man took a pull from his straw as he waited for Norman to finish, then shifted on his feet, looking like he'd rather eat glass than make small talk with the stranger standing idly by.

Finally, he said, "Not from around here, are you?"

"That obvious?" I asked.

Thin gray clouds began to drift apart, revealing glimpses of cobalt-blue skies as he gave me a quick once-over. Then his gaze drifted toward my car—the only one parked nearby. My hatchback with its Ohio license plates screamed exactly how far I'd traveled to chase this particular wild goose.

"Not many wear wool around here, especially this time of year."

As a smile warmed his eyes and chased away the somberness, I guessed him to be in his early thirties. He wore a wrinkled short-sleeve button-down shirt patterned with miniature red crabs, and blue twill shorts. On his feet were well-worn boat shoes but no socks.

"I know it's a little out of place here at the beach, but it's my lucky blazer." I tugged at my vintage speckled purple jacket. It was an expensive piece that I'd found on a Goodwill rack years ago for a steal because it had a rip in the sleeve, a tear that had taken me no time at all to mend. I'd been offered every job I'd ever applied for when wearing this jacket to the interview. Granted, that had been all of two jobs, but still.

"Are you in need of luck, then?" he asked, the soft twang of a southern accent barely noticeable.

I smiled, hoping he could see only my hopes and not my regrets. "Aren't we all?"

He glanced at his left hand, bare of any rings, and flexed his fingers. "Some believe you make your own luck."

As a butterfly drifted between us, a monarch, identifiable by its deep-orange-and-black coloring, I said, "Well, I'm not one of those people. I'll take all the luck I can get."

I noticed this particular monarch had a unique anomaly—its right forewing had a white tip, almost as if it had been dipped in paint. The unusual marking shimmered, looking opalescent, even in the gray morning.

The wind gusted and the man lifted his chin, inhaling deeply as if he'd been suffocating the whole time he'd been standing there. "I'm Sam, by the way, and this here is Norman." Norman had emptied the dish and was licking his lips with a tiny pink tongue. "Are you here on vacation . . . ?" With eyebrows lifted, he bent slightly forward and trailed off, obviously waiting for me to supply my name.

With him so close, I could easily pick up his scent. Hazelnut and citrus, deep woods and melancholy. "I'm Ava. And I'm actually here for a job interview."

Suddenly I felt queasy at the risk I had taken by coming here. Before yesterday, I'd never driven farther than an hour away from home. Heck, I'd only had a driver's license for a few years. Now I was in Driftwood, Alabama, all because of a ghos— I cut my thought off, silently revising it. All because of a mysterious letter.

When I'd opened that strange letter with that *everything you've always wanted* line, it felt like an opportunity to start life over, to take a leap of faith.

Which was why I was here, a stranger in a strange, charming land, ready to take a big, scary chance.

"I see," Sam said. "That explains the lucky blazer."

I nodded.

He turned his face into the wind again, breathed deeply. "I'm not sure you need that coat. I feel luck blowing in the air today. Blowing around you."

"It's the blazer, trust me."

He only smiled at that, as if he knew better but had the good manners not to argue.

The butterfly that had been drifting around had a herky-jerky way of flying, almost like it was drunk. It dipped and rose repeatedly before finally landing on my forearm. There, its wings opened and closed slowly, the whooshing sound nearly blocking out all other noises. "Are butterflies a sign of good luck, too?"

Sadness shadowed the gold flecks in his eyes. "I've never heard of a butterfly as a symbol of good luck, but who knows? In these parts, most believe they represent life—more specifically, life after death. Anyone else around here would tell you that when a butterfly chooses to land on you like that, it's a visit from someone in your life who's passed on."

I swallowed hard, thinking about the butterfly stamp on the letter and how the ethereal whooshing of the monarch's wings suddenly sounded like a heartbeat.

Was this butterfly . . . *Alex*?

A rush of emotion came over me, and I struggled with whether I wanted to blow the butterfly off my sleeve or hold it close.

"Anyone else would say that, but not you? You don't believe it?"

"I'm not sure what I believe in anymore."

The strain in his voice, the mournfulness, came through loud and clear, sharing a painful ending to a story but none of the early chapters. Using my fingertip, I lifted the docile butterfly toward him. "I'm more than happy to share the experience."

Confusion flickered in his eyes as he turned away to untie Norman's leash. Then he picked up the empty whipped cream dish from the ground and tossed it in a nearby trash can. "I don't think it works that way, but thanks. It's real nice of you. But if monarchs are lucky, you hit the jackpot by coming here—there are plenty floating around these days. In a month or so, the whole town will be full of them, the sky nearly orange as they migrate south for the winter. The town celebrates by holding Butterfly Fest in late October. It's a big to-do around here."

The thought of witnessing the migration filled me with a joy I hadn't felt in a good, long while. But if I wanted to stick around to see it, I needed a job. I checked the time: 8:58. I couldn't procrastinate any longer. "I need to get going. It was nice meeting the two of you."

The curious look was back in his eyes as he nodded. "Welcome to Driftwood, Ava. Maybe we'll see you around."

As they walked away, I carried the butterfly to a waist-high planter pot overflowing with flowers and gently placed the monarch on a pink petal. Its wings opened, closed. Again, it sounded to my ears like the beat of a heart.

No. It couldn't possibly be Alex. That was impossible. It was just a butterfly.

But between it and the letter . . . it had me wondering about the impossible.

As the church's bell started tolling the hour, I hurried toward the coffee shop's door, a line from the letter going round and round in my head.

Be yourself and it'll all be okay.

I wanted to believe it would all be okay. Wanted it desperately.

But how could it be, when I couldn't change the fact that *being myself* was what had led to Alexander's death?

CHAPTER 2

MAGGIE

"He's losing his dang mind. Maybe even lost it already. Wandered straight off along with the stuff that's missing from his house."

"Desmond's mind is fine, Maggie," Carmella Brasil said, looking across the counter at me as I filled a cup with ice and then reached for the milk. "Eccentric, perhaps, but fine. The items in his house had simply been misplaced—didn't he tell you he'd found them?"

He had, but I thought the admission proved, rather than discredited, my point about my father's wayward mind. He'd be seventy in a couple of years. Wasn't that too young for memory issues? It felt too young, but that might be because he rarely acted his age.

Desmond "Dez" Brightwell often behaved like a teenager, and more often than not, I parented him, rather than the other way around. It hadn't helped any that he and my son, Noah, had been best buddies, two peas in a pod, partners in all sorts of mischief until Noah had flown the coop for college last year, which had been an exciting time for him and a hellish one for me. *Empty nest* was such a sweet term for having your heart ripped out and relocated to another state.

"Though I admit, *eccentric* may be putting it mildly," Carmella said with a smile, faint lines crinkling the corners of her eyes.

At sixty-four, Carmella was va-va-voom gorgeous, curvy, and glamorous. She was the longtime owner of Driftwood Realty and had aged spectacularly well, for which she gave credit to working hard, eating right, and her Latina heritage. Her usual order was an iced dirty chai latte, a drink that wasn't even on the sparse menu. But sometimes exceptions were made here at Magpie's.

As I added chai syrup into the cup, the bells on the door chimed. I glanced over, ever hopeful that it would be my mama who walked inside. But it wasn't. She hadn't walked through that door in twenty-seven years.

I smiled at the newcomer. "Morning, Redmond. I'll be right with you."

My gaze drifted to Estrelle Cormier, who sat at her favorite table near the picture window. The sequins on her black gown glinted as she watched me closely. I was surprised she hadn't yet weighed in on the conversation about my father. Estrelle was a meddler by nature.

I gave her a smile and glanced around. The coffee shop was fairly quiet at the moment, which was a good thing since I was currently the only one working this morning. Beyond Carmella, Estrelle, and now Redmond, Mrs. Pollard sat at the back of the shop near the floor-to-ceiling blackboard.

"Take your time, Maggie," Redmond said. He leaned in close to the bakery showcase, squinting at the pastries that had been dropped off earlier by Donovan Quinlan from the Beach Mouse Bakery.

I shoved aside the thoughts that sprang up over Donovan's recent return to town as I poured a shot of espresso into the cup, put a lid on it, and gave it a swirl. When I set the drink on the counter in front of Carmella, I picked up our conversation. "Dad's eccentric, definitely, but this goes beyond that. He's given up Purty's pulled pork, his absolute favorite food on earth, and has been talking about becoming a vegetarian. He hates vegetables. I spotted him jogging on the beach the other day, too. *Jogging.* You know how he feels about regimented exercise."

Her eyebrows rose. "Jogging? *Really?*"

"Good for him," Redmond piped in. "Move it or lose it."

In his late forties, the redheaded, ultra-buff Redmond owned the local gym simply called Red's, and even though he eyed a blueberry cake donut with cream-cheese frosting with deep,

deep longing, he wouldn't be buying it. According to town gossip, his health-nut lifestyle was one of the reasons he was newly single—last month he'd had a massive argument outside of Mother of Pearl, the jewelry store belonging to his partner, Javier, over Javier's love of cinnamon rolls and mocha lattes. Both had stormed off in opposite directions and had barely spoken since, except to discuss custody arrangements for their beloved pet cockatiel.

Redmond turned his back on the pastries. He wore a utilitarian gray muscle shirt and gym shorts, his standard outfit despite Javier's continued pleas to snazz up his wardrobe a bit. "There's no age limit on wanting to get healthy. How old is Dez now?"

"Sixty-eight," I said.

In my head I could hear Dad's voice saying, *You're only as old as you think, my little magpie. And I like to think I'm in my forties. No, thirties. No, twenties. Hoo boy. My twenties were something, let me tell you.*

For most of his twenties, he'd traveled the world, but he liked to say those adventures paled to meeting my mother, Tuppence, at a Mardi Gras parade over in Mobile when he was twenty-eight. After spotting her standing along the route, he'd jumped off the float he'd been riding to give her a MoonPie and his heart. She'd accepted both enthusiastically. She did *everything* enthusiastically. After that they'd settled down here in Driftwood and had been inseparable. Well, until . . .

I shook my head. No need to go down that road right now.

"There's a class at the gym geared toward the over-sixties age range that he might be interested in. Drifters and Shakers. Dance moves mostly. Great for the heart." Redmond glanced at Carmella, and she narrowed her gaze at him as if daring him to say something about her fitness level. Being a smart man, he looked away.

"I'll tell him," I said, then punched Carmella's order into the register. "And it's not just Dad's new, healthier lifestyle that's bothersome. He's selling most everything he owns. I can't tell you how many times he's said he'd rather cut off a limb than get rid of any of his treasures, yet not only is he planning a big yard sale, but he has made it a whole community-wide event."

I'd garnered the nickname Magpie early on. As soon as I learned how to walk, I was off, picking up anything shiny or unusual—having watched both my parents do the same. It wasn't until I was older that the focus of my collecting narrowed to very specific objects. My father, however, had always collected anything that struck his fancy, with no rhyme or reason. Those items filled two large storage units and were stuffed into every nook and cranny in his house. He hadn't been able to bear parting with anything. Until now, apparently.

Carmella rooted around her tote bag for her wallet. "You know Dez likes mixing things up. Says it keeps life interesting."

Carmella had been in my life . . . forever. She'd been my mother's best friend, and from the time I was eleven years old she had tried to help fill the gaps in my life left behind by my mama's absence. It was an impossible task, but I loved her dearly for trying.

"And his talk about selling the coffee shop? That's not mixing things up. That's . . ." I searched for the right word.

"The dumbest idea I've heard in a month of Sundays," Mrs. Pollard called out.

"Thank you, Mrs. Pollard," I said. "That's exactly what it is. Dumb."

"Dez is selling Magpie's?" Redmond asked, his voice threaded with disbelief.

"No." I wiped water droplets from the counter and tried to will away the headache I felt coming on. "He mentioned something about it, is all. It's just talk."

When I'd questioned Dad on why he'd even *consider* selling, he only said, "Waves of change should be welcomed, Maggie. They can uncover beauty and treasures untold. It might be time for me to let go and move on."

I loved discovering treasures as much as the next person—maybe more—but I also knew how waves of change could be destructive, destroying anything in their path.

Especially families.

So why rock this particular boat?

Sympathy flooded Carmella's eyes. "I don't think it's just talk. He's planning on getting a business evaluation and is gathering revenue statements—things he'd need to get Magpie's on the market."

Redmond's dark eyes flared wide and he whistled low.

My heart rate skyrocketed. This didn't make sense. My father wouldn't sell the coffee shop. My *mother's* coffee shop. Magpie's was a fixture in Driftwood. It was the *heart* of this town. Closing it would be devastating.

It was where so many connected and reconnected. Where gossip was shared. Where business deals were discussed. Where friends laughed so hard they cried. Where Mermaids gathered. Where relationships began. Where some ended. It was where life was *lived*. It was also where magic happened when it came to the curiosities I'd collected.

The bells on the door rang out again, and if not my mama, then I hoped it was Rosemary Clark, the best employee known to mankind. She'd called earlier to say she was running late because of car trouble. Instead, it was Sienna Hopkins who breezed through the doorway.

The relatively slow morning was the proverbial calm before the storm, since I knew the Mermaids, members of Driftwood's beachcombing club, would be along soon enough. They arrived every morning around nine after having walked the beach with their buckets and bins, searching for treasures like driftwood, shells, fossils, and sea beans. Mostly, though, the Mermaids were on the hunt for sea glass, which was extremely rare on our beaches but chances increased after a big storm. Their usual numbers would likely be doubled today—maybe tripled— because of last night's bad weather.

I took a moment to scan the small dining room, knowing that there was no way to fit all the Mermaids inside. They'd come anyway, spilling out onto the sidewalk and into the park across the street after ordering. I felt a surge of love for my small southern town and how supportive they were of the coffeehouse— and all the businesses here in the square.

I couldn't ever imagine moving away, and especially not moving north like Effie Reyes, who'd quit on me last week to follow her boyfriend to a horse ranch in Wyoming. But then again, I wasn't so goo-goo eyed over a boy that I'd blindly follow him anywhere. Well, I hadn't been for a long time now at least—and where he'd gone I'd decided not to follow. I *couldn't* follow.

I was tied to this town, to the water. When I was away from the beach for long, the magic in my life disappeared, which felt a lot like losing my mama all over again. She'd been the one who'd shared her magic with me the day she disappeared. As long as I had the magic, I had *hope*.

Automatically, my gaze went to the Curiosity Corner. Stretching across a back corner of the shop, catawampus style, were driftwood shelves of varying widths that had been designed to resemble an oak tree. On the shelves were bits and bobs I'd collected that were awaiting their fated companions. Atop the tree sat a dark, sleek carved wooden magpie with a small pink bow on its head, looking calm and serene and proud of its odd collection.

A break in the clouds filled the dining area with a burst of sunlight. I glanced toward the front window and found Estrelle still watching me. She stared through her veil's netting, the look so piercing it felt as though she could see right into my heart, to the part where my deepest hopes and fears lived.

Feeling vulnerable, I looked away, focusing instead on Sienna. "Morning," I said brightly, trying to hide my gratefulness that Sienna didn't work here anymore. She was a sweet, cheerful girl but had been an absolute menace behind the counter.

Sienna glanced around the shop as she strode toward the bakery case. "Good morning, all."

Everyone chorused back a hello, and I smiled. It was one of the things I loved most about Magpie's. Because it had been a part of Driftwood for thirty-five years now—my mother had opened it when I was three years old—oftentimes mornings here felt more like a neighborly get-together, a time when even snowbirds and tourists felt a bit like family.

"No croissants today?" Sienna asked.

"Sorry," I said. "The bakery's a bit shorthanded right now, so they've cut some items from their menu."

Redmond threw another glance at the donuts, before saying, "Has Dez hired you, Carmella? Signed a contract?"

She swiped her credit card and pushed buttons on the machine, adding, as always, a generous tip to the order. "No. Not yet."

I slumped with relief. If Dad was serious about selling, he'd have signed a contract.

Sienna's head came up as if sensing the cloud of tension that had bloomed in the air. "What's going on?"

"Dez is selling Magpie's," Mrs. Pollard said. It was her recipe highlighted on the blackboard this week—mini vanilla scones—and she was sitting next to the board proud as a peacock, ready to offer baking tips should anyone ask. At seventy-something, she was a widow who had plenty of time on her hands and loved being in the thick of things.

Sienna's jaw dropped. "Selling? That's crazy talk."

"He's *not* selling," I repeated. "He's just mentioned something about it."

Sienna pressed her hands to her chest. "Oh, thank goodness. I can't imagine Driftwood without Magpie's." She grinned. "It's been here longer than I've been alive. It's a constitution."

We all stared at her.

"Institution?" Carmella ventured.

"Exactly." Sienna smiled.

Despite her vocabulary goof, she'd made me tear up. Exactly. Driftwood wouldn't be the same without Magpie's, without its heart.

Dad knew that, which was how I knew he wasn't serious, despite his talk of letting go.

Something else was going on. Something big.

Blinking the tears away, I faced Redmond. "Almond milk latte?"

He nodded. "To go, please."

"Do you think his talk about selling has something to do

with that sleepwalking incident a few months back?" Sienna dropped her voice. "People were wondering if he'd gone a bit soft in the head."

I rolled my eyes. Most people wouldn't talk openly about that kind of gossip, but Sienna was about as open a book as books came. In her early twenties, she had slowly been working her way through each shop in town, unable to find just the right fit and often leaving destruction behind. Truly, she was one of the most uncoordinated, bumbling, clumsy people I'd ever worked with. With her blond hair and brown eyes, she reminded me of a young Carrie Underwood fresh from her *American Idol* days, and I couldn't help wondering how often Sienna's family had asked Jesus to take the wheel of her life, to steer her onto the right path and out of harm's way. I'd certainly asked a time or two on her behalf.

"*I* didn't think he had," Sienna said quickly to me, as if suddenly realizing she might've been rude. "Now I have some doubts, though. Little ones. Hardly worth mentioning."

I'd been hoping everyone would forget that Dad had been found by Mrs. Pollard's neighbor wandering about in the dark of night wearing only a skimpy pair of underwear. But around here people had long memories. Nothing was ever truly forgotten.

Dad's nighttime adventure had opened a Pandora's box of concerns in my brain, and to calm a rising tide of fear, I'd broached the idea of me moving in with him. Not that I *wanted* to move—I rather liked my house and having my own space, but it seemed the best option for my peace of mind. And his potential safety.

He'd turned me down flat, though. Wouldn't even discuss the matter.

Mrs. Pollard let out a soft whistle, then took a sip of her coffee. "That sleepwalking was something else. Got myself quite an eyeful that night." She fanned her face with one of the recipe cards she'd had printed out *just in case* someone didn't have the time to write out or take a picture of her recipe.

For some reason, I sought out Estrelle. She sat quietly by

the window, watching and listening to everything going on. She lifted a thin eyebrow in my direction and I swore there was amusement dancing in her pale eyes, though it was hard to tell from across the room. I questioned again why she hadn't chimed in. Her silence was highly unusual. And slightly disturbing.

Redmond snapped his fingers. "The sleepwalking happened right around the time Dez began talking about ghosts, right?"

Trying to ignore the conversation, I went about making the almond milk latte. Usually work helped calm my inner turmoil. Here at Magpie's, I was in complete control and had been since I was nineteen years old. That was when my father, who'd been desperate for a change of pace, handed me the reins of the business, deciding I had enough experience to run the place on my own.

Today, however, being here was stressing me out. And stress, according to my doctor, was the last thing I needed in my life.

"Ghosts?" Sienna asked. "Really? I hadn't heard that."

Lord. How had she not heard? But then I remembered. She'd been out of town, visiting her folks, when he first started talking about it. By the time she came back two weeks later, the talk had turned to how sixteen-year-old Ambrose Symons had run his electric scooter off the road and into Mrs. Harlin's heirloom tomato bed after ogling a young bikini-clad woman heading to the beach. The crash hadn't hurt him at all but Mrs. Harlin had gone after him with a broom, and he'd ended up needing four stitches on his arm. No charges were brought against either.

"Just one ghost," I corrected, before the story got out of hand.

I tried to drown out the chatter between the two of them by steaming the almond milk, but I, unfortunately, could still hear the conversation.

Redmond said, "Dez has been talking about how his house is haunted, telling anyone who'll listen that a ghost has been showing up in the middle of the night, making noise, making a mess of the place. He doesn't seem bothered by it—in fact, he seems amused more than anything."

Carmella said, "He's always loved a good ghost story."

I didn't know what to make of Dad's supposed ghost. I'd tried to brush it off as him just having a bit of fun, but one afternoon I'd let myself into his house and had seen the mess with my own eyes. Dad wasn't persnickety with his cleanliness, but he wasn't a total slob either, so the quick deterioration of his home was completely out of character.

It had been unsettling, to say the least.

And impossible to ignore. Because he, mercifully, hadn't wanted *me* to move in, I'd floated the idea of hiring an in-home caretaker. I even offered to pay for the help, not that I really had the money to do so. He'd shut down the conversation with a hearty laugh that rolled on and on until he gently steered me toward the door.

"My ghost is messy, and I have better things to do than clean. All is well here, my little magpie. Stop worrying."

Sienna said, "Does he think the ghost is his w—" She suddenly cut herself off and looked helplessly around.

Carmella jumped in, filling the painful silence. "To me, Dez is acting only like a man who's ready for a change. And change isn't always a bad thing."

"Oh!" Sienna brightened. "Maybe he's selling Magpie's because he's planning on retiring. He once told me that he wanted to cruise around the world. That would be a *great* thing."

I wiped the steam wand clean and stared blankly at her. Why would Dad say such a thing? He'd already seen the world. He wouldn't leave Driftwood now. Not without my mama. And certainly not on a ship—he knew the kind of anxiety that would cause me. Plus, I talked to him only recently about retiring and he said he wasn't near ready. He liked working, staying busy. Ever since handing Magpie's over to me, he'd been renovating fixer-uppers in the area and turning them into rentals— all except for the home he'd sold to me on the cheap. The super cheap.

I wasn't sure what was going on with my father, but it went beyond the idea of retirement. A little over a month ago, we'd had dinner plans but he had stood me up. When I went to his house to check on him, I found it still a disaster area. Worse than that, though, was his neglect of Molly. His cantankerous cat's water dish had been bone dry. It had also been my thirty-eighth birthday. And he'd forgotten.

When he finally arrived home, full of apologies, he'd tried to play off his absentmindedness as no big deal and the conversation quickly devolved into an argument. When I once again suggested hiring someone to keep an eye on him, his house, *Molly,* his usually jovial face had clouded over with anger, something so rare it had stunned me silent.

"Enough, Magdalena," he had snapped. "*Enough.* Let it go. *Let it be.*"

Then his face softened, the anger vanishing as quickly as it had come. He grabbed a garishly painted porcelain monkey candlestick off the counter and used it as a faux microphone to wail about Mother Mary speaking words of wisdom—he was never one to pass up a chance to sing a song by the Beatles, especially when the lyrics were used to lighten a heavy situation.

Frustrated after that visit, I had marched myself straight to my office here at Magpie's and used my mama's old typewriter to create the worst possible help-wanted ad for an in-home care provider. I hung it in the front window where everyone arriving the next morning would see it first thing, and even had visions of scanning it and posting it in local online groups. My determination to hire someone had lasted approximately two minutes before I chickened out and took the notice down. I crumpled it up, threw it away in the trash can outside the shop, and went home to bed with a heavy heart.

Now Dad was talking about selling Magpie's, and I wished I'd kept the ad up, because I needed a spy. Someone who'd report any unusual behavior straight to me. Plus, I wanted to make sure Molly had a full water dish at all times. We had a contentious relationship, Molly and I, but I still cared about her well-being.

I passed Redmond's latte over to him and rang up his order.

He took a sip and let out a happy sigh. "Wonderful as usual, Maggie."

As he paid with a credit card, the bells on the door announced another visitor. The jingling was getting on my nerves, but I breathed a sigh of relief at the sight of Rose.

"Sorry I'm late!" she said as she sailed through the dining room and around the counter, a long, dark braid sprinkled with silver strands trailing behind her. She tucked her handbag away and grabbed an apron. "Good morning, everyone."

Again, a chorus of hellos went up and filled my soul.

"Who's next?" Rose asked, jumping right into work, even as her hands were still tying the knot on her apron.

While Sienna ordered, Carmella motioned at me with her chin, nodding toward the back hallway. I followed her there, and as soon as I was within reach, she gently touched my arm.

"When was the last time you had a vacation, Maggie? You might be worried about your dad, but I'm worried about you. You look ready to snap in half. You're always working or on the go, doing for others—never taking time for yourself to just be."

"There's no time for that," I said, hating that I heard my doctor's voice in my head, talking about slowing down. "Besides, it's hard to think of myself when I'm so worried about Dad. You know him almost as well as I do, Carmella. You have to have seen that something isn't right. If it's not his mind, then maybe it's his health? Do you think he got some terrible diagnosis? Is that why he's pulling out all the stops to get healthy?" I straightened, feeling like I was onto something. "I can absolutely see him hiding health issues from me, wanting to protect me. Oh lord."

Carmella grabbed hold of my hand, held it. "Stop, Maggie. Your blood pressure is going to go through the roof."

Nearly six months ago, I'd had a transient ischemic attack, sometimes called a mini-stroke, due to untreated high blood pressure. Luckily, TIAs rarely left lasting damage, but the doctor had warned that I now had a one-in-three chance of having a major stroke if I didn't make big changes in my life.

Changes like reducing stress.

"Dez is *fine*," she said. "The very picture of vim and vigor. I promise you."

I'd been well on my way to working myself into a fine frenzy, but her calm voice, her serene tone, pulled me back from the brink. She sounded so *sure*.

I eyed her. "You know something, don't you?"

The bells on the door grated as Sam Kindell came inside. Rose welcomed him with a hearty "Good morning, Sam!" and started pulling together his usual order: an iced hazelnut latte and a whippy cup to go.

Carmella shifted her weight on her high-heeled sandals and wouldn't meet my eye. "What? *No.*"

I laughed, but it sounded more like a cry to my ears. She might be the number-one real estate agent in these parts, but she was a lousy liar. "Tell me. *Please.*"

As she lifted her head, I saw resolve gleaming in her deep, dark eyes, and I held my breath, waiting, hoping, that I'd finally know the source of my father's odd behavior, once and for all.

"Magdalena Mae Brightwell, a word?" Estrelle stomped toward me, the sequins on her gown glinting like moonlight on water.

"Can it wait a second?" I asked her.

"No, it most certainly cannot."

Relief flooded Carmella's face at the reprieve she'd been given. "I should be going, anyway. I have a showing at nine thirty." She gave me a kiss on my cheek and practically ran to the door, shoving it open.

Sam soon followed her out, his order in his hands, the bells shredding my last nerve. I wondered why Dad, when he'd first taken over running Magpie's, had even added the dang bells to the door in the first place. Mama would hate them.

Trying my best to ignore my troubles and my throbbing head, I forced my focus away from Carmella's hasty retreat and onto the elderly woman standing in front of me.

Estrelle owned the fabric and notions shop next door, Stitchery, and also offered tailoring services and custom work. No one seemed to know her true age, but she had to be eighty if a day. Her thin, pale skin was practically translucent, a maze of blue veins easily visible. Her fingers were gnarled, her manicured nails painted hot pink. Her crystal-clear silvery stare was unwavering behind the black netting of the veil on her pillbox hat. Her back was hunched, which pitched her head slightly forward, as if she was always leaning in to hear better, not that she seemed to have hearing issues. In fact, all her senses seemed as sharp as ever.

As the church bells began tolling the nine o'clock hour, Estrelle, her gravelly voice firm and strong, said, "You *will* hire her."

CHAPTER 3

MAGGIE

The hair stood at the back of my neck.

Estrelle had the *knowing*—the ability to know things about the past, present, and future that she shouldn't. She'd known that Daisy Fern Jensen was expecting before Daisy did. Twins, at that. Estrelle's baby gifts—two hand-stitched bibs and a warning to take bed rest seriously—had sent Daisy into a tizzy of excitement and worry. A few years back, Estrelle had brought a cane to Boomy Eldridge's house a few days *before* he sprained his foot. Once, when I was in high school and had snuck out of the house to hang out with Donovan, the next day she'd asked, eyebrow raised as high as it could go, if I'd enjoyed my late-night lark. When Noah was in his early teens, she'd awoken me in the middle of the night with a phone call that he was in danger—a call that likely saved his life. Two years ago she'd somehow known that Kitty Bethune had badmouthed her at the town's annual blueberry festival even though Estrelle hadn't been standing anywhere nearby. The ensuing confrontation was legendary around these parts.

More often than not Estrelle offered advice or issued orders without asking, or caring, if the interference was welcome, but when she'd approached me just now, I'd been *hoping* she'd say something about my dad. Surely she had some insight into the matter.

Caught off guard by her demand to *hire* someone, I said, "Pardon?"

Estrelle lifted a thin eyebrow. *"It has been said."*

Giving me a stiff nod, she then turned on her clunky heels.

"Wait!"

She slowly pivoted, her body stiff with irritation.

The door opened, the bells screaming in sharp tones. That was it. I'd had it. Those bells had to *go*.

Wincing, I said to Estrelle, "Do you know what's going on with my dad?"

The sequins shimmered. "Perhaps I do. Perhaps I don't."

Behind me, Mrs. Pollard snorted. "That means she don't."

Estrelle narrowed her gaze.

Mrs. Pollard quickly stood and patted her short gray hair. "I'm just going to freshen up in the powder room. Will you keep an eye on my recipe cards, Maggie?"

"Of course," I said, watching her hurry off.

By the time I looked back at Estrelle, she was halfway across the room, her sequins flashing a hearty goodbye as they caught a thin shaft of sunlight. When she reached the door, she lifted the mysteriously silent bells off their hook, threw me a glance full of mischief and affection, then dropped the bells in the trash can before walking out.

My jaw fell clear to the floor. I glanced around to see if anyone else had noticed what she'd done but no one seemed to be paying the least bit of attention.

Rose called out, "Maggie? Someone here to see you."

I pulled my disbelieving gaze from the door, turning it toward a woman I didn't recognize, who stood at the counter. She was studying me, looking nervous as could be with her hands clenched on the strap of her bag. Her face was pinched with worry.

"Go on, sugar pie," Rose encouraged her, before pulling cups, prepping for the Mermaid onslaught.

The woman, mid-to-late twenties by my guess, was such a tiny thing that I had the feeling a stiff wind would blow her straight down the street if it caught her by surprise. She thanked Rose and returned her smile, which eased the tension in her perfectly heart-shaped face, revealing her to be quite pretty with her fair complexion and high cheekbones flecked with pale freckles. She didn't so much as blink as she walked slowly toward me on kitten heels, but her attention was now fixed upon the Curiosity Corner. Her big owlish hazel eyes had gone wide, the mix of green and brown reminding me of the moss that grew on the oak trees in the square. Her eyebrows were pulled low, as if she was trying to puzzle out exactly what she was seeing.

It was a common reaction to the space.

"Maggie?" she questioned as she neared, once again looking at me. "The plum-tuckered Maggie?"

I laughed, because it was wholly true. I was exhausted, and it was barely nine in the morning. "Hi, yes, I'm Maggie. Have we met?"

She didn't look familiar, and she certainly didn't dress like she was from around here. Wool. At the end of summer. She was all-out begging for heatstroke.

"We haven't met, no. My name's Ava Harrison." She took another step nearer and thrust out her hand to shake mine.

Being an arm's length from her brought an ever-so-slight wave of dizziness, a mild shock wave, as if my equilibrium had taken a hip check. It was a familiar sensation, as comfortable—and comforting—as a hug. I enfolded her small hand with both of mine and gave it a squeeze. "I'm glad you're here," I said, truly meaning it. "I have something for you."

I lived for these days when one of my curiosities found its forever home.

Hopefulness swept across her face. "You do?"

She had a quiet voice, light and feathery. "I do. Just give me a second to find it."

I hurried over to the elaborate driftwood display. To anyone else the knickknacks in the magpie's tree might seem like hodgepodge at its finest—or junk at its worst. To me it was all treasure, even though none of it was mine. It belonged to others. I was simply the patient middleman, the mystical matchmaker.

My mama had felt shock waves, too, having had the ability nearly all her life, just like her mama before her. When I was little, she'd tucked me in at night telling me stories of the matches she'd made. I'd been envious that I didn't feel vibrations like she did, but she always had faith that one day the gift would be passed along to me. That time had come when I was eleven, and it was forever tied to the worst day of my life.

I searched for Ava's match, rooting around in shallow bins and baskets until I felt a similar tremor to the one I'd experienced a moment ago. Finally, I pulled out a silver thimble, its rim embossed with butterflies in flight. I couldn't quite remember where—or how long ago—I'd found it. Had I picked it up while walking along the beach? At a thrift store? At a yard sale? I had no recollection of a thimble at all, which was unusual. Until today, I'd always recalled exactly where I found my curiosities.

I held the thimble out to her. "This is for you. No cost."

The items I'd collected for the Curiosity Corner were only valuable to the people they belonged with—and I never charged a dime for them. It wouldn't have been right, and honestly, they usually weren't pricy pieces to begin with. Their value was in the memories they stirred.

Tentatively, she took the thimble from me and examined the pattern before closing her fingers around it. "My grandmother had one similar to this, only hers had birds in flight and was dented on the top. I'd forgotten about it until just now."

The curiosities most often acted as reminders of something that had once brought joy that might now be missing from that person's life. Then they sparked a desire to seek that happiness again.

Ava ran a thumb over the crown of the thimble. "But I don't understand why you're giving this to me. Is it part of the job?"

"My job? I guess you could say so." My daddy had created the Curiosity Corner for me about six months after my mama disappeared, after it had become clear that I'd picked up collecting curiosities where she had left off. Here at the shop, where I spent so much time, was the best place to house them.

Rosiness bloomed in Ava's fair cheeks. "I meant, is this thimble for the job I'm applying for? I'm pretty good with a needle and thread, and I have to admit I have a fondness for sewing. My grandmother was the one who taught me." She held up her sleeve arm, showing off an embroidered hedgehog surrounded by flowers on the fabric. "There was a hole there when I bought this blazer."

The hedgehog was adorable, quirky, and charming, but I was still stuck on the part she'd mentioned about applying for a job, since I was down an employee. "Do you have any experience as a barista?"

Ava's big eyes blinked slowly. "I think there's been some confusion. I'm here to interview for the caretaker opening." She reached into her tote bag and pulled out a crinkled piece of paper and scanned it. "For the peculiar old man? *Oh no.*"

"What?"

"In my rush to get here—I drove through the night from Ohio—I didn't stop to think about how old this listing might be. Well, not in terms of the actual job, anyway. I was too busy thinking about—" She cut herself off. "I'm rambling. Sorry. The interviews were probably weeks ago. I feel so stupid." She let out a deflated sigh, then a second later lifted hopeful eyes. "I don't suppose there's any chance the job is still available?"

It took me a second to process what she was saying. *A peculiar old man?* My heartbeat kicked up a notch. "May I?" I motioned to the paper.

She handed it over.

```
           HELP WANTED
Patient, energetic, unflappable in-home caretaker
wanted for a peculiar, stubborn old man; a spoiled,
she-devil cat; and a cluttered, possibly haunted
beach house . . .
```

As I read, my heart started beating so loudly that it felt like everyone in the room could surely hear it. This was the want ad I'd put in the window a month or so ago, then torn down and thrown away. At the top of it, someone had scribbled a short message to her.

"Where did you get this?"

"It came in the mail."

A noise rose from outside, sounding like a flock of overexcited seagulls that had just spotted a beach picnic. The Mermaids had breached the square. "Who sent it?"

"There wasn't a return address, but I think . . . I think it came from someone I used to know. Alexander. An ex-boyfriend. That kind of looks like his handwriting at the top."

"Does he live near here?" I asked, trying to understand. Had the man gone through Magpie's trash?

Ava looked over her shoulder, toward the front window. A monarch butterfly was fluttering against the glass, looking like it was trying to get inside. Her face drained of color, and she turned back toward me, her eyes pained.

"No, he doesn't."

"This is all very strange. The want ad was just me venting mostly, not an actual job opportunity. I threw this away after typing it up. That's why it's crumpled." I handed the paper back to her. "I don't know how it found its way to you."

The clouds shifted. Ripples of light caught my eye. Sunlight sparkling on sequins. Estrelle leaned against a lamppost just outside the shop. She watched us through the window, and I easily heard her voice in my head, telling me, *You* will *hire her.*

Her being Ava?

Had to be, with the way Estrelle was looking on.

Good god. I certainly didn't want to be on Estrelle's bad side. I easily recalled the head-to-toe blistery rash Kitty Bethune had suddenly developed after denying she'd called Estrelle a creepy old hag. Some said the rash had come from a blueberry allergy or was simply swimmer's itch, but everyone around here knew that Estrelle doled out her own form of justice just as much as she handed out advice. I'd not heard Kitty utter a single bad word against Estrelle since. Or anyone else, for that matter.

"So there's no job?" Ava asked, her shoulders slumping.

As I stood there, I realized my headache had faded, barely pulsing now. It was as if my body recognized that Ava's presence in my father's life would help *my* stress levels.

And lord knew, I needed to lower those levels.

"I didn't say that. There are extenuating circumstances. But with that being said, I'm curious why this job even interests you. It wasn't the most appealing description."

"Alex, he, well, he . . ." Her voice was so quiet I could barely hear her and then she trailed off, the words falling into nothingness. Finally, she took a deep breath and pressed on. "You mentioned this was strange. It gets even stranger. Alex passed away a month ago, just weeks after we broke up."

She quickly explained about a letter falling off the counter yesterday, the smudged postmark, and the overwhelming need to *take a chance,* as the scrawled note at the top of the want ad had suggested.

"Do you know for sure that he was the one who sent the letter?" I asked. "You said it didn't have a return address and the note isn't signed."

"I have some doubts," she admitted, those mossy owlish eyes awash with apprehension, "but it sounds like him, and I can't think of anyone else who would have sent it."

"But how did he get it?" I asked. "I threw the want ad away."

"I have no idea," she said quietly. "But to me there's something that feels . . . *otherworldly* about this whole situation."

Goose bumps rose on my arms as the Mermaids began making their way inside the shop. The room burst full open with sound. Hellos and laughter and orders of lattes and tea and muffins and donuts.

I needed to go help Rose before all-out chaos ensued. "Otherworldly? Like . . . *ghostly?*"

I wasn't sure what to believe when it came to ghosts or spirits or even angels, though there was something comforting in believing there might be some sort of life after death.

She shrugged. "I don't know what to think."

I didn't, either. But then thoughts started filtering in about Dad's sleepwalking, his new healthier lifestyle, the yard sale, and now the talk of selling Magpie's. I made a quick decision. One I hopefully wouldn't regret.

"The timing *does* feel like more than coincidence. And how the letter fell off the counter like it did?" I made a show of shivering. "That definitely sounds a bit woo-woo to me."

She nodded, her face so earnest it almost made me feel guilty for playing up the ghost angle. *Almost.* My need to find out what my dad was up to overrode everything else.

"I keep trying to come up with another explanation but just can't quite," she said.

I took a deep breath. "Let me help take care of these Mermaids, then we'll go see my dad. He's who you'd be working for, by the way. Despite what he thinks, he does need help, and I think you might be the perfect person for the job."

The job she *was* going to get.

I knew this mostly because Ava had Estrelle's stamp of approval—Dad wouldn't dare cross the old woman, either. But also because what Carmella had said earlier was true. My father loved a good ghost story. He'd never pass up being part of one.

I glanced out the window to see if Estrelle was still watching, pleased at how all this had unfolded.

But the only thing near the lamppost now was a butterfly flitting about.

CHAPTER 4

AVA

An hour after I first stepped foot into Magpie's, I followed Maggie out of the coffee shop. The gray clouds had drifted off to the north, leaving behind a brilliant blue sky above us. We were on our way to meet with her father, Desmond, at his home.

Maggie shaded her eyes with her hand as she glanced at my blazer. She smelled of sweet cream and coffee, golden sunsets and generosity.

"Dad's house is about six blocks from here, so we'll take the golf cart over instead of working up a sweat by walking."

Sunshine had warmed the morning, and she was dressed more appropriately for the weather in her knee-length denim shorts and green Magpie's T-shirt. I definitely felt the heat in my tweed jacket, but I didn't want to take it off until after I met with Desmond. Until *after* I got the job. No use in jinxing my luck.

Earlier, Maggie had called her father on speakerphone to let him know we were coming, and I'd heard the conversation easily, even though the door to her office had been closed. Desmond hadn't been pleased about interviewing a helper until Maggie mentioned someone named Estrelle and a ghostly connection to the letter I'd received.

I didn't know what to make of his alarm at hearing Estrelle's name or the instant enthusiasm when told about a possible ghost, but I'd been warned, hadn't I? The job description had mentioned right up front that he was peculiar.

"Does he live near the beach?" I asked, hopeful.

"Direct beachfront with some of the best views of the gulf around." She looked at me, concern flaring in her eyes. "You don't mind the water, do you?"

"Mind? Not at all." Happiness swirled through me. "I've only been to the beach once before, but I loved it."

"I have a love-hate relationship with the water, myself. It's so beautiful—breathtaking, really—but incredibly dangerous. You'll never find me in it, but I'll admire it from afar."

A few of the Mermaids, as Maggie had called them, were still milling around outside the shop, chatting. As a full group, they'd been quite a sight to behold, thirty to forty strong, made up of men and women alike, young and old and in between. They'd come into Magpie's windswept and disheveled, but all had been smiling and laughing and showing off their beach-combing finds—including a few bits of sea glass. The smooth green and blue pieces had been passed around, hand to hand, table to table.

One of them now called out, "Will we see you tonight at the library, Maggie?"

"I'll be there," Maggie said to the woman. "Seven?"

"Six if you want to do some pre-sale shopping," the woman said.

Maggie laughed. "Six it is. See you later!"

I glanced around to see if the youngest Mermaid was still nearby but couldn't find her in the crowd. She was a chubby-cheeked baby who'd been strapped to the chest of a young woman with pink-streaked, wind-teased hair. Six-month-old Juniper, who wore a snug yellow romper covered in bold daisies, reminded me of a golden baby goose with her big eyes and tufts of pale floofy hair. When she cooed, testing her voice, I decided it was the sweetest sound I'd ever heard. It had been her mom, Gracie, who had gone out of her way to make sure I held the sea glass, too. I'd smiled the whole time, feeling included in the delight of the discovery, even though I was a complete stranger to the group.

I couldn't quite remember the last time I'd felt included in anything exciting, and it left me slightly buoyant.

As Maggie and I turned the corner, she said to me, "The Friends of the Library is hosting a rummage and book sale this weekend. Tonight, we're sorting and pricing. One of the benefits of being a member is first dibs. Do you thrift much?"

"Every once in a while. I like vintage clothes and fabric. Thrift stores are some of the best places to find them."

With each step I took, the thimble in my pocket pressed against my hip. I wanted to take it out, feel its dimples. Nostalgia hit hard and fast as I thought about my grandmother, Bunny, teaching me how to sew a zipper pouch, our first project together.

Hand-sewing had been a great hobby to ease the boredom of being homebound all the time. And though a sewing machine would've made easy work of the project, my mother forbade using one. The loud sound it made was a risk she wasn't willing to take, fearing it would trigger a seizure in me. Noises sometimes did.

My first seizure had been a terrifying incident that had left my whole family shaken. After a series of medical tests, I'd been diagnosed with idiopathic epilepsy, a disorder with no known cause.

Then, three years ago, the seizures simply stopped occurring. Last year, after two years of being seizure-free, I was slowly weaned off all medications and was officially considered to be in early remission. I was well aware that relapse was possible. Probable, even.

But seizures or not, no one knew better than I did that my body wasn't fully healed. Not a single specialist could tell me if my senses of smell and hearing would ever return to what they once were or if they would always be this way. *Extraordinary,* a doctor had labeled them. To me, they were just more things in my life that weren't normal.

Fortunately, over the years I'd learned how to tune out when needed in an overwhelmingly noisy situation, but it took a lot of energy, and I didn't do it often. I'd always been able to control my heightened sense of smell much better—sniff, identify, dismiss—but I'd never get used to being able to smell perfume from a block away. Nor would I ever understand how scent could reveal a glimpse of personality, but it did.

As Maggie and I walked toward a parking lot behind the coffee shop, I heard hurried footsteps behind us. Then a voice called out, "Maggie! Yoo-hoo! Hold up!"

We turned. A squat woman rushed toward us, her white-blond hair teased, her chin high, elbows out. Immediately, she reminded me of a beautiful, if slightly unusual, crested duck I'd read about in one of my wildlife books.

"I'm so glad I caught you!"

She wore sensible pink heels and a floral wrap dress that barely contained her generous curves. I had the feeling she was the kind of woman who hugged with abandon, practically swallowing you whole.

"Good morning, Bettina," Maggie said, her voice cheery.

Bettina's breathing, shallow and rapid, sounded like it was being squeezed out of fireplace bellows. "Ooh, goodness. I saw you leaving Magpie's and turned on the jets to catch up." She flicked a glance at me and pressed her hands to her heart. "Well, hello, there. I'm Bettina Hopkins Fish, and I surely don't recognize you, young lady. Aren't you pretty as a peach?"

"This is Ava," Maggie said. "She's from Ohio."

"That explains the outfit." Bettina smiled while quirking an eyebrow at my coat. "How long are you visitin' our lovely little town?"

I didn't bother explaining the lucky blazer. "I'm not sure, but I hope to stay a long while."

"A snowbird, eh?"

Bettina spoke the word *snowbird* like she had a chicken bone stuck in her throat.

Tucking a fleeting pained look out of sight, she added, "Usually our snowbirds are a mite older than you, but we welcome all with open arms."

It sounded to me like her hospitality only came with a great deal of determination on her part.

A jaunty breeze teased coppery curls out of the clip that held them off Maggie's face. "Ava is going to be moving in with my daddy. A housekeeper of sorts."

Bettina's eyes widened, revealing shiny blue surprise. "Oh

my stars! I had no idea Desmond was looking for help. You know Sienna would've been interested. My niece," she said specifically to me. "She's been picking up odd jobs here and there but is still looking for something long-term. As much as I try to steer her along, she seems destined to wander aimlessly. Bless her heart, she simply can't seem to find her passion in life."

The comment struck a little too close to home for my comfort. Data entry was the only work I'd ever done, which paid the bills and allowed me to save a little. But it hardly fed the creative fires that burned inside me—the passion in me.

I recalled Alexander once saying, *You can change jobs, Ava. What do you want to do? It's your choice, not the other way around.*

He'd had what seemed like a zillion jobs, and not because he'd been a little more than a decade older than I was but because he bored easily. When I first met him, he'd been a manager at a local restaurant. Our friendship had grown slowly. We'd chatted at length whenever I placed a to-go order. Then he quit that job and began working as a food and beverage manager at the baseball stadium. He left there not long after we started officially dating, having managed to talk a buddy of his, a brewpub owner, into letting him try his hand at brewing beer. Alexander was always eager to leap headlong into something new and had never understood my reluctance to uproot myself.

Maggie said, "Some people's paths are more winding than others, but eventually she'll reach her destination. She'll figure it out. Give her time."

I stole another look at Maggie. She didn't seem to notice how her words had worked into my soul, wrapped around my heart. Squeezed.

Bettina clasped her hands together. "Sure enough. It's a dang shame her stint at the coffee shop didn't work out. I'd had high hopes."

"Me too." Maggie made a show of looking at her watch.

"Oh!" Bettina exclaimed. "I don't mean to be keeping you so long. I need to ask a favor, Maggie, and I'm sure hoping you'll say yes."

Maggie's smile tightened, and I thought I detected a slight note of panic in her voice as she said, "What can I do for you?"

"The Happy Clams just found out a pipe burst in our Foley warehouse, and lordy mercy, it's a nightmare. All our décor is ruined! We've called an emergency meeting for tomorrow morning to discuss our options. Mardi Gras is a scant five months away. We're in panic mode."

I'd lost my way in her words at *Happy Clams* and was completely puzzled by the mention of Mardi Gras.

Maggie must've sensed my confusion, because she translated for me. "The Happy Clams is a Mardi Gras krewe—a social group—that has had a float in the Gulf Shores Mardi Gras parade for the last fifty years. Their float and décor are stored in a warehouse in Foley, a town a little north of here."

Bettina grinned. "If you're still here in February, you're in for a treat, Ava. I'd invite you to sit on our float, but we're an organization comprised only of *seasoned* women—women of a certain age—but I surely do hope you'll join the Snail Slippers, our walking group. The name is a play on the slipper snail," she added. "You'll find their shells all along the beach, don't even have to look too hard. All ages are welcome, men and women alike. Pets are allowed, too. We even have a chicken in the group. We meet on Mondays, Wednesdays, and Fridays on the green at seven A.M. We usually wrap up around eight, three laps later."

My brain calculated mileage. According to my GPS when I drove into town this morning, one length of the square was a quarter mile. A full lap would be a mile, so three laps would be three miles. Dare I walk three miles? In the southern heat and humidity?

I waffled, fighting old fears. But how fast could the group possibly walk if it had *snails* in its name? I was sure I could handle it. "I'd like to join in," I said, testing my wings. "Thank you."

"Splendid! Just find me in the crowd and I'll introduce you around. Now, Maggie, I know it's short notice, but we'd sure love for Magpie's to supply a light refreshment at the meeting tomorrow morning. Nothing fancy, of course. An assortment of drinks and nibbles for twelve. Is it possible? Could you? Pretty please?" she asked, pressing her hands together as if in prayer.

"I'm not sure it's— I need to check with—" Maggie sighed. "I'd be happy to help."

"Oh!" Bettina squealed again and gave Maggie an enthusiastic hug.

For a moment, I thought I was going to have to borrow the Jaws of Life to pull Maggie free, but Bettina finally released her.

"You're the best, Maggie Brightwell." She stole a look at her watch. "Ooh, I must get going. See you tomorrow. Nine A.M. at Delaney Parrentine's house. Lovely to meet you, Ava. Toodles!"

She spun away, rushing off the way she'd come, and I glanced at Maggie. Her smile faltered briefly before she shored it up again. "Fair warning, by noon, the whole town will know you're here and why."

"Is there really a chicken in the Snail Slippers group?"

"Sure thing. Cluck-Cluck is her name, chosen by Jolly Smith's four-year-old granddaughter, Hannah, who is eyeball deep in a Cinderella phase."

I smiled, recalling how one of the mice in the Disney movie called chickens cluck-clucks.

"Jolly's chicken walks on a leash and everything. It's a sight to see."

My smile widened, making my cheeks ache. "I can't wait to meet her."

"Bettina can be a little overwhelming," Maggie said as we started walking again. "If she gets to be too much while you're with the Snail Slippers, just duck into the coffee shop on one of your laps around the square to hide out for a while."

"I'll remember that. Thanks." I stepped over a flower that grew out of the brick sidewalk. "Is there a story behind Sienna's brief employment at Magpie's?"

She laughed lightly. "Sienna has what I'd call *coordination* issues. In one short four-hour shift, she broke the credit card reader and the grinder, knocked over the display case of beans and mugs, and burned Rose with the steam wand. She's a lovely girl, truly, but she isn't well suited for a coffee shop work environment."

Ahead, a bakery van turned the corner and Maggie lit up, her deep-blue eyes sparkling in the sunshine. She waved her arm, flagging down the driver. A window powered down, and a man leaned out. He had brown hair with a hint of gray at the temples, blue-green eyes, and a devilish smile.

"You were just the man I was hoping to see," Maggie said.

He clutched his chest. "I've been waiting years to hear those words."

I caught the barely discernable sound of her breath catching before she said, "Ava, meet Donovan Quinlan. His family owns the Beach Mouse Bakery. They supply Magpie's with its baked goods."

She quickly introduced me as well, again saying that I'd be working for her father. I wasn't sure how she was so confident I'd get the job, but her surety blared like a horn each time she spoke about it.

"I need a big favor," she said to Donovan. "A last-minute order of pastries for a Happy Clams meeting tomorrow morning. Twelve guests. Can you help me out?"

One of his thick eyebrows rose. "If I don't?"

"I'll be baking all night."

"If I do?"

"I'll be eternally grateful."

His face wrinkled playfully. "Listen, while eternal gratitude is nice, it's not what I want."

Electricity sparked between them, and I wondered if they had a romantic history.

"What is it you want, then?" she asked, a loud note of apprehension in her voice.

"A date." He smiled broadly, then glanced at me. "I've been asking Maggie out for years. She keeps turning me down. Why, you might ask yourself, when clearly I'm a catch. I ask myself the same thing. Why?"

Her whole face flushed and she sputtered. "You have *not*

been asking me out for years. You've only been back in town for a few weeks, and in that time you haven't said a single word about a date." She turned my way. "He recently retired from the Coast Guard and moved back home to Driftwood."

"It *feels* like years that I've been asking for a date. That counts."

Maggie crossed her arms. "It doesn't."

He looked at me, a question in his eyes. I shook my head. "I side with Maggie on that one."

"Well, I've definitely *hinted* at a date."

"Hinting is not the same thing as asking, Donovan," she countered.

"Well, I might've asked, but you blew off the hints. I have my pride."

She opened her mouth, then snapped it closed again.

He glanced at me. "What's a man to do?"

"Oh my goodness. Stop," Maggie said. "You'll give Ava the wrong impression."

"What impression is that?" he asked.

"That you're pining for me." She once again faced me and her words came out in a rush. "Donovan and I have been friends a long time now. Forever, really. Since he's been back, he's been working at the bakery, so now he's kind of like a coworker. It wouldn't be proper to date."

With the tumble of words, I saw what she was doing. Hiding behind excuses. Why? It was obvious she cared for him. It was evident in her body language, in the way her eyes had lit up when she'd seen him. Did she not feel it? Or did she simply not want to acknowledge it?

I said, "I don't think it's improper. He doesn't work for you. Not really."

"Thank you, Ava," he said. "Finally a voice of reason. So what say you, Maggie? Will you go out to dinner with me tomorrow night? *Please.*"

Maggie rubbed her temples. "Why now, Donovan? Why ask me now? Today? This is all so sudden. What's gotten into you?"

The humor fell away from his face, and his features softened.

He held her gaze. "I saw an opening and grabbed it. I'm tired of waiting for you to see that I'm not kidding. I wasn't joking twenty years ago, and I'm not joking now."

Twenty years ago? I looked between the two of them, hoping they'd elaborate, but they didn't seem to notice my blatant curiosity.

Maggie's breath hitched, held. "We aren't the same people we were then."

While I desperately wanted to know what had happened between them, suddenly I felt like I shouldn't be witness to this conversation. I stepped away, pretending to study the cute cartoony mouse painted on the van's side panel. One wouldn't think a rodent would be a good brand for a bakery, but looking at it dressed as it was in a tiny apron with a little whisk in hand, I was ready to hand over cold, hard cash for anything it wanted to sell me.

Donovan said, "I don't think we've changed all that much, but I wouldn't mind finding out for sure. A date. It's all I'm asking."

I could hear Maggie's heart pounding. I spared her a glance and saw her holding Donovan's gaze, searching for something only she could see.

Softly, she said, "Fine, I'll go on a date. *One* date. But nothing fancy. Drive-thru fast food is good with me."

He smiled wide. "Heck, I'll let you pay if you want."

She sighed loudly. "Please go away now."

He was laughing as he drove off, and I suspected Maggie couldn't hear the relief floating on the sound like I did, warm and velvety.

Residential areas fanned out from the square in a loose grid pattern. As Maggie drove nearer to the coast, green lawns with oaks and pines and vines and flowers slowly gave way to sandy plots with palm trees, tall swaying grasses, and pots full of overflowing flowers where hummingbirds and butterflies hovered.

Inland, near the village square, cottages and bungalows with cement or stone foundations were the norm, but closer to the water, houses rose up, lifted a good ten or twelve feet off the ground by piers. Yet, the neighborhoods all felt cohesive, tied together with a cool color palette, twining sidewalks, and narrow wooden bridges that spanned wetlands.

Along the drive, I was swept up in the sounds swirling around, confused as to why they weren't bothering me in the least. I hadn't had any sensory issues in Magpie's earlier, either. The scents had been heavenly. Coffee mixed with hints of cinnamon, chocolate, hazelnut, and clove. And the sounds? Usually spending an hour in a coffee shop would've been like there were a dozen radios blaring in my head, all tuned to a different channel.

But today the blender, grinder, steamer, rattling ice, clank of silverware, music, and voices hadn't been the least bit overwhelming. It all sounded . . . mellifluous.

Why did the *whole town* feel like a familiar song?

The wind gusted more fiercely closer to the beach. Sand dusted the streets and sidewalks. What remained of the fog was thin and ethereal, a misty veil that made my skin and clothes feel damp to the touch.

I listened intently, wanting to know which bird had the call that sounded like a rattle and which one whistled. I was intrigued with the way the sand crunched under the tires of the golf cart. I was fascinated with the many sounds of the gulf water—beyond the waves hitting the shore, there was rolling and lapping, ripples and splashing.

Maggie turned right onto Eventide Lane, a dead-end street dotted with homes lifted on stilts, each one colored like an Easter egg. Blues and pinks, yellows and greens, all lovely and cheerful, even in the lingering mist.

Just beyond a beach-access boardwalk that cut through rolling sand dunes, Maggie pulled into the gravel driveway of the last house on the road. She slowed to a stop behind an old truck that was parked in one of the three bays under the house. An identical golf cart to Maggie's was parked in another of the stalls, and the third held two bikes, a fiery red adult tricycle and a lime-green cruiser bike with a brown seat.

Behind the house high dunes dotted with tall grasses blocked views of the water. Somewhere seagulls squawked. A pelican flew overhead, the flap of its wings steady, smooth, fearless as it cut through the choppy air. Two red flags thrashed in the wind, their hardware clanking against a metal flagpole.

Maggie shut off the engine and looked at me. "My dad is . . . well, he's a character. A bit loud, a bit exuberant. He's excitable. He's also one of the nicest, kindest, most loving men you'll ever meet. You'll love him. Everyone does."

"I'm sure I will." I was nervous to meet Desmond, hoping he'd like me enough to let me live here in this paradise. As I climbed out of the golf cart, I looked up at the house. "It doesn't look haunted."

Haunted houses conjured up images of dark, foreboding mansards with busted, shadowy windows and creaky doors, not this two-story beach cottage, painted a delicate grassy green, trimmed in creamy white and royal blue. A flight of sand-dusted stairs led up to a white porch that wrapped around three sides of the house.

"It's not haunted. It's just inhabited by a man who likes to blame an imaginary ghost for his messiness and forgetfulness."

"That's good to know," I said, even though I heard uncertainty in her voice, as though she was trying to convince herself more than me. There was obviously more to this ghost stuff than she was saying.

"The house isn't even twenty years old—hardly old enough to be haunted." She glanced around, her eyes mournful. "Most of this neighborhood was wiped out by Hurricane Ivan in 2004. We lost just about everything except for what we threw in the car when we evacuated and what survived in Dad's storage units, which are farther inland. We rebuilt, obviously, and have been mostly spared from other storms, thankfully. Sally, a few years ago, was a doozy for other places along this coastline but didn't cause any major damage here in Driftwood. We were lucky."

I glanced from one charming house to another, trying to picture the waves and wind that tore apart so many lives. "I can't even imagine."

"It was—" She shook her head, shuddered. "I hope we never have to go through something like it again."

I studied the beach house, built so high off the ground, and had to disagree with Maggie about the ghost situation. After a storm like that, I could easily imagine this place haunted. The house had been built on old memories and fears, haunted by all the things that had been lost to an angry sea, the panic of fleeing a beloved home, the fear of the unknown, the fear that it could happen again.

That it could all be lost again.

But then I realized that this house had also been built on resilience and fortitude and hope, and it filled me with warmth and appreciation. Hard times *could* be overcome, given time. Given heart. Given determination. Life could be rebuilt.

Fresh starts were possible.

I held tightly on to that thought as I looked toward the right side of Desmond's house. The end of the lane was marked with three stubby concrete posts that were painted flamingo pink. Beyond them was a short stretch of sand dotted with spiky clumps of grass before a pine forest rose up, seemingly out of nowhere. A trail marker stood at the start of a path that cut through the low brush, leading into shadows. "Is that a nature trail?"

Maggie said, "Driftwood is bordered with nature reserves on its east and west sides. There're miles of trails if you're of a mind to explore, though keep a careful eye out for alligators and snakes—they're around but just as afraid of people as people are of them."

I wasn't afraid—I was intrigued. The trails sounded like quite an adventure—the perfect place for me to stretch my wings.

Above us, I heard a door open and footsteps on the porch boards. "Hello down there!"

A man peered down at us over the porch railing. He had shoulder-length white hair, a thick white beard, dark-brown eyes that sparkled with vitality, full cheeks, and a deep tan.

"I'm preparing refreshments," he said. "Meet me out back and let me hear this ghost story. I'm about to pop with curiosity!"

His footsteps faded away. The door squeaked open, then closed. The sound of the surf rolled through the air, a constant repetitive rumble of soft, loud, soft, loud as the water ebbed and flowed.

Maggie climbed the stairs. "Like I said. Excitable."

I followed her up. On the porch, high above the dunes, I stopped short. Even with the milky remnants of the morning fog, the sight stole my breath. Beyond a stretch of sandy white beach, the gulf reached far and wide, the water a deep gray blue capped with spots of white where waves broke along its choppy surface. A pelican, with its long beak leading the way, patrolled the surface of the water, its wings skimming the spray. Dozens of smaller birds scurried along the beach, dipping in and out of the swash.

"It's something, isn't it?" Maggie stepped up next to me. She lifted her chin into the wind. The loose hairs framing her face danced with wild abandon.

I clutched the railing tightly, my knuckles white. My heart fluttered in my chest as I breathed in the salty air. "It's . . ."

I searched and searched but couldn't find the right word. A *big* enough word.

Something had shifted within me at the sight before me, something that stirred my soul and told me I *belonged* here, near the water. "It's incredible," I finally said, settling for a word that hardly mined the depth of emotion I felt.

"Sometimes I forget exactly how beautiful it is until someone like you reminds me, so thank you for that." She gave me a smile, then waved for me to follow her along the narrow side porch.

I could barely take my eyes off the water as we made our way to the back deck, where there was an assortment of chairs, loungers, and end tables. All were coated with a fine layer of dirt and dried-on salt, obviously not used often.

A screen room filled the right half of the wide deck. Maggie pulled open its thin wooden door and stepped aside to let me pass. Inside the room, two French doors led into the house, and both stood open wide, revealing a mid-century-style dining table piled high with cardboard boxes, its thin legs somehow bearing the load. Somewhere farther inside, a drawer opened, then closed.

"Daddy?" Maggie called into the house. "Do you need any help?"

"No, no! I'll be right there. Make yourselves at home."

I tried to take it all in. In each corner of the screen room, gauzy white curtains floated in the breeze. A fuchsia rug anchored a round iron-and-wood table and four cushioned chairs. In the center of the table stood a green folk art face vase, complete with buck teeth and bulging eyes, that held three pink dahlias.

Peculiar, I reminded myself.

Three place settings had been put out, each holding a dessert plate with a colorful chameleon pattern, a cloth napkin, and golden flatware. A pitcher of iced tea sat on a round tray along with three glasses—blue, green, and yellow. Large pillows were strewn about, and a telescope was aimed at the water.

On the wide threshold between the house and the screen room sat a fat cat, its tail swishing rhythmically. Left, right, pause, left, right, pause. The pause, I noticed, matched the ebbing of the waves.

I assumed this was the spoiled she-devil cat Maggie had mentioned in the job description.

She was the biggest cat I'd ever seen. Fluffy and creamcolored, she had a pale tangerine nose and ears that twitched as she watched me. I wanted to scoop her up and snuggle, but the look in her pale blue eyes warned me that would be a mistake. A huge mistake. If I was being completely honest, she kind of looked like a miniature lion eyeing its prey.

My parents hadn't been pet people and my pleas for a dog or cat or *anything* cuddly and furry had been answered with only books upon books about animals, both fictional and non. On my ninth birthday, Bunny had taken pity on me and gifted me a hamster. Mr. Whiskers. But he was only around a few months before he escaped his cage and disappeared.

The experience had traumatized my mom, who freaked out about a rodent being loose in the house, and subsequently forbade any gifts of living creatures. I'd always told myself that once I moved out on my own, I would march myself straight to the nearest shelter and adopt, but life hadn't quite cooperated. The little apartment I rented didn't allow pets either, so I was still left longing.

I was fairly giddy at the thought of finally having a pet to care for, even though this kitty didn't belong to me. By that look in her eyes, I suspected she didn't belong to Desmond, either. In fact, she might possibly be the one who was running this house.

"Welcome, welcome!" a voice boomed as Maggie's father swept out of the kitchen, taking care to step over the cat. He carried a platter of cellophane-wrapped chocolate cakes that he set on the table before kissing Maggie's cheek, then mine, as if he'd known me all his life. He smelled of sawdust and coconut, old books and mischief.

"Daddy, this is Ava Harrison. Ava, my father, Desmond Brightwell."

From the ankles up, he was dressed in what I could only describe as upscale cruise wear. Loose off-white linen pants and an oversized white button-down silk shirt. But his feet were clad in black Converse sneakers, the tongues slightly frayed, the canvas faded, the laces finessed to make the shoe a slip-on.

He had a heavy build, nearly perfectly spherical, and with his snow-white hair and dark eyes he reminded me of a harp seal pup, which made me smile.

"Ava, please call me Dez. All my friends do."

He was so inherently charming and welcoming that I was immediately taken with him. After the cheek kiss, I thought it silly to offer a handshake, so I simply said, "It's nice to meet you."

"The pleasure is mine." His gaze dropped to my blazer, his eyes widening a fraction as he studied the hedgehog I'd embroidered. An eyebrow lifted. His head tilted. "Is that vintage Chanel you're wearing?"

I nodded.

"Did you do the custom mending?"

I nodded again.

He laughed, a sound so cheerful and boisterous that I found myself smiling.

"You've got big nerve for such a tiny thing, don't you? I love it. You might just fit in here after all, Ava Harrison, ghost or not."

CHAPTER 5

MAGGIE

A date. A *date*.

Those were the last words I'd expected to hear from Donovan Quinlan today.

Or ever.

We'd never been on a date. Not a *real* one, at least. Despite our age difference—he was two years older—we'd been best friends as teenagers, growing especially close the summer he worked at the coffee shop when he was seventeen. Until he graduated high school and immediately enlisted in the Coast Guard, we'd been nearly inseparable.

"This is Molly," Dad said to Ava, gesturing toward the cat sitting in the doorway. "Do you like cats?"

I tried to pull myself out from my thoughts of Donovan in order to pay attention to what was going on around me. It was near impossible, though. I'd barely been able to think of anything else but him since he'd asked me out.

A *date*.

The young girl in me had been fairly jumping with joy at the thought of us getting a second chance. But I was older and wiser now and questioned whether our rocky past could truly be overcome.

Ava said, "I love cats. Is she a Ragdoll?"

"Dr. Eiderman, her vet, believes so," Dad said, the deep lines between his eyes furrowing, "but I think she might have Maine coon in her lineage as well."

Truly, Molly was the most ill-tempered, feisty, aggressive cat I'd ever met. Currently, her eyes were closed, but I knew she was somehow watching us. She was always watching. Waiting. Biding her time before sticking a paw out to trip someone or flexing her claws to inflict a deep scratch. She wasn't above biting, either, and I had the scars to prove it.

Dad said only, "Molly is reserved with her affection."

I smiled at his vagueness. As I poured us all a glass of tea, my thoughts wandered back to Donovan and those blue-green sea eyes of his, that impish smile.

The summer after my freshman year of college, he'd come back to Driftwood on leave to see me. The visit had ended badly. So badly that I could hardly think about it now without bursting into tears.

I'd broken his heart. And I'd broken mine. Smashed them both to smithereens, really.

"Hey, hey!" Dad said, reaching out with a napkin to dab the tea I'd spilled, my hands suddenly shaky, my memories jarring. "Coffee jitters?"

"I guess I had one too many espressos this morning," I lied, not wanting to explain about Donovan. In truth, since my health scare, I allowed myself only one coffee a day. "Sorry."

Dad eyed me as though he knew I'd fibbed. "No big deal. Sit, sit."

I carefully put the pitcher on the table and forcefully banished thoughts of Donovan, our past. As I sat, my gaze fell on the platter Dad had set on the table. Of course he'd served MoonPies. Not homemade ones, either. These came straight from the box, still in their plastic packaging. They were his signature dessert, the one he served at every party he hosted, the one he brought to every gathering.

It was actually somewhat reassuring to see them. If there had been something healthy on the plate like banana oat muffins or yogurt parfaits, my concerns about him would've only grown.

MoonPies were my daddy.

Not the person who was talking about selling Mama's coffee shop.

I studied him, searching for any signs that he was ill, but

Carmella was right. He looked the picture of health, especially since he had lost a few pounds—weight he'd been trying to take off for years.

Dad glanced at his watch. "I hate to be a boorish host, but I have an appointment at eleven I cannot miss, so forgive me for rushing us along."

"What kind of appointment?" I immediately asked, hoping for a clue as to what was going on in that head of his. There had to be a *reason* behind his behavior. All these changes weren't based on whim, his usual way of making decisions.

"The kind that is none of your beeswax," he answered with a cheeky smile. "Now, Ava, Maggie has filled me in on the job posting that brought you to town. I have to say I was quite surprised, as I *emphatically expressed* to my daughter that I was uninterested in a housekeeper or caretaker or however she phrased it."

"Uninterested," I put in, "doesn't mean *unnecessary*. And, Daddy, I told you I took down the job listing, threw it away. I don't know how Ava ended up with it. It's part of the mystery."

"Right, right," he said. "The mysterious letter. My condolences on the loss of your friend, Ava. I should've started with that. Please forgive my rudeness."

"No need for apologies," she said graciously. "This is an unusual situation, and I recognize we caught you off guard today."

"Unusual, yes. Quite. Do you have the letter? May I see it?"

Ava handed it over while giving him a quick rundown on what had led her here to Driftwood.

My cheeks heated as he read. *Hoo boy*. Never before had I ever wished so hard for a splash of vodka in my sweet tea. This moment called for alcohol fortification. Pulling in a deep breath, I sat tall, ready to stand my ground.

Dad glanced my way, a bushy white eyebrow lifted. *"Peculiar?"*

I shrugged.

His eyes widened. "She-devil?"

I flicked a glance at Molly. "I fully stand by that one."

His voice rose. "Bats in the belfry?"

I couldn't stop the grin if I'd tried. "I'd be happy if you proved me wrong."

Huffing, he rolled his eyes, then turned his full attention to Ava. "Do you believe in ghosts, Ava?"

Suddenly the air around us exploded with the scent of seaweed.

The curtains stilled.

The world around us fell eerily quiet.

Molly let out an unnerving *meow* and darted into the house.

Slowly the air cleared of the briny scent and stirred with life once again. I rubbed goose bumps from my arms.

Ava glanced around. Her eyes widened at the sight of a butterfly perched on one of the deck chairs. "I'm starting to believe."

Dad had straightened, his gaze darting. Then he laughed. "Don't that beat all. Ava's got herself a ghost."

She paled. "I don't—"

I gave her a barely perceptible head shake, a warning not to finish that sentence. The ghost was her ticket to landing this job.

She snapped her mouth closed.

"You believe it was your ex-boyfriend who sent this note?" Dad said, leaning toward her, fully invested. "How long did you date?"

She fidgeted in her seat. "Not very long, only three months. But Alexander and I were friends for a year before that."

My father put his elbows on the table. "How did you two meet?"

Ava fussed with the cuff of her blazer, tugging at a loose string. "The restaurant where he worked was just around the corner from my apartment and had some of the best food in town. I'd order takeout a few times a week, but I hated going inside to pick it up. It was always so *loud*. The music, the voices. It flustered me. I have sensitive ears. After a while, Alex noticed my discomfort and offered to meet me outside with my order when I called."

"That was kind of him," Dad said.

She nodded and smiled sadly. "It was. And it was nice to be *noticed*, you know? He asked me out early on, but I wasn't ready. Instead, we built a friendship. Every few weeks, we'd go for a long walk, or to a quiet movie, or on a picnic lunch. He was funny as anything, always making me laugh, and he was whip-smart, too. He entertained me with his past adventures—he was a drifter at heart and had lived in a dozen different cities, at least. And he was always traveling, quick getaways. It felt like he was getting on a plane every few weeks."

At the mention of his travels, I wondered if it was possible he'd been here, in Driftwood, when I typed the want ad. Summer was the height of our tourist season. But even if he had visited, it didn't explain how he'd gotten hold of a piece of paper I'd *thrown away*. Unless he'd somehow seen it in the two minutes it had been posted and then fished it out of the trash can.

Smiling, Dad said, "I was once a drifter as well. I sure do miss those days. I hope to get back to it eventually."

Wait. What? He'd never told me that. But he had mentioned it to Sienna, hadn't he? Telling her he longed to travel the world again.

"The stories I could tell," he went on, his eyes flashing with delight. "But do go on. This isn't about me. I want to hear more about Alexander."

Oh, but it was about him. Anger sparked and sputtered. How could he even *think* about traveling? Leaving Driftwood? My gaze went to the water, lingered there. As I watched the currents, my anger fizzled, replaced with a deep yearning to go back in time.

Ava said, "I'm pretty sure Alex knew a little something about *everything*. He was respectful of my sensitivities. I envied the way he never looked before he leaped, since I'm more of a baby-step kind of person. He was always encouraging me to be more outgoing, to be more like him. After a year, he asked me out again, and I said yes, finally ready to test those waters. But it didn't take long for me to realize that we'd been better off as friends."

Dad sipped his tea and said, "If you don't mind my asking, what made you come to that realization?"

"*Daddy*," I said on a sigh. He might possibly be the nosiest man on earth. Plus, he loved gossip. Couldn't get enough of it.

"No, it's all right," Ava said. "I don't mind sharing. I thought I knew everything about Alexander before we started dating. But I learned there are just some things you don't discover until you're spending *all* your free time together, opening yourself up more. Little things like how he left the cap off the toothpaste, the toilet seat up, and never cleaned up after himself. Bigger things like his increasing pressure on me to be more adventurous, and his obsessive need to check his phone all the time. He'd even wake up every couple of hours during the night to check it."

Dad whistled and shook his head.

"It was unsettling," she said. "He had such a big fear of missing out on life that he couldn't settle down. Even in his short bursts of sleep, he was restless. He had a master's degree in business but preferred to job hop than settle into a long-term role. He moved every one to two years because he bored easily. He felt like if he didn't learn something new *every* single day that he'd wasted the day. He had a hundred hobbies, at least. Stunt kites, photography, blacksmithing, guitar playing, rock climbing. The list felt endless. He'd see something intriguing, learn all about it, master it, then move on to the next thing."

One or two of the things she mentioned could probably be overlooked or compromised on. But as a whole? It was a lot to overcome. No wonder they hadn't lasted.

"When he confessed he didn't want pets or children because they'd tie down his adventurous spirit," Ava said, "I knew I absolutely had to end it with him. Those are deal breakers in my book."

Dad flicked me a glance, and I knew immediately what he was thinking about—because I'd been thinking it, too.

Noah.

His father hadn't wanted kids, either. Well, not at nineteen years old at least. My heart ached whenever I thought about

Theo and me, two terrified college kids, holding our breath while watching for lines to appear in the small window of a pregnancy test, the rest of the dorm loud and rowdy and carefree.

Dad sighed, deep and heavy, and asked Ava, "How did Alexander handle the breakup?"

She took a sip of tea, then said, "For the most part, fairly well. He'd also come to the realization that we weren't compatible as a couple. The breakup was amicable. Friendly, even. I think we were both more relieved than anything. He was going to move to Amsterdam."

"The most part?" Dad's eyebrow went up.

Suddenly, I was grateful for his nosiness, because I'd caught that too and wanted to know more. I leaned in.

The wind gusted, teasing light brown hair from her topknot. "After we broke up, he kept texting me, trying to get me to go here, there, wherever. Roller skating. Bowling. A concert. A riverboat tour. You name it. There was almost an obsessive tone to the texts that made me realize that at some point during our relationship, I'd become one of his hobbies. A challenge to master. I was a puzzle he hadn't been able to solve, and he wasn't going to be able to move away until he finished what he'd started in Cincinnati. He was bound and determined to get me fully out of my comfort zone. But I still wasn't ready to be that adventurous. And then he passed away—he was hit by a car late one night a couple of weeks after the breakup."

Dad smacked the table with his hand, making Ava and me jump. "Is that why you think he sent the letter? He's still trying to get you out of your comfort zone?"

Looking pained, she nodded. "After reading that letter, something came over me, and I knew it was finally time to make my own leap, to start an adventure of my own. So here I am."

After hearing what Ava had to say, I was starting to believe the letter *had* come from a ghost. It made a strange sort of sense. Yet . . . "But why would Alexander send you *here*? Why *this* town? *This* job? There has to be a reason."

"Did you not see the note written at the top?" Dad asked.

"Ava is destined to find happiness here. Many do, you know," he said to her.

"Really?" she asked.

"I've lost count at how many people have visited and end up staying. That number includes me. My wife and I honeymooned here and loved it so much we ended up buying a house." He laughed at the memory, then the sound fell away, and he looked out toward the water.

Today was a double-red-flag day—absolutely no one was allowed in the water due to the dangerous riptides. Twenty-seven years ago, before the flag system had been implemented, it had been the same kind of day. Without realizing the danger, my mama ventured into the surf to swim with a squadron of manta rays and hadn't come back yet.

I clenched my fists tightly, my short fingernails digging into my palms to refocus the pain, to control it so I didn't break down into a puddle of tears.

Ava was perceptive—she'd caught the shift in the mood. She glanced between my father and me, seeking the source of the sadness.

My gaze went to my father's ring finger to find a glimmer of comfort in the thin gold band my mother had once placed onto his finger. A symbol not only of love but of our family unity, our bond. I blinked. There was no ring.

"Daddy," I blurted, "where's your wedding band?"

He glanced at his hand, then at me. Fidgeting, he seemed to be searching for what to say.

"You lost it, didn't you?" I said, turning toward the house, a headache flaring to life. "Do you think you lost it inside? Or on the beach? Or at one of your work sites?" It was going to take a miracle to find it. My breath caught at the thought that the ring might be gone forever. No. I refused to believe it. We'd find it.

"Now, now, Magpie, don't go getting all riled up. My ring is with Javier, being resized." He patted his remarkably diminished double chin. "If you haven't noticed, I've dropped a few pounds. My ring was loose."

Of course I'd noticed the weight loss. I also suspected, by the look in his eyes, that he wasn't telling me the whole truth about the ring. He'd been losing track of his belongings left and right for the last few months, blaming the misplacements on a nonexistent ghost. "It's lost, isn't it? Just tell me so I can start looking."

He laughed. "Calm down or you'll be on the fast track for another stroke."

Ava's head whipped my way, her eyes full of sympathy.

I held up a hand. "It wasn't a stroke. It was *mini*-stroke. A TIA. And I'm fine. It didn't cause any damage. Dad's just trying to deflect from the fact that he lost his ring."

Despite a history of headaches, I'd been as shocked as anyone the day my left side went numb in the coffee shop and my words had come out as gibberish. Rose rushed me to the emergency room, but by the time I got there, I was back to normal.

Normalish.

My blood pressure had been through the roof. I'd been put on medication, had to make changes to my diet, and had been given an exercise plan. I'd also been warned about the dangers if I kept spreading myself too thin.

"It is *not* lost," Dad said. "It's at Mother of Pearl. Feel free to check with Javier. Have a MoonPie. Have you eaten today? You always get out of sorts when you're hungry."

I wasn't hungry, but the roaring in my head was enough for me to lean back, take a deep breath. I blew out a sigh and made a mental note to stop by to see Javier Blanco at his jewelry shop.

"Let's get back to the matter at hand, shall we?" Dad tapped the letter. "I'd like to hear a little more about you, Ava."

She pulled so hard on one of the strings on her sleeve that it broke free. "Me? Let's see. I've lived in Cincinnati my whole life, in the same neighborhood, though not the same house. My parents divorced when I was a teenager, and my dad and my older brother moved to the West Coast, where they still live. My mom eventually remarried and is now living in Florida."

Dad leaned in, clearly seeking more. "And?"

Her hands stilled as she met his gaze. Something unspoken

passed between them. Her voice wavered slightly as she said, "I was a sheltered child. I was tucked away in a safety zone that eventually became a comfort zone I rarely left, even though I longed to. Fear has held me back. I have to confess that being here now, I'm scared to death. But I'm also excited and ready to see what life has to offer."

Compassion filled Dad's eyes, softening them. He drummed his fingers on the table for a moment before saying, "I believe your ghost has sent you to exactly the right place, Ava, but before I make a decision about hiring you, there's one big wrinkle to iron out."

"A wrinkle?" she asked.

Out of habit, his hand dipped inside the collar of his shirt and he picked up the pendant he wore on a leather cord that hung around his neck. I was thankful to see he hadn't lost it. At least not yet.

"Yes," he said. "You see, tidying up after me is *not* a full-time job."

"I beg to differ," I piped in, rubbing my aching temples. "Going through all your boxes is a full-time job in itself."

"Hush now. It isn't." Dad tucked the pendant away. "The house is cluttered, yes, but all that will be gone in two weeks, after the yard sale is over. Here's my proposition for Ava: two part-time jobs. One in the mornings at Magpie's, the other here, helping around the house in the afternoons. The coffee shop is busiest in the mornings, and Magpie's can use some extra help since an employee recently moved away."

"Dad, that's ask—"

He held up a hand, silencing me. "That's my offer. Take it or leave it."

"But," I said, "don't you remember earlier that Ava mentioned restaurant sounds bothered her? The coffee shop is no better. We shouldn't put her on the spot. This isn't about me needing help. It's about *you* needing help."

I needed Ava here, full-time. How else was I ever going to discover what was going on with him?

"I beg to differ," he said, serving my words back to me on a smug platter.

Here and now it was hard to uphold any theory that he was losing his mind. He wasn't struggling to find words. His mental acuity seemed sharp. Razor sharp. His humor was intact. His empathy. However, I couldn't simply dismiss his forgetfulness lately.

"Actually," Ava said, her gaze darting between us, "I was okay in the coffee shop this morning. The sounds were . . . surprisingly pleasing."

"Then it's settled?" Dad asked her.

Ava smiled, big and bright. "It's a deal."

I let out a sigh of defeat on the Magpie's front even as relief swept through me. By living here, she was going to be able to keep a better eye on him than I ever could—even if she was only technically working for Dad part-time. And then she could report back to me on anything that might seem amiss.

It seemed as soon as my body felt the swirls of relief, thoughts of Donovan popped back into my head. I tried to push them back out, but it was of no use.

What had I been thinking by saying yes to a date? I didn't want to rehash our past, relive that pain. I should cancel. Yes. Definitely. I'd call him up and tell him I changed my mind.

But . . .

I wanted to go.

I wanted to sit next to him, stare into those mesmerizing eyes, and believe we finally had a chance. I wasn't a scared young girl anymore. He was back in town for good. Once we worked our way through old hurts, there wasn't anything to hold us back.

We could take our time, get to know each other again. See if there was still something between us worth reviving. And I hoped we could do it quietly, without the whole town finding out. At least at first. I didn't want the pressure, the scrutiny.

"Oh! I almost forgot." Ava's mossy green eyes sparkled with joy, making them shine like emeralds as she dug into her bag. "I brought references."

"Yes, yes," Dad said, taking them from her and immediately passing them to me. "Formalities only. I trust my instincts, and they're saying you're trustworthy. Plus, the Chanel doesn't hurt. You'll have to tell me about the mending—" He glanced at his watch, winced. "Later."

Ah yes. He had to get to his none-of-my-beeswax appointment.

"Before I leave," he said, "there is one other small wrinkle we should work out. A crease, really."

"What now?" I asked, eyeing him warily.

He took a sip of tea, taking his time to answer. Finally, he said, "It's going to take me at least a week to sort through the guest room to make it livable. Ava will need another place to stay until then."

"I'll book a hotel," Ava said quickly. "I passed quite a few of them on my way here."

"Nonsense," Dad said. "You can stay with Maggie since Noah's room is currently unoccupied."

Ava blinked. "Noah?"

Trying to decipher the look in my father's eyes—and failing—I said, "My son. He's currently away at college."

For a change, I was glad Noah wasn't home. This way, he didn't know about the changes in his grandfather. There was no need to stress him out—or for him to see me stressed out. He'd only want to come home, to help. He didn't need to be pulled away from the life he was building at college or be distracted from his studies. I could handle what was going on with my father on my own. Well, with a little assistance from Ava.

"Of course you'll stay with me, Ava. I'm happy to have the company."

"Wonderful!" Dad clapped and stood up. When he walked around the table to give Ava a hug, a piece of paper fluttered out of his pocket.

I bent down to pick it up. It was a business card for Orrel Gibbs. On the back of the card in Dad's scribbly penmanship was written, *Monday 11 A.M.*

I slipped the card onto the table and watched as my father pointed out a dolphin fin not too far offshore. As Ava laughed with delight, I fought to calm a storm brewing within me.

Because apparently whatever was going on with Dad involved a probate attorney.

CHAPTER 6

AVA

"Why in the world would Dad need a probate lawyer?" Maggie asked Rose early the next morning as she poured coffee beans into a grinder. "He clammed right up when I asked him. Didn't he, Ava?"

Across the dining room, where I was busy removing chairs from the tops of tables, I nodded. Dez definitely hadn't wanted to talk about the lawyer.

Faint music—'80s classics—played from overhead speakers as Rose carefully poured half-and-half into a slim stainless steel carafe. "Can't say I know why," she finally said to Maggie, as if she had been weighing her words, trying to find the perfect balance.

I heard evasion in her undertones. She can't say? Or *won't* say?

I set another chair on the floor. There were eight tables in all. Each had a dark-stained wooden top with a white apron and legs, which reflected the color palette of the whole shop: black, white, and wood, with touches of gold here and there, like in the bakery case.

The timeless, classic décor didn't match Maggie's style at all—at least not from what I'd seen at her house. There, the bright and airy space had been done in pale greens and blues and creams, reminding me of a sea that reflected a cloudy sky. Thick area rugs covered tiled floors, squishy accent pillows dotted sofas and chairs, and plush throw blankets were draped invitingly. None of that *softness* was present at Magpie's, yet somehow both spaces felt inviting.

The menu didn't seem to represent Maggie, either. At her

place, her spice cabinet held a wide variety of tins and her fridge had been full of foods and condiments with big flavors. The menu here was minimalist to say the least, offering only a sprinkling of drinks in just two sizes, small and large. There were hardly any specialty flavors and none that appeared to be seasonal, like pumpkin spice. It was September, after all. There were only two choices for milk: 2 percent and almond. No cold brew. No pour over. No frozen drinks.

On one hand, I questioned why the menu hadn't been expanded over the years, but on the other, I was grateful that it was going to be easy to memorize. Currently the plan was that I'd work here Tuesdays, Thursdays, and Saturdays, opening till noon. The pay was decent but there were no benefits other than all the coffee I could drink, which was a perk I appreciated because I wasn't used to waking up so early.

The chirpy alarm I'd set on my cell phone had woken me at the crack of dawn, and I had automatically pressed the snooze button. When I finally blinked open my eyes, it had taken a second to remember where I was and why there had been dinosaur diagrams hanging on the wall.

Maggie's son Noah was at Vanderbilt, studying earth and environmental sciences with hopes of being a paleontologist one day, something Maggie had told me he'd dreamed of since he was a small boy. I was impressed—and a little envious. What was it like to know what you wanted at such a young age? I was twenty-seven and still didn't have a clue.

There had been only two photographs in Noah's room, both tacked to the mirror above the dresser with yellowed tape. One was of Dez and a young boy, who I assumed was Noah, standing on a dock, wearing matching smiles and a look of pride as they lifted a scrawny-looking fish high in the air. The other picture was of an impossibly young Maggie holding a baby out in front of her, a comical look of what-in-the-hell-did-I-get-myself-into on her face as spit-up oozed down her shirt. She couldn't have been much older than eighteen or nineteen, and the way she stared at the baby had filled me with warmth. It was as if, even in that distressing moment, she was saying with her eyes that she'd willingly let him spit up on her every minute of every day if she had to, because that's just how much she loved him.

I set another chair on the floor of the coffee shop as Maggie said to Rose, "It's strange, though, right? Something else to add to the long list of bizarre things going on with my father these days."

After today's shift, Maggie and I were going back to Dez's house, and I was eager to see inside, since I hadn't had the chance yesterday. In his rush not to miss his morning appointment, he had all but kicked us out, telling us to come back today for a full tour.

Maggie hadn't out-and-out said so, but she had been worried about that appointment. I supposed I'd be worried too if it were my father who suddenly started acting strangely. Before she rushed off to the library last night, we'd shared a pizza for dinner. While we ate, she'd explained why she'd written the want ad in the first place and her hopes that I'd be able to help shed light on his odd behavior lately.

To me, Dez didn't seem like a man who was failing in any way, shape, or form, but sometimes health troubles were well hidden. I knew that better than most. I had looked perfectly healthy when I was younger, but I hadn't been. Not by a long shot.

Across the street, slivers of early-morning sunlight fell across the tops of the oak trees in the park. People were already headed toward the beach, pulling wagons of fishing gear. I'd seen a few Mermaids heading that way as well, and I hoped they'd bring their finds to the shop later on.

I caught my reflection in the picture window and smiled at the purple Magpie's shirt I wore. It was going to be hot today, in the low nineties, so I'd thrown on a pair of shorts to complete the outfit. I was more than ready to start the first day of my new normal. My *normal* life.

Rose put the lid on the carafe, and the threads squeaked lightly as they tightened. "Might could be he's getting his affairs in order. He's sixty-eight now. Long past time to have it done. I'm fifty-two and had my will drawn up long ago."

According to Maggie, Rose had worked at the coffee shop since it had opened, and just from the short time I'd seen her bustling about, I had little doubt she could run the place on her own. She'd given me a big hug when Maggie officially introduced us earlier, and also gave me her life in a nutshell: divorced with two grown children who both were raising families in the area, lived in Lower Alabama her whole life, loved the beach, coffee, and people.

Laughing, Rose added, "Made my kids co-executors instead of choosing one over the other. They can fight it out after I'm gone and then I don't have to listen to the bickering. You've never seen two siblings who like to squabble so much. Felt like I was moderating a debate team more often than mothering. Do you have any siblings, Ava?"

The evasiveness I'd heard in her voice had now been replaced with diversion.

Curiouser and curiouser.

"An older brother. He lives in Oregon." I kept in touch with texts and video calls but had yet to make a trip out to see him, since in my old life I didn't travel. But now? Now I decided I should book a flight to see him. My first flight ever.

Maggie, however, wasn't so easily distracted by Rose's tactics. "Dad getting his affairs in order would make perfect sense if he was seeing an estate-planning attorney. But a probate one? Probate is only for handling estates *after* death. Right?"

Rose glanced up as she set the half-and-half container on the counter and sent me a silent plea, her eyes all but begging for help.

At seeing the look, I let a chair slip out of my hands. It crashed against the floor, the sound hurting my ears. "Sorry!"

Rose rushed around the counter, mouthing *thank you* as she did so. She bent and lifted the chair, setting it on its feet. "You should grab yourself a cup of coffee before we open. No offense, sugar pie, but you don't look like you slept all that well last night."

I didn't take offense, because I hadn't slept well. After

Maggie had left for the library, I'd gone down to the beach and walked along the shoreline, reveling in the lap of the water against my ankles and the wind in my hair until the sun melted on the horizon. Back at Maggie's, I'd watched her two goldfish, Mac and Cheese, swim around for a while. Then I'd texted with my mom, letting her know a little more about my new job with Dez—but not about the job at the coffeehouse. Or the fact that I was in Alabama. Not yet.

I'd tried to turn in early, but couldn't fall asleep, so I watched old Esther Williams movies on my phone until almost midnight. When I finally settled in, unfamiliar noises kept me awake. The squeak of a strange mattress, the dull whirr of the ceiling fan, the whisper of curtains against the window frame. Outside, wind chimes had clinked, bugs chorused, and the waves, two blocks away, slapped against the beach in their endless ebb and flow.

And somewhere in the night a fiddle had cried, sounding like an elegy meant for my ears only.

"I'll get the coffee," Maggie said. "Is drip okay? Or I can make you an espresso? Or a latte?"

I supposed some of my exhaustion came from simply being here, in Driftwood. Everything was new here. *Everyone.* I'd spoken to more people yesterday than I had in years. Adjusting to normality was going to take time.

"Drip is great," I said, smiling. "Thanks."

I didn't really want any more coffee—I'd already had two cups—but it was keeping Maggie's mind off Dez for the time being, which I decided was a good thing. Worrying so much couldn't be good for her health. I'd done a little research on TIAs last night as well. Because she'd had a mini one, she was now at risk of a major stroke.

"Are you hungry?" Maggie asked. To Rose, she said, "She didn't eat this morning."

"I'll get you a muffin," Rose said. "Chocolate? Banana?"

I smiled, deciding to be amused rather than annoyed by the mothering. "Thank you, but coffee is enough. I don't have much of an appetite in the mornings."

Or at all lately. I didn't dare mention not eating well since Alexander had died—I'd lost seven pounds in the last month. I could only imagine their reaction to that.

Give it time, my mom had said.

I drew in a deep breath, repeating the words over and over in my head.

Rose narrowed her gaze at me. She smelled of jasmine and sugar, of a sunny garden and affection. For some reason, I wanted to sit down and spill my whole life story out to her.

"I'm okay, I promise," I said.

Something buzzed from behind the counter and she turned toward the noise. "All right, Ava, but you just grab yourself something if you get hungry."

I nodded. "Thanks, Rose."

Giving my arm a gentle squeeze, she leaned in and whispered, "Thanks again," before heading to the counter.

She passed Maggie on the way, who hurried toward me with a cup of coffee in one hand. In the other was a set of old Tupperware measuring spoons, mustard yellow and in fairly good condition considering their age. She'd come home from the library with them last night, all smiles.

After taking the cup of coffee she handed me, I politely took a sip. She'd already memorized how much cream and sugar I liked. I suspected she knew the orders of everyone in town by heart. "Thank you. The coffee here is really good, not that I expected anything less, considering."

"It's a local blend. Do you remember Donovan?"

How could I forget? "From the bakery."

Nodding, she walked over to the Curiosity Corner and set the measuring spoons on one of the driftwood shelves. "His older brother owns Little Lagoon Roasters, where we get all our coffee."

"Talented family."

There was no rhyme or reason to the collection that I could discern, but Maggie must've seen something I couldn't, because she beamed at the mishmash of objects with pride.

The church bell started tolling the seven o'clock hour and

almost immediately someone pulled open the front door and came inside.

"Morning, Mrs. Pollard," Maggie and Rose said in unison.

"Morning, ladies!" She shuffled in, her gaze on the blackboard at the back of the shop. "How's my recipe doing?"

"Pictures are being snapped left and right," Rose said.

Mrs. Pollard beamed.

Maggie looked at me. "Ready to learn how to make an Americano?"

I nodded, and as I passed by the driftwood tree, I felt the thimble Maggie had given me in my pocket. I wasn't sure why I'd even brought it with me today. Or why I'd been given the gift at all. Or, most especially, why there was a murmur deep down when I held the thimble, as though it was speaking directly to my heart.

CHAPTER 7

MAGGIE

"Gossip is making the rounds, Maggie," Mary Carole Adkinson said as she floated around the teal-and-walnut sideboard where I was setting up the coffee service for the Happy Clams.

The coffee shop received a lot of business from private events. In the past I'd set up in schools, churches, wedding venues, hair salons, offices, the beach. Just about anywhere, really. So far the only place I wouldn't go was on a boat. Not a yacht. Not a pontoon. Not a party barge. If it floated, it was out of the question.

I'd been hoping to be in and out of Delaney Parrentine's house before many of the other members arrived, but between getting Ava situated at the coffee shop and prepping for this last-minute order, I'd been running late this morning.

I wasn't the only one.

Donovan had texted earlier. The bakery's short-staffing issue had caused a delay with the order of scones, muffins, and cookies for the Happy Clams. He'd promised a special delivery to drop the pastries off here as soon as they were ready, which he assured me would be *before* the meeting was set to begin.

I hadn't seen him since he'd asked me out yesterday, and I was jittery with nerves, which was all kinds of silly. It was Donovan. Donovan, who I'd known my whole life. We'd made mud pies together. Played tag. Fished. Rode bikes. Hunted blue crabs. Swam—until I no longer went in the water. We snuck out together. Shared secret kisses. Held hands. Watched movies. Dreamed together.

But then I realized that was exactly why I was nervous. He wasn't some random guy I'd been set up with. This wasn't a casual date.

"Gossip?" I repeated, hoping I sounded clueless.

While Magpie's was hands down the best place to hear the latest news in town, it had never been the *subject* of the gossip. Until today. Nearly everyone who'd come in this morning had weighed in on my father possibly selling the coffee shop *and* had also quizzed Ava on the mysterious letter that had brought her to town.

It was no surprise at all to me that I had a headache.

A gauzy maxi dress drifted around Mary Carole's legs as she moved about, adjusting a picture frame, the basket of napkins. "I hear there's a newcomer in town who's going to work for Dez and is also working at the coffee shop? Is that true?"

Mary Carole, a retired microbiologist, was the grandmother of thirteen little ones, the oldest in graduate school. She'd seemingly dipped herself in the fountain of youth, because she didn't look a day over fifty.

I filled a creamer jug. "It's true. Her name is Ava Harrison."

Mary Carole's blond hair was pulled into a fancy twist held in place with a long tortoiseshell comb. Clear blue eyes watched my every move as I set out stir sticks, an assortment of tea, and three airpots—regular coffee, decaf coffee, and hot water. A tiered cake stand sat empty, waiting on Donovan's arrival.

"She's from Ohio?"

"Yes." I rearranged the coffee cups that Delaney, the hostess, had supplied. She'd taken up pottery late in life and had created all the mugs herself. Each was unique, though had the same beachy glazed design—a sandy-brown bottom, swirling blues in the middle, lighter blues at the top, all flecked with gold. Stunning works of art, each of them, and I felt a rush of pride at seeing them.

The first time I met Delaney, I'd been compelled to give her a loop tool, one used for sculpting, from the Curiosity Corner. It had rekindled in her a long-buried interest in making pottery. Now she had a thriving pottery business, and it filled me with happiness knowing I had played a small part in its success.

"Don't you think someone from within our own community would've been a better choice? Someone who's known your father her whole life?"

Obviously, Bettina had bent Mary Carole's ear.

"No." I smiled as sweetly as I could. "Ava is the best person for the job."

I could only imagine the havoc Sienna would wreak in my father's cluttered house.

"You barely know her. She could rob him blind."

"I know enough." Anyone who met Ava for longer than two seconds could easily see her kind heart shining in her eyes. She'd be more likely to give him the shirt off her back than take his.

Mary Carole smiled, her gaze softening. "I've always admired the strength of your convictions, Maggie. At least I can tell Bettina that I tried. If she's being intrusive, it's only because she's worried about Sienna."

We were all a little worried about Sienna. We'd watched her grow through the years as she spent each summer at the beach with her aunt. After she graduated high school in South Carolina four years ago, she'd been at a loss what to do with herself, so Bettina had taken her in, hoping a change of scenery would be inspiring. And even though she couldn't seem to hold a job, she'd sure found a place in all our hearts.

"I'll keep an ear out for anyone hiring," I said, though most of the town was keeping an ear out already, all of us looking for a soft place for her to land, a *safe* place. Somewhere she couldn't break anything or accidentally hurt anyone.

As I lined up a row of tea bags, I felt Mary Carole's warm gaze holding steady on me. I glanced at her, a question in my eyes.

She shook her head, laughed. "I was trying to decide whether to mind my own business, but I've never been any good at that, so I'm just going to ask flat-out: Is Dez selling the coffee shop? I've been hearing talk this morning that he is."

"He's *not* selling." I needed to print a T-shirt with those words on it, because I did not want to have this conversation ever again.

She exhaled so deeply she bowed backward. "I'm relieved to hear it. I was worried for you. What would you do? It's your livelihood! And what would happen to your precious Curiosity

Corner? And Rose? She's worked there since the very beginning. Visiting that shop without seeing both your wide, welcoming smiles would be like the sun not coming up."

My heart pounded. I hadn't allowed myself to think about
questions like those because Dad *wasn't* selling. He wasn't. But
now that they'd been spoken aloud, they hung in the air like
neon signs, like *warning* signs.

"Perhaps Dez is having a delayed midlife crisis?" she spec-
ulated.

I fought off a wave of dizziness and smiled wanly. "He may
just be."

She put a hand on my shoulder. "Maggie? You've gone pale.
Why don't you sit down? Delaney?" she called over her shoulder. "Could you bring a glass of water for Maggie?"

I shook my head and waved her off. "I'm okay. One too
many espressos this morning," I said, pulling out my usual excuse. It was coming in handy lately.

She made a clucking noise. "Espresso might not be the best
choice for someone with your blood pressure issues."

"But it's so good."

She laughed. "That it is."

Delaney rushed into the room, a glass of water in hand.
"What's wrong?"

"Maggie's blood pressure just spiked." Mary Carole took
the glass and handed it to me, obviously seeing through my
espresso-coated lies.

Delaney crossed her arms. "Well, it's no wonder with Dez's
fool talk about selling the coffee shop. Don't you worry, Maggie dear, we all have a mind to give him what for."

"I'm certainly going to let him have it next time I see him,"
Mary Carole said. "Hell, I might even go looking for him."

"I'll go with you," Delaney said. "He needs to know we'll
stand by you any way we can. We know what that shop means
to you, Maggie. If it comes to it, many of us are always on the
lookout for a good investment opportunity, and we know our
money would be in good hands with you."

Feeling tears threatening, I took a sip of water, glad my hand was steady enough not to spill. "I don't understand why he's even contemplating it. Magpie's is the heart of this town." I took a deep breath. "Do either of you know why he might visit a probate attorney?"

Mary Carole's eyes flared in surprise. She waited a beat, then two, before tightly saying, "No, not a clue."

Delaney shook her head. "Me, either. Not unless—"

Mary Carole not-so-subtly elbowed her, and she snapped her mouth closed.

"Unless what?" I asked, suddenly alarmed.

Delaney waved a hand. "Unless he was estate planning. But that's the wrong type of attorney. My mistake." Her eyes were bright with lies.

Why would she lie? What was I missing?

Outside, a car door closed. "That might be Donovan."

Delaney and Mary Carole shared a look, then Mary Carole said, "Ah, yes, that's another piece of gossip I heard."

"What? What did you hear?" I asked, suddenly bone weary.

"That there's love in the air between you and Donovan Quinlan," Delaney said, fairly bouncing up and down with delight.

I put the glass down before I dropped it. "Where did you hear that?"

Delaney grinned. "A tall, handsome mousy told me when I was at the bakery yesterday."

Donovan? Had he been telling people about our date? Why would he do that? Didn't he know the ramifications of a statement like that in a town this size?

Delaney added, "I always thought you two would make the perfect couple. You were always glued at the hip in your teens. Everyone thought . . . well, we all thought you were meant to be and hoped you'd find your way back to each other. It's lovely to see the spark between you rekindled."

My cheeks were burning. I held up a hand. "Let me stop you right there."

"No, no," a deep voice said from behind me. "Do go on. I heard something about being meant for each other. I like the sound of that."

I was surprised I hadn't heard him come in. He was the type who commanded a room, filling the space with his energy, his mischievous personality. There wasn't a time I could remember that I hadn't been aware of him walking into a room.

Until today.

I blamed the headache.

He stepped up to the sideboard carrying double-stacked white boxes, each printed with the Beach Mouse Bakery logo. He glanced at me, a twinkle in his teal eyes. "Hi, honey. Sorry I'm late. These are for you."

Honey?

I might have to kill him with my bare hands.

But, oh lord. Why had my knees gone weak?

Tongues were going to be wagging all over the town. And once they started, they wouldn't stop until they had us married off. We weren't going to have a moment's peace. He had to know that. He *had* to. Why was he stirring the pot?

"A big, strapping, handsome man who brings me pastries?" Delaney pressed her hands to her heart. "You're a lucky woman, Maggie."

"The luckiest," I murmured as I set chocolate muffins on the stand.

"Where are y'all going for dinner?" Mary Carole asked. "The Outrigger? Honeysuckle?"

They were two of the area's most popular upscale restaurants, and the thought of dining with the eyes of many neighbors upon us filled me with dread. We'd be like bugs under a microscope, every move examined, analyzed, and then reported to the rest of the town.

I just wanted to be alone with him. I wanted to get to know him again. I wanted to see if we had a fighting chance.

"I'm thinking along the lines of something more *intimate*," Donovan said. "I'd share, but I'd like it to be a surprise for Maggie."

Both women faux fainted.

I gaped at him, and he shot me an innocent smile.

He was only forty, but I suddenly questioned if it was possible *he* was having some sort of midlife crisis, only early.

Or maybe he'd simply lost his mind.

The same way I was going to lose mine if he kept yammering on about anything intimate.

As I set the last of the pastries on the stand, my headache hammered my temples so fiercely I thought my head might explode.

I needed some fresh air, and fast. "That completes setup on my end. Please remind Bettina that the airpots need to be returned by closing time this afternoon. I'll see y'all later." I gathered up my things and headed for the door.

"That's my cue to leave, too," Donovan said. "Have a nice day, ladies."

"You too," Mary Carole cooed. "Especially have a nice night."

I groaned as I pulled open the front door, trying to ignore Donovan, who was suddenly so close that I could feel his body heat.

Outside, more Clams were coming up the front step as I rushed down them. Bettina and Carmella and Mrs. Pollard. As much as I wanted to talk to Carmella, to pick up our conversation from yesterday, I hurried past, intent on making my escape. "Have a good meeting, ladies."

The quicker I could get out of here without more questions from the women or more innuendos from Donovan the better. I was woefully unprepared for his banter. I didn't know what to say or how to respond to his romantic insinuations. Just yesterday morning I'd had no idea he even wanted to date me.

Only, when I stepped off the last stair and looked toward my golf cart, I saw that the Beach Mouse delivery van had been parked diagonally across the end of the gravel driveway. I was blocked in.

I felt Donovan—and his blasted heat—step up directly behind me. I pasted on a smile, spun around, and looked up at him. "Would you like me to murder you now or later, *honey*?"

His eyes danced with amusement, glinting like sunlight on water. "I didn't know you had such a violent side, Maggie."

"I'm a woman on the edge."

"I know." He said it softly, so softly I almost didn't hear him, even though his breath stirred the hair on my head. "But"—he glanced over his shoulder at the house—"right now there are witnesses. So, perhaps the murder should wait?"

There were several faces in the window watching us, being openly nosy.

"I've got to run. More deliveries. And since you're planning on killing me later, I'm just going to go ahead and do this now." He leaned down and kissed me on the lips. A soft kiss. Gentle. One full of hope and promises.

Then he hotfooted it to his van, got in, and drove off.

I held my hand to my lips, then threw a quick look back at the house and saw all the women cheering.

Lord have mercy.

I gave them a quick wave, hopped in the golf cart, and headed back to the square, wondering the whole way there why my lips were still warm and tingling, but knowing exactly why they tasted of chocolate.

Thanks to an iridescent paint additive, the Mother of Pearl jewelry shop sat like a lustrous white pearl in the middle of the storefronts that made up the east side of the square. It was sandwiched between the Salty Southerner, a margarita bar and tapas restaurant that didn't open until four, and Stitchery, Estrelle's shop, which seemed to be open only when it struck her fancy. To the right of Stitchery sat Magpie's.

I angled the golf cart into an empty parking spot in front of the jewelry store. Even though the shop was closed at the moment, I knew Javier would be along in the next ten minutes or so to open for the day. According to my father, his wedding band was here, being resized. I'd know soon if that was the truth. Or if he'd lost the ring, like I suspected.

While I waited, I glanced around the square. The wind blew

gently. The birds sang loudly. Butterflies flitted. It was Tuesday, so Redmond was leading a yoga class on the green, and there was lots of stretching and lunging going on. Across the square several people were dining on the patio of the Break an Egg diner. The church parking lot was full of cars and golf carts—most likely belonging to participants of an early Bible study class. Tourists walked from shop to shop, peeking in windows of the stores that weren't yet open.

Soon my gaze drifted to the coffee shop, to the hanging shop sign above the door. On a white wooden board, *Magpie's* was spelled out in a simple black font, and a magpie was perched on the wide hook of the lowercase *g*. The bird wore a pink barrette, just like the one I used to wear in my hair when I was a toddler.

In my mind's eye, I tried picturing my mama sitting at her desk sketching the logo, but the image was fuzzy. I drew in a sharp breath, wishing my memories of her weren't fading.

Wishing she'd come home.

The coffee shop had been her dream. A place for people to gather, to sit, to sip, to while away the time. I tried to imagine the shop gone and Rose and me working different jobs. Tried to imagine a different shop here, an ice-cream parlor, a candle shop, *anything*, Mama's décor replaced with something trendy or modern. Her blackboard torn down. The driftwood tree dismantled. I couldn't picture it at all, as if my mind found the idea too ludicrous to even consider.

Nothing belonged on this corner except for Magpie's.

It might be time for me to let go, my daddy had said.

But letting go of my mama's shop was not an option. It had never been an option. Not when she went missing and certainly not now. It was hers. Not ours. Dad and I were simply the coffee shop's caretakers, waiting for the day Mama came back.

I heard footsteps and saw Estrelle walking toward her shop. Today she wore a high-necked, long-sleeved black lace dress that hung to her feet. Her stocky heels peeked out of the hem as she strode along. Her pillbox hat wobbled. She stopped in front of the golf cart and stared at me through her birdcage veil for a long moment, a tender, thoughtful expression in her silvery eyes, before continuing to Stitchery. Keys jangled as she found the correct one for the front door. As she pulled it open, she glanced back at me, looking like she wanted to say something, but she remained silent and went inside.

I wished she *had* stayed and talked with me. She'd been a guiding force in my life for a long while now, often giving unsolicited advice when I hadn't thought I needed it. But looking back now, those were some of the times I had needed it most. Somehow she always knew. I watched her walk around her shop, her movements clipped and perfunctory. I was still watching her, hoping she'd come out and tell me what was going on with my father, when Javier stepped out of the coffee shop carrying a to-go bag and a coffee cup, its sleeve stamped with the Magpie's logo. Without question the cup held a mocha latte with 2 percent milk, and the bag held a cinnamon roll. He had never once ordered something else.

"Hello there, Maggie!" Javier called out when he spotted me.

He was perhaps the most elegant man I'd ever met. Impeccably dressed in designer trousers, a custom-tailored shirt, and a silk tie. He had a thick shock of black hair that was slicked back atop his head. His dark beard was exquisitely groomed. He spoke with an English accent, though he originally hailed from Italy. He was often seen with Alistair, his pet cockatiel who liked to perch on his shoulder, but the bird wasn't with him today.

I climbed out of the golf cart and he kissed both my cheeks. From the corner of my eye, I saw Estrelle watching us from her shop window.

He said, "Delighted to see you indulging in a moment for yourself. Lovely day for it. Nary a cloud in the sky. Might I suggest the beach to be a better place to bask?"

I noticed the way his gaze kept darting toward the green, toward the yoga class. It had been a month since he and Redmond had broken up, and most of the town was still hoping they'd reconcile. Only Donnie Dufresne was holding out, but only because he'd had a crush on Redmond for years.

Basking sounded delightful, and for a moment, I considered

playing hooky for the rest of the day. It had been a long time since I had an afternoon to myself with nothing at all to do. But there was simply too much on my schedule. Ava needed training, I had vendor calls to make, the guest room at my dad's house needed cleaning. And, of course, there was my date with Donovan.

"Actually," I said, "I was waiting for you."

His eyes lit. "To what occasion do I owe the honor?"

As I stood there, trying to figure out what to say, all I could hear was my father's voice in my head.

Now, now, Magpie, don't go getting all riled up. My ring is with Javier.

All of a sudden, being here felt wrong. Dad had never lied to me before. Embellished, yes. Evaded, yes. Lied, no. Why did it feel like a betrayal to check up on him? It didn't make sense. Especially since *he* told me to ask Javier if I had doubts.

I dragged the toe of my tennis shoe across the bricks in the sidewalk and made yet another decision I hoped I wouldn't regret. "Carmella's birthday is coming up soon. I was thinking of getting her earrings."

I glanced Estrelle's way. She met my gaze, held it for an uncomfortable moment, before I looked away.

"Soon?" He laughed. "Her birthday is in two months. Oh, I do love how you plan ahead. I have just the pair of earrings in mind. When I unboxed them, I thought of Carmella right away. Silver filigree in a half-moon design. They were screaming her name. Come, come. Let me—" He stopped abruptly and spun around, his gaze on the sky. "Alistair!"

The cockatiel had come out of nowhere, swooping low in front of us before landing on a high oak branch. It let out a string of warbled chirps, like it was telling Javier off.

"Alistair, perch," Javier called, whistling as he held out his arm. The bird didn't budge.

"Is there anything I can do?" I asked.

"If you can figure out how Alistair is escaping not only his cage but also the confines of the house or the shop, I'd be obliged.

He's become a regular Houdini. This is his sixth breakout in the last month!" He whistled again, more sharply this time.

Alistair stuck his beak under his wing and started preening.

"Bloody hell. Don't make me climb that tree, Alistair. I've barely recovered from the last time."

"You climbed a tree?" I couldn't picture it. He wasn't exactly a slim man and didn't seem the athletic type. But now that I took a good look at him, he did look trimmer, his rounded stomach a bit flatter.

"Desperate times, Maggie. Fortunately for me, it was past dark and most of the town had already turned in. It was not my most graceful moment."

Alistair let out more chirps, then suddenly took flight, heading down the block.

Javier pushed his Magpie's order into my hands. "Hold on to that for me, will you? I have to catch him before Redmond sees him and accuses me of being an unfit pet parent. You won't tell him of this, will you?"

"My lips are sealed."

"Thanks, Maggie." He took off, sprinting down the block, knees high, his chest leading the way, his tie flapping in the wind. "Alistair!"

I glanced across the street, toward the yoga class. It turned out that Javier didn't have to worry about me blabbing to Redmond, because he was standing on the edge of the green, watching the chase with his own eyes.

I turned to Stitchery's window to see if Estrelle had been watching as well, but the shop was dark and she was nowhere to be seen.

CHAPTER 8

AVA

"I'd like a small iced matcha latte, add a double shot of espresso, add chai, add lavender syrup. Please."

An older gentleman—I guessed him to be in his early sixties—stood on the other side of the counter. He had kind dark eyes, bushy eyebrows, and waist-length graying dreadlocks. He flashed a wide, friendly smile as he finished his order. A smile that slowly faltered as my hand froze in mid-air as it reached for a cold cup.

"Is there a problem?" he asked.

I said, "Can you repeat that, please?"

"I'd like a small iced matcha latte." He paused. "Add a double shot of espresso." He paused again. "Add chai and add lavender syrup."

It had been a busy morning of learning machines and recipes and procedures and a new vocabulary. Words like *extraction* and *portafilters* and *knock boxes* and *pucks* and *purging* among many others.

Then there had been the names of the customers. So many names. Everyone in town seemed to know of my arrival, my two new jobs, and that it had been a ghostly letter that brought me here. I'd always heard about how news spreads quickly in small towns but never realized exactly how lightning fast it traveled.

It was something of a relief, though, to have the letter out in the open rather than have to share it myself, one person at a time. I imagined it felt a little like jumping into the deep end of a cold pool instead of wading in carefully. Not that I'd know. I'd been taught to be a wader. A slow, extremely cautious wader.

Suddenly, I was angry about that. About the slow, cautious

life I'd been forced to lead. Navigating the difficulties of my disorder had been challenging enough without also having to deal with my mother's over-the-top smothering. I should've been allowed to test my limits, find my boundaries. I shouldn't have had to live a life of fear. *In* fear. Life was about balance. And the scales of mine had been tipped the wrong way.

"Ma'am?" the man said. "Did you get that?"

I blinked, his voice pulling me out of my thoughts. "Matcha, espresso, chai, lavender. Got it."

I thought I'd been fitting in quite well here at Magpie's until this man had come in. Earlier, when the Mermaids, only ten strong this morning, had stopped by, I'd worked alongside Rose to fill their orders with no problems at all, her confidence shoring up my own.

I'd been thrilled to see Gracie and Juniper, the mom and baby I'd met yesterday, return with the group. As I made Gracie's vanilla latte, I'd learned that she worked part-time as a stylist at Wild Hairs, a salon on the south side of the square. And when she told me that her husband, Ben, was in the middle of a three-week shift on an oil rig off the Mobile coast, I'd immediately recognized the loneliness in her eyes. So when she extended an open invitation to join her and Juniper on a Mermaids excursion when I had the time, I'd only had to think about it for a second or two. How strenuous could it be?

After only a day in this small southern town, it seemed like I was already fitting in. For someone so used to being the odd one out, it was an amazing feeling. Magical, even. I'd been on cloud nine since the Mermaids left, but this man, with his matcha chai lavender concoction, had brought me crashing back down to earth.

"Just give me a second," I said to him as panic bubbled up. Did matcha come in a powder? A syrup? I threw a look at the menu board. Matcha wasn't even an option.

"Titus." Rose, who'd been wiping down tables, stepped behind the counter and scooted in close to me. The man's name came off her lips like an admonishment. "Ava is new here. Have some compassion."

"I have compassion," he countered merrily. "I didn't ask for an iced latte with half oat milk and half almond milk, with sugar-free vanilla syrup and raw sugar, now, did I? I recognized that might be a complicated drink for a newcomer. Welcome, by the way."

Rose shook her head at him and said to me, "I got this, sugar pie."

It seemed Rose called nearly everyone sugar pie, and not one single customer seemed to mind the endearment. I didn't mind, either. It felt like she was sharing her innate sweetness, which somehow seemed like a gift.

She grabbed a small hot cup, took two steps to the drip brewer on the counter behind us, a high-volume commercial machine that wasn't so very different from the old-school model sitting on Maggie's countertop at her house. Just bigger and fancier.

The silver strands in her black hair glimmered under the lights as she stuck the cup under the coffee spout and pushed down its black lever.

She filled the cup nearly to the brim with black coffee. Then she popped on a lid and sleeve and pushed the drink across the counter. "Here you go, Titus Pomeroy."

He laughed softly. "This will have to do, but I will take a moment to remind you that the matcha drink is an order I've requested at least three times a week since I moved here a year ago, always to be denied. I don't think I ask too much. This is a coffeehouse, after all. And you're a talented barista."

"You can always move back to Atlanta," she said in a syrupy tone, "and resume your patronage at the fancy boutique coffee shop you used to frequent before you decided to grace us with your presence by retiring to our humble town where you support our simple shop."

"And deny myself the pleasure of your delightful customer service? I couldn't possibly."

There wasn't a trace of hostility in the undercurrent of their voices—only cheer. They enjoyed this back-and-forth, and I knew without asking that this was a frequently repeated conversation between them.

"That'll be two dollars for the coffee," she said sweetly, wiping her hands on her waist apron. "Pay the woman."

No *sugar pie* for Titus, I noticed, despite their playful banter.

Arching a bushy eyebrow, he handed me two singles. As the cash drawer popped open, I said, "Thank you. Have a nice day."

"You too, Ava." He smiled—that big, friendly smile—and dropped another single into the tip jar. "One day, Rose, I'll get that matcha out of you." He lifted the cup in the air in a cheers motion.

"Don't hold your breath," she tossed back as she grabbed a rag and wiped down the already clean countertop.

He laughed and headed out the door.

As soon as he was gone, I turned to Rose, smiling. "He liiiikes you."

She flapped the rag at me. "Hush your mouth. That's nonsense. He is handsome, I admit, but I could never date him, even if he asked."

"Why's that?"

"Matcha, chai, *and* lavender? That's too pretentious for my blood. Coffee says a lot about a man, Ava. He probably folds his underwear and irons his jeans. I can't do persnickety."

"I'm actually surprised Magpie's doesn't have matcha or lavender. They're common flavors."

Sadness flashed across her eyes. "Despite encouragement from many, Maggie's reluctant to make changes to the menu. It's basically the same as it was thirty years ago. The whole place is the same, really, except for updates to machines that have broken. And the magpie tree. You've never seen me so happy as the day our ancient credit card machine called it quits. The new one is much more efficient."

I glanced around. "Why is Maggie reluctant?"

"It was her mama who came up with the menu and designed the space. It's . . . homage, I suppose," she said, but there was concern lurking in her eyes, her voice. She tossed the rag on the counter. "I'll be right back. I'm going to pop into the restroom, then get more cups from storage."

Had Maggie's mom passed away? Yesterday after Dez's melancholy when talking about his honeymoon and Maggie's concern about his wedding ring, I'd suspected something tragic had happened, but I hadn't wanted to assume. I still didn't, but I didn't know how to ask outright.

It seemed as soon as Rose was out of sight, the front door opened, whooshing just the slightest bit differently, as if cautioning me.

The patron who stepped through the doorway was the old woman with the birdcage veil—the one who'd scowled at me yesterday. She was wearing the same hat and veil today, along with a long black dress with lace trim.

She stood just inside the entrance, as if allowing her eyesight to adjust to the lighting before taking a step forward. Over her shoulder, I noticed the white-winged monarch flapping its wings against the front window before rising out of sight, still flying in a topsy-turvy flight pattern.

The woman glanced over her shoulder toward the window as if she had heard the butterfly as well. A thin eyebrow was arched as she turned back to face me. Slowly, she stepped up to the counter, her footsteps somehow sounding like fanfare, theatrically announcing her arrival.

I wasn't sure at all why she made me nervous, but she did. Glancing toward the back hall, I hoped Rose would suddenly reappear, but apparently I'd used up all my luck yesterday.

I plastered my voice with false cheer. "Good morning! May I help you?"

The woman's silvery eyes narrowed behind the veil. "A small hot chocolate with whipped cream and a sprinkle of cinnamon, if you will. To go."

She'd caught me by surprise. I hadn't expected her to order hot chocolate. She looked more like an espresso drinker to me. Or perhaps an Americano—espresso diluted with hot water. Something strong. And dark. Quite dark.

"Coming right up." I could do this. This morning someone had ordered an iced chocolate, which was basically milk chocolate with ice, and Maggie had walked me through the steps of making it hot as well.

I readied a cup and set it aside. Then I added two pumps of chocolate syrup to a stainless steel steaming pitcher, then added cold milk.

Taking a deep breath, I faced the espresso machine and tried to scrounge up some courage. The steam wand terrified me, especially after hearing the story of what happened with Sienna. Earlier, I'd used it only with Rose or Maggie by my side. Never alone.

"Is there an issue?" the veiled woman asked in a tone that suggested she knew exactly why I hesitated.

"Not at all."

"Hm."

Taking a deep breath, I turned on the steam wand to purge it of air and jumped when the burst of steam came out, just as it should. I glanced at the darkly dressed woman. Now she had the other eyebrow lifted high.

She terrified me almost as much as the steam wand.

I could do this. I was in charge of my life now. I had to be braver. Take more chances. Believe in myself. Stop letting my fears get in the way.

Before I lost my nerve, I positioned the pitcher and carefully made my way through the steps Maggie had taught me. A few seconds later, after the correct temperature of the milk had been reached, I shut off the steamer, pulled the pitcher free, purged the wand, and wiped it clean.

I wanted to do a happy dance but controlled myself as I poured the hot liquid into the to-go cup, added whipped cream, and asked, "Would you like a lid or extra whipped cream instead?"

Her thin lips pursed. "A lid. Don't forget the cinnamon."

I smiled. "I'd never."

She harrumphed as I shook cinnamon on top of the whipped cream. I secured the lid and slid the drink across the scarred wooden counter. "That'll be three dollars even, please."

She picked up the cup, took a sip, and nodded. "Remarkable what can result from letting go of one's fear, is it not?"

Goose bumps popped on my arms. It was as if she'd somehow heard the pep talk I'd given myself. I opened my mouth but realized I had no words, so snapped it closed.

From her black clutch, she took out a credit card and then tapped it against the card reader. That tap reverberated as much as her heels had when she came in.

She reverberated. One big quiver housed in a black silk–wrapped package. I'd never heard a sound like it. Had never met anyone like her. I took a deep breath, trying to pick up her scent, which might give me a clue to her disposition, but there were only the normal scents of the shop floating around.

Which was unusual.

Everyone I'd met since my sense of smell had become enhanced carried a unique scent, one that revealed hints about them, their personality. This woman did not.

Her thin eyebrow arched again. "You will come to my shop this evening. Six P.M. Do not be tardy. I cannot abide tardiness." She gave me a firm nod. *"It has been said."*

She took her drink and turned away, her heels now oddly silent as she walked out. Stunned, I could only watch her go.

Rose sidled up beside me, holding a sleeve of cups in her hand. Her gaze immediately went to the woman in black passing by the front window. "I see you've met Estrelle."

So that was Estrelle. No wonder there had been alarm in Dez's voice when Maggie had mentioned the name on the phone yesterday.

She *was* alarming.

I rinsed the steaming pitcher. Maggie had drilled *clean, clean, clean* into my head straight off the bat this morning. "Not formally, though she wants me to be at her shop at six tonight."

Both Rose's eyebrows slid upward and surprise rounded her eyes. "Best you don't be late."

"I don't even know where her shop is. And what happens if I *am* late?"

"Her shop is right next door. Stitchery. I don't want to know what'll happen if you're late. You don't either. Trust me. The last person who stood her up suddenly developed body odor that lasted nearly a week."

My jaw dropped. "I mean, that's just a coincidence, right?"

"Estrelle is . . . well, you'll see for yourself the more you get to know her."

"But I don't particularly want to get to know her. She didn't even *ask* me to meet her tonight. She demanded it."

"Be that as it may, I wouldn't stand her up if I were you. Her demands are not to be taken lightly."

I glanced out the window again—the woman, Estrelle, was long out of sight at this point, but one big question lingered. What in the world did the old woman want with me?

When I had first met Dez Brightwell, I hadn't thought him a man in need of assistance. He'd been well groomed, articulate, and openhearted.

And perhaps *he* wasn't in need.

His house, however, most definitely was in dire need of help. I'd come to the beach house straight from Magpie's, arriving sooner than expected because Maggie had let me off early, claiming I'd learned enough of the coffee business for the day.

When I first got there, I thought perhaps I'd come *too* early, because Dez didn't immediately answer the ringing doorbell. Finally he appeared, looking flustered and sounding exasperated.

"Molly's playing hide-and-seek." He'd wiped a hand across his damp forehead. "I need to find her before Maggie gets here and thinks I've done lost her, too. That's a lecture I do not need."

"When was the last time you saw her?"

I focused on listening to the sounds inside the house, filtering each, identifying, moving on, hoping to hear a cat's meow or scratching. But I heard only the usual sounds of a home, the creaks, the electrical hums, plumbing burbles.

"An hour ago? Two?" He scratched his chin. "Could be

three or four now that I think about it. Time gets away from me sometimes."

He ushered me down a long, wide hallway that had been narrowed by dozens of boxes. The hallway spilled into the back of the house, an open space that contained the great room, the kitchen, and the dining area. French doors in the kitchen were open wide to the screen room, letting in the sea breeze. Behind the house, the gulf was a sea of endless blue.

I heard the slightest movement, a whisper of air, really, and looked to my right. On the stovetop, Molly's head stuck out of a large stockpot that sat among a collection of copper cookware. For a horrifying second, I thought she was being made into soup. Then I realized the stove wasn't on. "There she is."

Dez turned. "Molly," he said, full of outrage.

She twitched a dismissive whisker and ducked back into the pot.

That had been a few minutes ago, and I still stood in the same spot trying not to let my shock show on my face. How did he live like this? Where did I even begin in cleaning this place?

Dirty dishes were stacked high in the sink—rinsed, at least, I noticed. Dust bunnies scattered with each footstep, diving for cover under couches and chairs. Here and there, clumps of cat hair latched together, looking like throw rugs. Dust piled thick and heavy on drapes, windowsills, side tables. There were boxes and bags everywhere. Running a vacuum in here would be impossible until some of this stuff was moved out.

"It's a tad messy," Dez conceded as he looked around. "My collection has grown a bit out of control."

An understatement if I'd ever heard one.

"What is it you collect exactly?" It seemed an odd assortment to me, part antiques, part junk.

In the immediate vicinity were vintage milk bottles, a hen cookie jar, a box of linen postcards, jadeite lamps, a Southern Comfort bank, a stack of old concert T-shirts, a tin whistle, three turntables, a mercantile scale, cake pedestals, a Howdy Doody doll, a brass crawdad, wind-up chatter teeth, a butter churn, and an old jump rope. I couldn't even imagine what was *in* the boxes stacked about.

"Whims, mostly." He grinned. "Whatever strikes my fancy."

I wandered into the living room, one side of which was being used as a gallery wall. From what I could see, there was no rhyme or reason to the subject matter or aesthetic of the artwork. The odd assortment of images included a fruit bowl, a ship at sea, pecking chickens, tap shoes, a can of peas, and a foggy road. In the midst of it all was one empty square that held only dusty shadows.

"Your fancy seems to be struck quite a lot."

Dez laughed. "That is true. There's something satisfying in the hunt for unusual pieces." He glanced around. "And they make for good company."

His hand went to the pendant he wore at his neck—a penny set into a silver mount. There was wistfulness in his voice as he spoke those last words that struck a sad chord within me. Did his collecting have more to do with loneliness than whims?

"But I've decided it's time to let them go. The yard sale the weekend after next is sure to be a doozy. I've been sorting and pricing for weeks now. Everything goes!"

"Everything?"

"Everything!" he said again, his voice full of resolve and a touch of elation.

"Why?"

He chuckled. "Why not? Change is the spice of life!"

Even though he laughed, I heard an undertone of secrecy. There was most definitely a reason for his big cleanout, one he didn't care to share with me.

"Let me show you around. We'll make it quick like, and then I'm going to put you straight to work. I want to bring a load of these boxes to one of my storage units—that's where I'm doing most of the sorting. A little more elbow room there."

There'd be just about a little more elbow room *anywhere* else but here.

"There is a method to my madness," he said. "I keep a detailed inventory and the boxes are labeled."

I was grateful that most of his collection was in boxes. Sturdy ones, too, not beat-up banana boxes from the local grocery store like I used when I moved out of my mom's place. There were just so *many* boxes it was hard to believe he'd been keeping track of it all.

Narrow pathways had been carved through the forest of cardboard. To my untrained eye, I saw no trash hiding among the stash. No piles of newspapers, food wrappers, and other junk associated with hoarder houses. There were no terrible smells—the primary scent being staleness, which told me he didn't spend much time at home. No signs of mice, either, thank goodness. I supposed Molly could possibly be the reason for that, though she looked too prim to be bothered to hunt.

I threw a look toward the pot on the stove, where her head was once again poking up. Her whiskers twitched as she watched me. I had the uneasy feeling she was sizing me up and finding me lacking.

Dez gave me a quick tour of the downstairs, the open layout at the back of the house making the tour quite simple. In the front of the house, on one side of the entryway, was Dez's bedroom, a suite that was also filled with clutter. On the other side of the hallway, a powder room was tucked under the stairs. Next to it was a laundry room, which was so stuffed with clothes, towels, and bedsheets that it was hard to fully open the door.

The second floor had three additional bedrooms, the biggest being a suite at the end of a long hallway.

"This suite will be your room," Dez said, "once it's cleaned out."

Right now it was decorated primarily in cardboard boxes and plastic bins. In the middle of the space, I could just make out the footboard of a queen-size bed. I eyed the unusual assortment on one of the nightstands: a tall metal cactus sculpture; a set of (somewhat creepy) Beatles dolls, each with a guitar; a stubby shaving-cream brush; a music box; and a brass whale ashtray. Whims.

"Oh ho! There you are, you sassy devil. I was wondering

where you'd gotten off to." He was studying a framed painting on the wall. "This belongs downstairs. It's been missing since Sunday from the gallery wall."

Another *misplaced* item. Interesting. "You didn't move it here?"

"It's probably my ghost playing tricks on me."

I looked at the picture and froze. It was a framed monarch butterfly print from an old book, the page yellowed along the edges. One of the monarch's wings had a white tip.

"If the ghost wants the picture to stay here, that's fine by me," he said. "It suits you, I think, seeing how butterflies represent new beginnings and transformation."

I barely heard him as I tried to tell myself that it was coincidence that this print went missing the day I opened the mysterious letter that had a butterfly stamp. That it featured a butterfly with the same anomaly as the one I'd been seeing since I arrived. That the frame had *somehow* ended up in a room destined to be mine.

A chill went down my spine, and I turned away from the picture. As I did, I caught a strange scent in the air. Something that was faintly fishy. No, not fishy, necessarily. It reminded me more of nori. Seaweed. Exactly like the scent that had engulfed us in the screen room yesterday when we talked about ghosts. Just like yesterday, the smell faded as quickly as it had come on.

Dez didn't seem to notice the scent or my dismay. He rubbed his hands together. "Best we dive right in."

To save my sanity, I decided not to dwell on the seaweed scent or the butterfly painting and to throw my energy into the task at hand instead. "All this is going to the storage unit?"

"Yes, ma'am. We'll load up my truck and make as many trips as necessary. Maggie can join us when she gets here. Now, grab a box and let's go."

I picked up the box closest to me and headed for the door. Dez followed close behind. We were in the hallway when above our heads came a high-pitched honking noise, sharp and staccato. It was quickly followed by creaking. Then silence. Dez's gaze shot upward. Mine, too.

"What was that?" I asked.

"Maggie would tell you it's sparrows in the attic."

"And you? What would you tell me?"

"It's my little ghost, of course. Now, come along. We have much to do."

The ghost. Of course.

Only . . . I didn't think ghosts *walked*. They floated. Or at least that's what movies had always led me to believe.

So I didn't understand why the creaking sound in the attic sounded just like footsteps.

CHAPTER 9

MAGGIE

By five thirty, my bed was strewn with clothes, tried on and then dismissed. Every time I questioned why I was having trouble picking out something to wear tonight, I could hear Donovan's voice in my ear, saying *something more intimate*. It was followed quickly by a rush of heat flooding my cheeks, my veins.

Unbidden, Delaney's words from this morning came drifting back to me.

We all thought you were meant to be.

At one point, I had thought so, too. I believed my love for him was enough to stop him from enlisting in the Coast Guard right after he graduated high school, so impatient to get started that he hadn't even considered applying for the Coast Guard Academy.

My love hadn't been enough, though.

I recognized now it had been too much to ask of him. I'd been only sixteen at the time, too young to understand that sometimes love meant letting people go so they could follow their dreams. No matter how much those dreams terrified you.

In order to save what was left of my threadbare sanity, I told myself to stop thinking of tonight as a date and start thinking of it as dinner. Dinner with an old friend. That was it. That was all.

With that mindset, choosing an outfit was easy. I grabbed a pair of jeans off the pile on the bed and shimmied into them. Striding to the closet, I yanked a blouse off a hanger and pulled it on over my head. The shirt was loose and flowy and utterly feminine with its ruffled cap sleeves and delicate embroidered flowers. With a dressier pair of sandals, the outfit could work for both a casual restaurant, something a bit fancier, or even—I gulped—something intimate.

In the full-length mirror propped against my bedroom wall, I applied a thin coat of lip gloss. I'd gone simple with my makeup. Just mascara, the gloss, and some concealer to hide my exhaustion. My hair was down tonight, a rarity, and it fell to mid-back, the curls soft and shiny. I desperately needed a haircut but had been too busy to fit one into my schedule.

How had I allowed that to happen? Who's too busy to get a *haircut*? I sighed, feeling annoyed with myself all of a sudden. The headache I'd been dealing with had abated some, but I could still feel it pulsing gently, like a dormant volcano waiting to erupt.

As I turned away from the mirror, my gaze fell on the framed photos atop my dresser. I smiled at Noah's graduation picture, at his toothy, droll grin. Oh, how I missed him. I had been so hyper-focused on raising him up right and good and fulfilled that it felt an awful lot like grief when he went off to college.

Because I'd hated coming home to a quiet house, I worked overtime at the coffee shop and stepped up my activity in various clubs and organizations around town, never turning down an opportunity to support my neighbors or this community. Doing so helped fill an ever-present emptiness within me—a chasm that had developed not long after my mama disappeared and deepened when Noah went away.

Being busy, super busy, was the only way I knew how to cope.

I let my attention linger on one of the few photos I had of my mother—all the others had been lost in the fury of Ivan. Mama sat on the beach, awash in a golden glow, her face turned toward the setting sun, her eyes closed, her expression utterly peaceful. I sat at her side, a plastic shovel in hand, my wild curls standing on end, despite the pink barrette in my hair that tried to hold them down. In the photo, I was watching her, my gaze adoring. With a deep ache in my chest, I looked away from her serene face and pulled open the bedroom door.

Ava was curled up in a corner of the couch, reading the Magpie's employee manual. She glanced up when I walked into the kitchen. "Well, hello, pretty lady!"

I reached for a glass in the cabinet. "Thanks, Ava."

As I took the water pitcher from the fridge, I noticed my hand trembling, a slight waver. Whether it was my blood pressure or nerves about tonight, I wasn't sure. With the increase in headaches this past week, I needed to call my doctor for a medication adjustment. And start hauling myself more often over to Red's to get in better shape.

"Do you know where Donovan is taking you?" Ava asked.

"Nope."

She put the manual down. "How long have you two known each other?"

"Since we were babies, really, small towns being what they are. He's a couple of years older than I am, but we went to the same schools, hung around the same people. The summer he was seventeen, he worked at the coffee shop in a quest to work anywhere but the bakery, and we became the best of friends."

At the time, he'd been feeling the heat from his parents about leaving town, leaving the bakery. They'd been planning for him to take it over one day, and he'd rebelled against having his future mapped out for him. Now that he was back and doing what his parents had wanted all along, I wondered how he was feeling about it. He didn't look like he minded, but then again, I knew how well true feelings could be masked.

She tipped her head. "I hear something in your voice when you talk about him that suggests you two were more than friends."

I scoffed dramatically. "What? No." I shook my head for good measure, not wanting to talk about it. Even now, I tried to block the memories, slamming the door on them in my mind. Somehow, though, the pain leaked out of the cracks and crevices, flooding my brain.

The pain. And the regret.

They were tangled up together, like thorny vines.

Her thoughtful, mossy eyes narrowed and she tipped her head, silently calling me out on the lie. It was rather disconcerting, to be honest, that she'd heard more in my voice than I'd intended.

"Well, maybe," I conceded. "But we wanted different things in life, so it didn't work out. We've stayed friends, though. He visits his family a lot, so I see him a few times a year."

Those meetings were always a mix of tension and happiness. We enjoyed each other's company, but the shadows of our past always followed us around.

"We exchange birthday and Christmas cards. He sent flowers when I had my TIA, even though he was on a boat in the middle of nowhere at the time. He's a nice guy. A great guy. I hope—" Suddenly, I shook my head, laughing lightly. "I don't know why I'm telling you all this. I'm not usually such a blabbermouth. You're easy to talk to."

She smiled. "I've always been a good listener."

I walked over to the dining room table and fussed with the care package I planned to send off to Noah soon. So far it had socks, three gift cards—gas, food, and music—hand sanitizer, and four bags of Golden Eagle caramel corn, which was his favorite snack. I tried to send a package once a month, a small reminder of home and that I was thinking of him.

On impulse, I snapped a pic of the box and wrote:

Not sure there's enough caramel corn

A moment later, he returned the text.

Never enough!

I smiled.

"Noah?" Ava asked.

"How'd you know?"

"The look in your eyes. It's the same one in the framed picture on his dresser. Pure love. How old were you when you had him?"

I slipped my phone into my pocket. "I was eighteen when I found out I was pregnant, nineteen when he was born. Having a baby definitely wasn't something I'd planned on, but as soon as I knew about him, as soon as those lines showed up on that pregnancy test, I loved him. It's something I can't even really explain, the immediacy. His father hadn't quite felt the same. By that time we'd been broken up for a couple of months, and he begged me not to have the baby. Or to put him up for adoption. But I was already a goner. There was no going back."

There I went again, jabbering on. She really *was* a good listener.

"Did his dad ever come around?"

For a moment, I let my mind wander back to a late-spring day in Theo's dorm room—I'd been a commuter student—at the University of South Alabama over in Mobile. I'd rocked on the bed, my arms around my legs, wondering how I was going to tell my daddy that I was pregnant. Theo's eyes were red, his skin blotchy from trying to hold back tears, hold back his fears. Eventually, both spilled out. He talked about how he was supposed to spend the next year studying abroad. About his career plans. About how he was too young to be a father. That he didn't know *how* to be a father.

Then, when he asked if we should get married, I all-out panicked. I didn't love him. Had never loved him. He'd been a good friend, one who for a short time helped me forget how much I missed Donovan. But that was it. Marriage was out of the question.

Instead, I'd urged him to go abroad. I assured him that I could raise the baby on my own until he got back, then we could come up with some sort of financial and visitation arrangement that would work for all of us.

He'd kept in touch for the first couple of months of being apart, still talking often about how scared he was to be a dad. Then contact became more sporadic. Then there was nothing. Not even after Noah was born. Theo had let his fear win.

I probably should have tracked him down. After all, he had a responsibility to our child. But at that point, I didn't want someone in Noah's life who didn't want to be there.

I still didn't, but that choice was out of my hands now that Noah was older. So far he hadn't sought out Theo, but if that day came, I'd support it. Because I loved Noah.

"No," I said quietly. "Fortunately, Noah had my dad as a father figure. I don't know what we'd have done without him. Without this whole town, really. They truly rallied around me when

I decided not to go back to school. And if you asked Noah, he'd tell you he has hundreds of aunts and uncles even though I'm an only child."

She smiled. "I can only imagine the offers to babysit."

I laughed. "Don't think I didn't take people up on it, either. Noah was only six months old when I took over running Magpie's." I looked at the clock. "Estrelle, of all people, was probably the biggest help. Noah adored her. Still does. She'd sit in a corner of the coffee shop and rock him or play games with him or read. It was all kinds of sweet. No doubt, babies bring out the absolute best in her." I smiled at the memories. "Now that I've talked your ear off, did you eat? I can make you a quick grilled cheese. Or a PB and J? The mom in me needs to feed you."

"Thank you, but I'm not hungry."

I leaned a hip on the table. "You've barely eaten since you've arrived."

"I haven't had much of an appetite since what happened to Alexander. I'll be sure to grab something later on, though."

"If you ever want to talk about him, I'll try to be as good a listener as you are."

"Thanks. I'll remember that." Standing, she stretched, then walked to the door to slip on her shoes. "I should probably get ready to go. Estrelle warned me not to be late."

"I'd take that to heart."

"No one really believes, like truly believes, she can give someone body odor, do they?"

"The question isn't really if we believe it to be true. The question is do you really want to risk it?"

"I'm not going to lie, she scares me."

I laughed. "She scares *everyone,* but under her gothic exterior, there's a good heart. She's always the first to donate to a fundraiser, the first to send a gift to someone who's ill or newly engaged or pregnant." I didn't add that Estrelle often knew of those events before they were announced to the general public. "She always seems to know when someone needs any kind of help, whether financial, emotional, whatever. If she can't physically help, she finds a way to get it done. She makes things happen."

"Has she always lived here in Driftwood?"

"No, like a lot of people, she came here on vacation and ended up staying. I remember clearly the first time I saw her. It was on the beach when I was eleven." I swallowed hard, searching for the right words. I didn't want to talk about what had happened to my mother, not tonight. "She was there, dressed in a black bathing suit straight out of the forties, the kind with thick straps and full skirt. She had a swim cap on, too. It was covered in puffy black flowers. Mind you, this was in the nineties. She stood out. Way out."

Ava smiled. "I can picture the outfit so clearly. I'm surprised the swim cap didn't have a veil."

"Me too. There's rarely a day when she doesn't have it on."

Thinking of that day always brought tears to my eyes. I turned toward the sink to hide them. That afternoon on the beach, amid the panic, I'd raced into the water to swim out to where the manta rays had gathered, hoping I'd find my mama with them. Estrelle had gone in after me, hauling me straight back out.

"No," she'd said firmly once we were safely back on shore. "It's too dangerous. There's another way."

She'd guided me to the end of a fishing pier, where we sat down. The magnificent manta rays had swum over to us, gliding around the pilings, their movements almost ethereal in their beauty.

My mama hadn't been with them.

Still, Estrelle and I sat there a long time that day. We watched the manta rays swim while search teams scoured the water, the beach.

"Does she have family nearby?" Ava asked.

"Not that I know of. For as much as she meddles, no one knows all that much about her. But one thing we do know is not to cross her. Unless you enjoy getting boils. Or pox. Or bad breath."

Deep lines formed between Ava's eyebrows as she frowned. "I'll keep that in mind."

I dropped a couple of flakes of fish food into the goldfish bowl and watched Mac and Cheese swim about for a moment, grateful as always that Noah hadn't taken them to school with him, since they were technically his pets. He'd won them at a fair a couple of years ago. Having them here made my empty nest just a little less lonely.

Ava stretched again, reaching her arms over her head. She groaned slightly, then yawned. "I didn't realize how out of shape I was until I lugged those boxes around today at Dez's. I wore myself out."

When I had finally joined her and my dad at his house, they'd already cleared half the guest room and had taken two trips to his storage unit. Both of them had been filthy, absolutely covered with dust and dirt, and I'd declined the bear hug my father had so generously offered.

"You've had quite the day. Are you settling in okay? Here in town?"

I could only imagine how overwhelmed she must be. New town. New people. New jobs. It was a lot, even though she seemed to be taking it all in open-armed stride so far.

"I am. Everyone's been so kind and welcoming. I didn't burn myself—or anyone else—with the steam wand at the coffee shop, either, so I count that as a win for the day."

"Definitely a win. And you and Dad? Did you get on well?" I asked, glad to finally have a moment to ease into this conversation.

"Like you said, he's quite the character." She smiled. "I like him."

"Did you notice anything that seemed off?"

She knew what I was asking. "Physically, he seems fit to me. He was lifting boxes, loading and unloading, barely breaking a sweat. Cognitively, there was only the issue about a misplaced picture and, well, he thinks the house is haunted, which you already know."

I really needed to talk to Carmella again, because I suspected she knew exactly what was going on with my father. I'd call her tonight, after I got home.

Ava fidgeted, shifting foot to foot. "About that ghost. I should probably tell you we did hear some noise in the attic."

"Sparrows always seem to find a way inside," I said.

"Dez told me you'd say that. But to be fair to him, it didn't sound like birds to me. It sounded like—"

She was cut off by the doorbell. Donovan waved through the glass panel. We both whipped our heads to look at the clock: 5:52. He was early.

Ava let out a panicked squeak. "How did it get so late? I need to go." She made a dash for the door, then called over her shoulder, "Have fun tonight."

I heard her say something to Donovan as she rushed by him and rocketed down the porch steps.

I walked over to the door. Donovan stood there with a bouquet of zinnias in hand, watching her sprint down the street.

"What's got into her?" he asked.

"She's running late to meet with Estrelle."

His eyes widened. "Say no more."

I hooked a thumb over my shoulder. "Let me just grab my purse and I'll be ready."

He thrust out the flowers. "Wait. These are for you."

My stomach squeezed. "Thank you. You didn't have to do that."

I quickly put the flowers in water, grabbed my purse, and closed the door behind me. Out on the porch, I glanced around for his truck but saw only my car and Ava's hatchback in the driveway. "Am I driving?"

"We're not driving." He grinned. "We're walking."

"Where? To the Salty Southerner?" Suddenly, I realized I could do with a margarita. Or two. I started down the steps. At the end of the walkway, I turned toward the square.

Tugging on my arm, he turned me around. "This way."

There weren't any restaurants in that direction. Only houses and the beach.

"Just follow me," he said. "You do trust me, right?"

I looked deep into his ocean eyes, saw glimpses of the boy I'd loved. I had trusted him then, and I trusted him now.

But he knew as well as I did that I had limits to where I'd follow him.

Minutes later, our footsteps echoed hollowly on the wooden boardwalk, gray and weathered, that cut through rolling dunes covered in sea oats and beach grass. I took off my sandals at the end of the platform and sighed with happiness as my toes sank into the soft white sand, still warm from the day's heat.

The water was calm this evening, looking pale green in the evening light. Waves rolled gently onto the beach, and the wind blew calmly as the day prepared to turn into night. Even after all these years, I scanned the water in all directions. Searching for my mama had become habit.

Two men stood along the shore, surf fishing, their poles anchored deep in the sand, their fishing lines extended beyond the point where the waves broke before coming ashore. Sanderlings darted in and out of the swash, surprisingly fast for their tiny size.

"Are we catching our own dinner?" I asked Donovan. We'd done it before, a long time ago, when the space between us wasn't filled with what-could-have-beens.

"Maybe next time."

Next time.

Oh lord. I'd hoped there'd be a next time.

"We're set up over there." He pointed to the right, where the beach stretched westward, bathed in coppery light.

Not too far away a white beach umbrella canopied a low wooden table surrounded by pillows. As we walked nearer, I could see the table was dressed with a linen runner, its ends weighted down by thick tassels. A brass lantern held an electric candle, its flicker barely visible in the golden lighting. There were also two vases of flowers, a wine bucket, glasses, and a silver cloche.

Nearer still, I could see the pillows had been set on large

beach mats, protecting them from the sand. There were two place settings, each comprised of a round braided-grass place-mat, an elegant glass plate edged with gold beads, and a white napkin tied with a seagrass bow.

My heart tripped about. "You did all this?"

"Well, not personally, but I arranged it. Does that count?"

It counted.

As I lowered myself onto the soft pillow, he kept hold of my hand, only letting go when I was fully settled. I tucked my hands into my lap and tried to memorize every detail.

As far as dates went, so far this was pretty perfect.

"Wine?"

I nodded and he filled a glass and handed it to me, then filled his own and sat down.

This was my favorite time of day, this golden hour, when the sun started its descent. Along the waterline, the light caught on crushed shells and pebbles, making them glitter.

"Do you like it?" Donovan asked, his hand sweeping over the table and umbrella, then extending toward the beach and water.

A blue heron walked lazily along the shore on an evening stroll, and I was surprised it—and a dozen of its seagull friends—wasn't creeping in on us, curious as to what was un-der the cloche.

"I do," I answered honestly, suddenly feeling like I could cry. "I could sit out here all night."

"We could. If you want."

I injected a teasing lilt into my voice and said, "I told Ava I'd be home by six thirty."

He glanced at his watch, then laughed. "Then you'd better eat fast."

Glancing around, I tried to soak in everything I could, letting it imprint on my mind, my heart. I was grateful that he hadn't arranged for music to be playing. The sound of the waves and the calls of the birds were the song of my heart.

But suddenly I had the feeling he knew that.

He lifted the cloche with a flourish. "I hope you're hungry."

I laughed loudly at what he'd revealed—an assortment of fast-food burgers and grilled chicken sandwiches and onion rings and French fries, displayed neatly on a small cordless warming tray.

My doctor would have a fit, but I couldn't have been happier.

"You seemed like you had your heart set on fast food, so . . ." He shrugged. "I aim to please."

He aimed to please my heart.

I couldn't wrap my head around the notion, but the heart he'd *aimed to please* was doing a weird dance in my chest, flipping and flopping like a fish out of water.

A boat sped by and laughter from its passengers carried on the wind.

"Perfect day to be out on the water," he said, hearing it, too. Then he quietly added, "I took a few boats for test drives earlier. Nothing too fancy. I want one mostly for . . . fishing. Maybe a sunset cruise or two. That kind of thing."

The flip-flopping in my chest turned into panicked thudding.

Suddenly I wasn't at all sure what it was that my heart wanted. I had thought it was looking for a second chance, but now it was acting like it wanted to be locked up tight, safe and protected.

A boat. He wanted a boat.

Of course he did. He loved the water. Always had. The more he was in it, on it, the happier he was. Retirement from the Coast Guard hadn't meant he left that love behind. Why had I thought otherwise?

"Maggie?"

My hand shook, so I set my glass down. "Hmm?"

He looked out at the water. "You know what? I don't really need a boat. I've served my time on the sea."

I snapped my head to look at him. "What? No."

"No what?"

"Of course you need a boat."

He shook his head, held my gaze. "There are other things more important. That's a lesson I learned a little too late."

Me. He was talking about me. And oh my lord, I wanted to cry. To sob.

Because I couldn't ask him to give up something he loved for me.

Not again.

CHAPTER 10

AVA

"Hey, now. Whoa!"

I comically skidded to a stop before I smacked into Sam and Norman in front of the coffee shop. Sam extended his arms straight out in a protective stance, the leash stretching with the motion.

My lungs burned and my breath came out in ragged puffs. "So sorry. Didn't see you."

Tunnel vision at its finest, because otherwise the pair was hard to overlook. Especially the beautiful Norman, who excitedly wagged his shaggy arched tail and greeted me with one of his adorable *quabarks*.

I bent down and petted his head, and his fur was as silky as I'd imagined. "Hi there, handsome."

His tail wagged even harder and he licked my hand. I contemplated a dognapping as I fell in love right there in front of Magpie's.

"You all right?" Sam asked.

I stood up, full of regret that I couldn't sit with Norman awhile longer. "I'm fine, thanks. Just out of shape."

Strenuous exercise had been on my list of avoidances most of my life, and I quickly checked for warning signs that I'd overdone it. I was queasy, a touch dizzy, and more than a little sweaty. All were slightly troubling symptoms, but I told myself they could be chalked up to the mad dash I'd just made, not anything having to do with an impending seizure.

I took deep, even breaths, trying not to worry, but breathwork wouldn't prevent a seizure. Nothing, other than medication, could truly prevent one. And sometimes not even that. I'd had plenty of seizures while on medication.

Tonight, the town square was hopping with activity, the evening full of chatter and laughter. The green was dotted with chairs and blankets, and a band was setting up their instruments on a makeshift stage.

Magpie's was closed, the shop dark except for the dim shafts of late-day sunlight that spilled across the dining room. I found I was already looking forward to my Thursday shift, and I smiled inwardly, unable to believe I'd ever look forward to working in a busy, noisy coffee shop.

"At least you're not wearing the heavy tweed," Sam said. "I heard the job interview went well."

Tonight, he wore a ball cap that shaded his eyes, and the ends of his dark hair curled around the brim. I smiled, once again thinking about gossip in small towns. "I guess you were right about the luck in the air."

"About that." He reached into his back pocket.

The church bell pealed, and I let out a yip. "Sorry, I need to go. I'm going to be late for a meeting with Estrelle. I'm supposed to be there at six."

I had only five peals left before I was officially late.

Sam's eyes widened, and he rushed ahead of me to pull open Stitchery's door, which was unlocked even though it sported a "Closed" sign. "Hurry!"

From the street, the shop looked inviting, welcoming even, with its pale sea-green facade and blue trim. Mellow orange light glowed warmly in its window. There was nothing about it at all to suggest that a scary old woman owned the place.

As I passed by him, sweeping into the store, I couldn't help but notice the look of concern on his face as the bell tolled again. "Thanks."

"Good luck. Not that you'll need it. Probably," he added with a mock grimace.

At least I hoped it was mock.

My god, what had I gotten myself into?

I nodded and smiled as confidently as I could—which wasn't saying much—and said goodbye to Norman as Sam released the door. It closed slowly with a prolonged whoosh, as if exhaling after a deep, meditative breath. He gave a quick wave before he and Norman walked off.

The church bells finished marking the six o'clock hour with an echoing ring. Adrenaline raced as I called out a tentative hello, proud that my voice didn't crack.

A gravelly voice came from a back room, strong and sure. "One moment."

Trying to calm myself, I breathed in, held the air, then released it.

Time ticked slowly by. A minute. Two. I noted that Estrelle wasn't too concerned about keeping *me* waiting.

Biding my time, I took a good look around the shop. Because I'd seen Estrelle only wearing black, I'd pictured the inside of Stitchery to resemble Morticia Addams's walk-in closet, so I was quite surprised to find it looking more like Rainbow Brite lived here.

There was hardly any black at all in the space, which was awash in colorful fabrics, décor, and fixtures. The walls had been painted in a curving, curling, multicolor geometric design. The greens, blues, corals, and yellows were somehow both energetic and soothing.

The space felt . . . cheerful.

Serene.

I listened—it was almost always my first instinct. I expected to hear the rattle of the air-conditioning through metal ductwork or footsteps in the storeroom or the hum of the computer on the counter that also held the cash register. But there was nothing. Only silence.

Which was odd. There was no true silence in the world. Sound lived everywhere. It was in my breath, in the blink of my eye, in the flow of my blood through my veins. It was in the creak of drywall, the birds on the roof, the stir of the air.

Yet in here . . . silence.

I wasn't sure if the lack of sound was blissful or disturbing.

Finally, I decided it was neither.

It was peaceful.

One side of the wide shop held bolts of fabrics, a cutting station, notions, and a display of sewing machines. The other side held a long pink worktable, a dress form that had swaths of white fabric pinned in place. Three tiered bookcases were filled with patterns as well as sewing and quilting books. There was an embroidery nook at the front of the store, cram-jammed with floss, hoops, needles. Scattered throughout the shop were hand-sewn goods for sale. Beach bags, tea pouches, potholders, hair scrunchies, bibs—all done in bright, happy colors.

I could easily imagine Bunny in here. Leafing through the books. Buying thread and buttons. She'd encourage me to pick a favorite fabric and then we'd make something out of it. A pillow or purse or book cover. We'd even made a stuffed Mr. Whiskers once, which wasn't quite the same as having the real thing, but I loved it just the same. It was one of my most treasured possessions.

I turned at the sound of heavy footsteps. Estrelle walked out of the back room carrying two medium-size carpetbags with dark leather handles. Both were fashioned in a fabric that matched the wall's geometric design and had the name of the shop stitched near the clasp.

She set the bags down on the worktable. Then she narrowed a shrewd gaze on me. "To be early is to be on time. To be on time is to be late. To be late is to disturb me greatly."

I took a deep breath. Nope. She still had no scent. Her face was pinched with irritation, all the fine lines scrunched into a scowl. For some reason, in this calm, soothing shop, she didn't terrify me as much as she had at Magpie's. No one who created such a tranquil space could be *too* scary. I made a point to look at my watch. "By my calculation, you're three minutes late to our arranged meeting. Are you disturbed by your own tardiness?"

Her right eyebrow rose. Stormy eyes darkened. "I'm deeply disturbed *all* the time."

There was a twitch of her lip that hinted at a smile, but it disappeared nearly as fast as it had appeared. Suddenly I was convinced Estrelle had a sense of humor. One that was smothered in doom and gloom and fright, but still.

"Enough of the chitchat. I despise chitchat. Take these." She picked up the carpetbags and thrust them toward me. "You will return these bags to me in exactly two weeks at ten A.M. Do not be late."

I took the bags from her. One was much heavier than the other. "I don't understand."

She walked toward the front door, pulled it open, and said, "Goodbye, now."

Stunned, I didn't know what else to do but leave.

As I reached the doorway, I said, "But—"

Her pupils slitted like a dragon's, and I snapped my lips closed and hurried onto the sidewalk. She closed the door, locked it, and walked away, soon disappearing into the storeroom.

And as I walked back to Maggie's, I couldn't help but notice that the monarch butterfly with the white wing followed me the whole way there.

CHAPTER 11

AVA

Back at Maggie's, I carried the carpetbags into Noah's bedroom, set them on the bed. Full of curiosity, I flicked open the clasp on the lighter of the two bags. I peeked into its depths, my whole body tight with tension, not sure what to expect. Upon seeing a teddy bear inside, I immediately relaxed, my uneasiness replaced with interest.

When I pulled the bear out, it hung limp in my hand. It was missing most of its stuffing. It also lacked an arm, its nose, and an ear. It had large gashes all over its body.

"What in the world happened to you?" I asked, even though I suspected I knew the answer.

It looked like someone had taken sharp scissors to the poor thing. I'd seen it before.

When I was eight years old, I'd been in my bedroom trimming a piece of fuzz off my favorite teddy bear when my parents' raised voices slid under my door and filled the space with their heat, their anger, their bitterness.

So entangled in their words, I hadn't realized I'd accidentally snipped a big hole in the bear's chest, slicing it wide open. The last thing I'd wanted at that moment was to ask for my mother's help. So I sat on my bed with the sewing box Bunny had given me and carefully made the repairs. The stitches were uneven but surprisingly strong for being held together with nothing but the thinnest thread, sorrow, and salty tears.

Here in Noah's bedroom, I ran my hand across the bear's wounds, then looked into the bag to see what else it contained. I found a plastic baggie of stuffing and the bear's missing pieces, minus the nose. At the bottom of the bag was a small sewing kit and an assortment of thread and needles.

I quickly opened the other bag, the heavier one. It was filled with old clothes and fabric scraps. On top of the pile was an infant's daisy-printed romper, which reminded me of the one Juniper had been wearing yesterday. There was also a woman's skirt printed with crows that had a drooping hem and broken zipper, and a ripped sweater patterned with the outlines of cartoonish dinosaurs. There were embroidered napkins. An assortment of vintage remnants. A single yellow cotton curtain with a pom-pom fringe. And even a floral tablecloth that had a big pink stain on it.

The whole lot looked like laundry-gone-wrong. What did Estrelle expect me to do with it? The skirt would be an easy fix, though that stain on the tablecloth was likely permanent. But what about the baby clothes? And the scraps of fabric?

I wasn't sure. I also didn't know why I felt the stirring of excitement when I looked at the mishmash pile of material.

I was trying to puzzle it all out when my phone rang, the ringtone assigned to my mother distinct: "Don't Worry, Be Happy" by Bobby McFerrin.

"Hello!" I answered, turning my back on the carpetbags so I wouldn't be distracted.

"Well, hello there," my mother said. "Everything all right?"

"Sure," I replied, overly bright as I made my way through the house and stepped out to the front porch. A steady breeze blew as I made my way to a rocking chair and sat down. Maggie's house faced west, and the sunset was a sight to behold. As the sinking sun neared the horizon line, it colored the sky a glorious mix of brilliant orange and deep purple.

"How's the new job going?" she asked.

"So far so good," I said, still unwilling to share that I had *two* new jobs. "The room that I'll be sleeping in is full of boxes, so those need to be relocated before I can officially move in."

"You're not doing any heavy lifting, are you?"

"Not too heavy. There's a cat at the house. Molly. She's

part Ragdoll. She's beautiful and, oh my gosh, so fluffy. It's hard to believe there's even a cat under all the fur. She's stand-offish, but I think she'll warm up to me."

My mother was not one to be easily sidetracked, especially by a cat. "Did you tell the old man you're working for about your condition?"

When I'd told her about the job, I might have exaggerated Dez's age and frailty. Partly so she wouldn't worry about me working for a man. Lectures about the dangers associated with being female had been included in the diet of cautionary tales I'd been raised on, each and every story composed of her endless fears. I'd lived a life avoiding risks to appease her worries. And though I recognized some of those concerns were justified, on the whole, they'd been suffocating.

"Yep," I fibbed. And the lies kept coming as I added, "He had an epileptic cat once, so he figures he knows what to do in an emergency."

She let out a soft *harrumph*. "I don't think it's quite the same, but it's better than nothing. It's good he knows what can happen. Just in case."

Just in case the seizures came back, she meant.

"Are you sure, absolutely certain," Mom said, "that you're ready to take on such a challenging job? I know you're lonely, sweetie, but is this position the best choice for you?"

I had been lonely, it was true. Alexander had really been my only adult friend. I was a loner by nurture, not nature, so the hole his absence had left in my life was as wide and deep as the middle of the ocean.

"It's good for me to leave the house, Mom. To stretch my wings. I've been . . . too careful."

"There's no such thing as too careful, Ava. Not when your life is at stake."

"There is when it doesn't really feel like you're living."

It was the most I'd ever pushed back with her, and my heart was pounding as I waited for her to lovingly remind me that I was very much alive *because* we'd been careful.

"Is that how you feel? That you haven't been living?"

I wiggled in my seat. Across the street, a neighbor watered the flowers on her porch and waved to me. I waved back and said, "Yes."

I didn't add *for a long time now,* though I wanted to.

"I hope you realize that you are living, Ava. It might look different, your way of life, but you are living."

Shaking my head, I stood up and walked to one end of the porch. From this vantage point, I could see a narrow span of darkness in the distance that I knew to be the gulf. "Mm-hmm," I said.

I'd pushed a boundary I'd never dared to before. Next time we talked, maybe I'd push a little harder. Perhaps I'd even come clean about where I actually was living these days.

"Did you talk to your landlord about terminating your lease early?" she asked, as if she somehow knew I'd been thinking about my location.

The lies popped into my head and out of my mouth before I could think to stop them. "I did. I'll have to forfeit my last month's rent and the security deposit, though."

I had no idea if that was the case at all. In fact, I actually hadn't made any plans for my Cincinnati apartment—I'd been waiting to see how things would pan out here in Alabama. I'd need to make some decisions soon. It was silly to pay rent there if I was living here. And I'd need to go back to collect the rest of my things at some point, too.

"How's *your* work going?" I asked, redirecting the conversation as the sun sank out of sight. It left behind a thin band of tangerine sky and a deep purple that bloomed like a night flower unfolding its petals.

"Great!" Her voice became light and floaty, her worries briefly forgotten. When she moved to Tampa with her new husband, she quit her job as a legal secretary. Now she worked for a florist and loved every minute of it. Her Instagram page was full of the colorful arrangements she created, and I saw the pride in each of the photos she posted. "We have a busy weekend coming up. Four events—three of them weddings."

Gone was the stress in her tone, the anxiety, replaced with a giddiness that made her voice sparkle and shine. Her happiness brought a lump to my throat. She never would have dated Wilson, her husband, if I was still having seizures. She never would have married him. She never would've left a job she didn't like but was one where she could work from home three days a week that had good insurance coverage. She never would've moved away from me. She wouldn't be experiencing the joy she was now. She wouldn't be living the life she had deserved all along.

A seagull squawked overhead, and she said, "Was that a seagull?"

I frowned up at the bird as it headed for the beach. Tattletale. "Blue jay, I think."

She laughed. "When you live by the water, all the birds start sounding like seagulls."

"I can imagine." I laughed, too, so she wouldn't get suspicious.

"You're drinking plenty of water, taking your vitamins, and eating some vegetables, right?"

Instead of rolling my eyes like I normally would when she gave me these reminders, I was surprised to find my throat thick with emotion. Even though she could be suffocating, she'd given up a lot in her life to take care of me. Simply because she loved me.

My voice cracked slightly when I said, "You know how I feel about vegetables."

The full truth of it was that I hadn't been taking good care of myself since Alexander died, a sorrowful effect of grief and guilt. I needed to do better. For my mom. For myself.

"Ava Laine," she said softly, her voice so full of compassion that it nearly broke me wide open, "if you can't eat, at least take the vitamins and drink the water."

"I will. I promise."

"All in all, everything else going okay?"

Suddenly, I wanted to confess everything. The otherworldly letter. The road trip. The overwhelming desire to do *all* the things. The strange butterfly that might or might not be Alex.

I knew, however, that if I did, she wouldn't sleep tonight. "I'm good. Really."

"All right. But remember if it doesn't work out with your new job, my offer still stands."

She had been trying to lure me to Tampa since she left Ohio, and after Alexander passed away, I'd actually been tempted to take her up on the offer once or twice. But I knew if I moved near her, she'd fall into old habits of watching over me twenty-four/seven. Neither of us needed that again.

"I'll remember. Thanks, Mom."

"Call if you need anything. Anything at all."

We said our goodbyes and I hung up. Somewhere in the distance, I heard a fiddle. It wasn't crying like it had been last night, but the song was still full of melancholy and heartache.

Without really thinking about what I was doing, I tucked my phone in my pocket and followed the sound. As I walked along, I soaked in the gorgeous sky, the sound of the waves, the call of a chickadee, the trill of frogs. Only when I turned onto Eventide Lane did I notice the fiddle had quieted. I glanced toward Dez's house at the end of the lane. It sat dark and his truck wasn't in the driveway, either. Where was he? Was it my job now to know?

I worried about that for a moment before I heard the jingle of dog tags and a soft *quabark,* so quiet it was nearly drowned out by the sound of the waves and the sighs of the wind. I squinted and smiled when I saw Norman wagging his tail from the gravel driveway of the home across the street from Dez's. The one-story house stood proudly on piers and its pastel-yellow paint glowed like moonlight in the growing darkness. A newer-model truck was parked in the carport.

I walked over to Norman, crouched down, and let him lick my chin.

"Hey," Sam said, coming down the steps with a leash in hand. "Didn't expect to see you here tonight. I heard you weren't moving into Dez's for a few days yet."

No doubt he knew my whole life story already. Most of it, anyway. "I was just out for a walk and couldn't resist saying hi to Norman when I saw him. I didn't mean to trespass."

I caught a flash of light out of the corner of my eye coming from Dez's house. I looked that way. A white light flickered in the attic. I blinked, sure I was seeing things, and the light disappeared.

"I'm not sure what all mean streets you grew up on in Ohio," Sam said, "but around here it's called *neighborly* when people stop and say hi, not *trespassing*."

I smiled, thinking about the street I'd grown up on, lined with crabapples and picket fences. Hardly anything mean about it, unless you counted the time one neighbor chopped down another neighbor's sweetgum tree because its branches stretched into his yard and he was sick of the spiky pods littering his lawn. That incident had been talked about for years.

"Besides," Sam added, "I'm fairly sure Norman would've run off to meet you if you didn't stop. He's taken a liking to you. He's shy, so that's saying something."

"Really?" I bent and took Norman's face in my hands, then ran my thumbs up the bridge of his silky snout, up to his forehead, and over his oval eyes. There was a hitch in my voice when I said, "I've taken a liking to him, too."

Norman nudged his nose into my stomach and wagged his tail, and I fell just a little bit harder in love with him.

"I'm glad you stopped by, actually," Sam said. "I have something for you."

Reluctantly, I stood. "You do?"

He reached into his pocket and pulled out his wallet. From it, he took out a dollar bill and handed it over.

"What's this for?" I asked, perplexed.

"After we talked yesterday morning about luck, I hopped in my truck and drove over to Perdido Key—just over the border in Florida—and bought a dollar scratch-off lottery ticket. We won two dollars. That's your half of the win."

"But it was your ticket."

"But it was your luck," he said.

I laughed. "All right, then. Thanks."

My attention drifted back to Dez's house, specifically to the attic, and listening intently, I swore I heard something moving up there. Sparrows, I told myself, glancing away. Sparrows.

"Well, I should be getting back." I had the shivers all of a sudden. The sky had started looking like a bruise, all traces of the orange glow gone now.

Sam's knuckles whitened as he gripped the leash. "We were just heading out to get dinner. Did you want to join us?"

He had excellent manners but a lousy poker face. It was obvious he'd asked only because he was a nice guy. The invite was the *neighborly* thing to do. "Thanks, but I already ate," I lied, waving away a mosquito from my face. "But I'll walk back toward the square with you, if you don't mind. I'm lousy with directions. I can get lost in a grocery store."

His shoulders relaxed as he clipped the leash to Norman's collar. "No worries there—if you got lost, Norman would find you. He's the best unintentional search dog around. Kids in my old neighborhood loved to play hide-and-seek with him."

"Good to know," I said as we started walking. Porch lights had started coming on, glowing deep amber. Moths flitted. Frog chirps grew louder and cicadas screamed. Gulf waves provided a pleasant backdrop to their raucous symphony. "Where did you move from?"

At the end of the street, I looked over my shoulder, back toward Dez's house. Again, I saw a white light flicker in the attic. Goose bumps popped up on my arms as I thought about ghosts and tried to convince myself there was a logical reason for that flash of light. A light fixture on the fritz, perhaps.

"A small town outside Nashville."

There was hardness in his voice, thick as armor. He didn't want to talk about his old home. I could take a hint, but to keep from asking nosy follow-up questions as we walked, I turned my attention to the dollar bill, folding it this way, that.

One block north of the beach, Sam finally broke the silence between us. "You're staying with Maggie, right?"

The tongues around here had to be mighty tired by now. "She's been really kind, taking me in like she has."

"The Brightwells are good people."

I nodded. "Seems to me there are lots of good people around here." Some unusual ones, too. Like Estrelle. And now me.

Norman trotted in between Sam and me and kept looking my way as if checking to see if I was really there. For a foolish second, I almost asked to hold his leash, stopping myself only because I didn't want Sam to think I was some crazy dog lady. Though, honestly, I might be. I just hadn't been around enough dogs to know for sure. I bent another corner of the dollar bill, smoothing it with two fingernails. "Florida seems a far way to go for a lottery ticket."

"It was either Florida or Mississippi, and Florida's a far sight closer. Only half an hour in good traffic. There's no lottery here in Alabama, though that might change soon."

As we turned another corner, Maggie's house came into view, looking inviting with the soft yellow light filling the windows and spilling out onto the porch. I stopped at the walkway and faced Sam. His face was bathed in the light thrown from a lamp-post. I said, "Are you still feeling luck blowing around me?"

He tilted his chin upward and breathed deeply. "There's *something* blowing. Why?"

I held up my hand. In my palm was the dollar bill. "What do you think about letting our luck ride, see how far we can take our winning streak?"

Leaning in for a closer look, he said, "Did you fold that bill into the shape of a dog?"

"It's basic origami. I had a lot of time on my hands as a kid."

Laughing lightly, he took the money from my hand. "All right, Ava. Count me in on letting it ride. I was heading back that way in a couple of days anyway. I'll pick up another scratch ticket."

"Headed that way for work?" I asked, curious about him. What had brought him here to Driftwood? What happened in Tennessee that he didn't want to talk about? Did it have anything to do with the sadness in his eyes?

He shook his head. "Appointment in Orange Beach—only minutes from Perdido Key."

"Don't suppose you need a dog walker while you're gone?" I asked, unable to stop myself. I bent down to rub Norman's ears again, and his tail thrashed about.

"Nah. Norman will be okay on his own."

Disappointment flowed, thick and heavy. "Well, if you change your mind, you know where to find me."

"That I do."

"I guess I'll be seeing you two around." I gave Norman one final pat and started up the sidewalk. Halfway, I turned around, readying to call out, expecting to see Sam much farther up the street. But he still stood where I'd left him. I realized that he was waiting to make sure I got inside safe and sound, and for some reason the gesture had me blinking back tears.

"Something wrong?" he asked.

"No. I was just going to ask if you know who plays the fiddle around here. I heard it late last night, then again just a little while ago. And well, I'm curious is all. It's beautiful."

His chin jutted and he pulled his ball cap lower over his brow. "Can't say I do."

I tried to figure out what it was I saw in his eyes, but couldn't quite.

However, as I walked into Maggie's I knew full well it had been a lie I'd heard in his voice.

CHAPTER 12

MAGGIE

"Look at her go," Rose said, her voice full of humor as we stood side by side at the front window of Magpie's, looking out onto the square.

Across the street a battery of Snail Slippers had just turned the corner closest to the shop on their first lap of the square. We were watching Ava, who was leading the pack of walkers, but only because she was being pulled along, pell-mell style, by Cluck-Cluck, Jolly Smith's feisty chicken. Little Hannah Smith, fully decked out in a Cinderella ball gown costume, ran after them in pink sneakers that lit up with every step, her tulle skirt billowing behind her.

Rose laughed. "Ava's going to break her dang neck stumbling around like that."

"I don't think she'll mind if she does. Look at that smile on her face."

It was the biggest, sunniest smile I'd ever seen, full of pure, sweet joy. I had the uneasy feeling that Ava hadn't felt much joy in her life. There was something about her, something frail and fragile, that made me want to bubble-wrap her and hug her tight. My motherly instincts were to protect her—I just didn't know what I was protecting her from.

The front door opened—I didn't miss those bells a single whit—and a rush of warm air swept in along with Titus Pomeroy. His gaze went first to the empty counter, then over to us at the window.

"Good morning, Maggie. *Rose.*"

His voice dropped when he said her name, and he stretched

the single syllable for an extra beat, almost as if he was singing it.

It was plain as day to anyone who saw them together that something was brewing between them—and it wasn't coffee. I'd been waiting months to see if he'd ask her out, but he was apparently a patient man.

A smart one, too, because taking his time was to his advantage. Rose needed those months to warm up to him, to defrost the heart she'd put in cold storage a good ten years back after her no-account husband ran off with a vacationing hussy.

Sure, she acted disinterested in Titus. Offended, even, sometimes. But I knew her too well. I saw the softening happening, slow and gradual. Titus was the first man I'd ever seen her give more than a passing glance. The only one she bantered with. The only one she watched walk away until he was out of sight.

I had little doubt that Titus Pomeroy was going to be the man to change her mind about loving again. It made my own heart do a happy dance for her. She deserved all the love in the world.

"Good morning," we responded in unison, though Rose's voice had a hint of haughtiness in it and mine was full of hopeful anticipation.

Something was different about him today. Determination radiated, wafting as sure and strong as his woodsy cologne. His dreadlocks were held off his face by a cloth band at the nape of his neck, and it looked like he'd had a fresh shave. There wasn't a wrinkle to be seen on his short-sleeve button-down or knee-length shorts. He held a single daisy in his hand as he stepped up to the counter and glanced up to study the menu board, even though the options hadn't changed in decades.

Rose pulled her shoulders back, headed for the counter, and there was extra swing in her hips as she passed him by. "What can I get for you today, Titus?" she asked.

I scooted over to the end of the counter and busied myself by rearranging a display stand that held an assortment of Magpie's mugs and bags of coffee while I eavesdropped. I realized I was grinning and tried to stop, but the corners of my lips kept turning up.

Titus kept hold of the daisy with one hand and scratched his chin with the other. His gaze dropped from the menu board to her face and held steady. "Let's see. Hmm. I'd like a small iced matcha latte, add a double shot of espresso, add chai, add lavender syrup. Please."

Rose pursed her lips, tipped her head, and flashed him a tight smile. "Sure thing. Coming right up."

She grabbed a hot cup from the stack, pivoted, and filled the cup with black coffee from the drip maker. She stuck a lid and sleeve on the cup, pivoted again, and slid it across the counter to him. She stabbed buttons on the register screen as if she were trying to kill the machine. "That'll be two dollars, please."

Slow as could be, he pulled several bills from his pocket, handed her two, then put the third—and the flower—into the tip jar.

She stared at the flower like she'd never seen a daisy before. "What's that for?"

"Do I need a reason to give a lovely lady a flower?"

His voice was smooth as silk, sweet as honey. I gave up all pretenses of minding my own business and openly watched the two of them. I didn't worry about them noticing my nosiness. They only had eyes for each other.

Her eyes narrowed. "Is that a bribe or something? If so, you're wasting your time. I'm still not making you that fancy-schmancy drink."

Full cheeks rounded as he smiled. "Time you enjoy wasting is not time wasted, as the saying goes."

I heard the back door open and looked over to see Donovan coming down the hallway, carrying three white boxes—today's pastry order.

My heart rate doubled at the sight of him. The phrase *aim to please* kept bouncing around my head, knocking me a little off-balance. In truth, our date had thrown me for a dizzying loop, and I was still feeling the warmth of it all.

And the confusion as well.

There are other things more important. That's a lesson I learned a little too late.

I couldn't deny that I'd had a nice time with him last night, but I couldn't stop thinking that our new relationship was headed nowhere fast.

All because of a boat.

I waved him over to me, then held a finger to my lips and jerked my head several times toward the drama unfolding at the cash register.

Donovan's eyes widened knowingly and he oh so casually tiptoed around Titus and stepped up behind me, as if suddenly having a deep interest in purchasing a bag of coffee his brother produced.

Rose was now looking at Titus like she'd never seen *him* before. Crossing her arms over her chest, she lifted her chin. The haughty tone was back in her voice as she said, "Most men trying to butter me up bring me roses."

"I would hope you'd know by now that I'm not like most men." He picked up his cup and gave her a slow nod, never taking his gaze from her face. He didn't even *blink*. "You have a good day now, Rose."

With that, he turned. Donovan and I suddenly looked up, down, all around, as Titus's attention fell on us. He gave us a nod, too. "See y'all tomorrow."

With that, he walked out.

As soon as the door closed behind him, I fanned myself and let out a *"Whoo-ee."*

Rose blinked as if just now realizing there were other people in the shop. "Oh, hush now," she said sharply. "Not a word. Not a single word."

I made the motion of zipping my lips, but I was certain my eyes were flashing my delight as brightly as a lighthouse lantern.

She turned and marched to the restroom, her hands pressed to her cheeks.

I took the boxes from Donovan. "I'm glad you were late so you could witness that. I'm not sure anyone would believe me otherwise."

"Rose will skin you alive if you tell another soul what just happened."

It was true—she would. But it might be worth it, because I was fit to bust with happiness for her.

As I set the boxes on the counter, I saw Estrelle walk past the front window. Through the black netting of her hat, she looked our way, lifted her eyebrows, waggled them, and kept going in the direction of her shop.

I frowned at her reaction, hoping she hadn't gotten her hopes up too high where Donovan and I were concerned because I wasn't at all sure it was going to work out between us.

"Listen, I need to run," Donovan said, "but can I interest you in dinner tonight? Maybe a real restaurant? We can go over to Gulf Shores or up to Magnolia Springs if you want privacy."

"Sorry," I said. "There's a park commission meeting tonight."

"Tomorrow?"

I wrinkled my nose. "I'm working at the Driftwood Museum fundraiser."

"Friday, then."

I bit my lip. "Euchre club."

"Maggie. Is this about the boat? Because I told you—"

"Of course not." The dejection in his tone nearly did me in. Because it *was* about the boat.

The boat was all I could think about. Even last night, while we talked about most everything else under the sun, I was thinking about the dang boat.

It was on my mind when I told him about what was going on with Dad. When I'd shared all my best coffee shop stories. While he told me stories of people he met during his career. When I talked of Noah.

The boat sat between us like an elephant in the room as we chatted about his family, his reluctant return to the bakery, Butterfly Fest, the questionable beach mouse population, my father's hoarding issues, Ava's strange letter, the way the moonlight looked on the water, and how the mosquito, not the northern flicker, should be the state bird.

The boat, the boat, the stupid boat.

Even when he walked me home and stood on the front porch

talking about how everyone on the street was probably peeking at us from behind their curtains, I was thinking about Donovan being on the open water. Of him falling in. Of him disappearing.

As he gave me a hug and walked off into the night, I knew I had a big decision to make.

Keep dating him, knowing that in doing so, he would have to give up a huge part of himself.

Or let him go. For good this time.

I knew how he felt about the situation, but I wanted a little more time to decide. I *needed* more time.

"All right, all right. You're busy, I get it." He drummed his fingers on the showcase. "But I'm not going to give up easily, Maggie."

I opened a box full of muffins. My hand was, yet again, shaking. I glanced up at him.

"I'll wait," he said, staring into my eyes. "I'll wait forever if I have to." He gave a final tap on the showcase. "See you later. I've got to go strategize."

"Strategize what?"

"How to win you over, of course." With a wave, he walked off.

I watched him go, his voice echoing in my head. My heart thumped crazily.

Little did he know that he'd won me over a long time ago. That wasn't the issue here.

I went back to unloading pastries, and only a moment later, the front door opened. A warm breeze raced into the shop just ahead of Mark and Trixie Davies.

"Good morning!" I said, my voice a bit shaky. "What can I get for the two of you?"

They were all smiles, dressed nearly identical in loose black trousers, sunflower-yellow dress shirts, and white bow ties. Trixie's blue hair was pulled up in twin topknots, and Mark's black hair had zigzag lines buzzed into it. They were jugglers by trade, their daytime schedules filled with school and library visits. Soon, they'd be on stage at Butterfly Fest as well. Everyone loved them.

Rose reappeared at my side, said her hellos, and helped fill the order: two iced mocha lattes with almond milk and two chocolate-nut muffins to go.

Mark said, "Maggie, word is Dez is selling Magpie's. True?"

My fondness for Mark dropped a notch. I pasted on a smile and felt the beginnings of a headache as I bagged the muffins. "Nope."

I'd been hoping that the talk would've died down by now.

Trixie leaned in and dropped her voice. "Really? Everyone we've run into sounds so sure."

"I'm positive." I broke down the empty pastry boxes using more force than necessary. I glanced at Rose, who was watching me with remorseful eyes as she made the drinks.

Trixie grinned. "I'm glad to hear it. Do you remember that Mark and I met here? I'd been on vacation with my family when I saw him sitting in the corner with a set of juggling bags. Tall, dark, and nerdy. Be still my heart."

I remembered, especially since I'd gifted Mark the juggling bags only moments before Trixie had come inside. The bags had been on a curiosity shelf for years at that point, and I'd been over the moon to finally match them.

"You saw me watching him, Maggie, and encouraged me to go over and strike up a conversation."

They'd been young. In their teens. And oh so adorable.

"You nearly spilled your drink on your way," I said softly, my irritation about the boat vanishing.

She laughed. "I was nervous. I didn't just go up to boys, talk to them. But somehow I knew if I didn't, I would be making the biggest mistake of my life."

"We had our first date here at Magpie's, too," Mark said.

Trixie glanced fondly at him. "It was really more of a getting-to-know-you cup of coffee than a date."

"She had to make sure I wasn't a total weirdo before she agreed to dinner." He laughed.

"Luckily, he's just a little weird." She bumped his shoulder with hers, her adoration of him shining brightly in her eyes.

After she and her family left town that summer, she and

Mark had kept in touch. A few years later, I'd been invited to their wedding.

"And look at us now," Mark said.

Rose pushed their drinks across the counter. Mark paid and Trixie added, "There wouldn't be an *us* if it weren't for Magpie's. Or you, Maggie. When we heard that Dez was selling, I couldn't remember if I ever thanked you for all you do here. For all you provide. So, thanks."

It wasn't me. It was this shop. My mama's heart pulsed in here. Her spirit. Her love of matching things—which sometimes included people.

I swallowed over the lump in my throat. "You're welcome."

No sooner had they walked out than Redmond and Sienna came inside, talking about Alistair. From what I gathered, the small bird had once again escaped, this time ending up at Red's, where Redmond had been sleeping since his breakup with Javier.

"*Aw,*" Sienna said. "He misses you."

"Javier?"

She blinked. "Alistair. But probably Javier, too. Do you miss him?"

Redmond shifted foot to foot. "It's complicated. If only he'd make better health choices . . . I don't want to lose him to a heart attack because he can't put down a cinnamon roll."

Sienna smiled dreamily. "I like cinnamon rolls. Pillowy soft dough. Sweet vanilla icing. That gooey center? Heaven."

"Yeah, they're great if you like six hundred calories of fat, cholesterol, and sodium."

She sniffed, annoyed. "Now I understand."

"What?"

Crossing her arms, she glared at him. "Why Javier looks for sweetness elsewhere. He sure ain't getting it from you."

Rose murmured, "Amen."

"Hey now!" he exclaimed. "No ganging up. I'm sweet."

"When was the last time you had a cinnamon roll?" Sienna asked.

Glancing at the bakery case, his gaze went straight past the rolls and landed on a blueberry donut. His eyes flared with longing. "A long time."

The front door flew open. A mighty gust of wind blew through the shop, bellowing a warning as it rattled tables, chairs.

"What in the world?" Rose asked, looking around.

Then suddenly Estrelle appeared in the doorway, seemingly out of nowhere.

Sienna sidestepped to hide behind Redmond, a sapling in the shadows of a giant oak.

Estrelle clomped inside, the sound of her shoes echoing. She looked from face to face. When her gaze landed on Redmond, it stayed there.

Sienna tripped over her words as she said, "I'm just, I'm going to—" She looked around. "Go get a picture of that recipe." She hightailed it across the room to the blackboard.

Rose squeezed in close to me.

Redmond gulped as Estrelle stepped up to him, the top of her head only reaching his chest. Slowly, she looked upward, the hump in her back seeming extra round. She arched an eyebrow. Then she reached out with her gnarled fingers and squeezed his massive bicep.

Sienna gasped. Rose grabbed my hand and whispered, "Lordy mercy."

Redmond flinched but otherwise held still.

It was an impressive show of courage. If I were him, I'd have been out the door and down the block by now.

Estrelle glared at him from behind her veil. "You'd think one so strong would understand the benefits of flexibility."

Confusion filled his eyes, and his voice quavered as he said, "I'm flexible. I teach a yoga class."

Estrelle's gaze narrowed dangerously.

He gulped and started scratching at a hive that had popped out above his knee. He glanced at it, horrified.

"Denying your true desires will lead only to a lifetime of heartbreak." She let go of his arm. *"It has been said."*

The silence lingered.

Finally, Redmond muttered, "I—ah, actually, I need to, ah, I forgot . . . I mean . . . Bye!" He sprinted toward the door.

Estrelle smirked. Then she glanced at Sienna. "I believe you're next in line."

"No, no," she said quickly. "You go on ahead." She snapped another shot of the recipe.

Mrs. Pollard would be beside herself if she were here and not doing laps around the square with the Snails.

Rose let go of my hand and somehow sounded as though nothing unusual had just occurred as she said, "Hot chocolate, Estrelle?"

Instead of answering, the older woman's silvery gaze turned on me, and I had the uneasy feeling she was going to lecture me about Donovan's boat and my inflexibility where it was concerned. She'd been gently trying for years to get me to make peace with the water and my mama's disappearance, but not even the risk of boils could make that happen. Fortunately for me, she never pushed hard. If she had, I feared I might just have broken.

I quickly picked up the empty pastry boxes and glanced at Rose. "I'm going to run these out to the recycling bin. Be right back."

As I made a dash for the back hallway, Estrelle said, "There are a few around here who could benefit from a little more bending, don't you agree, Rose?"

Rose's voice finally cracked. "Yes, ma'am."

"I'll take that hot chocolate now, if you will. Do not forget the cinnamon."

I didn't dare look back at the counter. But as I passed Sienna, who still stood near the blackboard, I felt a little vibration. I stopped short and backed up. Closer to her, I felt it again. That familiar shock wave.

"Is something wrong?" Sienna asked. Then she dropped her voice. "I mean, other than Estrelle being scarier than those creepy-crawly earworms that sometimes pop out of the bathroom drain." She shuddered.

It took me a moment to figure out what she meant. "You mean *earwigs*?"

"Right. With all those legs and those pincers? Ugh."

I shuddered, too. Those things were terrifying. "No, nothing's wrong. Just the opposite." I smiled. "I have something for you. A curiosity."

I'd been within arm's length of Sienna dozens of times and had never gotten a vibration, so I knew her curiosity must be new. I set the boxes down on the table by the blackboard. Since I had only added one thing to the shelves in the last week, I knew just what to look for—and right where they were.

"You're serious?" She tucked her phone in her pocket and clasped her hands together. "I've always wanted one!"

It never failed that matching a curiosity lifted my spirits. Joy rippled. As I picked up the measuring spoons I'd found while sorting donations ahead of the library sale, I closed my eyes momentarily and silently whispered thanks to my mama, wherever she might be, for giving me this gift.

"These are for you," I said, holding out the mustard-yellow Tupperware measuring spoons.

Sienna blinked at them, doubt in her eyes. "Are you sure? I had my heart set on that Cranberries vinyl on the top shelf." She started singing about zombies.

Estrelle chuckled. I threw her a look, and she responded only by lifting an eyebrow.

I pushed the spoons into Sienna's hands. "I'm sure."

She pouted. "I mean, okay. Thanks. I guess."

"Do you cook?" I asked, trying to lead her in the right direction.

She shook her head.

"Do you like baking?"

"I don't know. I've never really done any cooking or baking. The kitchen has always been off-limits."

Had her family kept her out of the kitchen on purpose out of fear she'd burn the house down? If so, it was probably a wise decision.

"I do like eating vanilla scones, though," she said thoughtfully, looking at the blackboard. "Earlier this week, Mrs. Pollard offered to teach me how to make them."

I thought that exceedingly brave of her.

"I think that's a great idea." I sent silent apologies to Mrs. Pollard and hoped her house was well insured. "You should take her up on it."

"Maybe I will. We'll see." She threw a look at the counter. "I should get my coffee now that the coast is clear. And I think I'll get a cinnamon roll, too. I might even bring one to Javier. Just because."

I glanced over my shoulder. Estrelle had gone. Rose stood watching us, an amused look on her face.

As Sienna ordered, I once again picked up the boxes and headed for the back door.

It was unusual that Sienna hadn't felt a connection to the measuring spoons, but not unheard-of. Every once in a while, instead of evoking a trip down memory lane, the curiosities paved a path forward instead. I hoped beyond hope that the measuring spoons would soon guide Sienna in a direction that would lead to her finally finding her passion in life.

CHAPTER 13

AVA

By Friday I'd determined that *the Snail Slippers* was an ironic name.

These people took their exercise seriously. Hips swaying, elbows pumping, feet flying. Bettina led our pack, dressed in black spandex, her white-blond hair blowing in the wind as she soared along like a bat out of hell.

And much to my absolute delight, I'd discovered that Jolly Smith was a gossip.

She was fast becoming one of my favorite people here in Driftwood, and the first person I'd sought out early this morning, on my second foray with the Snail Slippers this week.

The big-haired, big-hearted woman was as friendly as she was chatty and hadn't thought twice about letting me have a go at walking her pet chicken when I asked upon meeting her this past Wednesday. When Cluck-Cluck, a beautiful black chicken with white markings, had taken full advantage of my naiveté, Jolly had laughed her head off, a full, radiant round sound that hadn't stopped until I happily (and breathlessly) handed the leash back to her after a wild lap around the square.

"Oh, there's Candi Chitwood, goin' into the bakery. The woman in the itty-bitty tank top?" Jolly motioned with her chin.

I glanced over and nearly tripped on my own two feet. It had been a long week, and I was tired, struggling to keep up with the rest of the group. Jolly had been nice enough to slow her pace to match mine, and I immediately loved her for the kindness. We were currently well into our third lap, and Hannah, Jolly's granddaughter, skipped ahead of us, singing "Bibbidi-Bobbidi-Boo" off-key, loud and proud.

No doubt, my new work routines, loss of appetite lately, and lack of regular exercise were the root cause of this exhaustion. Nothing else. Nothing else at all.

Earlier some of the Snails had been talking about the Butterfly Fest 5K walk/run. It would be an ideal goal—the walk, not the run (I hadn't lost my mind). With the race being just about a month and a half away, it would give me plenty of time to whip myself into some semblance of shape.

"Sweetest girl you ever did meet, that Candi," Jolly said, "but has no idea her bodacious cleavage has been the cause of more than one accident around here; most recently, one that resulted in a decimated tomato patch and a young man's trip to urgent care."

In our time together, I'd heard that Bettina lied about her age, having *added* years so she could join the Happy Clams. Misty Keith hosted a book club, but only as an excuse to have a themed party once a month—she'd never read a single one of the picks. Ernestine Aiken kept stealing her own garden gnome because she had a crush on Dodge Cunningham, a recently divorced police officer.

I smiled the whole time Jolly talked. I couldn't believe my dumb luck in landing here, in Driftwood, a picture-perfect, perfectly quirky town.

A place where someone like me, who had *extraordinary* senses of hearing and smell, could fit in. I was a square peg and Driftwood was proving to be a square hole.

But then again, it hadn't quite been dumb luck, had it?

I never would've known about this town if not for the letter I'd received.

I heard a *quabark* in the distance and instantly knew it was Norman. Which then made me think about Sam. I fervently hoped Jolly would spill what she knew about Dez's neighbor. Why had he lied to me about playing fiddle? I didn't want to openly ask her about him, though, because saying something like that to someone like Jolly would have the whole town theorizing that I had a crush. I didn't. I was just curious. *Beyond* curious.

"When do you move in with Dez?" Jolly asked.

She smelled of orange blossom and almonds, homemade biscuits and patience.

"Sometime this weekend." I wished I didn't sound so winded. My voice came out in thin, thready rasps.

Cluck-Cluck trotted in front of us, pulling her leash left and right to examine the trees and flower beds along the sidewalk. Every once in a while, she'd stop to peck the ground, her red comb wobbling, and come up with a wriggling bug or worm.

Hannah had switched to singing about dreams and wishes and hearts, using the lights on her sneakers to add emphasis to certain words. *Asleep,* flash. *Rainbow,* flash. *True,* flash. She was a one-woman show in the making.

"What I'd give to live beachfront," Jolly said. "It's a dream."

Hannah, who might have hearing as good as mine, shouted, "Mawmaw, don't you know a dream is a wish your heart makes!" The last word was followed by a foot stamp and a flash of pink light.

"That's right, honey. It sure is." Jolly leaned into me, dropped her voice low. "If I never see *Cinderella* again, it'll be too damn soon. I'm startin' to root for the evil stepmother." In her regular voice she picked up our conversation where she'd left off. "I'm sure you've already figured out that Dez is a hoot and a half. His wife, Tuppence, was, too. A real firecracker. That woman could command a room like no one's business."

My heart pounded, my pulse sounding like a bass drum in my ear. "Did she pass away?" I asked, finally finding the courage to say the words aloud.

Jolly nodded. "She was lost to the sea. It was one of those days where the water looked calm but wasn't. She got caught in a riptide and couldn't get out of it. They never did find her body. Terrible tragic." Jolly looked at me, her plump face suddenly sharp and stern. "You need to be careful in the water, Ava. The beach here didn't have warning flags back in those days but it does now—they were actually put up because of what happened to Tuppence. Pay attention to them. If they're yellow, you best be extra careful in the water. If they're red, you'd be a damn fool to go in. If they're double red, you have a death wish or a fervent desire to pay a big fine or even get arrested—it's illegal to go in the water when double reds are flying."

"I'll pay attention," I said, my heart breaking for Maggie. "I promise. How long ago did all that happen?"

"It's been a good twenty-five years now, thereabouts. Maggie hasn't stepped in the water since. And she tried to keep her boy out of it, too, but sometimes he'd sneak off with friends to swim. Maggie about lost her mind when she found out. Have you met Noah yet?"

I shook my head.

"He's a darling boy. Smart as a whip. Studying dinosaurs at college. Dinosaurs, of all things. Did you know you can find fossils on the beach? Sure enough. Shark teeth, sand dollars, and plant . . . stuff." She waved a hand. "Noah'll tell you more about it when you meet him, I'm quite sure. He knows all the fancy terms."

Jolly's words had started to swirl in my head, and I stumbled on a crack on the sidewalk. I righted myself before I fell, but my feet suddenly felt leaden. My vision clouded, and I blinked to clear it.

I hadn't eaten before coming out today, and that had been a mistake. I'd stop at Break an Egg, the breakfast diner, to get something to eat after we were done walking. The thought of eggs, though, soured my stomach. Pancakes? My stomach rolled. Hash? No. Definitely not. I'd figure something out, but for now I needed to stop thinking about it or risk getting sick right here in the flower beds.

I suddenly heard the whooshing of a heartbeat and looked around. The monarch with the white wing was floating nearby, dipping and rising, turning and tilting. The poor thing looked to be having terrible trouble flying.

If the butterfly was Alex, that made sense, I supposed. He'd been a terrible driver. The absolute worst.

But if it was him, why was he still here? Following me around?

Jolly *tsk*ed, throwing a glance at Magpie's. "All this talk about Dez selling the coffee shop has the town up in arms. No one knows why he's even contemplating it, considering how Maggie feels about her mama coming back. You can already see the stress it's causing her, which she does not need, considering her blood-pressure issues. Dez has received several strongly voiced phone calls this week, I can tell you that. Maggie has more surrogate mamas in this town than you can shake a stick at."

"What do you mean, considering how Maggie feels about her mama coming back?" I asked, the words catching in my throat, sticking there.

"Oh, bless her heart. The only way Maggie was able to cope with her grief was to believe Tuppence had simply gone missing and would come back one day."

Oh no.

"It's why she keeps the shop the same," Jolly says. "She wants it to be just as it was when her mama left."

My heart broke. Simply split wide open.

"At first, Dez held out hope, too, praying that Tuppence would be rescued or found clinging to a piece of driftwood or washed up somewhere having amnesia or *something*. After a while, reality set in, but he kept up pretenses for Maggie's sake. They never had a memorial service or funeral or nothing."

Terrible tragic, Jolly had said. It didn't even come close to describing this situation.

"So the town goes along with it, too?" I asked, knowing even as I asked that they did. It explained why Rose had been avoiding Maggie's questions the other day.

Jolly nodded. "At first it was so she simply didn't break from the grief of it all. Then, it never seemed the right time. After a good while, some wanted to say something, just to get it out in the open. An intervention of sorts was planned, then canceled. No one could quite bring themselves to do it, because we knew it'd hurt her. Then we stopped trying altogether because somewhere along the way, Maggie got us hoping, too. Why not? Why not hope for a miracle? If nothing else, she's taught us a thing or two about love."

I swiped a tear from the corner of my eye. I wanted to run to the coffee shop, hug Maggie.

"Miz Ava," Hannah said, skipping back to me. "When'll Junebear be done? I miss her."

I mustered up a smile. "Junebear?"

Jolly explained. "Estrelle told Hannah she'd turned Junebear's care over to you."

"I didn't mean to hurt her!" Hannah cried, her blue eyes filling with tears.

My foggy brain realized the bear in the carpetbag must belong to Hannah. I threw a look at Stitchery, expecting it to be dark this time of day, but I saw Estrelle framed in the window, watching us. Anyone else might think it eerie the way she popped up like she did, but for some strange reason I was starting to find comfort in it. I gave her a smile and waved. She awkwardly lifted her hand as if she'd never waved a day before in her life and then abruptly turned away.

Jolly cupped Hannah's head and drew her in close. "What happened to Junebear was an accident. Hannah found my kitchen shears and got caught up in wielding their power. I've been there a time or two myself."

Cluck-Cluck bopped over and started pecking at my shoelace as I crouched down to Hannah's level. "I promise to take good care of Junebear and get her back to you as soon as possible."

Jolly said, "We were worried she wasn't fixable. That's some kind of magic you'll need to put her back together."

I kept my gaze on Hannah. "She might not look quite the same on the outside, but on the inside, where it truly matters, she'll be just the same as she always was."

With her head pressed into her grandmother's round stomach, Hannah nodded. "Will you tell her I love her? And that I'm real sorry?"

"I sure will."

Knowing the bear belonged to Hannah made me want to get straight to work, my mind already thinking of creative ways to patch her up.

Movement across the street caught my eye. It wasn't Estrelle this time—Stitchery's window was now empty, the store dark. Instead, it was Sam and Norman, heading for Magpie's. I waved and Sam waved back. Norman's tail started wagging a mile a minute.

I petted Cluck-Cluck before I stood up, and she kept on pecking at my laces. As I straightened, the world spun and I wobbled.

"Hey now." Jolly grabbed my arm. "You've gone white as a ghost."

Woozy, I smiled weakly. "I think I should call it a day. I'll remember to eat breakfast before walking next time."

This was bound to happen with my lousy diet. But still . . . I wondered where the closest emergency room was. Did this area have a neurology practice? Did any of the doctors in it specialize in epilepsy?

My mind spun as Hannah intoned, "Breakfast is the most important meal of the day, Miz Ava."

"Sure enough." Jolly kept tight hold of my arm and watched me with worried eyes.

A series of *quabark*s sounded like squeaky fireworks. Cluck-Cluck started panic *bawk*ing and running this way and that. Norman darted across the street, heading straight for me. Jolly released me to scoop up the chicken, who continued to wail like a broken siren.

As chaos reigned, I took a couple of steps and latched on to a tree. "I just need to get something to eat, I think," I said so quietly I didn't think anyone heard me.

But someone had.

"I know just the place." Sam stepped up next to me. "Just lean on me. I've got you."

MAGGIE

Friday morning had dawned bright and sunny, the sky dotted with wispy clouds. But there was a sharp wind blowing, whispering ominously and stirring up trouble.

As I carried a bag of trash to the dumpster behind the shop, I glanced around, looking to find anything that might explain the disturbance.

I found it quickly in the Beach Mouse delivery van that just turned down the alleyway, heading my way.

I hadn't seen Donovan since Wednesday, when he left the coffee shop to strategize how to win me over. The sun glinted off the windshield, blocking the view of his face, but my heart knew it was him. It increased its tempo, flooding me with warmth.

With dread.

Because for the past two days all I could think about was how Estrelle told Redmond that denying true desires led to a lifetime of heartbreak.

If I continued to date Donovan, wasn't that what I would be doing?

Denying him his love of the water?

I didn't want to be the cause of his heartbreak. Been there, done that when he'd come back to town on leave the summer after my freshman year of college. He'd heard the news that I wasn't returning to school. At that point, however, no one had known *why*.

He'd told me how much he'd missed me. How much he loved me. He wanted me to leave with him, to join him in Florida, where he'd been stationed. He talked of getting married, of starting a family.

I'd had to tell him the truth.

I'd *had* to.

He'd been stunned by the news. Heartbreak had glittered in his ocean eyes like shattered glass.

And yet . . . he said that a baby didn't change how he felt. He still wanted to marry me. That he'd adopt my baby. Love him like his own.

But Noah hadn't been the reason I couldn't marry Donovan.

The old memories brought tears to my eyes. I blinked them away as the van rolled to a stop feet from me. Donovan shut off the engine and pushed open the door. "Fancy meeting you here."

I held up the trash bag. "The glamorous life of managing a coffee shop."

"I think you do more than manage it, Maggie."

Managing summed up my job description perfectly, but I didn't want to debate it with him, not with that troublesome wind blowing. I tossed the trash in the dumpster and faced him.

He eyed my chest. "Nice shirt."

I felt a blush rising as I glanced down. HE'S NOT SELLING was printed on my T-shirt. "My craft room comes in really handy once in a while. What brings you by?"

The wind tousled his hair, and in the early-morning light, I noticed a few sparkling silver strands standing upright amid the soft brown waves. I wanted to reach out and smooth them.

"A proposition: you, me, and an antique mall. What do you say?"

Antique mall? I tipped my head, intrigued. "Go on."

He took another step closer to me. "I heard about a new antique market that opened this week near Daphne. Thought you might like to go with me on Sunday to check it out. You have the day off, right?"

I did—the coffee shop was closed on Sundays. But my schedule was still full. I had a garden club get-together that afternoon, then a Butterfly Fest meeting in the evening.

But an antique mall might be worth playing hooky for, something I'd never once done in my whole life. The thought of possibly finding a bauble to add to the Curiosity Corner made my blood hum with happiness and anticipation.

Donovan jammed his hands in his pockets and rocked on his heels. He didn't take his eyes off mine as he sweetened the deal. "The mall is eighty thousand square feet. Has *five hundred* booths."

My knees turned to jelly just thinking about all the possible treasures.

However, as I looked at Donovan, into his hopeful eyes, I gave myself a good mental shake, rattling loose my senses, which had seized up.

I needed to keep my head about me. There might be five hundred booths, yes, but Daphne was also a good hour and a half away. We'd likely have to stop to get something to eat while we were out, or risk getting hangry. Also, it would just be him and me. Me and him. Alone. All day.

My palms started to sweat, because I wanted to go. Not just because an antique mall was my idea of heaven but because spending all day with Donovan suddenly sounded a little like heaven, too.

But no. *No.*

I had to let him go.

I had to.

Guilty heat infused my face. "Sorry, Donovan." I practically choked on the words. "I have a couple of meetings on Sunday."

"You can't skip them?"

I shook my head, unable to trust my voice.

"You sure?"

"Yeah," I croaked.

"Do you ever feel, Maggie, that you're *too* busy?"

Lately, yes, I had been feeling that way. I found myself wanting to slow down, to simply enjoy life as it was. But I couldn't let that sway me now, when I needed busyness as an excuse. "Not at all."

"Okay, then." He kicked at a rock, blew out a breath. "I guess I'll go."

I swallowed hard. "I should get back inside, too."

He pivoted toward the van, then abruptly turned around.

My heart bounced around my chest.

"Just one more thing," he said.

"Yeah?"

Why did hope flicker in my chest? It had no right. None at all.

Clouds darkened his eyes. "I got caught up in talking with Roscoe Dodd earlier at the bakery."

Confused by the switch in both his tone and the topic, I said, "Well, he can certainly bend an ear."

Donovan's eyebrows dipped low, and he looked up at the fronds of a palm tree as they whipped about.

Warning flags popped up left and right. "Is something wrong with Roscoe? Or the Dodds?"

Roscoe was a sweet old man, mid-eighties, who lived with his son's family not too far from my dad's house. He was a talker, yes, but beloved around here.

"He's fine. Just fine," Donovan said. He tossed another glance at my T-shirt, then added, "Like everyone else in town, he was talking about your dad selling Magpie's."

If I never heard another word about selling Magpie's, I'd be a happy woman. Ecstatic, even.

"Did he have anything worthwhile to add?" I asked, still curious about Donovan's serious tone.

I was hoping so, especially since it had become clear that Carmella was avoiding me. She wasn't answering my calls and hadn't been in the shop in days.

Donovan crossed his arms. "Roscoe asked something I didn't have the answer to, but you might. About the coffee shop's deed."

"The deed? What about it?"

Donovan stiffened, looking pained. "Not completely sure. Roscoe thought if Dez does plan to sell, it might have something to do with the lawyer he went to see."

The statement knocked me backward a step. I wasn't 100 percent sure, but I thought the shop was in both my parents' names. It was how Daddy had so easily taken it over when Mama went missing.

If Dad did plan to sell, would he have to get Mama's name removed from the deed?

But he didn't plan to sell.

I was certain of it.

Mostly certain, leastways.

Suddenly, my skin hummed with panic.

Donovan hooked a thumb over his shoulder. "I'm going to go now. Listen, my offer still stands if you change your mind about the antique mall. And Maggie, I hope you know I'm here for you if you want to talk about your dad or Magpie's or *anything*."

A little dizzy, I said, "I won't forget, Donovan."

His wide shoulders rounded as he stuck his hands in his pockets. A rock skittered as he kicked it far across the alley. He climbed into the van.

I wanted to call out, to tell him not to leave, to stay. Stay and tell me more about the antique mall. Tell me more about his plans for us.

I pressed my lips together, keeping in all the things I wanted to tell him. All the things I thought he ought to know. Like how much I loved him. How much I'd loved him since I was fifteen years old.

The van roared to life and he turned and gave me a sad smile before driving off.

I felt like crying. Full-out, body-shaking sobbing. It took a good minute and every ounce of willpower to hold the tears at bay, to keep my composure.

When I finally turned to go back inside, I found Estrelle standing in Stitchery's back doorway, an empty cardboard box in her hands. I didn't know how long she'd been standing there, and I supposed it didn't really matter. With her *knowing*, she likely had plenty of insight into my sad love life.

Her voice was rough and rock hard as she said, "Magdalena, are you not now denying *yourself* of your true desire? If you continue to allow yourself to be haunted by your past, if you continue to allow fear to run your life, you will *never* have the future you yearn for, the happiness you've dreamed of. You must make peace with your past in order to move forward. Stop hiding from your pain. The only way out is *through*."

Despite her rigid tone there was softness in her eyes behind the veil, and at the sight of it, my composure threatened to break. Tears pooled in my eyes.

A diaphanous black chiffon dress billowed as she clomped to the recycling bin in her chunky heels, tossed the box inside, then shuffled back to the doorway, and looked at me. *"It has been said."*

CHAPTER 14

AVA

"How was it?" Sam asked an hour after I nearly fainted in the square.

Norman slept at my feet, snoring softly, as I sat at Sam's round wooden bistro table. He'd just cleared my empty plate. "Honestly? The toast tasted like sawdust, but the jam was the best thing I've tasted in months. I could happily eat it with a spoon." I picked up the unlabeled mason jar, held it to the light, admiring its ruby glow. "Is it made out of rainbows and unicorns?"

"Close. Raspberries from my mama's garden."

I watched him move about the kitchen, his lanky body smooth and fluid as he put the plate in the dishwasher, wiped crumbs from the counter around the toaster, and hung a dish-towel on the oven handle.

Sam's house had a similar footprint to Maggie's place, only bigger and more airy, with its vaulted ceiling. Light poured in from the south-facing windows, which had stunning views of the gulf across the road.

The windows were closed but I could still hear the waves, that endless push and pull. A ceiling fan whirred noisily; one of its blades was slightly out of balance. Down the hall, a washing machine behind a closed door entered a spin cycle.

"Do your mom and her magical garden live around here?" I asked.

The open space was decorated in light neutrals and was minimalist yet somehow cozy, done in beiges and blues. A thick area rug sectioned off the living room, covering a white oak floor. Four throw pillows topped each of the two couches, which were arranged in an L shape, one facing the TV, the other facing the front windows and the gorgeous view. A sleek oak sideboard acted as a TV stand, its remote the only item on a round coffee table. There were no photographs except for a snapshot of Norman tacked to the fridge with a magnet. The only artwork was a series of three large framed posters—blueprints for musical instruments. A guitar, a violin, and a banjo. They hung side by side next to the bistro table. Those prints were the only things in the space that hinted about the musical nature I suspected Sam of hiding.

"North Alabama, not too far from Huntsville."

"Is that where you grew up?"

His body stiffened, his motions no longer loose and limber as he checked Norman's food and water dishes before rejoining me at the table. He sat and folded his arms across his chest. "Yep. Mom, Dad, my sister, and me. Everyone's still up there."

"Except for you."

He looked toward the front windows. "Except for me."

Across the street, alongside the boardwalk, sea oats were swaying in the wind like they were dancing to a tune only they could hear.

"What brought you here?" I asked, pressing my luck.

He swept a hand over the table, brushing away invisible crumbs. "Chasing happy memories. My grandparents used to have a place down here when I was a kid. I tried to buy direct beachfront, but those houses don't come up on the market often. I spent a lot of summers on that beach, playing in the water, letting the soothing lullaby of the waves lull me to sleep."

"As far as lullabies go, I don't think you can get much better."

My gaze flicked to Dez's house. How soon would he hear about my little episode this morning and reconsider hiring me? Maggie had already called my cell phone—apparently she'd been one of the first to hear the news—and had gone all mama bear on me, not hanging up until she was assured by both Sam and me that I was okay. In my head, I could easily picture the spandexed Bettina flying into the coffee shop to share the news, all fluffed up and flapping away.

Sam eyed my water glass, which was nearly full, because he'd been refilling it every time it dropped below half. "Can I get you anything else to eat?"

He'd already offered everything under the sun. Toast with butter and jam had been the only thing that sounded palatable. I'd eaten two slices, choking them down. It wasn't much, but it was a start. I shook my head and said, "I can't thank you enough for all you've done."

Waving away my gratitude, he mumbled something about being neighborly, then said, "The color's come back to your face."

Norman snuffled, and I bent to run a hand over his head. "Are my cheeks bright red? Because I'm thoroughly embarrassed. I can only imagine what people are saying."

I'd wanted so badly to hide my health problems, then I ruined everything by getting lightheaded from not eating. Now everyone was going to be on alert around me, wondering if I was going to faint at the drop of a hat.

It hadn't been a seizure. I was certain of it. I didn't black out. At all times I knew where I was, who *I* was, who I was with— all things that were always fuzzy after previous seizures.

"You would be the talk of the town," he said breezily, "except you already were."

"That doesn't make me feel better."

He laughed, a low, gentle rumble. "Welcome to small-town life."

I took a sip of water. "It doesn't seem fair. Everyone knows everything about me, but I hardly know anything about them."

Well, except for what Jolly had shared.

"It'll come around to you eventually. Always does."

How many people knew his story? I had the feeling it wasn't many, no matter what he said.

I slid off the chair. "I should get going. I'm real sorry for taking up most of your morning."

"Don't be. I'm glad to help."

Norman bounced to his feet, his tail wagging lazily. I crouched down to give him a good petting and let him lick my chin.

Sam stood, too, watching. "He's shameless."

"I love him. Yes, I do," I said to Norman, dropping a kiss on the top of his silky head. "You're the goodest boy ever, aren't you?"

His whole body shimmied with joy.

I gave him one last pat, then stood, glad my legs held. I felt better, yes, but not great. Obviously two pieces of toast weren't enough to cure what ailed me, even with the amazing jam.

Over Sam's shoulder, I studied the trio of instrument prints and zeroed in on the violin—which, depending on what kind of music was played on it, was also called a fiddle.

"The other night when I asked you about the fiddle, I had the feeling you lied to me. Why would you lie about playing? Especially when it's lovely?"

I needed to get the lie out in the open if there was going to be any kind of friendship between us. I wanted to trust him.

"I'm sorry for that, truly, but you caught me by surprise with the question." Sorrow filled his dark gaze, highlighting the golden flecks. "It's not . . . It's not something I'm ready to share yet."

That look in his eyes tore my heart to pieces. I headed for the door before I did something stupid like hug him. "That's okay. Maybe one day. Just no more lying, okay?"

"Promise," he said solemnly, his long strides beating me to the door. He pulled it open. "But before you go, Ava, I'd really like to know how you heard me playing. I only play in a sound-proof studio. Hardly any noise gets out. I double-checked."

It was my turn to be taken by surprise. Flustered, I stepped out onto the porch, buying some time. I didn't want to tell him about the seizures or how one of them, a big one, had altered my hearing and sense of smell. I didn't want anyone here to know about the epilepsy. I wanted to be *normal*. But I didn't want to lie, either. I opened my mouth, closed it again. Felt tears rising in my eyes.

"That's okay. Maybe one day," he said, echoing my words.

Slowly, I nodded and turned to go.

"Oh, wait a sec." He ran to the kitchen, opened a cupboard, and pulled something out. He hurried back and thrust the item toward me. "For you."

It was a full, unopened jar of raspberry jam. I curled the warm jar into my chest, hugging it tight. "Thank you. For everything, Sam."

"You're welcome, Ava."

I walked across the sandy street knowing he would watch protectively until I was inside. As I slowly climbed the steps of Dez's porch, I couldn't stop thinking about how Sam hadn't thought twice about taking care of me this morning, taking me in. He made sure I ate something, got a little strength back. He'd shared his mom's magical jam and Norman and a little of himself, too.

The wind gusted, nearly knocking me off-balance as I used the key Dez had given me to unlock his front door. A blast of cool air-conditioned air poured over me as I pushed the door open. But before I went inside, I turned to wave at Sam.

He waved back, then ducked inside his home and closed the door.

I kept tight hold of the jar he'd given me as I stepped through the doorway, knowing without a doubt that the jam was the least of the gifts Sam had given me this morning.

MAGGIE

"She's sound asleep." I stepped off the bottom stair as quietly as I could.

I'd arrived at Dad's house only moments ago and had gone straight upstairs to see how Ava was feeling and found her curled up on the unmade bed. I'd resisted the urge to tuck a pillow under her head, spread a blanket over her, and check her forehead for a fever, forcing myself to let her be.

I almost hadn't gone upstairs at all, still hearing Estrelle's voice in my head, telling me I let fear guide my choices. But sometimes fear was warranted. Like when you were worried about someone, worried about *losing* someone. I was astonished at how quickly I'd become attached to Ava, caring about her, her well-being.

Dad adjusted a box on the stack next to the front door, then headed for the great room. "The tiny sprite has done wore herself out. She's been nonstop since she got to town."

My head ached. I'd been on edge since Donovan's visit this morning, because of his sad smile. And because of what he'd said about Roscoe, too. About the coffee shop's deed.

I eased my way through a maze of boxes in the hallway, which had seemed only to multiply in the last few days. Molly appeared out of nowhere, dashing past me toward the stairs, and I stumbled in an attempt to not trip over her.

I could practically hear her laughing as she sat down halfway up the stairs and curled her tail around her paws.

"Not amusing," I said to her.

Her whiskers twitched as though she disagreed.

I left her there, gloating, and followed Dad into the great room.

"Ava mentioned she's not been eating well since Alexander died," I said, "but I'm starting to wonder if there's more to it."

It was so strange to talk about the man like I knew him personally. Though, I supposed I did, in a way. Ava had painted such a vivid picture of him, his personality. Everyone knew an Alexander. A free-spirited adventurer. Like how Dad used to be.

"Grief sure can tear you up, inside and out. I lost ten pounds after your mother . . . went missing." He let out a huff. "I couldn't eat seafood for years—it reminded me too much of the smell of that day. Don't know if you recall how bad the sargassum was that year."

I recalled. The smelly seaweed had stunk up the beach on and off for several months. And I still had nightmares about my mama getting tangled in it.

As much as I didn't want to think about that day, or how

my mama was still missing, I recognized this was the perfect opening to talk about the shop and the deed. Especially since Dad hadn't yet noticed my custom T-shirt.

He crouched down in front of another box. "Ava will find her way through just like we are."

I sat on the arm of the sofa, took a deep breath, and took the plunge. "Is that what's going on with you lately? You're finding your way through?"

He glanced at me and finally noticed the shirt. A bushy eyebrow raised in disapproval. "Some."

"Listen, I wouldn't have had to make a T-shirt if you'd put an end to the gossip."

Listen. I was starting to talk like Donovan. How easily he'd worked himself into my subconscious. Though, I supposed, he'd always been there, hadn't he? Lurking.

I pressed on before I lost my nerve. "Now there's talk going around about how you went to see the probate lawyer about the shop's deed. What do you say about that?"

"About the deed?" He shook his head. "I can assure you, Magpie, that I did not visit Orrel about the deed. Hand to God."

Truth gleamed in his eyes, but hiding in the shadows was a flicker of deception. He was dancing around why he'd really been there.

His gaze narrowed thoughtfully. "Though I suppose if I decided to sell the shop, I would need to discuss the matter with him."

My hackles rose. "It's time for you to stop this madness. I'm tired. I'm sick to death of answering the same question over and over. We both know you're not selling the shop, because it's not yours to sell. It's Mama's."

He looked at me with such disappointment in his gaze that I felt as though I'd somehow failed a test I didn't know I was taking. The look broke my heart and made me angry all at the same time.

He picked up a box. "It *was* your mama's shop. Once. It

hasn't been for a long time now. Like I've been saying, it might be time to let go."

My head throbbed. "What're you talking about? Of course it's still her shop."

"Hmm." He started walking the box to the front door.

My face heated as I followed him, trying to keep my temper in check. Outside, a car door slammed, and I looked out and saw Carmella's SUV in the driveway.

She was headed for the stairs with a Driftwood Realty folder in her hands. Whatever was in it had to be important since she avoided coming to Dad's house as much as possible—because she was highly allergic to cats.

Molly, the spiteful beast, seemed to know about the aversion, too. Every chance she got, she twined herself around Carmella's legs. Even now she crept down the steps and stood near the door, ready to generously share her dander.

I kept my voice low, so I didn't wake Ava. "Why is Carmella here with a real estate folder? What is going on with you?" I pushed. "Something is. Don't deny it."

Worry flashed in his eyes. "You've gone pale, Maggie. Do you need to sit down?"

I was shaking. "Do not change the subject."

"Take a deep breath, Magdalena," he said calmly. "I'll get you some water."

"I don't need water. I need the truth. I need you to stop protecting me."

He looked upward, then shook his head. "I will protect you until the day I die, and maybe even after that." He snickered. "I'd make a dandy of a ghost, wouldn't I?"

He started playing air guitar and began singing the Beatles' "I'm Looking Through You."

Red-hot anger sparked, then flared to life. How dare he try to joke? At a time like this? I grabbed my backpack from the hall tree, slung one of the straps over my shoulder. "I'm leaving."

"Maggie, come on now," he said. "Stay."

If I stayed, I was going to say something I would regret. I

didn't fight with my father. I couldn't even remember a time when we'd raised our voices to each other. We were peacemakers, the two of us.

In fact, I couldn't quite remember the last time I truly blew a fuse. Oh, wait. Yes I could. It was when a fourteen-year-old Noah had snuck out of the house to go with his buddies to scope out the Sand Island Lighthouse in the middle of the night. They'd had to be rescued by the Coast Guard when a thunderstorm popped up and sank their boat. If not for a phone call from Estrelle warning me of the danger, who knows what would've happened.

I'd needed a sedative to calm down after that incident.

I pulled open the door, catching Carmella as she was about to knock.

She pulled her hand back and held it to her chest in surprise. "Maggie! I didn't realize you were here. What's wrong, sweetie?" She looked between Dad and me. "Oh dear. How about we sit and talk abo . . . about—" She sneezed. "This?"

Molly had snuck out of the house and was executing impeccable figure eights around Carmella's ankles.

"Unless someone's ready to tell me what is truly going on, I'm not interested in what you have to say."

I looked at the folder in her hands, then between the two of them.

Both gazed at me with worried eyes, their lips firmly sealed.

I blew out a breath of frustration and hurried down the steps. My feet had just touched the gravel driveway when I heard my father's voice drifting down from above.

"The only thing going on here, Maggie, is me trying to help *you* find your way through."

I looked up at him.

He said, "You keep asking me why I'd consider selling the coffee shop, but I think the bigger question is why you haven't once offered to buy it. Is it because subconsciously you've realized it's time to do a little letting go of your own?"

I turned and walked off, thinking that it was interesting that Dad had chosen "I'm Looking Through You" to sing moments ago. The song wasn't about a translucent ghost. I knew it to be about how sometimes, as a relationship fails, a loved one starts to disappear before your eyes, becoming unrecognizable.

In hindsight, Dad's song choice now seemed appropriate.

Because if he thought I'd let go of my mama's shop, her dream, then maybe he'd become someone I didn't know anymore.

CHAPTER 15

AVA

On Saturday morning Titus walked in the coffee shop door holding a slim pastry box in his hands. The second I saw him, I grabbed a rag and scurried out from behind the counter. "Rose! Someone here for you," I yelled toward the storage room.

Titus flashed me a conspiratorial smile, which completely vanished when Rose came hurrying toward the front of the shop. At the sight of her, he adopted a serious, contemplative look, lowering his eyebrows and pursing his lips. He turned his attention to the menu board.

Rose's steps faltered when she saw him standing there, and she turned slightly to throw daggers my way.

I grinned and gave her two thumbs up.

Rolling her eyes, she wiped her hands down her apron and scooted behind the register. "Good morning, Titus. What can I get for you this fine morning?"

I glanced at Mrs. Pollard, who sat next to her recipe. She'd been a fixture here this past week, but I suspected today would be the last day she'd camp out at that table. On Monday, a new recipe would go up on the board. She winked at me, propped her elbows on the table, and put her head in her hands as she openly watched Titus and Rose.

"Good morning, Rose. Let's see, let's see." He tapped his chin. "I think I'll have, oh, *hmm*, a small iced matcha latte, add a double shot of espresso, add chai, add lavender syrup."

There was a feisty light in her eyes when she said, "Matcha, chai, lavender? A wonderful choice. One of our most popular. Give me a sec, and I'll get that ready for you, lickety-split."

As she went about pouring him a cup of plain black coffee,

outside the wide front window I saw Sam walk by, leash in hand. He glanced into the shop and saw me watching him and smiled. I waved. He bent low, and I imagined him tying the leash to the hook next to the door.

Warmth flooded my cheeks. I was still a little embarrassed by what had happened yesterday.

Last night I'd done my best to convince Maggie that I was feeling much better, but I sensed she knew I was lying. Part of me—a big part—wanted to tell her everything, but I held back. People would eventually forget my near-fainting spell, but if they knew about my history of seizures, I knew they'd hover, checking on me constantly.

I'd hoped I'd feel better today, but after having to practically drag myself out of bed this morning, I'd searched online for the local neurologists.

Just in case.

Beyond my exhaustion and lack of appetite, there were other symptoms that I'd been ignoring all week. Slight dizziness. An upset stomach. Pins-and-needles feeling in my legs.

All were prodromal warning signs.

And as much as I wanted to believe they were caused by something else, I had to be prepared to face the fact that my break from seizures might have been only a temporary reprieve.

Emotions churned as I thought about going back to a life filled with fear, wondering when my brain might misfire. And when it did, what part of me would be changed afterward? Because something always was. Whether it was my hearing or sense of smell or a long-lasting headache, confusion, or fatigue, I rarely came out of a seizure the same person as when I went in.

Then I shook the thoughts free, not allowing them to take root. Even if the epilepsy had reemerged, *I* wasn't who I used to be. I didn't have to be so scared. I didn't need to hide in a safety zone. I didn't need my mother to watch over me day in and day out. I just had to be careful. Cautious. Aware. Hyperaware. I could deal with the physical side effects. But not the fear. Not anymore. I refused to clip my newfound wings.

At least my room was finally ready at Dez's, which would

make it easier to hide my health issues from Maggie, since I didn't think I'd see her over there anytime soon. At least not while Dez was at home. She'd told me they had a big fight.

I glanced toward her office door, even though she wasn't in there. Earlier, I'd heard her on the phone and knew it was Noah she'd been talking to. Her voice changed when she spoke with him, becoming round and full of love. I could tell by her side of the conversation that he had no idea about the fight between her and Dez. They talked about classes, a new restaurant off campus, a study abroad possibility.

Then, I'd heard her say, "What? Nothing's wrong. Why do you ask? Sad?" She'd laughed, phony and brittle. "I'm fine, honey. Just fine."

Lies, of course. But something he said must've touched a nerve. Because as soon as she hung up, she marched herself out of her office, told Rose and me she'd be back in a while, and walked out the front door, determination in each step she took.

She hadn't come back yet, now an hour later. We were actually slightly relieved she left. She'd been out of sorts all morning, getting orders wrong and even burning *herself* with the steam wand.

Rose placed the cup of coffee on the counter in front of Titus. "That'll be two dollars, please."

He pulled three one-dollar bills from the front pocket of his wrinkle-free twill shorts. He handed two to Rose and put one in the tip jar. He then slid the box across the counter toward her.

Rose looked at the box as if it were a snake that might strike. Carefully, she reached out and picked it up. "What's this?"

"A little something that reminded me of you."

Carefully, she lifted the top, then an eyebrow. "Three whole chocolates? Mighty generous of you, Titus."

Sam pulled open the door, took in the scene at the counter, and headed for the Curiosity Corner, where he picked up a hand-carved spoon with a curvy handle.

Titus was undeterred by Rose's sarcasm. "They're dark-chocolate truffles with a white chocolate, mango, and cayenne pepper filling. Sweet with a hint of heat. A perfect combination, if I do say so myself, and not just because I made them. I hope you enjoy." He picked up his coffee cup. "Good day, Rose." He tipped his head, turned, and walked toward the door.

Rose was still staring into the box, and I thought she was too dumbfounded to even say thank you, but then she lifted her head, looked at Titus's retreating form. "Thanks for stopping in. Have yourself a nice day, sugar pie."

Titus froze as he reached for the door, and in the glass I saw the reflection of his smile before he pushed the door open.

Rose glanced at me. She smiled shyly before giving herself a good shake. "I need to finish up in the storeroom."

She practically ran down the hallway, still clutching the box of chocolates.

Mrs. Pollard said, "What do you think the chances are she'll share the chocolate?"

"Not good, I suspect." I turned to Sam. "It's like I'm living in a romance novel. I wish Titus would come in three, four times a day."

"Was that his first 'sugar pie'?"

"Sure was," Mrs. Pollard said. "Dang near brought a tear to my eye."

Mine too. I smiled and motioned Sam to the counter. "Iced hazelnut latte and a whippy cup?"

"Yes to the whippy cup, but I think I'm going to mix it up today. How's the caramel latte?"

"It's my favorite," I said, reaching for a cup. "I'm a sucker for anything with caramel in it."

"Then I'll give it a go." He cast a quick glance over me. "How're you feeling?"

Everyone had been asking this morning. So much so that I was almost hoping Candi Chitwood would take pity on me and strut around town in her bikini and cause another tomato incident.

Almost.

It was sweet that people cared about me. And I really didn't want Mrs. Harlin to cause any bodily harm to whoever dared desecrate her garden.

"I'm . . . so-so." I didn't want to lie. "Your mom's jam is just about the only thing that tastes good." I had eaten it again on toast in the morning and on vanilla ice cream last night.

"I'll get you another jar."

"You don't have to do—"

"I want to, Ava."

I glanced at Mrs. Pollard. She was now watching us with her head in her hands. I channeled my inner Rose and rolled my eyes.

The door opened and Jolly filled the doorway, speaking to someone still outside. "Yes, yes, I know you love Norman, but I thought you wanted some chocolate milk and a cinnamon roll."

"Bye, Norman, byyyyye!" Hannah said in a loud singsong voice, then squeezed past her grandmother into the shop. She was once again wearing her Cinderella costume and her light-up sneakers. "Hi, Miz Ava!" she shouted.

Jolly looked to the heavens and followed her in.

"Good morning, Hannah! Hi, Jolly. I'll be right with you."

I finished making Sam's drink, then filled a dish with whipped cream for Norman. Sam swiped his credit card and said, "Thanks, Ava. I'll be seeing you."

"Give Norman a hug for me."

He smiled and walked outside.

"I'll be off now, too," Mrs. Pollard said, stuffing recipe cards into her purse. "Got an appointment soon with someone who wants to look at my rental house. Can you let Maggie know I have more recipes if she needs one for next week?"

I nodded. "I'll let her know."

"Bye!" Hannah yelled.

"Bye, little darlin'," Mrs. Pollard said, tapping Hannah's head as she passed by. Once outside, she stopped to pet Norman and chat with Sam, who laughed at something she said.

"That Sam Kindell is a good egg," Jolly said, watching them as well. "Quiet as they come and likes to keep to himself more than most, but quick to lend a hand if need be." She squinted at the menu board. "Are you offering pumpkin spice yet?"

Kindell. I hadn't known Sam's last name till now. I could kiss Jolly for her gossip-loving ways.

"Not quite," I said. "Maggie's waiting till October."

Jolly *tsk*ed in dismay. "I'll have a chai latte, then, please. Maybe throw in some extra cinnamon? I'm craving autumn flavors."

Chai wasn't technically on the menu, but Maggie once told me that sometimes the shop made exceptions for special customers. To me, Jolly fit that description perfectly.

"And a chocolate milk!" Hannah shouted. "And a cinnamum roll. *Please*," she added when Jolly whispered the word to her.

"That'll be to go, Ava." Jolly rooted around in her big handbag for her wallet. "Hannah and I have things to do, people to see while her mama's at work today."

"Coming right up," I said, knowing that forever onward, cinnamon would be pronounced *cinnamum* in my head.

Hannah ran to the doorway, pressed her hands to the door, and peered through the glass. "Hi, Norman!" she yelled. A moment later, Norman stood in front of the door, wagging his tail.

Jolly shook her head at the antics, but she was smiling. "Did you know you can see a man's heart reflected in his dog? Most of the town wants to adopt Norman. And there are quite a few who'd love to get their hands on Sam, too." She waggled her thin eyebrows. "A brokenhearted divorcé? Lordy be. He's prime pickin'."

I swallowed over a sudden lump of emotion. I'd known his heart was broken and could've guessed at the divorce, by the way he often looked at his bare ring finger, but my heart hurt for him just the same.

I didn't want Jolly to think I was one of the people ready to pluck him clean, so I said, "Are men's hearts reflected in cats, too?"

"Oh, hell no. Cats don't let anyone tell them what to do with their hearts. Fickle creatures, those."

I laughed, thinking of Molly as I added ice to a small cup, poured in milk, then added chocolate syrup. I gave it a good swirl and set it on the counter before starting Jolly's drink.

Jolly turned her back to the door, and leaned in, putting her elbow on the counter. She dropped her voice. "I don't mean to nag, but I was wondering how much progress you've made with Junebear?"

Yesterday, after finding out Junebear belonged to Hannah, I'd been so gung ho to get started on fixing her up, but I hadn't had the energy last night.

Before I could tell her I hadn't even started work on the bear, Jolly went on. "We'd love to get her back before Hannah goes into the hospital for her operation."

Hannah was jumping up and down, showing Norman the lights on her shoes. He was *quabark*ing in appreciation. "Operation?"

"You haven't heard? Lord, honey, the way this town talks, I thought you knew. Hannah'd been having headaches. I thought it was on account that she's always singing so loud, but a brain scan showed a tumor."

My heart stopped, freezing up for a good second before it kick-started again. "No," I whispered.

"The doctors are fairly confident it's benign, but they gotta go in and do some testing before they know for sure."

My voice cracked. "When?"

"Friday, up in Birmingham at Children's. We'll be leaving on Thursday afternoon and spending the night up there."

I didn't have very long to get the job done, but I'd work through the nights if I had to. "I'll make sure Junebear is ready for the trip."

Jolly reached out, patted my hand. "It'll mean the world to Hannah."

I blinked back tears and went about finishing the order, all the while hoping and wishing and praying Hannah would be okay.

"Bye, Ava, bye!" Hannah yelled when they walked out a few minutes later. I watched through the door as the little girl stopped to give Norman a hug before they finally headed off.

Not a minute later, Sam came back inside.

"Did you know Hannah was having surgery on Friday?"

The words slipped out of my mouth before I could even think to filter them.

"I heard that. I can't even imagine what the Smiths are going through. Norman's been giving Hannah extra love. He seems to know when people need it most."

My voice cracked. "She'll be fine, right?"

He looked my way. "I sure hope so."

I swallowed hard, met his gaze, and realized suddenly that I wasn't being the least bit professional. "Sorry. I was just caught off guard by the news. Did you forget something? Or need another dish of whipped cream?"

"I did forget something, actually." He pulled out his wallet, slapped a twenty-dollar bill on the counter. "Your half of yesterday's scratch ticket win."

"Get out! Really?"

"I only lie about fiddle playing."

I smiled. "And what about guitar playing? Are you going to lie about that?"

I hadn't heard a fiddle last night. Instead, as I fell asleep I'd heard a sweet but sad melody being played on a guitar.

His gaze narrowed. "Don't suppose you're ready to tell me how you can hear me playing in a soundproof studio?"

"I don't suppose you're ready to tell me why you don't want anyone to know you're playing?"

After an eternal second, he looked down at the money on the counter. "So, twenty dollars is a good day's win, I think. Don't you?"

I laughed. "It definitely is. But . . ." I slowly pushed the money back toward him.

"Let it ride?"

"Let it ride."

CHAPTER 16

MAGGIE

It was sheer stubbornness that pushed me through the town square, steering me along like a strong set of hands on my shoulders.

If they were anyone's hands, they were Noah's.

When I'd talked to him earlier, he'd told me that I'd sounded sad.

I turned my face upward, toward the sun, hoping the light would dry the sudden tears in my eyes.

I *was* sad. Sad and tired and angry. I wanted a little happiness. And I was on a mission to see if Estrelle was right about finding it.

Forcing one foot in front of the other, I marched myself over to the Beach Mouse Bakery. I felt my resolve weakening as I passed in front of the display window and saw Donovan inside, restocking a bakery case with cinnamon-streusel muffins.

I smiled at the sight of him. He never thought he wanted the bakery life, but he looked perfectly at ease. Like he belonged right where he was.

I was still frozen in my spot when Lily Kirkpatrick stepped out of the bakery carrying a white box with the mouse logo. She smiled. "Maggie, I'm so glad I ran into you. I had a few questions about—"

So help me if she said the sale of the coffee shop.

"The Butterfly Fest," she finished as if she knew better than to ask about Magpie's.

Lily was a freelance photographer, one of the best. She could often be found snapping photos around town, and she worked local events as well, like the Butterfly Fest. Her bread and butter, though, were the sessions booked by tourists requesting photo shoots on the beach.

"Do you have a minute?" she asked, squinting against the late-morning sunlight.

Ordinarily, I wouldn't think twice about answering a few questions, but right now the nerves in my body felt fit to snap, and if I didn't go inside the bakery right this minute to see Donovan, I was going to chicken out.

I reached for the door handle and tried not to feel guilty when I said, "I really don't have time right now, Lily, but there's a committee meeting tomorrow night. You can bring up any questions then."

"Okay, sure." She glanced into the shop. "Are you here to see Donovan? I heard you two were an item now."

Dear lord.

"The minute he moved back to Driftwood," she added, "everyone knew it was just a matter of time. See you tomorrow!"

For a second, I thought about abandoning this foolish mission, but then thought about what Estrelle had said about the things that haunted. I grabbed the door handle and pulled.

The scents of vanilla, almond, and chocolate washed over me as I stepped inside. The shop was a dream, done in sophisticated shades of pink. Four bakery cases stood front and center, full of mouthwatering treats. Cakes and tarts and cookies and tortes and turnovers and muffins. The only thing out of place in the beautiful space was Sienna Hopkins, who was working the register. That was a new development.

"Hey, Maggie," she said, "I'll be right with you."

She was in the middle of boxing up Boomy Eldridge's order, what looked to be a peaches-and-cream cupcake, and I prayed he hadn't heard her say my name. I just wanted to talk to Donovan, then get back to the coffee shop.

Boomy turned. "Maggie! How's that young woman staying with you? I heard she passed out and fell face-first onto the sidewalk and broke her nose."

The man didn't know how to talk. He shouted. It was how he'd earned his nickname. Fluffy white hair topped his head and puffed out of his dark ears. Watery brown eyes watched me expectantly, waiting for my response.

"Ava didn't pass out or fall or break anything." I cursed small-town gossip. "She was just a bit faint and is fine now. Thanks for asking after her. How's Rascal?"

Rascal was Boomy's geriatric Jack Russell terrier and the love of his life.

"Not getting around like he used to," Boomy said. "Much like me. These old bones are creaking to wake the dead. I'm surprised there's not a ghost or two haunting me at this point."

I laughed like I was supposed to, but the mention of ghosts caused one of my nerves to break clean in half. Because I realized even if my father *was* selling the shop, it still didn't explain the other odd things going on with him.

I told myself not to care. To *let it be*, as he'd advised me when his strange behaviors started. But I couldn't. Because even if he was becoming someone I didn't recognize, I still loved him.

I winced at the headache suddenly hammering my temples and slid a pleading look toward Donovan, who was concentrating mighty hard on those dang cinnamon muffins.

"Oh! That reminds me," Boomy said. "Do you think you can watch Rascal a couple of days next month? My granddaughter is gettin' married in South Carolina, and as much as I want him to come with me, I don't think it's wise to be taking him on a long trip. You know I don't trust many to take care of him."

My jaw ached as I gritted my teeth and took out my phone to pull up my calendar. "Sure thing. What days?"

As I typed in the dates, I slid another imploring look at Donovan, catching his eye this time. I held his gaze, silently begging for mercy.

Instantly, he rushed around the counter. "Hey now, I didn't realize the time, Maggie. So sorry to keep you waitin' on me." He glanced at Boomy. "Maggie and I have a special order to iron out so I need to steal her away from you. I hope you understand."

"Oh, I understand, all right. A *special* order." Boomy gave us an exaggerated wink. "Been a long time comin'."

I could only shake my head. Donovan and I'd had only one date. *One.*

Donovan laughed and put his arm around me. "Too long, am I right, Boomy?"

Heaven help me.

"Don't know about that," Boomy said loudly, nodding to the cupcake sitting pretty in a clear plastic cocoon. "Take a peach, for example. Picked too soon, and it's sour. Hardly worth a damn. Only with patience comes the sweet reward."

"I like that," Sienna said on a lofty sigh. "The sweet reward. I heard old people were really smart. You must be, like, a genius, Boomy."

Donovan dropped his head and groaned.

But Boomy only laughed. "Most people can't see past my good looks to spot the brains. Thanks for noticing, young lady." He picked up his cupcake and shuffled to the door. "Y'all have a good one now."

I teared up, watching him go, suddenly so full of love for the people of this small town that I could hardly breathe. I snuffled.

Donovan glanced at me and instantly started steering me toward the back hallway. "Sienna, will you be okay out here alone?"

I picked up on the trepidation in his voice.

In my opinion, he had good reason to worry.

Though I wasn't really one to talk today. Just this morning, I'd burned my arm on the steam wand.

"Sure!" She looked around as if not knowing what to do with herself.

His steps faltered but he forged onward, guiding me down the hallway, through the kitchen, then into an office. He closed the door behind us, leaned against it. His intense gaze swept over me.

The room was jewelry-box small. Just enough room for a desk, chair, and filing cabinet. It was tight with two of us in here. And hot.

"What's with the tears?" he asked, tipping up my chin.

I wiped my wet eyes. "Just emotional. It's been a rough week. You're a brave man, hiring Sienna. A kind and brave man."

He smiled. "She needed a job, we needed the help, and we keep the sharpest knives away from her. She's been here for a couple of days now and so far, nothing catastrophic has happened."

I thought about the measuring spoons I'd given her, and wondered if they had led her here. Was the bakery where she'd find what was missing in her life?

"She's fitting in quite well, actually," he added, "which has been a nice surprise to most everyone."

There was flour on his arms, dusting the fine hairs. The loose wave in his hair had started to curl with the heat and humidity. He smelled of vanilla and birthday cake.

I wanted to lean into him, melt there against the heat of his skin, and lose myself for a while. I clasped my hands instead and met his gaze.

His voice was tender as he said, "I heard you had a fight with your father."

Of course he had.

"Why don't you tell me about it while I tend to your arm. Is that a burn?"

I nodded. "Steam wand."

"Ouch."

"I'm not usually so clumsy."

"You have a lot on your mind these days."

An understatement. "I thought I saw relief in Ava's and Rose's faces when I left the shop a few minutes ago. I think Rose, especially, was having Sienna flashbacks."

"It's probably just relief that you're taking a minute to yourself." He gently took me by my shoulders and walked me backward, to the edge of the desk. "Have a seat. There's a first-aid kit around here somewhere."

"The burn isn't that bad. It just stings. I don't need—"

"Will you please sit and let someone take care of you for once?"

"I—"

He arched an eyebrow. I snapped my mouth closed and sat on the edge of the desk.

Crouching low, he opened a drawer of the desk, rooted around inside, and pulled out a small plastic box.

His leg brushed against mine as he stood up again and sorted the supplies. "Now, tell me about Dez. Was the fight about the coffee shop?"

I nodded. "It's a long story, but the fight ended with him basically asking why I hadn't offered to buy Magpie's if I was so afraid of him selling it. But why would I do that if I didn't think he'd been serious about selling? It's illogical thinking."

Illogical seemed a good word to sum him up lately. *Infuriating* worked as well.

Donovan lifted my arm, blew across my skin, chasing away the sting of the burn. It probably wasn't the most sanitary thing to do, but the whisper of his breath on my arm had released all kinds of tension so I wasn't about to complain.

"Is Dez serious about the sale, after all?" he asked.

I thought about the folder in Carmella's hands. "I think he is. So I guess I'm buying a coffee shop."

It was the first time I'd allowed myself to think the words, let alone speak them. But as soon as I said them, I knew it was the right thing to do. I just had to figure out *how*. It wasn't as though I had a nest egg big enough to buy it outright. My nest egg would belong to a hummingbird.

In the past if I'd needed a loan, I'd always gone to my father. But that was out of the question now. I'd look into getting a commercial mortgage. If that didn't work, then I wasn't sure what I'd do. But I'd find a way. For my mama, I'd find a way.

He pulled out a tube of antibiotic ointment and squeezed a blob onto a square of cotton gauze. "Let me know if I can help at all."

"I will. Thanks."

He wrapped my wound, taped it off. His hands lingered, his fingertips brushing against the delicate skin on the underside of my arm. "Better?"

I didn't trust my voice. "Mm-hmm."

I'd missed his touch. Honestly, I'd missed him. I'd been missing him for twenty years now.

"You know I aim to please."

My heart started thumping—in a good way for a change. I pulled in a breath, gathering up all the courage I could muster. "I came by because I was wondering if your offer to go to the antique mall tomorrow is still open?"

His fingers stilled, and his gaze searched mine. I wasn't sure what he was looking for, but there was warmth in his blue-green eyes, shimmering like the gulf water on a hot summer's day. "Of course it's still open. But why'd you change your mind?"

My voice was raw when I said, "I've been hearing a lot lately about letting go. And I'm not saying that's necessarily a bad thing. But maybe, sometimes, when something feels good, feels right, it's best to hold on."

As I said the words, I let go of some of my fears, watching them drift away like a toy boat caught on a wave.

Speaking of . . .

"I do have one condition to our date, however."

"What's that?"

"I won't go unless you promise you'll buy yourself a boat. Maybe not today. Or tomorrow. But one day. I refuse to be the reason you give up something you love. You're not the only one who learned a painful lesson from our history."

"Maggie, I told you—"

"It's a deal-breaker, Donovan."

He looked deep into my eyes and must have seen my resolve, because he said, "All right, Maggie. I promise." He abandoned the bandages and cradled my face in his large palms. "Listen, now that we have that out of the way, can we get back to talking about you wanting to hold on to me? I really liked that part." His eyes flashed. Heat lightning.

As I sat there, basking in his attention, my fears poked me, prodded, but I did my best to ignore them, letting my heart lead the way. Because Estrelle had told me that I'd never have the future I yearned for otherwise.

And the future I wanted—the future I'd *always* wanted—was with Donovan.

As I left the bakery, there was a skip in my step, hope in my heart.

Donovan and I had a date tomorrow. A full day with him, of not holding back, of not keeping it all in. It was all I could do not to dance my way back to the shop.

I had just crossed the side street near Magpie's when I heard my name being called. I turned and saw Javier jogging my way from the parking lot behind our shops.

"Have you perchance seen Alistair?" he asked as he neared, breathless. "The blighter has once again escaped."

I blinked in surprise. He wasn't dressed in his usual fancy clothes. He had on a pair of gray, slim, sleek athletic pants, stretchy yet breathable, along with a black polo shirt in a similar fabric. And he was wearing tennis shoes. Tennis shoes!

"Sorry, no, but I'll call you if I see him. Can we talk about you for a second, though? I'm loving the outfit."

Glancing down at himself, he smiled. "I decided that if I'm going to be running all over town, I might as well dress for it."

"Well, you look great."

"I do, don't I?" He laughed. "I feel better, too. It's also why I haven't been into Magpie's as often this past week. It's time I cut back some on the things that aren't so good for me, health-wise. It's sickening, really."

"What is? Cinnamon rolls?" I hoped Sienna didn't hear him saying so.

"No, cinnamon rolls are God's gift to humans. It's sickening that Redmond was right that I'd feel better if I ate better and exercised more. I hate that. Him being right."

I smiled. "He cares, is all."

"Hmph. He doesn't need to be an overbearing stick-in-the-mud about it."

I tucked a loose curl. "I have the feeling he's going to be more flexible going forward."

As he scanned the sky, he pulled a handkerchief from his pocket and patted his forehead with it. "Really? What makes you think so?"

"A small, veiled meddlesome bird suggested it."

His gaze slid to Stitchery, which was closed. "You don't say."

"I also heard Alistair went to Red's the last time he escaped. Did you check there already?"

He nodded. "First thing, but he wasn't to be seen. I'll check again. He does end up at the gym more often than not."

"While you're there, it might be a good time to talk to Redmond about . . . things."

"Things. Yes." His gaze went upward again. When it came back down, he caught sight of my bandaged arm. "What in the world has happened to you, my dear? Did that fluffy terror of your father's get ahold of you?" He let out a low whistle. "She's drawn my blood on more than one occasion. I don't know how your father lives with her."

"No, no, it wasn't Molly. This time. It's just a little burn. Hazard of the job." At the mention of my father, I sighed. I knew I should just let the situation be, but I couldn't leave it alone. "Speaking of Dad, do you know when his ring will be ready for pickup?"

"His ring?" he asked, confusion shining in his dark eyes.

"Dad's wedding band."

A gust of surprisingly cold wind shook oak branches. I glanced around and saw Estrelle standing in front of her shop, looking our way, caution and sympathy shining in her eyes.

Javier shook his head. "I'm confused. Why would I have his wedding band?"

"He brought it to you to be resized. Didn't he?" My heart hung on the words.

Before he could answer, a flash of gray and yellow flew past, caught in the breeze, and Javier whistled sharply. "Alistair, perch!" When the bird didn't obey, Javier said, "Sorry, Maggie, I have to go."

"But Dad's ring . . ."

"I don't have it, darling. Desmond hasn't been in the shop for a few months now."

CHAPTER 17

AVA

It was strange and weirdly wonderful to look out the window and see nothing but endless darkness while hearing the movement of the water, the gentle lapping.

The lullaby.

I couldn't help thinking that a week ago, I'd gone to bed in my apartment in Cincinnati, not knowing how my life was about to change, thanks to one crinkled letter. Now, here I was in my room at Dez's house, listening to a murmuring sea.

I worked two jobs. I swam in the Gulf of Mexico. I talked with Mermaids. I walked with Snail Slippers. I sewed. I'd talked more in the past week than I had in my life. I'd laughed just as much. I had met so many interesting people and was enjoying their company.

Life was good. Better than I ever imagined it could be.

You'll be happy in Driftwood.

The letter had certainly been right about that.

The moon and stars were hidden deep behind thick clouds, and I smiled as I looked out into the night, thinking of Sam. Earlier, he'd come by with welcome-to-the-neighborhood gifts of a plant and another jar of jam. He'd stayed to help me empty my hatchback, bringing boxes up to my room.

When he left for home, he said he hoped I'd enjoy the lullaby tonight as I fell asleep.

It had taken me a moment to remember that we'd talked about the sea's lullaby, and I'd run upstairs and opened my bedroom's back window so I didn't forget. Then I quickly set about unpacking my things, wanting to feel fully moved in as soon as possible. Wanting to create a space of my own. Comfortable but *not* a comfort zone. More like a nest.

Dez had let me choose several pieces from his collection to decorate with in addition to the painting of the butterfly that still hung on the wall by the door. I hadn't dared move it.

I'd chosen an area rug done in a floral print, a hand-knitted throw blanket, a cast-iron cat doorstop that Molly kept hissing at, several throw pillows, a few classic books like *Watership Down, The Tale of Peter Rabbit,* and *Charlotte's Web,* and linen curtains with an embroidered hem.

I'd placed my stuffed Mr. Whiskers on one of the bookshelves and imagined adding more of my belongings once I retrieved them from my apartment in Cincinnati.

Dez had gone above and beyond to make sure I'd be comfortable here, and it showed, with the room having been transformed from cluttered to cozy in less than a week.

Still, I felt a little out of place. I'd gotten used to staying in Maggie's house. I knew its sounds. Its quirks—like how the dishwasher door tended to stick and how the faucet in the bathroom dripped. I knew its smells—coffee and sunshine.

And I had to admit, here at Dez's, I was a little lonely, even though Molly watched me from the doorway. I'd grown accustomed to having Maggie around, which seemed all kinds of silly because I'd stayed with her for only a little while. Yet, in that short time she'd become a dear friend. In a way, she'd started to feel like family. An older sister.

Earlier, Maggie had apologized profusely about not being able to help me move in, but she had been busy with the library's rummage sale. Tonight, she'd also volunteered—or had been volunteered, as I was coming to understand—to work the ticket window at the local theater production of *The Wizard of Oz* and hadn't been able to get out of it.

I hadn't seen Dez at all today. He'd been busy with work, then he'd texted that he had dinner plans and told me not to wait up for him.

It was probably for the best, though, that neither was here. I had work to do.

I glanced at the carpetbags on the floor next to a wide dresser. Molly rested atop one of the bags.

"I hope that's not the bag with Junebear in it, because I suspect we'll both be upset if it is."

She swished her tail.

I approached slowly, almost tiptoeing. "I'm just going to take the bag that's sitting right next to you."

Her ears flattened.

"You're okay. You're fine. You stay right there. You look comfy. Do you need a snack?"

Her whiskers twitched.

"Okay, it's a no on the snack. Maybe later, though?"

I slowly reached out my hand and nearly jumped out of my skin when I heard a crash in the attic.

Molly *reow*ed and shot like a missile under the bed.

With my hand pressed to my pounding heart, I stared at the ceiling.

Listening intently, I stepped out of my room. The scent of seaweed hung heavily in the air.

I stared at the door at the far end of the hallway. Behind it, I could easily picture the turned staircase that led up to the attic. Earlier this week, Dez had showed me the space, which had been designed for maximum storage. During my brief tour, I hadn't seen any sign of sparrows. Or the light I'd seen in the dark. Or anything that would explain a bump in the night. But there had been plenty of footprints in the dust.

Currently, aside from my hammering pulse, I didn't hear anything out of the ordinary. No footsteps. No squeaking. No nothing. Dez had been taking boxes down from the attic all week, so it was likely something that had been nudged off-balance by him had finally given in to gravity. I should probably check it out, but I'd seen enough horror movies to know that I wasn't going anywhere near that door. Certainly not when I was here alone, at night, in the dark. No. Nope. No way.

Leaving the seaweed scent behind, I scurried back into the bedroom, closed the door, and locked the handle. I grabbed the carpetbag with Junebear in it, and as I carried it to the bed, a paw reached out from behind the dust ruffle and grabbed my ankle. Sharp nails sank into my skin.

"Hey now!" I jumped back. "That's not nice. That noise scared me as much as you."

Molly's paw darted out again, swatting blindly.

Apparently, she wasn't one to see reason. Also, winning her affection was proving to be harder than I thought. I glanced at my ankle, happy not to see any blood. I fairly leaped into the bed to avoid another attack and settled on top of the fluffy duvet, sitting cross-legged.

As my heart rate returned to normal, I used the remote to turn on the TV that sat on a high chest of drawers in front of the bed and logged into my Netflix account. I clicked through movie options and settled on *My Fair Lady,* a movie I'd seen at least a dozen times.

As Henry Higgins sang about people speaking English correctly, I carefully laid out Junebear's pieces on the bed, along with all the supplies Estrelle had provided. I'd start with the easiest mending, the simple whipstitches that would close the slightest of Junebear's injuries. I looked through the spools of thread Estrelle had provided, my hand closing on the brown before setting it back into its place in the box. I then picked up a Cinderella-blue color instead. If Junebear was going to have scars, I might as well make them pretty ones.

I grabbed the thimble Maggie had given me to have at the ready, and as I sewed, I wondered once again, for what felt like the hundredth time, why Estrelle had given me this task. I wasn't sure, but I was grateful she had, knowing how happy Hannah would be to have her favorite teddy with her on a scary day.

I'd spent many days and nights in the hospital, and it never got easier to be poked and prodded or to sleep in a strange room with people coming in at all hours. It had always helped me to have a familiar stuffed animal to hold on to, to keep at my side, a reminder of home.

On a whim, I took a picture of the flotsam on the bed and sent it to my mom with a text.

> **Me:** Working on project *Fix Junebear*. Trying to get her
> finished in time for her sweet owner's hospital visit on Friday.

Little bubbles popped up on my screen, then my mom's message came in.

> **Mom:** Whoa. What happened?
> **Me:** A four-year-old with kitchen shears
> **Mom:** Say no more. Bunny would be so proud of you
> tackling a project like that. I have complete faith that
> Junebear will be back in her girl's hands soon

A sudden rush of emotion took me by surprise.

> **Me:** Thanks, Mom. I should get back to it. Love you.
> **Mom:** Love you too.

I set the phone down and looked up to see Molly, now sitting on the bed, batting around Junebear's ear. I didn't really think she could cause it any more harm, so I let her have her fun as I got back to work.

The next time I looked up, the movie was almost over, Molly was asleep on one of my pillows, and I was yawning so widely that my eyes watered.

In fact, I could hardly keep my eyes open. I packed up the carpetbag and quickly got ready for bed in the attached bathroom. Molly was still on the pillow, and I didn't dare try to kick her out. I unlocked the bedroom door and opened it just enough so that Molly could leave when she wanted. I turned off the light and climbed into bed, listening for any noises from above, but there was nothing to be heard.

Molly hissed as I settled in next to her, but she didn't bat at me or hop off the bed. I wanted desperately to reach over to scratch her ears, to get her purring, but kept my hands to myself so I didn't lose any fingers.

The rhythmic crashing of the waves was lulling me to sleep when a new sound registered. I leaned up on my elbow, listening intently. It took me a second to realize that it was the electric whine of a keyboard, and I smiled in the darkness as I recognized the song being played. I drifted off to sleep, listening to Sam playing Brahms's lullaby.

Early the next morning, I woke in a blind panic, hearing a sickening crunch, smelling smoke. A scream stuck in my throat.

I bolted upright in bed, my hands pressed to my chest as I glanced around, grateful for the night-light I'd plugged in before I went to sleep.

Curtains puffed lazily, the air humid. Molly was nowhere in sight. The hallway was dark. I glanced at the time on my phone. Almost four.

I took a deep, shuddering breath and willed my heartbeat to slow. Tears gathered.

I'd been dreaming about Alexander, about the accident that had cut his life so tragically short.

Sulfur had hung in the air that night as a storm front neared. It was late when he'd shown up at my apartment unannounced, past ten. I'd already been in bed, tucked in and binge-watching TV. I'd startled when he'd knocked loudly on my door, nearly jumping out of my skin.

"Ava, open up. It's me! There's a midnight tour of a local castle. Yeah, who knew there are castles in Ohio? Supposedly there are ghosts. You know you want to find out."

Inside, I'd pulled the covers up to my chin and shook my head. I had zero interest in going out in the dead of night, a stormy night at that, to a haunted castle. No thanks.

Also, his words were slightly slurred. I suspected he'd been drinking. It only added to my resolve to stay put.

He said, "Come on, Ava. The night air is good for you!"

That's when a neighbor had come out of his apartment and told Alexander to bug off or he'd call the police.

I'd breathed a great big gusty sigh of relief when Alexander did as he was told.

Alex had been laughing as he left. "I'll get you out of that comfort zone, Ava, if it's the last thing I do!"

I believed him. He was tenacious in his puzzle solving. But this had to stop. I decided I'd call him the next day, when he was nice and sober, and talk it out with him. Make him see reason. Encourage him to get on with his life. To finalize his plans to move overseas.

I'd heard his retreating footfalls on the stairs and the creak of the building's door as he pushed it open. I got out of bed, padded toward the front window to make sure he wasn't hanging around, planning to climb the fire escape or something equally as foolish. It was then that I heard the squeal of tires, a sickening crunch, the crack of a windshield shattering, a loud crash.

Heart pounding, I'd raced the rest of the way to the window. Peered out.

A streetlight highlighted the scene below. A car smashed into a telephone pole, its engine wheezing thick, dark smoke.

A crumpled body lying in the street.

Alexander's crumpled body lying in the street.

Now, I closed my eyes against the memories. Shook them away.

But the guilt wasn't so easily banished.

If only I'd opened that door.

If only.

A sea breeze whistled through the open window and swirled around me as if giving me a hug. Trying to comfort me.

There was no comfort to be had.

It was my fault Alexander had died. There was no changing that.

Wiping tears in my room at Dez's house, I slipped out of the bed and headed for the bathroom.

Halfway there, I stopped. Sniffed.

I *still* smelled something burning, the scent acrid, bitter, almost chemical in nature. It reminded me of the time my dad had plugged a portable air conditioner into a surge protector instead of directly into a wall outlet. It had taken only minutes before the protector started smoking and sounded an alarm.

Suddenly fearful, I listened intently, trying to focus. Deep in the distance, I heard sizzling and popping. The fire wasn't here, in the house. It was blocks away.

I grabbed my robe and ran down the stairs. "Dez! Dez!" I banged on his bedroom door.

A second later, he pulled the door open, his hair a mess, his eyes heavy with sleep. "Sprite! Oh my days, what's wrong?"

"There's a fire. In town. I'm not sure where." I sniffed again. "But I can smell it. I think it's an electrical fire. It smells like burning plastic."

His sleepy gaze focused. "You're sure?"

I nodded. "Positive."

"Then let's go find it. I'll call for help on the way."

It took only a minute more before we were in his truck, headed toward town, my face hanging out the open window. I listened for the crackling of flames, tracked the scent of smoke. Once we reached the square, we circled around until I pinpointed which building held the fire.

It was the bakery.

CHAPTER 18

MAGGIE

By late Monday afternoon, I was ready for a long nap.

I felt like I'd been going nonstop since hearing about the fire at the bakery yesterday morning.

If not for Ava, the destruction could've been catastrophic. As it was, the damage had been minimal because the fire hadn't had time to spread. The bakery would be closed only for a couple of days for cleanup.

I glanced at Donovan, who was dragging a broom around the coffee shop. I caught him looking out the window, toward the bakery. He'd been doing so all day, as if checking to see if it was still there. Reassuring himself.

The town had rallied around the Quinlan family yesterday. I'd set up a coffee service on the town green. Others brought food. Casseroles. Barbecue. Biscuits. Salads. Desserts. There'd been many offers to help with the cleanup or to fundraise to help cover the loss of income. It did my heart proud to see the town come together to help a neighbor in need.

For someone usually so chatty, Donovan had been quiet while fire investigators toured the bakery. Something had shifted within him yesterday. Something profound. I'd seen the change in his eyes every time he talked about what could've been lost. I didn't yet know what that change meant, however.

It had been an electrical fire, caused by faulty wiring in one of the refrigerators, and for some reason the fire prevention system had failed. How Ava had smelled the smoke had been the most asked question of the last twenty-four hours. She said only that she'd woken early, and the breeze must've been blowing just right for her to catch the scent. She'd mentioned before she had a sensitive sense of smell, but I now thought *sensitive* was putting it mildly.

The coffee shop had been packed today with gossip seekers, and overwhelmed, I'd almost closed early. Especially since I'd been working alone at the start of the day.

Rose, who'd gone out of town yesterday on a day trip to visit family in Georgia, was stranded there, her car having broken down. I hadn't wanted to call in Ava. Dealing with curious busybodies wasn't a stress she needed. The deep shadows under her eyes and near-constant yawning told me all I needed to know about her health these days. I was going to suggest she visit my doctor for a checkup. Just to make sure something else, other than grief, wasn't going on.

But just as I was ready to throw in the towel, help had arrived in the form of Donovan, who'd slipped on a Magpie's apron and jumped into the fray. He seemed to recall everything he'd learned the long-ago summer he'd worked here, and I could've cried I was so grateful for his help. How well we'd worked together would surely be the talk of the shop tomorrow. Maybe for the rest of the week.

Standing on a step stool, I used a chalk marker and my best hand-lettering to write *Boomy Eldridge's Vanilla Cream Tartlets* on the blackboard at the back of the shop.

Mondays meant a new recipe on the board, and I found comfort in the familiar routine. My head was currently pain-free, which was a small miracle considering how chaotic the day had been.

"I haven't seen one of these in years." Donovan set the broom against the wall as he rummaged through the contents of the Curiosity Corner, nudging aside a battered, water-damaged hardcover copy of *Travels with Charley* to pick up an old Polaroid camera, white with a classic rainbow stripe.

He aimed the camera at me, pretending to snap a picture. "Say cheese."

"Don't make me fire you."

I wouldn't. I was enjoying his company too much.

"You're a tough boss." He put the camera back where he found it. "How long has that been sitting there?"

"Nearly a decade."

If the camera worked, it might have some monetary value, but it had been broken when I bought it at a flea market nine years ago and it remained inoperable to this day. Not that it was for sale.

Donovan resumed sweeping, sliding the broom around the base of the magpie's tree, the bristles spreading wide to capture every dropped crumb. "What if the person it's meant for never comes in?"

"They will."

"How're you so sure?"

I shrugged. "I just am."

It wasn't something I could explain, the feeling deep inside me. It just was. *Is*. I was as certain of it as I was of the sun rising and setting.

Sometimes I imagined the person who'd be a match for the camera. That person might say, "I owned one of these when I was younger. Spent a fortune on film and took pictures of the most mundane items. Somewhere, I still have the Polaroid of a toothpaste tube, circa 1979. I used to love taking pictures. Not sure why I ever stopped."

I glanced at the Steinbeck book. I imagined its match longed to take a meandering road trip with his or her dog and just needed the push to go.

For a moment, I thought about the thimble I'd given Ava. I still didn't remember where I'd discovered it, but it was easy to see why it had been destined for her. When I stopped by yesterday to have a late lunch with her, she showed me the progress she'd made in mending Hannah Smith's teddy bear. There had been such sweet joy in Ava's eyes as she talked about the stitches she used and the patches she planned to add. Sewing had been missing from her life, and rekindling her love for it was clearly bringing her happiness.

"I'm sorry about yesterday," Donovan said. "I'd have loved to see you in that antique market, looking for these kind of treasures. How's this Sunday look for you?"

"The yard sale," I said simply. It was to be held Friday, Saturday, and Sunday, and I also planned to open the shop on Sunday, a rarity, to take advantage of the crowds.

He frowned. "The Sunday after?"

"I don't know off the top of my head. I have to check my calendar."

"Is it wrong that I want to chuck your calendar out a window?" he asked, sticking the broom under a table.

"What? Why?"

"When do you relax, Maggie? When do you have time just to yourself? Just to do the things *you* want to do? The things you enjoy?"

My eye twitched. "The things in my calendar *are* things I enjoy."

He simply smiled at me, and I had the feeling he didn't believe me. I didn't blame him. I was starting to wonder if it was true, myself.

I filled my schedule to keep loneliness at bay, but lately I was finding myself becoming annoyed with all I had to do. Sometime in the last month, my quiet house had become a refuge, instead of a painful reminder that Noah wasn't there.

"All right, because I'm a glutton for punishment, do you have anything going on tomorrow night?" Donovan asked.

I had a Community Christmas Decoration Committee meeting. Planning always started in September. "What time were you thinking?"

"What time are you free?"

I winced. "Nine?"

"We can make that work. How about dinner at my place?"

"At your brother and sister-in-law's house?" I asked. He'd been staying with them since coming back to town. "Isn't that too late? They have little ones."

He lifted his chin. "I have a place of my own now."

I nearly dropped the marker. "Since when?"

"Signed the papers on Saturday."

My heart fluttered. "You bought a place?"

"I'm *renting* Mrs. Pollard's guesthouse."

"The Pink Peony Cottage?"

"Stop that grinning."

"I can't help it. That place is so . . ."

"Available and cheap?"

The cottage used to be a pool house but had been converted into an apartment for extra income after Mr. Pollard passed away a few years ago. "I was going to say quaint. And pink. Very pink."

"I like pink."

"I didn't know that about you."

"There's a lot still for you to learn."

The heat in his eyes made my cheeks flame, and I turned back to the recipe so he wouldn't see just how much I was looking forward to those kind of lessons. He went back to sweeping, and I was hoping he'd also volunteer to mop. I despised mopping.

We worked in silence for a few minutes before he was once again at the Curiosity Corner, this time with a rooster-shaped biscuit cutter in his hand.

"Do you remember the first time you ever matched an object with someone?" he asked.

I wrote ½ *c. flour* on the board and said, "I was eleven. It was a penny, bright and shiny as could be. I found it on the beach the day my mama—well, that day, and I felt a strange sort of dizziness. When I ran over to show my father, I felt the same kind of vibration. I knew instinctively that it was meant for him."

My mama had told me that it would happen that way. I'd just *know* when I'd found a curiosity, and also know who it was for. I could hear her voice now, whispering memories into my ear.

When the time comes, pay attention to the vibrations, Magdalena. They won't lead you astray. And I promise you that wherever I am, I'll help guide you. Always and forever, I'll help guide you.

I blinked away tears and sighed, thinking about the penny I'd found. Thinking about how my father's pet name for Mama had been Penny. He liked to say she'd sent us the penny as a way of letting us know she was okay, wherever she was.

I glanced around the coffee shop. If I really concentrated, I could see her, walking around, smiling, welcoming everyone with open arms and a story to be shared. I recalled her saying many times, "Did you hear?" as she filled coffee mugs and leaned on the counter to talk. And talk. Mama didn't have an off button. I had never minded. I'd loved growing up here in the coffee shop, in her shadow, listening to her stories.

She'd always been the first to accept a dare, to try a new food, to learn a new dance, to test a new recipe, to give a hug, to embrace a challenge, like opening a coffee shop in a small town.

Dad had once confided in me that Mama hadn't even liked coffee much, only able to drink it with lots of milk and plenty of sweetener. Mama opened the shop because it filled a need in the town as a place to gather, to share life. Its good, its bad, and everything in between.

Very little had changed in here since she'd been gone. She could walk straight in and take over like she'd never even missed a day, which was exactly why I kept it this way. And I knew some around here thought I was naïve or even delusional for believing she was still coming back, but I was never going to give up hoping that she'd return to me, someway, somehow.

I said, "It's kind of a magical feeling, the joy that matching gives me. Helping others connect to something missing from their life, something that brings them happiness, helps take away some of the sadness that comes with my mama being gone."

Donovan had stopped sweeping again. He looked at me with such tenderness that I almost climbed down from the step stool to give him a hug. I got that look a lot when I talked about my mama.

He cleared his throat and said, "The penny? Is that the one Dez wears around his neck?"

I nodded. "About a month after Mama went missing, he asked Javier to make the penny into a pendant. My next experience with my curiosities was actually a match *for* Javier. It was a small chipped ceramic bird I'd collected from a yard sale. It turned out he'd always wanted a pet bird, and he told me I'd inspired him to finally get one. Soon after, he got his first cockatiel, Marcos, and he loved that bird more than life itself. After Marcos went to the big perch in the sky, he got Alistair."

Donovan smiled. "Ah, yes, the escapee. Some in town are starting to suspect Javier is the one letting Alistair out, knowing he'll eventually land at Redmond's."

I suspected something else entirely. I had the feeling the little bird's partner in crime was none other than Madame Meddlesome herself, Estrelle. I knew of two times now that she'd been in the vicinity when Alistair made an escape. If I asked around, I'd bet she'd been nearby each time.

I wrote *1 c. sugar* on the board in swirly letters. "I suspect there's going to be a reconciliation soon."

"I hope so," he said. "I do like a happily-ever-after."

I glanced at him. "I didn't know that, either."

"Like I said, lots to learn." Donovan picked up the dustpan, waved it around. "I have to admit I'm a little put out that you've never had a curiosity for me."

"Do you feel like something is missing from your life?"

When he didn't say anything, only kept staring at me, my heartbeat soared.

Finally, he said, "No, I don't, actually. Not anymore. What about you? Do you feel like something is missing from your life?"

My heart, I was certain, was doing jumping jacks inside my chest, banging around, making me so lightheaded I wanted to sit down.

I was saved from responding by the sound of a key in the back door. I leaned to my right to look down the hallway. The door swung open and Ava came in carrying a small box, followed by my father, who was saying, "You can set that right there, Sprite. Do you think you can manage the other bin in the truck?"

I adored the nickname he'd given her. It fit.

Ava saw me immediately. "Hello! Don't mind us. Just some boxes for the storeroom."

As she bent to put the box down on the floor, my gaze met my father's, and I was taken aback by the misery in his eyes.

"Didn't realize you were still here," he said. "We'll be out of your way in no time at all." One of his eyebrows went up when he saw Donovan crouched low, herding sweepings into the dustpan. "Afternoon, Donovan."

A wave of emotion swamped me. Dad and I hadn't spoken since the fight, not even on the green yesterday in the fire's aftermath, and it was breaking both our hearts. I climbed down off the step stool, capped the marker, and stuck it in my back pocket.

"Actually," I said, "if you have a second, I'd like to talk to you."

Surprise lit Dad's eyes.

Ava hooked a thumb over her shoulder. "I'll go get that other bin."

Donovan dumped the contents of the dustpan in the trash, then heaved the bag out of the can. "Let me help. It's the least I can do after you saved the bakery from going up in flames."

I suspected he'd meant his words to sound lighthearted, but I heard the hitch in his voice.

She said, "I'm glad I was awake, is all."

Dad watched them go. "We really know how to clear a room."

He balanced the blue plastic bin he held on his knee and opened the storeroom door. I picked up the box Ava had carried in, which wasn't heavy at all, and followed him inside. As I placed it among the many others he'd already brought here, I noticed the writing on the side of the box read NOT FOR SALE.

The bin he carried also had a NOT FOR SALE label stuck to it. I bit my tongue to keep from asking about why he was storing items here and not his storage units, but I didn't want to start a fight. The washing machine whirred and whined as we faced each other. Finally, I said, "I want to buy the coffee shop."

His eyebrows slid upward. "That so?"

I nodded. "I still need to figure out some of the math but I think it's doable. Delaney Parrentine's daughter, Amanda, works for a mortgage company. I'm hoping she can pull some strings, fast-track my application."

The financial aspect of buying the shop scared the stuffing out of me. I was already stretched thin. Paper thin. I was afraid the mortgage company was going to see that, plain as day, and think I wasn't worth the risk.

"I won't budge on an asking price," Dad said. "Fair market value."

"I'll get that money one way or another," I said, holding back cranky words about his attitude.

Dad crossed his arms. "Tell me why, Magpie. *Why* do you want to buy the shop?"

"I told you—"

"Don't you dare tell me it's because this is your mama's shop."

I wasn't at all sure what he wanted to hear. "As much as you want to let go, some things are worth holding on to. This coffee shop is one of those things. I cannot let her dream go."

Letting out a heavy sigh, he headed for door. But before he walked out, he glanced back at me. "Holding on is all well and good, as long as you're holding on for the right reasons. But, Maggie, you're only holding on because you're too scared to let go."

AVA

It was just a door.

A door that opened to a staircase.

A staircase that led to storage space in the attic.

The attic that might be haunted.

"I'm not scared," I said to Molly as I stood at the end of the hallway. "I'm just"—I yawned and stretched—"taking a breather before I go up there."

Molly's whiskers twitched.

The cat had been pretty much glued to my side since I'd moved in two days ago, and I was starting to wonder if her behavioral problems were related to loneliness. I'd barely seen Dez since I moved in, and had the feeling he didn't spend much time at home.

Molly still didn't welcome touching of any sort, but she'd been sleeping with me. She also kept me company while I cleaned the house or worked on Junebear.

The teddy was coming along. Her ears were now lined with a cotton print of vibrant flowers. I'd embroidered a purple rose, the birth flower associated with June, to cover a gash on a shoulder. There was still a huge hole in her chest I needed to figure out how to patch, and her face was still a work in progress. I'd tried embroidering a pink nose, but it hadn't felt right, and I'd ended up tearing out the stitches.

I'd been working on Junebear a few moments ago when I heard *something* in the attic. I wasn't sure what. It wasn't a crash. Or a squeak. Or footsteps. It had sounded like a . . . rattle.

I had been avoiding the space since hearing the crash the other night, but I decided it was time to check things out.

Molly *reow*ed.

"I am not stalling," I lied.

She blinked those beautiful blue eyes of hers and tipped her head as if saying, *Go on, then.*

I frowned at her. Then I took a deep breath, put my hand on the knob, and with one swift move, yanked it open. A wave of heat blew out, carrying with it the scent of seaweed.

Molly darted behind my legs.

"Chicken."

The enclosed stairwell echoed my heavy breathing. I flipped on the light switch, even though there was plenty of ambient sunlight filtering through the attic's dormer windows. Dust motes floated lazily.

Taking one step, then another, I closed my eyes and listened. I heard my own breathing, quick and shallow. I heard Molly's whiskers twitching. I heard the creaks and groans of the house siding. I heard the whisper of wind.

At the top of the steps, I looked around and was surprised to find sea glass scattered across the dusty floorboards, glittering like precious jewels. The glass had spilled from a tin that lay on its side next to a blue plastic tub labeled NOAH'S BABYHOOD in what I recognized to be Maggie's fancy handwriting.

The crash I'd heard on Saturday night had to have come from the spilled sea glass, but I wasn't sure how it had fallen, unless it had been perched on the tub of Noah's baby things. The lid to that container was askew. Before I tightened it, I glimpsed inside and *aww*ed over a tiny pair of overalls, a well-loved stuffed dog, and a knitted blanket.

Then I crouched down and used my hand to sweep the sea glass back where it belonged in its tin. I duck-walked along the floorboards, making sure I didn't miss a single piece. I'd take the tin downstairs, and later on ask Dez if he'd sell it to me. The glass was just so beautiful, I hated to think of it hiding away in the attic.

I was almost done cleaning up when something glinted in the shadows of the eaves, shining like a lighthouse beacon at night. I reached for it, my hand closing tightly around the object. Coolness seeped into my palm, despite the heat of the attic.

As I pulled it into the light, I quickly discovered it was a tarnished silver rattle imprinted with a sailboat. I gave it a shake.

Goose bumps rose on my arms. It was the sound I'd heard minutes ago—this rattle, the beads inside bouncing around inside the silver head. I shook it again. Yes, it was definitely the rattle I'd heard. But who'd shaken it?

Still crouched, I suddenly heard a fluttering that sounded like a heartbeat.

I glanced around, noticing for the first time that one of the dormer windows was open an inch, letting in the faintest breeze. The monarch butterfly that had been following me around sat on the windowsill, its wings opening and closing slowly. Its right forewing was now fully white.

As I watched it, the butterfly suddenly took flight, gliding gracefully under the window sash, leaving behind a glittery golden trail as it flew away.

CHAPTER 19

AVA

By the next afternoon, I was wiped out physically. I left Magpie's after my shift, and instead of turning toward the beach, toward Dez's, I veered right, practically dragging myself down the sidewalk. Stitchery's door was open wide, held in place by a kickdown doorstop. I was happy the shop was open at all. I'd yet to figure out the hours Estrelle kept. They seemed to be chosen by the same method Dez used to pick out his treasures: whim.

Immediately upon stepping into the shop, awash in its soothing colors, some of my tension drained.

It had been a busy day at the coffee shop. Neighbors were still coming in droves to get a firsthand account of Dez and me sniffing out the bakery fire, most still unconvinced that Sienna had nothing to do with it. Then there were those who hoped to see Donovan and Maggie working side by side again, because apparently it had been a lovely sight to see.

Everyone, it seemed, had wanted to hear the latest scoop on what was happening with the sale of the coffee shop. Mrs. Pollard had come by to critique the new recipe on the blackboard. The Mermaids had shared their treasures, including a sand dollar and a mermaid's purse—the horned egg case of a sting ray. Estrelle had been by for her hot chocolate with cinnamon. Redmond had peeked in the front window, and when he saw her inside, kept on walking.

Rose was still out of town because the mechanic working on her car was waiting for a part. Concern had been stamped all over Titus's face when he'd found out Rose hadn't yet returned to Driftwood, and I heard him mumbling that he ought to go get her himself.

I wouldn't put it past him if he did.

During lulls, Maggie sequestered herself in her office, filling out an online commercial mortgage application, and I tried to rest as much as possible.

Inside Stitchery an electric hum filled the air, the only sound I heard. Estrelle sat at a sewing machine, expertly guiding fabric patterned with cartoony dogs under a metal foot. It looked like she was making a toddler's shirt or perhaps a dress. She didn't look up from her work as she said, "You're late. You know I can't abide tardiness."

I actually looked over my shoulder to see if anyone else had snuck into the shop behind me without my noticing. But no. I was the only one here.

"I wasn't aware we had an appointment. The carpetbags aren't due back until next Tuesday. And they'll likely be empty when they come back, which I suspect you already knew."

The sewing machine fell quiet as Estrelle stood. She was once again dressed in black. It was the first time I'd seen her in pants, however—a pair of wide-leg culottes that swung as she walked to the cash register counter. Completing the outfit was a black satin blouse with a bow at the neck, her regular pillbox hat and veil, and chunky heels.

"It was an unspoken appointment."

I moseyed over to the counter, smiling. "Oh, right. That explains it. I do hope you'll forgive me."

"I'll take it under consideration." She picked up a paper Stitchery bag and handed it to me.

Confused, I glanced inside to see a roll of tracing paper and a package of embroidery stitch-and-wash paper. They were the items I'd come here to buy. How had she possibly known?

I slowly lifted my gaze to meet hers behind that black netting. "You're spooky."

She started to smile, then quickly pursed her lips, as if not wanting to get caught enjoying herself. "I prefer *surprising*."

I noticed she still carried no scent. "I suppose that works, too."

"I'll add those items to your tab."

"I have a tab?"

"Yes. I'll let you know when payment is due."

"Why does that scare me?"

Her eyes flared. "That is for you to determine, not me."

"You really are a kooky old bird, Estrelle."

Slowly, she came around the counter and trundled back to the sewing table. "I've been called worse."

Holding the bag tightly, I headed for the door. "Thank you for having this ready."

"You are welcome. I know you're busy and have a lot on your mind, denying what's plain as day in an attempt to be *normal*."

She said the word as though it was the most revolting word imaginable.

I shouldn't be surprised she knew of my health history, not with the way she somehow had insight into that kind of thing, but I certainly didn't want to verify it.

I tried to keep my face neutral. "I don't know what you're talking about."

She made a squeaky noise, and I realized it was a laugh. "Ava, your strength lies in the fact that you *are* different. Normality is tedious and dreary. Why hide the extraordinary?"

She certainly didn't hide how extraordinary she was. How she knew things, how she read minds, still baffled me.

But I wasn't her. And while I recognized that extraordinary could be worthwhile, could *help* people, I didn't necessarily want the attention that came along with it. After the bakery fire, I'd been so incredibly grateful, humbled even, to have caught it before it did serious damage, but I'd been unprepared for the questions. I'd been quickly overwhelmed by nosy, if not well-intentioned, neighbors.

Estrelle said, "Do you not see, child? There would be no questions if your abilities were widely known."

I frowned at her, wishing she'd stay out of my thoughts.

"I speak only the truth."

With a sigh, I said, "I need to get going. Long night of sewing ahead."

When I reached the door, the monarch with the white wing came fluttering inside. It flitted near my face with its topsy-turvy flight pattern. I gulped.

Estrelle suddenly appeared at my side, held out her hand. The butterfly landed on her gnarled finger. I noticed that *both* the wings on the butterfly's right side were now white, shimmering iridescently.

"You've traveled far in such a short time."

I looked up, thinking she was talking to the butterfly, but her silvery gaze was holding steady on me. "There is still a ways to go, however. You are being weighed down by the past. You must let it go. It wasn't your fault."

The butterfly's wings opened, closed. I heard a faint heartbeat.

I wanted to reach out, touch the butterfly, but I didn't dare. Tears pooled.

She knew.

She somehow knew about my guilt over Alexander's death. "How can I possibly let that go?"

She lifted her veil. "Because it is not a burden you are meant to carry."

"But if I had opened the door . . ."

She held the butterfly up, lifting it into the light. "What *if* he hadn't gone to see you? *If* he hadn't been tipsy? *If* the driver had taken another route. *If, if, if.*" Her tone softened as she added, "Life is too short, too fragile, too precious to hide in the shadows of what might have been. If continuously looking behind, you risk missing the possibilities that lie ahead."

She carried the butterfly outside, and it lifted off her hand and flew to a nearby flowerpot.

When she came back inside, she reached out, touched my chin, lifting it. Calm flowed through me as she said, "Tragedy, accidents especially, rarely come with reasons why. Yet, we look for them everywhere. We blame. We deny. We carry guilt, regrets. Sometimes, and this is hard to accept *but you must,* it is simply that person's time to go. We are all here on borrowed time."

"But"—I sniffled as I gazed at the butterfly—"if it was truly

Alexander's time to go, why isn't he gone? Why is he still here, following me around?"

Her eyebrow lifted. "That, Ava, is *not* Alexander. It has never been."

Not Alexander?

She moved toward the doorway, nudging me out as she went. She released the doorstop and said, "But until you stop looking behind you, until you stop letting fear hold you back, that butterfly will not be able to fly free. *It has been said.*"

With that, she walked inside. The door closed quickly behind her.

"Wait!" I cried, turning to follow her. "If it's not him, who is it?"

Because that was no ordinary butterfly.

But Estrelle had disappeared. The store was dark. The door locked.

And all I could hear was the slow whooshing of the butterfly's wings, still sounding just like a heartbeat.

MAGGIE

On my way to Donovan's cottage, I walked in the shadows, cursing the paper gift bag I carried, the one stuffed with extra tissue paper. It seemed determined to make as much noise as possible, to rat me out when I was trying my best to be sneaky.

I was a rule follower for the most part, so sneaking around went against my nature. However, I could only imagine the gossip if someone saw me going to Donovan's this time of night. Sure as I breathed, there would be wedding speculation by first light. Since I didn't want to add fuel to that particular fire, here I was creeping around like a thief in the night.

The Pink Peony Cottage sat three blocks from my house, closer to the town square than the beach. For two of those blocks, I'd walked normally along the sidewalk like I was just out for an evening stroll. But when I turned onto Sandbar Lane, the road Mrs. Pollard lived on, I took to the shadows.

I sprinted between crape myrtles and magnolias and cabbage and pindo palms. I darted behind bougainvillea, hydrangeas, and camellias. In my head, I could hear the *Mission: Impossible* theme song playing, and I realized I was having fun.

I tried to think back to when I'd last had true, pure fun.

It had been a while. When Noah was last home. With Noah, period.

I always had fun with him. Playing games. Going on adventures. Just being with him and his exuberant personality. I wasn't sure when it happened that I'd tied my happiness to him. It had been gradual, and it was one of the big reasons his leaving for school had hit me so hard. I didn't know how to have fun without him. I still didn't.

But as I scurried around in the darkness with a smile on my face, I suddenly realized how important it was for me to learn. I'd missed being happy. I missed this bubbly, goofy, could-break-out-laughing-at-any-minute kind of joy.

It was an eye-opener for sure.

I pressed my back to a live oak in the front yard of the house next door to Mrs. Pollard's and took a quick survey of my surroundings.

Mrs. Pollard lived in a lemony-yellow one-story stucco bungalow with a slab foundation, wide front porch, plantation shutters, and a hip roof. Lights glowed dimly behind closed drapes. An American flag flapped from a pole attached to a porch column. It was obvious that Mrs. Pollard took pride in her home. It showed in the neatly trimmed shrubs, the freshly cut grass, the recent paint job on the shutters, which was highlighted by a luminous porch light, the kind that wasn't allowed on homes closer to the beach this time of year because of sea turtle nesting.

The backyard, which housed an in-ground pool and Donovan's cottage, was enclosed by a five-foot-tall black aluminum fence. The gate didn't appear to have any kind of lock, just a latch.

I pressed the noisy gift bag to my chest and made a run for the shadows of the side yard. Mrs. Pollard's pug, Gus, barked from inside the house. Adrenaline surged, and I couldn't wipe the silly grin off my face if I tried.

I was thirty-eight years old and having the time of my life sneaking around my hometown.

I needed to sneak around more often.

With Donovan here, maybe I would.

I crept over to the gate, lifted the latch as quietly as possible, stepped inside the backyard, closed the gate, then darted back into the shadows. I inched my way along, contemplating my next move like I was playing a life-and-death game of chess.

A concrete path twined from the gate to the patio that surrounded the pool. The globe light in front of the Pink Peony Cottage cast circular shadows against its pink exterior, and light shone in the windows. My best hope of reaching the front door unseen was to keep to the fence line, which was dotted with magnolia trees, then make a mad dash to Donovan's doorstep.

Gus was still barking his fool head off, so I stayed where I was until he quieted. Then I waited a good two minutes before making a run for the magnolia closest to me.

I'd made it two steps before the floodlights flashed on, illuminating me mid-step. Gus started barking again, and next thing I knew, he was racing around my feet, yapping loudly.

"Maggie Mae Brightwell!" Mrs. Pollard shouted. "What in the tarnation are you doing?"

I slowly turned and said, "Hi, Mrs. Pollard."

I should've been horrified, terrified, but oddly, I felt like laughing.

Getting caught out here might be more fun than the actual sneaking.

"Are you having a sleepwalking episode like your daddy?" she asked. "Do I need to call him to collect you?"

Gus sniffed my feet, his ears perked, as I debated whether to lie. Then I heard the cottage's door creak open.

"Sorry to disturb you, Mrs. Pollard." Donovan stepped into the light. "Maggie's here to visit with me."

"At this hour?" she asked, clearly taken aback. "Well, I

never. Well, not often at least. Not anymore, sadly. But why the devil aren't you using the walkway? Are you having a mental break? Wouldn't surprise me with what all is going on these days."

A little giggle escaped. "Maybe?"

Donovan appeared at my side, put his arm around me, and guided me toward his front door. "She's fine, Mrs. Pollard."

"Best she call Dr. Jackson, just to make sure."

He pushed me through the open door. "Good night, Mrs. Pollard!"

He closed the door behind us, and I broke into gales of laughter. Tears leaked down my face.

Donovan looked at me, his eyes bright, and said, "What *were* you doing?"

Thumbing away happy tears, I smiled broadly. "Having fun."

Donovan had cooked chili and cornbread. I was seriously impressed with his culinary skills, even though he insisted this was the only meal he knew how to make.

We'd finished eating ages ago but had stayed at the table, chatting.

I told him all about my mortgage application, everyone asking about us at the coffee shop, and how I was worried about Ava's health.

He'd told me cute stories about his nieces and nephews, how he initially thought Sienna had somehow started the fire at the bakery even though she never went into the kitchen, and how he'd broken a sweat when signing the lease for this cottage.

I glanced toward the window, in the direction of the beach. "I never thought you'd leave life on the water."

"For a long time, I didn't either." He leaned back in his chair, crossed his arms. "Did I ever tell you that it was your mom who inspired me to join the Coast Guard?"

By his tone, he knew full well he'd never told me. "No."

Now I wondered why he hadn't.

"I've never felt more helpless than the day she went missing.

I wanted to be *in* the water, searching. From that day onward, I knew I wanted to be someone who *could* help if something like that happened again. I'd have done anything to bring your mom back to you, Maggie."

Tears filled my eyes.

He ran his finger along the edge of the table. "I still dream about that day sometimes. In my dream, I do go in the water."

"And do you find her?" I asked, my heart in my throat.

"I see her, and I keep swimming, trying to reach her. I'm always so close, so close, and she sees me, and this is the strangest part: she smiles—she smiles so big, like the way she did that time she found us playing in mud when we were little and joined us."

A tear slid down my face. In my mind, I could see that smile so easily.

"She stretches her hand out to me, and I stretch my hand out to her, and there are manta rays gliding all around, and when our hands finally clasp tightly, I always jolt awake."

I said softly, "Did you save many people in your Coast Guard days?"

"My fair share."

Emotion clogged my throat. "My mama would be happy to know that."

"I think she does know it somehow."

I was suddenly ashamed of my sixteen-year-old self who wanted nothing more than to squash his dreams of saving others so he could stay with me. I had been so blinded by the fear of losing him that I couldn't see the good he could do. I wanted to apologize, to beg his forgiveness, but I could feel the emotion, like a boulder on my chest, and didn't trust myself to talk about it without bursting into tears. Finally, I squeaked out, "Why did you decide to retire so young if you loved your job?"

Yes, he'd completed the required twenty years of service to retire, but he could've stayed in the service well into his sixties if he'd wanted.

"There were a couple of reasons. One was a training accident. I was knocked out and thrown in the water."

My heart pounded, my palms dampened. It was what I'd been so afraid of.

"I was lucky. Damn lucky. I was found and pulled out quickly. When I came to, alive and fairly well, I instantly knew I wasn't where I belonged. Not anymore. When you look death in the eyes, you start seeing life a lot clearer."

I shuddered, thinking for a moment of him lifeless in the water. But he'd survived. He'd *survived*. My chest ached as I asked, "Where was it you belonged?"

"Here. In Driftwood."

"But what about saving people?"

He said, hesitantly, "I've been thinking about forming a search-and-rescue group based out of Driftwood, partnering with the fire department."

Realization hit. "The boat?"

He smiled. "The boat. I'm sure there are a million hoops to jump through, but I think I'm up for the challenge. There's no group like that around here, and the police and fire departments don't have the water-rescue training or the equipment needed. They're already stretched so thin that it would be impossible for them to get it." He watched me closely. "How would you feel about that?"

My emotions cracked open and tears filled my eyes. He was talking about working on the water again. About risking his life. To save others, I reminded myself sharply. He would be *helping* people.

"I know it's asking a lot of you," he added.

In my head, I heard Estrelle, warning me about my fears. I curled my hands into fists. "That would be incredible. There are too many senseless drownings every year."

I'd learn to live with him being out on the water. Learn to live with the danger. Because loving him was worth the fear that came along with it.

"You'd really be okay with it? Because if not, just say the word and I'll let the idea go."

"I was told I need to start letting go of some of my fears. This seems a perfect opportunity." I tore the edge of my napkin and looked at him, studying the planes of his face, those blue eyes. "Does this mean you're done with the bakery?"

He leaned back in his chair. "That was the plan, initially. Then the fire happened and I decided I'm also going to stay on at the bakery. I'll do both."

I'd noticed a change in him after the fire but wanted to know more. "Why the change after the fire?"

He blew out a breath. "The fire kind of knocked the wind out of me. When I got the call, I pictured the worst, and I was *devastated*. I've been taking the bakery for granted my whole life, fighting against following in my parents' footsteps. After the fire, I realized how many footsteps *I've* taken in that bakery. It's a part of me as well. I don't know why I was rebelling. Because, to paraphrase something you said, sometimes it's important to hold on. All this clarity lately." He laughed, then stood. He picked up our bowls and carried them to the sink. "It's almost too much to handle."

It had taken him almost losing the bakery to realize how important it was to him—and had steered him in an unexpected direction. I understood that perfectly. Loss had been a guidepost most of my life.

I followed him to the sink with our cornbread plates and tried to lighten the mood a little. "Well, if you ever want another job, just let me know. There will always be a spot for you at the coffee shop. You have quite a fan club."

"*We* have quite the fan club. But I don't know how well that'd work out. I'd drink your profits and distract you with my wholesome good looks."

I laughed. "Just like the summer you were seventeen."

"It's good to see you laugh," Donovan said.

"It feels good to laugh. Thanks for asking me over."

"Thanks for accepting."

"I wash, you dry?" I nodded to the dishes piling up in the sink.

"I wash, you dry."

"Deal."

Working together, we got through the dishes quickly. I

glanced at my watch and sighed, thinking about my early morning wakeup. "I should get going. But before I do"—I grabbed the gift bag—"I have something for you."

"A curiosity?" he asked, eyes alight.

"Not a curiosity, but I loved it the minute I saw it and thought of you."

Humor shined in his eyes. "Did you just admit that you think about me?"

"Focus," I prompted.

He dug into the tissue paper, making a show of it by throwing each piece over his shoulder. He lifted out a bronze octopus. The ends of each tentacle curled up to form a hook.

He laughed. "Is this because of that one time . . ."

"Of course."

"I can't believe you remember that."

"I think you were hoping I'd forget."

"I can't argue with that. What was I? Ten? Eleven?"

He'd been fifteen, but I was willing to play his game and pretend otherwise. "Give or take."

We'd been shelling. When he'd picked up a conch shell, he'd been taken by surprise when an octopus slid out of the shell onto his arm. He'd let out a startled squeak and jumped back, as if it were a deadly snake. I'd laughed myself silly. The boy who aspired to be a brave coastguardsman had been startled by a tiny octopus.

"I love it," he said. "Thank you."

"You're welcome." I walked toward the door, reluctant to leave, but knowing it was time to go.

He followed me and leaned against the doorjamb, still holding the octopus key holder. "You know, it's funny. This reminds you of me, but it reminds me of you."

"I can't imagine how."

"The arms."

Pulling open the door, I gave him a look that suggested he'd lost his mind. "Last I checked I only had two and they're not covered with suckers, thank you kindly."

"Huh. Well, it seems like you have more. You use all of them to wrap around anyone and everyone, always. Looking out, taking care. You reach out, you grab hold, and pull people in close."

An unexpected rush of emotion made my throat tighten. I stepped outside. "That's actually kind of sweet. Maybe I don't mind being compared to an octopus after all."

"There is a downside."

I swatted away a mosquito. "What's that?"

"Your arms are always full, Maggie. Too full. I'm worried that you're being weighed down by helping everyone else. An octopus needs its arms to move forward, to move freely. Otherwise, it'll soon be buried by shifting sand and will eventually suffocate."

I knew he was worried about me. The concern glowed in his eyes as bright as Mrs. Pollard's floodlights. Still, annoyance flared, and my tone was sharp when I said, "There's nothing wrong in helping others. You of all people should know that." As soon as the words were out of my mouth, my lip trembled and I could feel tears gathering. My emotions were all over the place these days. Before I broke down, I quickly said, "Thanks for dinner," and walked away.

Leaving him behind, I hurried down the lit path and in the blue glow of a bug zapper saw Mrs. Pollard sitting in a patio chair, watching us. Gus started barking.

Donovan's voice chased me. "Maggie, wait a second. Please."

Clenching my fists, I stopped walking and faced him.

"That you help so many is one of the things I love most about you, but it's like how on an airplane you're supposed to put your mask on first, then help others. You're not wearing your mask. You're doing for everyone but yourself."

Suddenly, I was bone tired. I just wanted to go home, slip into bed, and pull my covers over my head and sleep until my alarm went off in the morning.

"Good night, Donovan." I rushed toward the side gate with Gus dancing around my feet, yapping happily. I bent and let him sniff my hands before I patted his head. "Good night, Mrs. Pollard!"

She threw a hand in the air in lieu of a wave, and I wondered how much she'd overheard between Donovan and me. I supposed it didn't matter. By this time tomorrow the whole town would know I'd been here tonight and that Donovan and I hadn't parted on the best of terms.

Once out on the sidewalk, I turned toward home and tried to take a deep breath but my chest was too tight. As much as I wanted to focus on Donovan saying there was something he *loved* about me, I was too worried that he might be right about the mask thing.

Because right now it really did feel like I was suffocating.

And I wasn't having the least bit of fun anymore.

CHAPTER 20

AVA

The morning sun sat low in the sky as the Mermaids finished their morning patrol of the beach on Wednesday morning. Most everyone was excitedly chattering about the storm system blowing in this afternoon.

The water gave no hint at what was to come. It was clear and calm, the waves rolling gently onto the sand. A group of seagulls squawked excitedly. Gracie had told me they were called laughing gulls, which fit perfectly.

I loved it here, on the beach, my toes in the soft sand. I often walked along the shore at night, watching the sunset. I'd been swimming only a few times, not liking to swim alone after what I'd heard about Maggie's mom. There was brave, then there was common sense. I needed to find a swim partner.

For some reason, my mind immediately chose Norman, and the thought made me smile.

Juniper, who was tucked into her baby carrier, was sound asleep, her chubby legs dangling. She looked as peaceful as could be as we headed for the boardwalk. My skin was tight with dried salt, my feet were caked in sand, and my hair was one massive knot from the wind.

And I hadn't felt better in days.

I'd found several shells that I'd tucked into a mesh bag that Dez had lent me. Gracie had stuck by my side during the whole excursion, telling me the names of the shells, but I'd already forgotten most of them. A few pieces of driftwood had been collected, some ceramic pieces, an arm of an old porcelain doll, and lots of trash, but no sea glass.

The other Mermaids were headed for the coffee shop, but

I was on my way back to Dez's. I wanted to give the kitchen and deck chairs a good scrub today, and I was still working my way through the mountain of clothes in the laundry room. I also needed to make a grocery run and check in with Maggie, because I'd heard some interesting gossip this morning about a late-night visit she'd paid to Donovan.

As we neared the boardwalk, Gracie turned and blew a kiss toward the water. When she saw me watching her, she said, "For Ben, who's out there somewhere. It's a thing we do."

"It's adorable. You must miss him terribly."

"I do. Juniper, too. And I know he misses us. But his is a good, steady job. Great benefits. Decent money. It's hard to complain when others might not have that kind of security."

The boardwalk groaned ever so slightly under our footsteps. I gave her a smile. "You can complain around me. I'm a good listener."

"I've noticed that about you. Thank you for that."

Dez's house loomed large next to the boardwalk. I automatically looked toward the attic in search of any strange lights or odd butterflies. I didn't see any, but I knew the butterfly with the white wing was nearby. I could hear it.

Which immediately started me thinking about Alexander, even if he wasn't the butterfly after all.

Since the last time I'd seen Estrelle, it had been impossible not to think about her saying *if, if, if*. What if I *had* opened the door to Alexander the night he'd died and agreed to go with him? Would it have been the *two* of us stepping in front of that car?

If.

I sighed.

The guilt that I'd hidden in my room when he knocked remained, but it didn't feel as powerful as it had. It had loosened its grip on my heart. I had become determined not to linger on regrets, instead choosing to focus on the good times we'd shared, his easy laugh and his kindness.

I was still puzzled by the butterfly not being Alexander. I'd been so *sure*. Perhaps it was my grandmother Bunny? Was she the one guiding me along on this trip out of my comfort zone?

She'd always thought I'd been too sheltered and had argued with my mom about it more than once. Although she'd been gone a long time now, nearly ten years, I was starting to believe in the impossible, so why not her?

I'd ask Estrelle the next time I saw her. Whether she'd actually answer and not mysteriously disappear remained to be seen.

As we reached the end of the boardwalk, Gracie smiled. "Will you be coming out with us tomorrow morning? The storm is probably going to uncover all kinds of goodies."

Oh, how I wanted to. I'd love to find sea glass of my very own. "I work tomorrow at the coffee shop."

"Well, consider it a standing invitation. You know where to find us. I have the feeling you'll be an official Mermaid soon enough. See you later!"

I liked the sound of becoming an official Mermaid. Very much so.

I waved goodbye as she headed off, and as I turned toward Dez's, I spotted Sam and Norman coming down his front steps.

I met them in the middle of the street and automatically dropped down to give love to Norman. He wiggled and jiggled and licked my chin.

I said, "I liked the xylophone. It was unexpected. Was that 'Mary Had a Little Lamb'?"

Sam dropped his head back and laughed.

For the past few nights, he'd been playing a different instrument and song. It had become a game for me to identify both.

"My xylophone skills are rusty."

"I thought it was a decent effort."

He nodded toward the mesh bag. "Did you score any good finds this morning?"

"Some shells." I glanced down the street, seeing Gracie turning toward the square. "And maybe a friend."

"The best find of all."

I glanced up at him, met his gaze, and nodded.

"Hey, Norman and I were just about to go for a walk on the trail. Did you want to come with us?"

I pointed toward the trees. "That trail?"

"The very same."

As I wavered, I heard Estrelle's voice in my ear.

If continuously looking behind, you risk missing the possibilities that lie ahead.

I recognized that this was a *possibility* I didn't want to miss. "Give me five minutes."

"I'll give you six. Don't go wearing yourself out."

Norman *quabark*ed as I fast-walked toward the stairs, ran up them and into the house. "Dez," I called out, "I'm going for a walk with Sam. Do you need anything before I go?"

"Not a thing, Sprite. Just beware of moving sticks out on that trail."

Snakes. I didn't tell him that I wouldn't mind seeing one—from a distance.

"Norman will be on guard, I'm sure."

I ran upstairs, dropped off my shells, grabbed a hat and pair of sneakers, and ran back down the steps. Outside, Norman and Sam were waiting near the trail marker.

Sam looked at his watch. "Impressive."

"Didn't you hear I'm the newest Snail Slipper?" I had officially joined the group.

"Of course I heard. Everyone's impressed you went back after your near-death experience."

I rolled my eyes. When it came to town gossip, somehow I'd gone from almost fainting to almost dying. "I wonder how long it'll take for me to get used to how this town talks."

"I've been here two years and I'm still waiting."

"Good to know."

We headed into the woods, welcomed by an army of evergreens. The trail split, offering the choice of going left, toward the beach, or right, into the woods. We went right. Tall grasses and spiky plants edged the wide, dirt pathway, but Norman didn't investigate them. He walked ahead of us a few steps, dead center, almost prancing.

"I have a favor to ask of you," Sam said after we'd walked in companionable silence for a few minutes. I'd been eyeing a lizard, some sort of gecko, and tore my gaze away to look at Sam.

"I'll do it."

"I didn't even say anything yet. Don't tell me you can somehow hear my thoughts, too?"

I smirked. "I'm not Estrelle. It's just that you've helped me so much I'll do just about anything to repay that favor."

"Just about? Are you already *qualifying*?"

"I just got to thinking about all the favors I don't really want to do. Like help you clean your sewer line or dig a trench."

He laughed. "Lucky for you, that's not what I was going to ask. The forecast has storms predicted for this afternoon, and I have another appointment in Orange Beach. If I'm not home when the storm hits, can you check on Norman? Maybe watch him till I get back? He's terrified of thunder."

"You're asking me to look after Norman?"

He nodded.

"That's not a favor! That's something I've wanted to do since I first met him. I'll definitely get him if the storm hits."

"Thanks," he said. "I'll leave the front door unlocked."

"So, another appointment in Orange Beach?" I glanced at him with the hope that he'd share what he was doing over there.

"Yep."

"For work?"

I scanned the brush as we walked. I hadn't seen any wildlife yet except for that gecko and a few birds.

"Nope."

Dirt plumed under our feet, the trail dry and cracked despite last week's rain. The air was scented with peat, decay, pine. I bumped his arm with my elbow. "I'm going to start thinking you're living a secret life there."

He said, "No, I live that *here*."

I adjusted the brim of my cap to see his eyes better. "Really?"

The gold in his eyes flashed with earnestness. He shrugged. "Well, I did before you came along."

I *had* unwittingly discovered that he played instruments. "Is there more beyond your musical talent?"

"Maybe."

"That's rather mysterious."

"I haven't been voted Driftwood's Mr. Mysterious two years running for nothing."

It took me a minute to realize he was joking. "You almost had me. Because you just never know around here."

I watched a cardinal flit in between trees, wondering about this man. Obviously he was kindhearted. Gentle. Giving. Why would he be keeping secrets? I wanted to push, to see if he'd open up to me, but it was a fine line I walked, because I didn't really want to tell him about the big secret I kept.

We walked along, the cardinal's chirp following us. The forest slowly thinned, giving way to wetlands. Spanish moss–covered branches stretched out over the murky water, casting shadows over the reeds and floating vegetation. Here, the air held a hint of sulfur, and I could hear the movement of creatures in the water, sloshing and splashing, but couldn't see any.

"I was married once," Sam said seemingly out of the blue.

I imagined the internal war he'd been waging whether to tell me, and I was humbled that he trusted me enough to share.

"To my high school sweetheart," he added.

I was trying hard to read his tone and struggling. It was a cross between disbelief and mournfulness. "She divorced me three years ago."

There was a long, heartbreaking story hiding in those words, and I could only tease out pieces of it. Some sorrow, some despair. But mostly regret. "I'm sorry."

As we kept walking, I picked up the strong scent of the beach. Soon, we passed a branch of the trail that led into tall dunes, but we kept to the dirt path.

"Then a year after that, I got word that she passed away."

My breath caught. That would have been right about the time he'd moved here, chasing happy memories. I debated what to say and decided on the absolute, plain truth of the matter. "Life shouldn't be so hard. It just shouldn't."

"Agreed," he said with a slight smile.

Norman *quabark*ed, pointing his nose toward a sand pine, and I saw another lizard trying its best to blend into the bark.

I didn't recognize what kind it was, but I'd do a little research tonight to see if I could figure it out.

"I've been going over to Orange Beach to meet with a lawyer. He's doing the legwork so I can set up a scholarship in her name at our old high school back in my hometown. A silver lining to a dark cloud."

I added *unselfish* and *compassionate* to his attributes. "You've got a big heart, Sam."

He shrugged. "It just felt like the right thing to do."

We rounded a bend, crossed a bridge, turned left, and realized we'd walked a loop. Ahead, I saw Dez's house. When we reached the pink pylons, I said, "Thanks for letting me join you two."

"Anytime, Ava. We enjoy your company."

I smiled at him, then I gave Norman a good petting before heading for the porch stairs. The wind had picked up, and the waves were hitting the beach with more force. I walked into the house and closed the door gently when I heard Dez talking to someone, whispering really.

I didn't want to interrupt, so I started up the stairs but stopped when I heard him say in a nostalgic, somewhat sappy tone, "Where have you been, my little ghost? I haven't seen you in a few days. I miss you."

I tiptoed down the hallway and spotted his cell phone charging on the kitchen counter. The house didn't have a landline. Goose bumps rose on my arms.

Dez's back was to me as he leaned against the doorjamb of the French doors, looking out at the water. He was alone.

Molly watched me from inside her favorite stockpot on the stove—I hadn't the heart to put it away in a cabinet. Her whisker twitched, obviously judging me for eavesdropping.

"Fine," I mouthed to her and slowly backed up, my mind spinning with what I'd heard.

My little ghost. Was he really talking to one? After what I'd experienced with the butterfly and the strange things happening around here, I couldn't dismiss it outright.

It didn't seem too concerning until I heard him say, "It

doesn't matter, I suppose. We'll be together again soon, my love. I promise."

Hours later, I was in my room, debating whether to tell Maggie what I'd overheard.

I had to tell her, didn't I?

It just sounded so fantastical.

Fantastical yet also worrisome.

If I told her, her blood pressure was sure to skyrocket, no matter how gently I tried to deliver the news. I didn't want to be the one to cause her to have another mini-stroke.

I sighed. I could only assume that the ghost Dez had been talking to so lovingly was Maggie's mother. It made perfect sense, especially with that seaweed scent I'd been smelling around the house. After all, her mom had been caught in a riptide. It would stand to reason her ghost would carry the scent of the sea.

While debating what to tell Maggie, I'd kept busy by working on Junebear, who was just about finished except for her nose.

As the wind buffeted the house, I stood up and walked over to the window. The skies had darkened. Low charcoal-gray clouds drifted quickly eastward. The water roiled, filled with whitecaps. Rain splattered the window.

Behind me, my phone started playing "Don't Worry, Be Happy." I walked back to the bed, scared up some energy, and answered. "Hi, Mom."

"You sound tired, Ava."

So much for that energy I'd mustered. "How can you possibly tell that from so far away?"

"I've been your mom a long time now. Have you been working too hard?"

"Not at all." I took a deep, fortifying breath. "In fact, I took a second job at a local coffee shop. It's just mornings, three days a week."

There was a long stretch of silence and I waited it out.

She finally said, "Is that wise? To take on so much?"

I took stock of my body, of the exhaustion, of the dizzy spells, of the lack of appetite. The answer to her question was a resounding no. No, it wasn't wise. But it made me happy. "I love the atmosphere and have met the friendliest people. Plus, there's coffee. We make this amazing caramel latte. You'd love it. My boss is the daughter of the man I care for, and they're the nicest family."

There was another stretch of silence. Rain drummed the roof. For some reason, I worried about the white-winged butterfly.

I waited for her to tell me that my health was more important than my happiness but instead she said, "All right, Ava, all right. I trust that you know when you're overdoing it. I'll try not to worry so much."

Her words were like small serrated knives of guilt in my chest, twisting and turning. If I didn't want her to treat me like I couldn't take care of myself, then I needed to *actually* take care of myself. I'd put off the inevitable long enough. I knew my body. I knew something was wrong. It was time to stop denying it out of fear of what I might hear, and take action. I'd call a doctor's office first thing in the morning.

We chatted for a while longer about her job, my brother, how my stepfather, Wilson, was doing with his retirement, and the Florida weather. I quickly realized I needed to get off the phone before it started thundering because there weren't any storms in the Cincinnati area currently, and it was only a matter of minutes before they hit here.

I promised to send a picture of Junebear when she was finished and we said our goodbyes. Electricity crackled in the air. I crossed to the windows at the front of my room and glanced across the street. Sam wasn't home yet.

"Should I go check on Norman?" I asked Molly, who sat on my pillow.

Her ears flattened.

"Don't be that way," I said. "He's sweet."

She hissed.

I stepped over to the bed and, before I could think twice about it, scratched under her chin. She curled her head into my palm, then must've realized what she'd done because in a huff, she quickly jumped off the pillow and disappeared under the bed.

I laughed. I'd win her over yet.

I picked up Junebear and ran my finger down her face, over the spot where her nose should be. I'd tried several nose options already. Embroidery and buttons and a plastic nose from a craft shop. None felt right. I had to turn the bear over to Jolly tomorrow if Hannah was going to be able to take the bear with her to the hospital, so I was almost out of time.

Underneath the bed, I heard Molly wiggling around. Her paws darted out from beneath the box spring, like she was pawing something, then disappeared again. She did it once, twice, three times. I dropped to my knees. "What's going on under here?"

In the shadows, she flicked me a glance as she batted something back and forth. I hoped to the heavens that it wasn't a bug she was playing with. "What do you have there?"

With a swing of her paw, she swatted the object out from underneath the bed and it landed next to my knee. It wasn't a bug. It was a piece of sea glass. I peeked farther under the bed. The tin I'd brought down from the attic the other day was now *under* the bed. With the lid on. As I pulled it out, the scent of seaweed plumed in the air, then quickly faded. Goose bumps popped up on my arms. Molly's fur rose.

The last I'd seen the tin, it had been on the bookshelf, next to Mr. Whiskers. Dez had laughed off my offer to buy the tin from him, instead giving it to me.

"Free to a good home," he'd said. "I'm not even sure where it came from."

I picked up the piece of pale green glass Molly had been playing with, turned it over in my palm. It was an irregular piece, one that looked like a trapezoid stretched out of shape. It had two tiny holes in its center, one slightly larger than the other.

The glass warmed in my palm as I stood up. Once again I caught the faint scent of seaweed as I looked between the glass and Junebear. I held the piece to the bear's face. The holes in the glass were the ideal spacing to use as a nose.

I glanced down at Molly, whose head was now poking out from under the bed. "Thank you for bringing this to my attention." I looked up, feeling kind of silly as I added, "And thank you, Penny, for helping me with Junebear. The sea glass is the perfect choice for her nose."

Just as the words came out, brightness suddenly filled the room, and I nearly jumped out of my skin, thinking I was about to meet a ghost face-to-face. Then I realized the flash had been lightning, not anything spectral. A few seconds later came the rumble of thunder, and I hurried to the front window. Sam's truck was nowhere to be seen. I grinned. "Be right back, Molly. I'm bringing back a friend for you."

A low growl came from under the bed in response as I made my way down the stairs. I flew out the front door into the rain, down the steps, across the street, and had to take a breather on Sam's porch before I went inside, realizing I might have overdone it with exercise today.

I knocked on the door even though I knew Sam wasn't home, and slowly pushed it open as another flash of lightning lit the sky. Thunder quickly followed. The storm was moving fast.

"Norman?" I called out.

Sam's place was as tidy as it had been the last time I was here, and the scent of grapefruit hung heavily in the air. A bowl of the fruit sat on the kitchen table, and I suspected that they might be responsible for his citrusy scent. A quick survey of the living room told me Norman wasn't hiding here.

"Norman, honey," I called out. "It's just me, Ava."

I glanced behind the kitchen island, in the bathroom, and guest bedroom, which had only a queen-size bed and nothing else in it. I checked under the bed but there wasn't so much as a dust bunny underneath.

At the far end of the hallway were two more doors. One was closed. The other open.

The closed one had to be his music studio. There was no

other space for it. As much as I wanted to snoop, I didn't dare. One day he'd tell me about the music, just like he'd told me about his divorce today. I could wait.

As I neared the open door, I heard the faintest whine. "Norman?"

Rain pounded the roof, and the wind whipped furiously. The lights flickered as I stepped into what had to be Sam's bedroom. It smelled of him—that nutty, citrusy scent.

The king bed was neatly made with a no-fuss thin beige blanket. Four pillows were stacked against a tufted headboard. A TV hung on the wall in front of the bed, and a dresser stood near the door. On the floor next to the door were a pair of well-worn black cowboy boots, and I was having trouble picturing Sam wearing them, having only seen him in his boat shoes.

I got down on my knees and glanced under the bed. Norman was shaking, his beautiful eyes filled with fear. I lay down on my stomach. "Hi there. Fancy meeting you here." I tapped the floor in front of me. "Come on out, come on."

He hesitated for only a second before he inch-wormed forward. Once out, he lurched toward me in one big burst, throwing himself against me. He kept pushing himself forward against my rib cage, as if he was trying to burrow into my body. I rolled and scooped him up.

He rattled in my arms, a full-body tremble. His tail was glued to his body, not even the slightest wiggle. "It's all right. You'll be okay."

Holding him tightly, I stood up and wobbled with dizziness. I quickly leaned against the dresser until I found my balance. I'd definitely overdone it today. As I waited for the faintness to pass, my gaze swept across the top of the dresser. There wasn't much on it. A folded T-shirt. A change tray. And . . . the origami dog I'd given to Sam last week, made from the one-dollar bill. I smiled. I didn't know why I liked that he'd kept it, but I did.

And I was still smiling as I finally headed for the front door, a trembling Norman tucked as close to my body as I could hold him. It had been a long, busy day with the Mermaids jaunt, the walk with Sam, overhearing Dez talking to a ghost, working sewing projects, and a Norman extrication, but as I hurried toward home, splashing through puddles as rain poured down, my smile turned into a full-blown grin.

It had been one of the best days of my life.

CHAPTER 21

MAGGIE

Last night's storm had blown northeast, but heavy clouds lingered. It was a dark, gloomy morning without even a hint of sunshine.

Carefully, I filled the bean hopper. I'd always loved the sound of the beans falling into place and the heady scent that wafted up. Over the years I'd become desensitized to the scent, so it was one of the rare times I could still smell coffee here in the shop.

There were still fifteen minutes until opening, and after the storm, I expected a full flock of Mermaids at nine. It was an all-hands-on-deck kind of day, but I was down a pair as Rose was *still* in Georgia. Thankfully the part she needed for her car was finally in, and she promised to be back at work by Saturday at the latest.

I was grateful I had Ava here to help out. She still didn't fully know the ins and outs of the shop, but she was a quick learner and a hard worker. But I hated having to rely on her so heavily, because she still didn't look well.

I wanted to scoot in close to her, feel her forehead to check for a fever. "You feeling all right?" I asked.

As I asked the question, Donovan's voice filled my head, saying, *I'm worried that you're being weighed down by helping everyone else.*

I shoved his words straight out of my thoughts. I couldn't stop being who I was. I couldn't stop *caring.* I was worried about Ava, and so help me, I was going to wrap my tentacles around her if I wanted to.

"I'm doing okay," she said. "But I do want to make sure

there's nothing more serious going on, so I'm going to call a doctor later, once the office opens. Dez recommended her."

I nearly slumped in relief. "Dr. Jackson?"

She nodded.

I tossed the empty coffee bag into the trash. "She's been my doctor for years. She's good. Better than most."

There was a knock on the front door and I glanced up, hopeful. For the first time in forever, the hope didn't come from the yearning to see my mama coming inside. I'd been hoping to see Donovan, even though he usually came in the back door with his deliveries. I hadn't seen him since dinner the other night, and I was regretting the way we'd parted.

My heart sank at seeing Sienna looking in. She smiled and held up three bakery boxes.

"I've got it." Ava rushed out from behind the counter. She hurried to the front door, threw the lock, and held the door open for Sienna. "Good morning."

My head was starting to hurt. "Morning, Sienna."

"Morning, y'all!" She set the boxes on the counter next to the cash register. "I've brought your bakery order."

I pasted on the fakest smile I'd ever faked. "I appreciate it."

"How do you like working at the Beach Mouse?" Ava asked as she came back around the counter.

"I like it," Sienna said. "I hope they let me bake eventually. Seems I love baking."

"Really?" I asked, my voice higher pitched than normal as I tried to hide my disappointment with Donovan's desertion by acting overly excited. "Did you take Mrs. Pollard up on her offer?"

I pretended not to see the way Ava looked at me. It was obvious she knew why I was suddenly super cheerful. No doubt she had heard the gossip about Donovan and me that had zipped through town yesterday like it had been caught on the sea breeze and deposited on the doorstep of every single neighbor.

"Sure did. She's been real kind about it, letting me use her kitchen to test new recipes. She says she fancies herself a baking consonant now. She's thinking about having business cards printed up."

I smiled, not even correcting her on the *consultant* slipup. I didn't want to interrupt the flow of happiness in her tone.

She went on, saying, "If you want, I can bring you by some Mississippi mud brownies to taste. I baked a mess of 'em on account of Mrs. Pollard and me are going to be selling them at her yard sale this weekend, so I have plenty. They're nothing but chocolate, marshmallow, and coconut delight."

"Ooh," Ava said.

"I'll bring some to you, too," Sienna said to her. "I owe you, since if you didn't catch that fire when you did, then everyone would be thinking I had something to do with it."

"That's really nice of you," she said, "but I can swing over to Mrs. Pollard's tomorrow and buy one."

"Me too," I said. "We want to support you."

She headed for the door, saying, "But you've already done that, Maggie. If you hadn't given me those measuring spoons, I never would've taken Mrs. Pollard up on her offer to teach me how to make those scones. I never would've realized what I've been missing. Baking just makes me really happy. So thank you. I need to be gettin' back. See y'all later."

Joy bubbled through me.

Ava said, "Seems to me, Maggie, the curiosities you find help others find happiness. That's a real special gift."

"It is, but I can't take all the credit for it."

"No?"

Since I was in a sentimental mood all of a sudden, I decided to tell her about the curiosities and how my mama had shared the gift with me.

"I didn't realize your mom had the same ability," she said, minutes later, a thoughtful look on her face, as she went about unboxing pastries. "It makes sense now."

"What does?"

"The sea glass," she said hesitantly.

"What sea glass?"

"The piece I used for Junebear's nose. It came from a tin in the attic." She took a deep breath. "There's something I should tell—" She cut herself off, shook her head, and then muttered, "Fantastical."

"I'm confused. What's fantastical?"

She studied my face for a long second before saying, "It's *fantastic* that I finished Junebear." She smiled. "And I'm working on a new project, too."

Her smile was something else when it radiated joy, but I couldn't help thinking there was something troubling hiding behind this one. "I can't wait to see them."

She carefully set donuts into the bakery case. "Did I hear that Sienna also dropped off yesterday's bakery order?"

"Hmm? Oh, yes, she did."

She slid me a look. "I hope Donovan's feeling okay."

"I'm sure he's just busy." It was obvious he was avoiding me, and even more obvious that Ava was trying to get me to talk about it. But I wasn't ready to share how I'd blown things with him, all because I didn't want to accept that I was stretched thin. I was. I didn't even want to look at my blood pressure numbers right now.

Instead of answering her, I flipped the tables. "Did I hear that Norman spent part of yesterday afternoon with you?"

Her cheeks turned a lovely shade of rose pink. "He's scared of thunder and Sam had an appointment, so I brought him over to Dez's. You should've seen Molly with him. At first, she was hissing to wake the dead, but no sooner had I put him on my bed than she was right next to him, snuggling up."

"Get out."

"I'm serious. I took a picture."

She pulled her phone out of her back pocket and pecked at the screen for a second before turning it toward me.

Sure enough, Molly was snuggled up close to Norman, practically lying on top of him. Perhaps she was trying to suffocate him, since to my eye, she was slightly bigger than he was.

"And she got in a huff when Sam showed up to take Norman home." Ava slipped the phone back into her pocket.

"That Sam is a nice guy."

Her cheeks turned from pink to red. "Sure is. Do you know much about him?"

"Hardly anything. He keeps mostly to himself." I filled a tray with sweetener packets. "Makes small talk but nothing deeper. Doesn't seem to have a job but seems to have enough money to get by. No one visits that I know of, but he does leave for long weekends every now and again. There's a rumor that he's divorced but I don't know if it's true—to my knowledge he's never confirmed it."

At the sound of a noise, a tap, on the front window, we glanced over in time to see Titus with his face against the glass, peering inside, a hand acting as a visor.

I shook my head at him.

He frowned and walked off.

Ava smiled. "Apparently drip coffee is only tolerable if it's Rose serving it to him."

"I'm not sure whether to tell her about his sulking or not."

"I have the feeling she knows," Ava said.

Not a minute later, the door opened again, and I glanced over, hoping once again that it was Donovan. But it was Redmond.

"Good morning," Ava and I said in unison.

Then I added, "Almond milk latte?"

"Yes, please." He glanced at the bakery case. "And I really, really want a blueberry donut. To go."

"Coming right up," Ava said, grabbing a paper sack for the donut. Her green eyes danced with happiness, and she had a big smile on her face.

That smile could light the world.

I quickly made the latte, and as I pushed it across the counter, it suddenly jumped out to me that Redmond had swapped his drab muscle shirt for a pretty blue moisture-wicking T-shirt. It brought out the color of his eyes. "I like your shirt, Redmond. Is it new?"

He nodded. "Does it say *flexibility*?"

I laughed. "Practically screams it."

My phone vibrated in my pocket just as the front door opened and Mark and Trixie came inside. I quickly glanced at the phone screen, and when I saw it was Noah, I panicked a little. He never called this early. I turned away from the counter and answered by saying, "You okay?"

He laughed. "I'm fine. Just had a minute so thought I'd check in with you. You're not busy, are you? You're off, right? It's Thursday."

I used to take Thursdays off, but it had been a long time since I'd done so. He wouldn't know that, though, because he'd been away at school. "Can you hold on a sec?" I glanced at Ava. "It's Noah."

"Go," she shooed. "I've got the shop covered."

"I'll try to be quick." I gave a smile to Mark and Trixie before turning toward my office. "I'm back," I said to Noah. "You sure you're okay?"

I stepped into the tiny room and closed the door. Sinking into my desk chair, I fought a yawn. I hadn't slept well since dinner with Donovan. He'd rattled me with his octopus talk.

"Mom, I'm fine. You worry too much."

I gritted my teeth. I really wished people would stop saying stuff like that to me. I rubbed my left temple as it started to pulse. "I'm a mom. It's what we do."

"Yeah, yeah."

My desk was a mess with receipts, invoices, brochures, and catalogs from companies that wanted me to buy new equipment. I powered on my computer. "How're classes?"

"Good for the most part. I almost fall asleep every time I have calculus. Numbers. Ugh."

"You know they have tutors available, right? If you need help?" There was certainly no way I could help him. Donovan, though, might . . . he'd always been good at math.

"Mom."

I sighed. "I know, I know. You can handle it."

There was a long pause before he said, "Heard you were fighting with Granddad."

Ah. The real reason for this call. "Did he tell you that?"

"Didn't have to. Joe mentioned it when we messaged last night."

Joe Rains, one of Noah's best friends growing up, still lived here in town. I was going to wring his scrawny neck next time I saw him for gossiping. "It's not a fight. It's a disagreement."

"I shouldn't have had to hear about it from Joe."

I tried to laugh it off. "It's not that serious."

"Does Granddad have a caretaker living with him? Is he talking about ghosts? Is he selling the coffee shop? Because all that sounds serious to me."

The pulsing in my temple slowly crept across my forehead, a little jackhammer delivering jolts of pain. It was hard to argue with him, because after hearing his side, he had every right to be mad. "I didn't want to worry you."

"I'm not a kid anymore. You don't need to keep things from me. To protect me or whatever."

And the hits kept coming. I didn't need the reminder that he was all grown up.

"Why is he selling the shop?" he asked.

"I'm not quite sure, but I'm going to buy it."

There was another pause. "How?"

I searched in my desk for a bottle of aspirin and had to stop myself from slamming drawers shut when I didn't find it. "Still working on that."

"What can I do to help?"

"Focus on school."

"Family's more important. I'll come home this weekend. See what we can figure out. *Together.*"

"The yard sale's this weekend, and your grandfather is running around like a chicken with its head cut off." I sent a silent apology to Cluck-Cluck for using that particular idiom. "Let's hold off a bit, okay?"

He let out a deep breath. "All right. But I don't want to wait too long."

"I don't know where you get this pigheadedness from."

He laughed. "Yes you do. All right, gotta go find some coffee if I'm going to make it through the day. Love you."

"I love you, too, Noah."

With a sigh, I hung up and then rested my forehead on the desk, clunking it lightly. When my phone rang again, I thought it was Noah calling back and was surprised to see it was Amanda Parrentine.

I answered quickly.

"Hey, Maggie." She let out a deep, weary breath. "You'll be getting an official call later from my boss, but I just wanted to give you a heads-up on your loan application."

My heart lodged in my throat. "Why don't I like the sound of your tone right now?"

"I'm sorry."

She didn't need to say anything else. My application had been denied.

"Thanks for letting me know, Amanda."

"Wish I had better news," she said.

"Me too."

I hung up, dropped my phone on the desk, and stared hard at the ceiling so the tears wouldn't fall down my face.

What was I going to do now?

CHAPTER 22

AVA

Maggie hadn't been the same since talking to her son on the phone, and when I asked if he was okay, all she said was, "Hmm? Oh, he's good."

Too busy with customers, I hadn't overheard her call through the closed office door and now wished I had. I wanted to help, because something had definitely gone wrong.

Since the call, she'd been distracted, putting things where they didn't belong, getting orders wrong, and her eyes were red-rimmed and glossy. I suspected she'd been crying.

Through it all, however, she smiled at everyone who came in, chatted with them, and made them feel welcome—even if she did give them the wrong coffee. The Mermaids had stopped by after scouring the beach, and more than one person had told me they missed seeing me out with them this morning.

Missed. Me.

It filled me right up with warmth and fuzziness, giving me the strength to work extra hard to cover Maggie's mistakes without letting on that's what I was doing. No need to make her feel worse.

While I worked, I also took mental notes on her graciousness. She spoke to everyone she knew by name, mentioned a child or pet, or a mama or daddy. She'd even asked one man about "Monty," who turned out to be a snake plant that had been rescued from the trash of a big-box store's garden center.

She knew this town inside and out, and it was apparent by everyone's reactions to her that they didn't come to the coffee shop solely for a caffeine fix. They came for Maggie. The way she made them feel.

I hoped she saw it. I hoped she felt it. And I hoped especially hard that her loan application was approved, because this town needed her here, exactly where she was, doing what she did best: serving up compassion and kindness, love and happiness to this small town.

Since that phone call, the only time I'd seen her perk up was when I called the doctor's office for an appointment and lucked out in getting one for the following week.

But since then, her smiles hadn't quite reached her eyes as people filtered in and out, talking about a rotted wooden boat that had washed up on the beach, the yard sale, and of how I'd taken in Norman in his hour of need.

Currently, I was wiping tables and chatting with Gracie as she tried to wrangle Juniper into her carrier. The baby was having none of it. Instead she wanted only to stuff a handful of her mom's hair into her mouth.

Gracie said to me, "She puts everything in her mouth these days. She's teething."

"Do you want some help?" I asked, trying not to notice the butterfly that kept knocking against the window. From here, it appeared that part of a third wing was now white as well.

"That's okay, I—" She was cut off by the sound of her phone, the ringtone a rendition of Elvis's "It's Now or Never."

"Oh, that's Ben calling. Don't judge the song. I'm an old-fashioned sap." Gracie shifted the baby onto a hip as she rummaged with one hand through the backpack on the table. Through all this, Juniper kept her death grip on Gracie's hair, pulling her head at an unnatural angle.

I held out my arms for the baby. "Why don't you let me hold her?"

"You're a lifesaver, Ava." She leaned toward me, and I slipped my hands under Juniper's arms. As soon as I touched her, she released her grip on the hair. I drew her close to me, one hand under her, the other around her, anchoring her to my side.

Gracie found her phone and breathlessly answered, "Hey, I'm here." Then she whispered to me, "I'm going to take this outside, okay? I'll only be a minute."

I nodded and looked at Juniper as if she were a tiny, loveable alien. I didn't quite know what to do with her.

I'd never held a baby in my life. It was yet another thing I'd been denied because of my disorder, this simple pleasure. It had been too risky. Or, at least, it had been deemed too risky by those around me. Those who worried I'd accidentally cause harm, even though there was usually enough warning time before a seizure to prevent that kind of thing.

Right now I wasn't scared of a seizure, but I *was* terrified I'd drop Juniper, so I quickly sat down. As soon as I did, she turned her dark-eyed attention on me, sizing me up like I was a buffet table at an all-you-can-eat restaurant. I was never so glad in my life to have worn my hair up in a messy bun.

She was heavier than she looked—and solid, too. She sat on my lap facing me, her legs stretched to span my waist. She gripped the top of my apron and tried to put it in her mouth, but it didn't have much give so she looked for something else to grab.

I glanced over at Maggie for help, but she was in the middle of taking Estrelle's order. I hadn't even heard the older woman come in, which was unusual because she clomped like a Clydesdale. As usual, she was dressed all in black—today it was a long-sleeve dress with a mock-turtleneck neckline and a lace hem. She wore her usual clunky heels and hat. Today, however, she'd accessorized with a necklace of large pearls—black, of course.

Maggie was saying something about the weather for the yard sale weekend, and Estrelle said, "A big storm's brewin'."

"No, don't say that," Maggie countered. "So much work has gone into the yard sale. I don't want to see it ruined by weather."

Juniper's silky hair was tied into the tiniest ponytail I'd ever seen. Her skin was rose-petal soft, and as usual she smelled of strawberries. She'd moved on from trying to eat my apron, turning her attention to my purple Magpie's T-shirt. She had it balled in her tiny fist and she was so determined to get it in her mouth that she leaned forward to meet her fist halfway. She bumped her head against my chest as she tried and tried again.

I laughed. "That can't possibly taste good."

She gurgled, leaving a wet spot on my shirt. When she gave me a drooly smile, she stole my heart.

I forgot about how scared I was to hold her. Somehow I'd been reassured by how her small body naturally molded to mine and by that all-encompassing trust in her eyes. She was a charmer and I'd been thoroughly charmed.

As she continued to gnaw on my shirt, I threw another look at Maggie. She was wiping down the espresso machine, deep worry lines creasing her forehead. I glanced around for Estrelle and found her sitting as primly as she could with curved shoulders at the table next to mine.

Amusement danced in her eyes as she openly watched me.

I frowned at her.

She made the squeaky noise that I was pretty sure was a laugh.

Maggie said, "Ava, I'm going to grab some more cups. Might take a hot minute. I think they're buried under the latest coffee delivery."

"All right." We didn't need more cups. There were plenty under the counter, so I knew she just needed some time to herself. It was probably best I waited on talking to her about what I'd overheard with Dez yesterday, especially in her current frame of mind.

Estrelle sipped her hot chocolate. "You're simply delaying the inevitable."

I wished she'd stay out of my mind. I used my best baby voice and said to Juniper, "Pay no attention to the spooky old woman, okay?"

In response, Juniper reached up and grabbed my lip, gripping it tightly.

Estrelle laughed again.

The door opened, and Gracie rushed inside. "Sorry about that."

I pried a tiny hand off my mouth. "Don't be. I enjoyed it."

She smiled. "Careful saying stuff like that or I'll be calling you to babysit in no time at all."

"Let me give you my number."

I stayed seated until Gracie effortlessly scooped Juniper up and wiggled her into the carrier. Suddenly, I wondered what would have happened if I'd stood up while holding Juniper and had another dizzy spell? I shouldn't have been so careless about holding something so precious. It was just . . . I sighed. I'd wanted to experience something I'd been denied for so long. I needed to get that checkup before Gracie took me up on my offer to babysit.

Gracie said, "You're a sweet one, Ava. Thank you so much for watching her for me."

"You're welcome so much. She's sweet as can be. Literally, I think. She smells like strawberries."

"Your sense of smell is amazing. That's her baby shampoo. It's strawberry scented."

I smiled. "Do they make an adult version? Because if so, I need it."

She laughed. "I'll check."

"Everything okay with Ben?"

"It is. He was offered some overtime and wanted to check with me about it. As much as we need the money, some things are more important. Aren't they, baby girl?" She kissed Juniper's head. "So he'll be coming home as planned." She wiggled into her backpack and headed for the door. "See you tomorrow at the yard sale."

As soon as she was outside, Estrelle said, "Lovely family."

I picked up my rag and started wiping tables again. "Seems to be an abundance of those around here."

"Yes, there is."

I glanced at her. She lifted an eyebrow, as if she knew what I was about to ask.

"Go on," she prompted.

I looked toward the front window. Unsurprisingly, the strange white-winged monarch hovered there. It was doing better flying these days, but it still had a bit of a wobble. "Is the butterfly that's following me around my grandmother?"

"No."

Well, there went that theory. Then I recalled how the butterfly had been in the attic when I found the spilled sea glass and smelled the seaweed. "Is it Maggie's mom?"

Her other eyebrow went up. "Most definitely not."

I sighed. "Is it . . ." I was having trouble finding the word I was looking for. Finally, I said, "It's *something*, right?"

"Indeed."

"You could be more helpful."

"I'm old. This is how I amuse myself."

I rolled my eyes. And because I was still thinking of the sea glass and seaweed scent, I said, "Do you believe in ghosts, Estrelle?"

"Do you, Ava?"

I thought long and hard on how to answer. "I believe in *something*."

Her silvery eyes glinted behind her veil. "As do I."

I glanced toward the storage area, where Maggie still hid. "She's going to take the news about Dez badly, isn't she?"

"You cannot stop the storm, Ava, but know the sun will shine again."

I winced, but when the door opened and someone I didn't recognize came inside, I forced a smile. "Welcome to Magpie's," I said, feeling like I'd been saying it my whole life long.

A half hour later, Maggie still hadn't emerged from the storeroom, Estrelle was on her second hot chocolate, and Sam had just passed by the front window. I'd been handling customers on my own and wasn't the least stressed by the responsibility. I barely recognized myself these days.

This suntanned, ghost-talking, fire-stopping, friend-making person. I'd taken charge of my health, was becoming more outgoing, and wasn't the least bit scared of the steam wand anymore.

Yet, at the same time, I didn't really feel like I'd changed that much. I was still *me*. I was just . . . spreading my wings.

As Sam came inside, I heard a soft *quabark* and said to him, "I really need to talk Maggie into letting pets in here."

"I think that's more a health department thing," he said.

"I'm sure they won't mind."

He laughed and ordered an iced caramel latte and a whippy cup. "Thanks again for taking care of Norman yesterday."

I started the espresso brewing. "Anytime. I love him."

He smiled. "I didn't think I was going to get him to come home."

"Molly's still mad he didn't stay." She'd been pouting under the bed when I left this morning.

"I think we can arrange a playdate."

I smiled as I pumped caramel into the cup. "I think she'd like that."

"Norman too."

I glanced up, met his gaze, and then we both looked away at the same time.

And I couldn't help thinking that maybe, just maybe, Juniper wasn't the only one stealing my heart around here.

"Oh," he said after an awkward pause, "I stopped to get a scratch ticket on my way back last night."

I picked up the milk jug. "How'd we do?"

Before he could say anything, the door swung open and Hannah ran inside in a flurry of blue tulle and flashing pink lights, saying, "Miz Ava! Miz Ava! Is Junebear ready?"

"Land sakes, child," Jolly said, laughing. "Say hello first. Wait your turn."

Hannah glanced up at her grandmother, then at me. "Hi, Miz Ava!"

"Good morning, Hannah, Jolly. Junebear is keeping me company back here, but she can't wait to go home with you. Just give me a second, okay?"

Excitement filled every inch of Hannah's face, which in turn filled my heart right to its tippy-top.

"Okay!" She bounced up and down, lights flashing.

I quickly finished Sam's drink and filled a dish with whipped cream. It seemed he swiped his credit card quicker than normal. Apparently neither of us wanted Hannah to wait a second longer than necessary to be reunited with her beloved bear.

As soon as the transaction was done, he walked over to look

at the recipe on the chalkboard, and I bent low to grab the package I'd put the finishing touches on last night. I cradled it carefully as I walked around the counter. "Here she is, Hannah."

I passed over the drawstring bag I'd sewed out of the pillowcase I'd found in the carpetbag. It was printed with ballerina bears wearing pink tutus. For the drawstring, I'd used purple ribbon.

"Oh, Ava, even the bag is adorable," Jolly said as Hannah plopped herself down on the floor and wrenched open the sack.

She reached inside and lifted Junebear out, and I held my breath, waiting for her reaction. She stared at the bear, then ran a hand over her head and back and then suddenly hugged the bear so tight I thought the stuffing might pop out.

"I missed you so much," she whispered.

Jolly crouched down. "Can I see her?"

Hannah held the bear out but didn't hand her over.

I watched as Jolly took in every inch of the bear, from the ear patches, the blue stitches, the rainbow embroidered on her back, the sea-glass nose, and the heart patch I'd carefully sewn on the front of the bear. There were tears in her eyes when she looked up at me, and it was all I could do to keep from crying myself.

Her voice was raw with emotion when she said, "What do you say to Miss Ava, Hannah?"

Hannah jumped to her feet, and before her shoes could even flash, she had wrapped her arms—Junebear still in one of them—around my legs. "Thank you, Miz Ava."

I rested my hands on her back, felt her delicate shoulder blades, and gave her a gentle pat while praying that her surgery would be nothing but a resounding success. "You're welcome, Hannah. Can you bring her by for a visit soon? I've grown quite fond of her."

"I will." She beamed up at me, then finally let go of my legs. "I promise!"

"I promise, too." Jolly gave me a hug as well.

I glanced over her shoulder, seeking Estrelle, but at some point she'd slipped out as quietly as she'd come in.

A few minutes later, Jolly and Hannah headed out, full of promises to keep me updated on the surgery. I watched them go, and through the closed door, I heard Hannah telling Norman that Junebear was all better. Norman *quabark*ed and I swore I heard happiness in the sound.

Sam stepped up next to me, and I wasn't sure why he'd waited around until I recalled he hadn't had a chance to tell me how we'd done on the latest scratch ticket before Jolly and Hannah had come in.

"So, did we win big with the scratch-off?" I asked.

There was a softness in his eyes I'd never seen before. "Unfortunately no, but we didn't lose any, either. We broke even."

I tipped my head side to side. "All right. I can deal with that."

He held up two twenty-dollar bills. "So the question now is . . ."

I smiled. "Oh, definitely let it ride."

He laughed. "Let it ride it is, then."

Since the shop was currently empty, I said, "I'm just going to say hi to Norman right quick before I get back to work."

"Right quick?"

I laughed. "All y'all are rubbing off on me."

He laughed and held the door open. Norman wiggled and waggled and whined happily when he saw me. I bent down and gave him a hug and pats.

"Hey, Ava?" The ice cubes in Sam's cup rattled as he swirled the liquid around.

"Hmm?"

"The heart shape you sewed on the front of the bear . . ."

A lump rose to my throat.

"It looked an awful lot like purple tweed to me." He paused, then added softly, "Did you use your lucky blazer to make that patch?"

I glanced up at him. He was a little out of focus because my eyes were swimming in tears as I thought about a little girl in a large hospital undergoing big, scary surgery. "I just wanted to make sure she had all the luck in the world with her tomorrow."

MAGGIE

I'd needed a minute.

Out of sight of everyone to just sit with my feelings.

I'd gone into the storeroom, closed the door, then slid down it to sit on the floor. I was quite sure Ava understood perfectly.

As I wrestled with my emotions, I propped my arms on my knees, then dropped my head on my arms. Maybe keeping the coffee shop wasn't meant to be. It was Mama's, after all, and never meant to be mine. Maybe Daddy had been right. Maybe it was time to let go.

Maybe, maybe, maybe.

I wrapped my arms tightly around my legs. This place had been Mama's dream. What would my dream have been if I hadn't always had the coffee shop in my life?

I racked my brain. I had my curiosities, of course, and while they gave me purpose and joy, they weren't a way to make a living. I didn't have my dad's passion for vintage or quirky finds. I only bought what literally moved me, giving me that little shove. I liked crafting. Could I make a living selling custom T-shirts and the like? I winced. That didn't feel right, either.

The only thing that felt right was doing exactly what I'd been doing.

Running Magpie's.

How was I ever going to let it go?

And how would I ever get over letting everyone down? Everyone who loved this place as much as I did. Especially Rose. And all my regulars. And even Ava, who seemed happy working here.

I wiped my eyes, sniffled.

Directly in front of me sat the bins and box my father and Ava had brought over the other day. On the bin nearest to me, I suddenly noticed a label I hadn't seen before. It simply read PENNY.

My mama.

Curious, I scooted over to the plastic tub and pried off the top. Oddly, it held only one item.

A plain black sketchbook, its cover frayed along the edges.

I took it out and carefully opened it. The first page was full of doodles: swirls and swashes and flowers and vines surrounding the words *Penny's Whims.*

My breath caught. This book had belonged to my mother. Why hadn't I ever seen it before? How had it survived the hurricane damage? Where had it been all these years?

I turned the pages. There were more doodles, a sketch—quite a good one—of a pier. One page had a scribbled grocery list—*eggs, milk, bread.* There was a page of baby names, both boys' and girls', and I smiled at the fact that neither Magdalena nor Maggie was on it. According to family lore, my name had been a source of contention between my parents. My father had his heart set on naming me Maggie Mae, after the Beatles' take on an old Liverpool folk song. My mama flat-out refused on account of the song being, in her words, *unseemly.* So they'd compromised somewhat.

Toward the middle of the sketchbook, the magpie logo first appeared, a simple line drawing. With each subsequent page, the drawings evolved, with more details added. The word *Magpie's* was written out many times in different fonts. The pink barrette soon appeared.

Quite a few pages held sketches of shop fronts. Wide windows, uneven bricks, frilly awnings. One shop was a pet shop. There was a candle store, a quilt shop, a bookshop, a bakery, a gift store, a coffeehouse, a pizza place, and a card shop. Each rendering took up two pages and included a floorplan and a short pro-and-con list.

I smiled at the list for the pizza place—pro: pizza; con: smell like pizza all day. The card shop's pro was that everyone needed cards. The con: bo-ring. For the coffeehouse, the pro was that it didn't need a lot of remodeling (which had three checkmarks next to it). The con: dislike coffee. The pages after that were blank. Her decision had been made. A low budget won out over all else.

I closed the book and hugged it to my chest, thinking about what I'd just seen, processing it.

All along, I thought Magpie's had been my mother's lifelong dream.

But it hadn't been.

It had been a means to an end.

A way for her to get the community engagement she longed for without a big financial commitment.

My father's answer about why he was selling the coffee shop rang through my head.

It might be time to let go.

I thought letting the shop go would feel like my mama disappearing all over again. But as I sat here, I realized I'd been afraid to let it go because it would be like losing *myself.*

Yes, this had once been my mama's coffee shop.

But it was my heart, my soul, my love for *both* my parents that was in this shop now.

Holding on is all well and good, as long as you're holding on for the right reasons. But, Maggie, you're only holding on because you're too scared to let go.

I wasn't scared anymore.

And I certainly wasn't going to let fear decide my fate.

I would find a way to buy this shop. Beg, borrow, steal if I had to.

Because Magpie's was *mine.*

CHAPTER 23

AVA

Summer was quickly coming to an end, but it wasn't going out without one last hot, humid hurrah. The first day of the yard sale had arrived with temperatures in the nineties and high humidity. The dew point was just plain cruel.

"What is this thing?" Sam asked.

The tarnished silver object looked like a cross between a scrub brush and a Slinky. "I have no idea."

"Huh." He put it down on one of the many folding tables Dez and I had set up this morning.

Norman slept under the table, in the direct path of the box fan I'd plugged in to try to beat the heat as I manned the cash box. The fan was a little like snow flurries in an inferno, but I'd take all the cool relief I could get at the moment.

There were only fifteen minutes left before we wrapped up for the day, and so far the community-wide yard sale was proving to be a big success. This morning, Dez's items had spilled across his driveway, the carport, porch, side yard, and the street—he'd even borrowed Sam's driveway as well. Now, most of that inventory had been sold.

But he still had more items in his storage units that he intended to sell tomorrow and Sunday.

"I'm spreading the love," he'd told me when I questioned why he wouldn't just sell it all in one day.

He was currently laughing it up near the pink pylons with a young couple who were bartering for a steamer trunk. Dez was in his element, wheeling and dealing. With his big personality, he was a natural-born salesman.

With seemingly endless energy, he hadn't slowed down at all

during the day, bouncing around like an excited child who'd eaten too much sugar. His face glowed with vitality, his skin glistening from the heat.

He looked perfectly healthy.

Normal, even.

Except he talked to ghosts.

Or, at least, one ghost.

I still hadn't spoken to Maggie about the conversation I'd overheard. With her mood, the timing hadn't been right. But I would soon.

Sam's gaze swept over me and twin worry lines creased the skin between his eyebrows. "How about I get you some water?"

I wasn't sure what he'd seen that prompted the offer, but I could imagine. My shirt stuck to my back. My skin felt like it was on fire, and I was in the *shade*. I held up my refillable, insulated bottle. "It's still half full from the last time you filled it up."

He tipped his head. "Something to eat, then?"

"I'm okay. I'm just tired and stressed about Hannah's surgery since I haven't heard from Jolly yet." I took a sip of water. "Have you seen Maggie today by any chance?"

"No. I skipped the coffee shop this morning to help Dez. Why?"

"I'm worried about her, too. She's been so anxious lately."

The couple who'd been bartering with Dez came over to my table to pay for the steamer trunk. When they asked for Sam's assistance in getting the trunk into their car, parked at the end of the street, he sprang into action without hesitation.

I knew he was worried about me. Dez, too. And Maggie. I hated that they worried—I had come here for normalcy, not to focus on any kind of disorder or illness, but here I was again, my health at the forefront of my life. It was probably time to come to terms with the fact that I'd never be normal.

And maybe that was okay. After all, I'd heard normal was tedious and dreary.

I was simply Ava. I had an extraordinary sense of hearing and smell and lived with a seizure disorder. I loved animals, the beach, moonlight, and the scent of strawberries. I loved to sew, read, and watch old movies. I loved this little town and the people in it.

My gaze drifted to Sam.

Some more than others.

I took another sip of water, suddenly feeling a little better. The day, health-wise, had started off so well. I'd been full of energy when I woke up early to help Dez set up. Then I'd walked around the neighborhood some, looking at everyone else's sales. I'd even bought a few things. Some fabric and notions, sea glass and buttons, a jewelry-making kit and a box of charms. And, of course, I bought one of Sienna's Mississippi mud brownies—which looked like heaven all wrapped up in a crinkly cellophane bag—even though she tried to give it to me. I hadn't eaten the brownie yet, though, unable to scare up any kind of appetite.

Then I'd grown tired, my limbs heavy, and Dez assigned me check-out duties.

So, here I sat in a folding chair in the carport, watching the clock. As soon as the church bell chimed two o'clock, I was going to help Dez clean up, then go inside to take a shower and a long nap.

Tomorrow, Dez would be here on his own, because I would be working at the coffee shop. But I honestly didn't think he needed any help.

Not with the yard sale.

Not with life.

Why had he hired me?

Yes, his house was a mess, but a cleaning service could've sorted that out once his collection of whims had been relocated. I'd made him only three meals since I'd been living with him. He wasn't a big breakfast eater, and he was often out for lunch and dinner.

I'd seen no sign of mental impairment, either, other than a few memory blips and the ghost thing, which who was to say he just wasn't talking aloud to a loved one who'd passed on? I'd done that myself with Bunny—and with Penny only a few days ago. I didn't really see anything *wrong* with it, other than

Dez's *we'll be together again soon* comment. That part was worrisome. Quite worrisome.

My gaze went back to Dez, to his big smile. His voice carried easily, rising above the sound of the waves in the background, as he talked to a woman about a cactus statue. He'd found it at a flea market in Texas and had to rent a U-Haul to drive it home because he couldn't leave without it.

Yet, he was selling it.

Selling most everything.

Suddenly this yard sale felt like an estate sale.

And selling Magpie's felt like he was getting his estate in order.

My stomach churned at the thoughts. Norman *quabark*ed as if sensing my discomfort and I reached down and patted his head.

The next half hour passed in a blur. Apparently the two o'clock end time for the sale had been merely a suggestion. Dez turned no latecomer away. We were collecting all the unsold items and corralling them in the carport when my cell phone rang. It was an Alabama number and I quickly answered. "Hello?"

"Ava, it's Jolly, honey."

A pit opened in my stomach, and I found myself perched on the edge of it, trying to keep my balance. "Jolly, oh, it's good to hear from you."

Sam looked up, and I pointed to the side yard, indicating that I was going that way, to get out of the wind—Dez had an outdoor shower with a slatted wall that would provide some cover.

"How's Hannah?" I asked.

"She's out of surgery and they're waking her up slowly. Samples were sent to the lab and we don't have them back yet, but the doctor is even more convinced now the tumor is benign. We'll know for sure tonight, tomorrow morning at the latest. I just wanted you to know that Hannah proudly showed Junebear to everyone who walked in her room. The doctor even made a little surgery cap for the bear. You gave Hannah something none of us could, and we all love you for it. Thank you."

Tears filled my eyes. "Let me know if there's anything else I can do. Anything. And please text or call and let me know when you hear for sure about those samples."

"I will, darlin'."

I hung up and hugged the phone to my chest and let out a deep breath.

I was still standing there, in the shadows of the shower, when I heard a high-pitched honk, sharp and staccato. Frowning, I looked up. I knew that noise. Had heard it coming from the attic when Dez first showed me around the house.

He had told me the noise was from a ghost.

I went on high alert, trying to focus my hearing to listen to what was going on above me.

"What are you doing here? You shouldn't be here," I heard Dez whisper in that maudlin tone of voice he'd used the last time I'd heard him talking to his "little ghost."

My heart hurt. And I knew I should walk away—it wasn't right to eavesdrop—but I couldn't quite bring myself to. Not after his *be together again soon* talk and suspecting this had been an estate sale.

I feared for him, his life. Was he considering doing something drastic?

Above me, on the back deck, Dez said, "Everything is going exactly according to plan."

My heart beat faster. Plan? What plan?

There was another strange honk, then I heard someone say, "I've missed you. I thought in the chaos of the sale, it wouldn't seem out of place for me to be seen here. It's been incredibly difficult to keep my distance."

My jaw dropped. The voice was *Carmella's*. I'd spoken to her a couple of times and would know her rich, silky sound anywhere.

"It won't be long now that we can be together all the time," Dez said. "No more hiding."

There was another high-pitched honk.

I realized it was a *sneeze*.

"Dez, you need to talk to Maggie before someone figures out

our secret. Ava's sharp. She's not going to buy your silly ghost story for much longer."

As they spoke, my head spun with what I was hearing and what I'd already known. Dez had first mentioned the ghost a couple of months ago, after he started neglecting his house. Now I realized the *ghost* was his way of hiding the fact that he wasn't spending much time at home.

"She almost caught us once already. Hiding in your attic is not something I want to do again."

So it had been Carmella in the attic the day I'd come by early, the day Dez gave me a tour. There must have been no way for her to get out without me seeing her. No wonder he had rushed me off to his storage units. And the day I'd come back from the trail? No doubt he'd been talking to her as well, probably using earbuds.

"*Silly*? I think not. I have half the town thinking this place is haunted." Pride flowed from Dez's words.

As I stood there eavesdropping, I wasn't sure if I was mad at him for keeping secrets from Maggie or impressed with his quick thinking. But how had I not put this together sooner? Why had I accepted the ghost explanation? Started to *believe* it, even?

But I knew why. The letter. The butterfly. The seaweed scent.

Sarcasm dripped as Carmella said, "That'll be great when we put the place on the market, by the way. Haunted houses sell so well."

He laughed low. "I have no worries about that. This place will sell lickety-split."

I could barely process what I was hearing—it was coming at me so fast. Dez's other behaviors that Maggie had been worrying about made sense now. Sneaking around. Losing weight. Not wearing his wedding ring. He was hiding a new relationship.

I'd been concerned by this yard sale, of him liquidating his belongings, thinking that he was planning his own death, but it had only been about downsizing, plain and simple.

He was moving in with Carmella—or perhaps they were getting a place together. Either way, this house wasn't going to be his much longer.

"You should've told Maggie already," Carmella said. "She's been worried for nothing. She went so far as to find help for you when you don't even need it. What's Ava going to do when the truth comes out? You're being unfair to her as well."

My chest ached. If this house wasn't going to be Dez's much longer, it wouldn't be mine, either.

Dez let out a sigh. "I'm working on a plan."

"No, no more plans. No more schemes. No more ghosts, for heaven's sake. You need to talk to Maggie, then Ava. Once this is all out in the open, then we can figure out the best course of action. All these secrets are only hurting people."

"I know." He sounded properly chastised. "And I will."

"When?"

"Soon."

"I've heard that before, Dez." Exasperation punctuated Carmella's sentence loud and clear.

"I need to tread carefully. You know how Maggie feels about Penny."

"I also know how she feels about *you*. She wants you to be happy. And you are happy, aren't you?"

"Of course, my little ghost."

I could practically hear her eye roll as she said, "Please stop calling me that."

He chuckled. "Of course, my *love*."

"That's *much* better."

There were some kissy noises, and I actually slapped my hands over my ears so I didn't have to hear them.

I needed to talk to Maggie. Now. Right now.

"Ava?"

I jumped a mile high at the sound of Sam's voice. Grabbing my heart, I said, "Sam!"

The noises above us quieted.

"Are you okay?" he asked.

"Um, actually, I need to go. Can you help Dez finish cleaning up?"

Confusion swept across his face. "Sure."

"Thank you." Impulsively, I leaned up and kissed his cheek. "I won't be long."

Norman *quabark*ed as I darted around him and headed for the square as fast as I dared in this heat. It took me nearly ten minutes to get to the coffee shop, and I knew to go to the back door and knock, since it was after two o'clock.

A second later the door opened and Maggie's eyes widened in surprise at seeing me. I said, "Can I talk to you a minute?"

"What's wrong? Get in here, sit down. I'll get you some water."

I was wobbly as I followed her into the front of the shop. Only half the chairs had been put up on the tables, so I sat down in one that was still on the floor and wiped my brow.

All the way here, I'd debated how to tell Maggie what I'd seen, what I'd overheard.

Maggie set a cup of ice water in front of me. "My goodness, what's happened? Do I need to call a doctor?"

"No, I just need a second. I wore myself out running over here. I don't know if I'll ever get used to this kind of humidity."

"You won't, trust me on that. But take as much time as you want. The longer I can put off mopping the better."

I smiled at that and my gaze fell on the Curiosity Corner. I bought some time by saying, "Jolly called with hopeful news." I quickly filled her in on what she'd told me. "Hannah might not have had the comfort of Junebear if you never gave me that thimble and Estrelle didn't give me those carpetbags. I might never have rediscovered my love for sewing. I just wanted you to know how thankful I am."

She smiled, big and bright. "I can't tell you the kind of happiness hearing that brings me. It is strange, though. The thimble is the only curiosity I don't remember collecting. I'm glad it found its proper home, though."

My chest was still aching, so full of uncertainties. What to say to her, my health, where would I go now that I knew Dez was moving?

In such a short time, I'd come to love Driftwood. I was no longer a stranger in this charming land. I adored the people that lived here. The coffee shop felt like a second home, and the people who frequented this shop had come to feel like family. It was a strange family, to be sure, but it was a happy one. I didn't think I could leave this place, this coffee shop of curiosities.

It was all something to think about later on. Right now, I had to focus on Maggie.

I took a sip of water, then said, "There's something I need to tell you."

"Oh my god, you're dying."

I nearly choked on the water I'd just swallowed. "What? No."

She slumped back in her chair, collapsing in on herself. "Thank goodness! You had me worried there with your heartfelt thank-you and your health hasn't been great lately . . ."

"I'm here about Dez."

Her eyebrows went up, and her eyes rounded. "What did you find out? Tell me everything."

I shook my head. "It really needs to come from him. Just push him. Tell him I overheard him talking to—" I didn't want to rat Carmella out. "His little ghost."

Maggie tensed. "Ava, no. You have to tell me. I've been worried sick for months."

I had to trust my instincts that I was doing the right thing by sharing what was going on with him—at least part of it. "You need to talk to Dez for the whole story," I said, "but I will tell you there's no ghost and he's not sick."

"Then what in the world is going on with him?"

"He's a man in love."

CHAPTER 24

MAGGIE

Love.

My father was in love.

I looked at Ava, at her pale, gaunt face, her big mossy worried eyes. "With who?" But as soon as I asked, I knew. I *knew*. "It's Carmella, isn't it?"

I pictured the softness in her eyes when she talked about Dad. The smile when she shared his antics.

Ava said only, "You really need to talk with your father."

Why hadn't he told me? Why, when he knew I was worried about his health, mental and physical, had he let this charade go on? Why?

"Are you okay?" Ava asked. "I'm worried about you. Your blood pressure . . ."

It felt like there was a weight sitting on my chest. I couldn't take a full breath. I couldn't think. I needed air. Jumping up, I looked about wildly. "Can you finish closing up for me? I need— I need to go."

"Definitely."

I gave her a nod and headed for the back door. I needed to talk to my dad. Or Carmella. Or Noah.

No.

I needed my mama.

AVA

It had been nearly two hours since I talked with Maggie, and I was beginning to regret saying anything to her at all.

After she ran out of the coffee shop, I fully believed that she'd gone straight to see Dez. But by the time I got back to his place, it was clear she hadn't been there. He had been sitting at the kitchen table working on his laptop, full of chitchat about the yard sale and acting like nothing out of the ordinary had happened.

I kept waiting for Maggie to show up. I paced, I cleaned, I tried to work on my new sewing projects, but I couldn't focus. Even Molly sensed my unease, and graciously head-bumped my leg on her way to the stove to hop into her stockpot.

I kept calling Maggie's phone, but the calls went straight to voice mail. The coffee shop's line kept ringing.

I debated whether to continue to wait or go look for her.

Then the image of me tucked into bed, ignoring Alexander's knock on my door, popped into my head, and I knew I had to do *something*. What if the stress of this week had been too much for Maggie's body to handle? What if she was out there somewhere needing help and I was just sitting here, waiting? Which somehow felt a lot like I was hiding out in my comfort zone.

Full of resolve, I ran downstairs and yelled to Dez that I'd be back soon.

In a flash, I was out the front door. From one of the bays under the house, I grabbed the lime-green bike to take a quick ride to Maggie's house. I was low on energy but adrenaline helped pedal the two blocks to her little cottage.

Since I considered breaking and entering to be the lesser of my evils today, I went inside the house through the unlocked front door and took a look around. Mac and Cheese watched me accusingly from their fishbowl as I darted from room to room.

Maggie wasn't home.

When I walked back outside, Donovan was coming up the walkway. As soon as I saw him, tears welled.

In my mind, I kept picturing Maggie crumpled up somewhere, in dire need of medical help. Rationally, I knew this situation wasn't even close to what had happened to Alexander, but I was worried sick. I felt helpless.

Alarm flared in his eyes. "Hey now, what's wrong?"

"Everything." My voice shook. "Can you help me look for Maggie? She was upset earlier. I want to make sure she's okay."

"Why's she upset?"

I swallowed hard, not even caring anymore who knew. "I told her that Dez has been acting a fool lately because he's in love. For some reason he was keeping a relationship with Carmella a secret. Maggie was pale and shaky when she left the coffee shop after I told her."

His face turned stony and determined. "How long has she been gone?"

"Since just before three."

He looked at his watch, winced, then pulled out his phone. "I know a few of her favorite places. I'll give you my number, and you give me yours. Does Dez know what's going on?"

I shook my head.

"Best you tell him. I'll check the coffee shop first, then head toward the beach."

We split up, and I pedaled back to Dez's house.

He looked up as I walked in. "There you are, Sprite! I wondered where you'd gotten off to."

Standing as tall as I could, I said, "I've been looking for Maggie. Long story short, she knows you've been keeping a secret about your love life and she's upset."

Swearing under his breath, he dragged a hand down his face, then his fingers wrapped around the pendant at his neck. The penny.

He hurried to the front door. "Where've you looked?"

I was hot on his heels, filling him in.

He said, "I'll go see if she's at Carmella's. Call me if you hear anything."

I nodded and followed him down to the carport. He got into his truck and drove off.

I stood there watching him go, unsure what to do now.

I heard a *quabark* and a leash-free Norman came charging at me. I bent down and opened my arms, ready for any affection

I could get out of the loveable dog. But he ran right past me, zipping down the boardwalk.

"Norman!" Sam shouted, nearly falling down his front stairs. "Norman, come!"

I ran after the little dog and Sam quickly caught up, a leash in hand. "He's never done this before. As soon as I opened the door, he took off. Norman!"

At the end of the boardwalk, Sam searched the sand for footprints, but there were none. Norman must have cut through the dunes.

Sam squinted left, then right. "We don't even know which way he went."

"He's that way." I pointed west.

"How do you know?"

"I hear him barking." I tugged his sleeve.

"Wait. You can hear him?"

"Yes, come on!"

We hurried as fast as we could through the shifting sand. Every once in a while, I'd stop, catch my breath, and listen. Then I'd motion Sam onward. We were going in the right direction. About a half mile up the beach, Norman's barks grew louder. "He's close."

"Lead on," Sam said, a strange look in his eyes.

Soon, doggy footprints appeared in front of us, coming out of the scrub and cutting across the beach, through the sand toward the wooden entrance ramp of an old fishing pier. Barely discernable was the figure of a woman sitting at the end of the platform, her legs swinging as they dangled over the water.

I nearly cried from relief. Maggie was okay.

Norman stood on the beach, his whole body vibrating as he *quabark*ed in Maggie's direction. I sank down in the sand next to him and gave him a hug. "Good boy, Norman!" I kissed his head. "I don't know how you knew she was lost, but you did such an amazing job of finding her."

"Wait, what?" Sam said. "Find who?"

I motioned with my chin toward the end of the pier. "Maggie. I've been looking for her. Earlier, she took off, upset, and I couldn't stop thinking about worst-case scenarios."

Sam's eyes widened.

"It's kind of my fault she's distraught. I told her something I probably should've kept to myself."

"Ava, knowing you the way I do, I can't imagine you meant to hurt her."

I shook my head. "Never. I just thought . . . I thought she had the right to know the truth. But I think I was wrong. Maybe the truth isn't always meant to be known."

"The truth is never wrong. Hard, yes. Wrong, no."

"I need to let Donovan and Dez know—they're out looking for her as well." I pulled my phone out of my pocket just as Donovan came rushing out of the woods, following a sandy path that had branched off one of the nature trails. He was drenched in sweat and had an anxious look in his eyes as he scanned our faces.

Norman barked at him, too, but the sound didn't hold any urgency. It was more of a welcome-to-our-party greeting. The little dog was enjoying himself.

I pointed toward Maggie, who was looking out at the gulf and hadn't noticed us yet.

Donovan bent double and sucked in a breath. I heard him quietly say, "Thank god," before he straightened. "Can I have a minute alone with her?"

I nodded. "Give her a hug for me and tell her I'm sorry."

I wiped tears from my eyes as I tried to text Dez. I kept hitting the wrong buttons.

"Why don't you let me do that?" Sam sat down next to me.

I handed him my phone as Norman climbed in my lap, licked my chin. I put my arms around the little guy, rested my cheek on his head. "Thank you, Norman."

"Dez is on his way." Sam handed my phone back to me.

I gave him a sad smile and kept wiping the tears as they refilled.

"It'll be okay, Ava."

I wished I believed that, but I didn't. This suddenly felt like an ending, and I didn't know how I was possibly going to be able to say goodbye.

I drew in a shuddery breath, feeling shaky and weak. I'd pushed myself beyond my limits today, and I was paying for it.

Sam clipped the leash on Norman, then dropped his forearms on top of his knees. "I meant what I said earlier, about truth always being a good thing, even when it's hard. I suppose I ought to practice what I preach."

I glanced at him, my heart in my eyes, because I knew, I *knew*, he was only trying to distract me from my pain.

"I know you've been curious about me," he said. "My secret life. Well, I'm a songwriter. Started writing when I was in high school and had my first heartbreak. Sang the song at a school talent show and caught the eye of the prettiest girl around. Eventually, we fell in love, got married, and moved to a suburb of Nashville, looking to make it big."

As he spoke, he faced the water, not me. I patted Norman's head and listened.

"Took a few years of barely scraping by but I finally got a break. Then another. And another. Signed a nice publishing deal under the name Sam Finch, which is my middle name. Quite a few of my songs were hits. My songwriting demos started making waves and one thing led to another and I found myself touring as a warm-up act. After a while, I was doing gigs on my own, but I wasn't happy. I loved the music but not the fame and all that came with it. The touring, especially, was brutal. The constant promotion was too much. I wanted quiet. Peace. I wanted a small house and a big family and beach lullabies."

I ran a hand down Norman's back. "That sounds pretty good to me, too."

He faced me, and I saw great big melancholy in his eyes. "It turns out it was the opposite of what my wife wanted. She loved the fame. The parties. The social climbing. I tried—I really tried to make it work, but the longer I was on the road, the more my creativity suffered. I stopped hearing the songs. I stopped hearing the music. I stopped being me."

The heartbreak in his voice made my eyes fill with tears once again. "I'm so sorry."

"We'd been divorced for a year when she and her new boy-friend, a big-name singer, went to some fancy party where she partied a little too hard. She went home that night and collapsed. Norman was there with her. And he barked and barked and barked all night. Finally someone called the building manager, who did a well check and found her body. She'd been gone for a while at that point. Norman had barked so hard that night that he damaged his vocal cords and lost his voice, so to speak. He hasn't barked with noise since. Only air comes out when he tries."

"No." I shook my head. "He has the sweetest bark. I call it a *quabark*. It's a mix between a quack and a bark."

Sam shook his head. "No sound comes out when he barks."

As I let that sink in, Norman wagged his tail at me, and I took his face in my hands and booped his long nose with mine.

I blinked away tears and said, "He does make sound, but there's a chance only I can hear him. I've had epilepsy since I was four years old. When I was nine, I had a particularly bad seizure. It's what the medical world used to call a grand mal seizure. It almost killed me. When I came out of it, I was in the hospital, and I could hear things others couldn't. A heartbeat from across the room. A conversation down the hall. And my sense of smell was heightened as well. The doctors ran many tests, but no one could tell me why it happened or if my senses would ever return to normal."

The monarch with the odd coloring fluttered past us. Its fourth wing had started to turn white. Its flight pattern was smooth, even, as it glided through the air.

What did the changing wings mean?

Sam took hold of my hand, held it tightly. His skin was warm, his fingers callused. "Epilepsy? Why didn't you tell me, Ava? Or anyone? Is that what's been going on with you recently?"

I dug my heels into the sand. "I'm not sure what's going on. I haven't had any seizures here—I haven't had any in years, actually. The doctors call it early remission. But having said that, I don't feel well. I have a doctor's appointment for next week. If the epilepsy has reemerged, the sooner I restart medicine, the better."

"But why didn't you say anything after you nearly fainted?"

I shrugged. "I wanted to be normal. I spent most of my life being babied and secluded and left out because of my health issues. Here, I wanted to know what it was like just to *live,* to be free." I half laughed, half scoffed. "That didn't quite go as planned. People are concerned about me here, too. I see it in their eyes. I see it in yours."

"It's only because we care about you. As for being normal, no you're not. You're anything but normal, and that's a good thing. You're—"

"Don't you dare say *special.*"

Different, I could accept. Special, though, still grated.

He laughed. "You're *amazing.* Kind. Compassionate. Caring. Your smile lights up a room. The joy you feel at living life shines in your eyes. Your medical condition doesn't define you. It's just a small piece of the greater whole."

I held his gaze, wanting to say so much but unable to find just the right words.

"It's because of you," he said, "that I can hear music again. The first day we met, when you offered me the butterfly? I heard a melody. You woke up *my* senses. You've made me realize that I wasn't doing myself any favors by hiding myself away."

There were tears in his eyes. Mine, too.

"Life's short, Ava. So short. I don't want to waste any more time being unhappy. I want—"

He broke off at the sound of huffing and puffing. I glanced over my shoulder and saw Dez jogging barefoot down the beach. Norman let out a short bark as Dez approached.

"It really is the most darling sound." I tried to copy it but failed miserably. At my attempt, Norman barked harder, as if he was insulted.

Dez wheezed as he reached us. "Did she already leave?"

His face was flushed, and if I didn't know he was a healthy man, I'd be worried. Sam and I pointed toward the pier. Maggie and Donovan were still deep in conversation.

Dez said, "Thanks," and headed that way.

"Can you hear what Maggie and Donovan are talking about?" he asked.

"I could if I focused, but I've done enough butting in today."

"It can't be all that bad."

I smiled sadly. "It feels like it is."

Sam stood and held out a hand to help me up. I nudged Norman off my lap, and his tail wagged excitedly.

"How about we head back?" he suggested. "It's been a long day and Maggie's in good hands."

Part of me wanted to stay, to explain myself, to give her a hug, but it might be best to let things settle down. It would also give me time to pack up before Dez got back, because one thing I knew for sure—I wouldn't be comfortable staying in his house any longer.

CHAPTER 25

MAGGIE

The clear blue-green water below me rippled and rolled but was relatively calm. A pair of dolphins played in the distance, and a squadron of manta rays was swimming around the pilings, lingering as if they were keeping me company.

This spot had always been one of my favorite places. It was where I felt closest to my mama, almost as if she were here with me.

Many times I've sat here and thought about her, wondering what she'd look like now. Would she have aged gracefully or fought it tooth and nail? Would she still love skydiving? Hate ketchup? Like roller skating? Be cranky that Mr. Floyd kept the milk at the far side of his market and not up close to the front doors? Would she still drop everything to watch a sunset? Or play in the mud?

I had often wondered what she'd think about my latest haircut. Or my grades in school. Or why I had to keep Noah. Or why I'd pushed Donovan away.

Why I seemed to keep pushing him away.

Sometimes I sat here wondering what *my* life would've looked like if she hadn't been swept off by destiny. Would my personality be the same? Would I have made other life choices? Would I be a completely different person?

The answer to those questions was always yes.

Losing my mama had completely reshaped my thinking, my life, *me*.

I didn't know how she would feel about that. Would she understand how profoundly I'd been affected? Or would she wag a chastising finger at me, because I'd allowed her absence to change me, my destiny, my future?

So lost in my thoughts, I startled when I heard a voice behind me.

"I should've known to check here for you first. May I?" Donovan asked, motioning to the space next to me.

I nodded. "You were looking for me?"

He sat down, his feet dangling the same as mine. He put his hands behind him and leaned back. "Ava got worried when you didn't show up at Dez's. She wanted to make sure you were okay. Are you? Okay?" He peered at me, studying my facial features. When I'd had the mini-stroke months ago, the left side of my face had drooped for a good half hour.

"I'm okay." Since I'd been sitting here watching the manta rays, my head had barely ached. My heart, however, was another matter. "I didn't mean to worry anyone. I just needed . . ."

"Your mama. I know. You always used to come out here to talk to her when your emotions were running high, happy or sad."

He knew me well. Better than I thought.

"Ava actually found you first, before I did." He motioned with his chin toward the beach.

Ava, Sam, and Norman sat in the sand. Ava kept wiping her eyes, like she was crying, and my heart broke that I'd scared her.

"Your dad's probably on his way," Donovan said.

It was obvious by Donovan's protective tone that he knew why I'd come here. Ava had probably filled him in.

Leaning forward over the safety board, I looked downward. The manta rays glided effortlessly through the water, almost like they were performing some kind of dance.

I felt Donovan's hand on my lower back, rubbing in gentle circles. The touch almost did me in.

"Aren't they beautiful?" I asked.

He leaned forward. "Absolutely. It's no wonder some people think they represent peace and tranquility."

I rested my chin on my arms, which were folded on the railing. "I can certainly use some of that right now."

"Some people also call them devil fish."

I faced him. "You're making that up."

He laughed. "I'm not. It's only because of their shape." He pointed downward. "See how the lobes alongside their mouths look like horns?"

"That's just not right. I'll never call you that," I said to the rays below us. "You're too lovely." We sat in silence for a minute or two before I said, "I should've known. About my dad and Carmella."

"How?"

"In hindsight, Dad voluntarily exercising was a big tip-off. If he were dying, he'd probably be eating his weight in MoonPies, not jogging off the pounds."

Donovan smiled. "Men do like to look good for their ladies. Take me, for example. I shaved today because I planned to see you."

I glanced at him, unsure what to say to that.

"I went by your house earlier," he said. "I wanted to apologize."

"You don't owe me—"

"But I do. I'm sorry I upset you. I stuck my big nose where it didn't belong."

"It's not a big nose. It's perfect. I shouldn't have been so testy. I've been"—I smiled—"a little overwhelmed by all the things going on in my life."

He had the good manners not to say *I know.*

I swung my legs. "I've been doing a lot of thinking about those things since I've been sitting here. Mostly about my father and why he didn't just tell me he was dating."

It might be time for me to let go.

My father's words floated into my head. I realized now he hadn't been talking about the coffee shop at all.

He'd meant it was time to let go of the hope that one day Mama would simply show up as if she hadn't been gone at all. That she'd return to the life she'd left as if nothing had ever happened. That she'd resume her place in our lives—as Dez's wife, Maggie's mama—and reclaim her rightful place at the coffee shop.

"After my mama disappeared, my dad and I used to come down to the beach every day. We'd walk. Long walks. Miles. Just looking. Hoping for a miracle. Praying for one. Time passed and we didn't walk so far. Then we'd walk only a few times a week. More time passed and we'd just sit on the beach and watch the water. Right here is where we feel closest to her."

We hadn't held a memorial for my mama. Or a funeral. Or anything that would make us officially say she was gone forever. Through the years of uncertainty, our hope that she'd one day return had anchored her to us and us to her.

But now I realized that I'd been holding on to the hope more tightly than my father had been.

My voice cracked as I said to Donovan, "I couldn't marry you because I couldn't move away from Driftwood. I had to be here in case my mama came back."

But she wasn't coming home.

She was gone. Lost forever to the sea.

A tear rolled out of the corner of my eye, and I thumbed it away.

"I know, Maggie. I've always known."

I gazed into his eyes. "You have, haven't you?"

"It didn't stop me from trying to get you to leave, though."

He looked out over the railing, watched the manta rays. I wondered if he was thinking about his dream of rescuing my mama.

"And I couldn't even fight you about it," he said, "because you made us all, everyone in town, hope that miracles *were* possible. None of us, especially not me, wanted to break your heart all over again."

A tear dripped off my face. "I don't know how you're even here now, after I broke *your* heart. I'm so sorry for all the years we lost that we could've had together. And I'm sorry that Noah missed out on you being his dad, because you'd have been a great dad. And I'm so very sorry I never even stopped to think about what you wanted out of life, what you needed, when I begged you to stay here with me."

He faced me, those ocean eyes filled with emotion. "I'll tell you why I'm here. Because I finally realized what I wanted out of life, what I needed was *you*. I tried to forget you, tried to move on. Then I'd visit home and fall for you all over again. Each time, I had to force myself to leave. Last time I was home—it was right around Christmas, remember?"

I nodded. We'd gone out of our way to avoid meeting under the mistletoe at his brother's Christmas party.

"When I saw you there in the glow of the lights, laughing at something Noah had said, I almost couldn't breathe, I was so full of regret. It hit me like a sucker punch that I'd made the biggest mistake of my life. For the last twenty years I had tried to convince myself that I loved my job more than you. It wasn't true. I shouldn't have been so stubborn. I could've found another career."

"No—I shouldn't have made you choose. Look at what you've done with your job. The countless people you saved. That's not a mistake. That could never be a mistake. My mama would be *so* proud of you. I know it. *I'm* so proud of you."

Moisture glistened on his eyelashes. "I hurt myself by choosing that life, instead of staying and compromising. But at Christmas, I realized it wasn't too late to change, to make other choices. That's when I decided to come back and win you over with my charm and wit." He batted his eyelashes and looked ridiculous doing it. "Is it working?"

I smiled through my tears. "It's not like it was a challenge. I loved you twenty years ago. I love you now. I never stopped."

He pulled me into his arms, held me close. "Maggie Brightwell, I've loved you since before I even knew what love truly was."

I sniffled and buried my face in his chest. "What now?" I asked.

"I vote we start making up for lost time as soon as possible."

I smiled into his shirt and nodded. "It's unanimous, then."

He held on for a bit longer before saying, "Now that we have that settled . . . What're your thoughts on your dad and Carmella? I was stunned when I heard."

Heartbroken was the word that came immediately to mind, and I tried to pinpoint the specific reason why.

"It feels like fresh grief. Like I just lost my mama all over again. Because I never truly allowed myself to believe she was gone forever, now I'm facing the cold, hard truth. And it hurts."

His voice was soft, gentle as he said, "It's common among people who've lost loved ones to the sea. It's called ambiguous loss. There's no physical closure. Emotionally, it's hard to accept what we can't see. The typical stages of grief don't apply."

I could tell he'd had this conversation with others before, and my heart hurt thinking of the tragedies he'd seen. "I can see now that over the last couple of months, my dad has been trying to ease me into facing reality, because he knew I was holding on to the past. Holding on to my mama. I have to let go of the hope, because she's not coming back. *She's not coming back*."

I had to face the truth, face my fears, find a way to deal with my grief. It was the only way I could truly move on, to live my own life, and stop trying to live *hers*.

His eyes were damp as he leaned in and kissed my forehead. "I'm so sorry."

I released a shuddery breath. "I want my dad to be happy. I want Carmella to be happy. I love them both. I'm feeling embarrassed that he's been treating me with kid gloves about the whole thing, but I know why he did. I understand. I truly do. I wasn't ready."

"And you are now?"

I smiled sadly at him. "I'm closer."

The boards of the pier vibrated underneath me and I glanced over my shoulder. My dad was walking this way.

"I'll let you two talk." Donovan pulled his legs back onto the pier. "But I'll be waiting for you when you're done."

I grabbed his hand. "Will you do me a favor?"

"Name it."

I glanced down at the manta rays. "I don't want to fear the water anymore. Once you get that boat of yours, will you take me out in it?"

"Listen," he said, smiling. "I'll take you anywhere you want.

Except if it's to a place that involves an octopus. I have to draw the line. I have my pride, after all." He pulled me in close and kissed the top of my head. "Never mind. I'll do it even if it involves an octopus. I'll do anything for you, Maggie."

In that case, maybe I'd also ask him to pack some peaches-and-cream cupcakes for that boat ride. Because suddenly all I could hear was Boomy Eldridge shouting about sweet rewards.

As Donovan walked away, I stood up and leaned against the top railing. My legs ached and there was the sting of a sunburn on the back of my neck and arms. But for the first time in a long time, my head didn't hurt, not even a little.

A lot of the pressure I'd been holding in had been released. I'd let go.

The air shifted as my dad stepped up next to me. He said, "I'm sorry, Magpie. Really sorry for not telling you about Carmella and me. I should have."

"If you had told me months ago, I don't know how I would've reacted. Not well, I'm sure. I needed you to ease me into it the way you did."

"After your mama disappeared, I should've found you someone to talk to. I saw what you were doing. Afraid to leave town, afraid of losing people you loved. So afraid, you just held on more tightly, dug your heels in, took on too much. But I didn't do anything. Because if you talked about it, then I'd have to as well. And talking about it made all those feelings come to the surface, and I'd gotten real good at stuffing them down, of filling that empty space with *things*. I'm sorry I failed you."

"You didn't fail me. I think we both coped the best way we could. We're still coping. We'll probably cope forever."

"Sure enough." His left hand wrapped around the penny pendant.

His ring finger was still bare, but the tan line was still visible. My chest squeezed, and I had to tell myself to just feel the emotions I was feeling. Jumping from denial, the first stage of grief, straight to acceptance, that last stage, wasn't possible. It was a well-known process for a reason, and I needed time to work through all the stages—something I should've done a long time ago.

"What now?" I asked. "Between you and Carmella?"

"We're going to be moving in together. We found a house down the beach, the old Kendrick place. We'll give it a good reno, make it ours. Something we built together."

It hurt. It hurt that it wasn't my mother by his side, taking on a new adventure, but he'd had enough pain in his life. If Carmella made him happy, that's all that truly mattered.

"I gather that's what the yard sale was all about."

"Clean slate," he said.

"But you love your treasures."

He said, "I love Carmella more. After we became a couple, I didn't need my collection to fill the lonely hole in my life anymore."

I swallowed hard. "Were you really sleepwalking the night you were found out in your skivvies?"

Grinning, he said, "No. I'd been at Carmella's. It was late, and I heard a noise outside. When I went out to investigate, I locked myself out. She didn't hear my knocking, so I was trying to sneak back home."

I couldn't help smiling, imaging the scene.

"I should've told you about us then and there," he said, "but I was scared of how you'd react."

I swallowed over a lump in my throat.

"I want to marry her, Magpie. *That's* why I went to see the probate attorney."

I sagged a bit from the weight of his statement. Technically, he was still married, because Mama had never officially been declared dead. That had to change if he wanted to marry again, and a probate attorney would need to be the one to petition the court.

I gazed out at the gulf, which stretched wide across the horizon. A sailboat in the distance sliced through the water, its vivid rainbow-striped sails a welcome pop of color against the cloudy skies. I wanted to tell him I was happy he'd found love again, but I couldn't quite say the words aloud. Maybe tomorrow, when my heart didn't hurt so much.

"It's time," I said quietly.

He nodded, his eyes full of tears. "What about you?" he finally asked. "What now? Still want to buy the coffee shop?"

"The bank denied my loan application."

He set his forearms on the railing, clasped his hands, and watched the rays. "So that's that?"

"I'm not giving up that easily. I'll find another way. Delaney mentioned that she'd be interested in investing if I needed help. I might take her up on it."

"You'd do that? Take on investors?"

I watched the manta rays. They were mesmerizing. "I love that coffee shop. It's *mine,* and I'll do what I have to in order to keep it."

Emotion washed over his face, darkening his eyes, twisting his lips, pinching his nose so that the skin on its bridge wrinkled. Once the wave passed, he smiled, slight at first, then big and toothy. "I see. I see."

I leveled him with a knowing gaze. "You put Mama's notebook in the storeroom on purpose, so that I'd find it."

His eyes twinkled. "I found it in my storage unit and thought you needed to know, to understand, that the coffee shop wasn't your mama's end-all, be-all. It was more of a lark. Another adventure. What it's become . . . that's not because of her. That's because of your hard work. Your dedication."

My eyes once again filled with tears as I watched the manta rays drift away from the pilings, swimming east, their wide, dark bodies effortlessly and beautifully gliding through the water as though they'd choreographed their departure. I wanted them to stay, but I knew it was best for them to keep moving forward.

Dad threw his arm around me. "Also, great news! The seller of the coffee shop has lowered his asking price. He's even offering seller financing to the right buyer."

The way he lit up when he was excited never failed to make me smile. I loved him more than he would ever know. "You don't have to do that."

"But Magpie, I *want* to. I didn't offer it straight off the bat, because I was waiting for you to see what everyone else has known for a long time now. The coffee shop isn't the heart of this town. You are."

CHAPTER 26

AVA

Titus Pomeroy was a man on a mission.

That much was clear by the way he impatiently paced the sidewalk in front of the coffee shop early Saturday morning, waiting for someone to unlock the doors to let him inside.

It was, after all, already five past seven. The church bells had long stopped tolling the hour. Foot traffic was picking up. Cars already lined the square, scoring prime spots ahead of the yard sale rush.

Titus kept peeking through the window, then glancing at his watch, then through the window again, hoping to catch someone's attention. He obviously knew Rose had returned from her unexpectedly extended trip.

"We should probably unlock the doors," I said to her, hearing the exasperation in his exhales through the closed door.

Rose and I had been busy since we'd stepped into the shop half an hour ago, setting up, accepting deliveries, and bracing ourselves for the long day ahead without Maggie's energy and guidance.

"A few more minutes won't hurt him none." Rose smiled as she glanced toward the door, a hint of anticipation in her voice.

A few other people joined Titus on the sidewalk, and I was glad I was here to help out Rose. I didn't think I would be. Last night, I'd had every intention of quitting both my jobs, effective immediately.

My exhaustion had other ideas, however. After Sam had walked me back to Dez's, I'd gone upstairs to pack my things. I'd done a decent job of it, too, until I ran out of steam and sat down on the bed to rest my eyes a minute.

Next thing I knew, my phone alarm was going off this morning. Molly had been curled up next to me, her fluffy head tucked under my chin. She let out a sharp *meow* as I reached across her to hit the snooze button, then hopped to her feet and sauntered toward the foot of the bed.

I'd grinned at her. "Were you snuggling?"

She turned her back on me and flicked her tail.

"You were." There was no mistaking the delight in my tone. "You were *cuddling.*"

Still ignoring me, she licked a paw and started washing her face.

I laughed until a sharp pain hit deep in my chest, an ache that had nothing to do with my physical ailments and everything to do with reality.

I had to leave. And I didn't know how to say goodbye to Molly. I had slowly gained her trust and was starting to earn her love. She was never going to understand.

I decided I'd go to my mother's house in Tampa, then figure out where to go from there. I wasn't going to move back to Ohio. I couldn't. Especially not now that I knew how magical the beach was. I'd find another coastal town and start over.

I could do it. I didn't want to, but I could. If anything had come out of this wild-goose chase, it was that knowledge.

When my snooze alarm beeped, startling me out of my thoughts, I cleared the alarm and noticed I had unread text messages from both Maggie and Dez.

I hadn't been at all sure I wanted to see what they had to say, but curiosity got the best of me. Gathering up my courage, I'd opened the message from Maggie first.

> Stopped by to see you but you're asleep and I don't want to wake you. I'm so sorry for scaring you. All is well. See you tomorrow.

The message had been sent with a bunch of heart emojis, and it was absolutely ridiculous how much those hearts meant to me.

All is well.

All. Is. Well.

Her words went round and round in my head, filling me with hope.

Holding my breath, I'd opened Dez's message.

I've got a job offer for you, Sprite. Staying at Carmella's tonight. Talk tomorrow.

Sprite. His pet name for me. Surely if he was angry, he wouldn't have used the special nickname, would he? Plus, a job offer. My broken spirit started stitching itself back together with strong sparkly thread.

"Molly, a job offer!"

She paused in grooming her tail and glared at me, her big blue eyes radiating sorrow.

At her look, my breath caught, and I deflated.

Most likely, Dez's job offer wouldn't be for a position at his home. It wouldn't be with Molly.

A mournful lump grew in my throat as I said, "I'll visit as often as I can."

With a graceful leap, she hopped off the bed and ran out of the room.

I'd searched for her before I left for work at the coffeehouse, but she clearly did not want to be found. "I'll talk to Dez," I said aloud in the great room, hoping she could hear me. "I'll see what we can work out."

As I stood there, talking to her, I could only imagine what my mother would say if she could see me now, trying to console a cat. The thought made me smile, despite my mood.

I needed to call her, my mom. All the talk yesterday about truth and secrets had worked its way under my skin. I shouldn't have kept the truth from her. Not about moving down here. Not about my health.

"I'll be back later, Molly," I yelled. "I'll see if Norman can come over for a while."

I waited for a hiss or a meow or anything but heard only my own voice reverberating off the tall ceilings.

I hated to leave, but I was already late for my shift.

When I arrived at the coffeehouse, I'd fully expected to see Maggie, but only Rose was there. Apparently, Maggie had called her late last night and asked if she could handle the opening, because Maggie wanted to take the morning off to sleep in.

Rose had wiggled her eyebrows suggestively. "I heard Donovan's voice in the background suggesting she take a whole *week* off."

Grinning, I had filled the grinder with beans. "Good for her."

The two of them had looked awfully cozy at the end of the pier yesterday, and I hoped whatever had caused their rift earlier this week was now behind them.

Rose made a test espresso to make sure the machine didn't need an adjustment. "I said the same thing. Nothing wrong with a little TLC. Not a darn thing."

I smiled at her. "Are we still talking about Maggie?"

She smacked me with a rag. "You hush your mouth."

"Yes, ma'am," I said, unable to keep the laughter out of my voice.

Now, at nearly ten past seven I walked through the dining room, taking chairs off tables. She stayed behind the counter, working diligently on getting everything up and running for what was sure to be quite the crowd.

Once all the chairs were down, I glanced at Rose. "Ready?"

"As I'll ever be."

I walked to the door, turned the locks, and pushed it open. "Good morning! Welcome to Magpie's."

Titus strutted in, but hung back as others streamed in around him, heading for the counter. His dreadlocks were tied back off his face, and he was dressed in a crisp short-sleeve buttondown and shorts that looked freshly pressed. He held no gifts. His hands were tucked into his pockets as he studied the menu board he probably knew by heart.

Rose's gaze kept flicking to him as we worked through the orders quickly and efficiently, clearing the queue. When she turned toward Titus, I heard her draw in a breath, as if bolstering her courage.

Titus met her gaze and they stared at each other for what felt like an eternity before he took a step toward the counter. Just when he was about to speak, the door opened yet again and Estrelle came inside. Titus huffed out a breath and stepped back once more.

Apparently, he didn't want an audience for what he had to say to Rose.

Estrelle said, "Good morning, Titus," as she stepped past him.

"Good morning, ma'am."

"You were here first." She swept a hand toward the counter.

"No, no. You go ahead. I insist."

She smiled as if knowing exactly why he was biding his time. Today she wore a floor-length black caftan with black lace detail at the collar. As she walked toward me, her curved shoulders led the way, and the dress swirled dreamily around her. From my spot behind the counter, she appeared to be floating.

"Good morning, Estrelle." I was already reaching for a cup. "You're out and about early."

Her silvery eyes glittered behind her black veil. "Who can sleep with all the metamorphoses happening around here?"

Metamorphoses. I didn't think it was coincidence that she used that particular term. I glanced toward the wide front window and was grateful not to see a white-winged monarch fluttering there. Even though it was long past its caterpillar stage, it was still transforming, wasn't it? What would happen when its fourth wing turned completely white?

"Your usual?" I asked.

"Make it a large." She stared at me, her gaze unwavering. "Long, stormy day ahead."

A shiver swept up my spine. I thought the *storm* she'd predicted yesterday had been Maggie learning the truth about Dez's relationship. What else was there?

"Whatever it is, just remember," she said. "The sun will shine again."

"I wish you'd stop doing that."

"Doing what?"

"You know what."

"As I've mentioned—"

"Yes, yes. *Old*. I know."

"Such impertinence." She shook her head.

Rose stared at me like she thought I was at dire risk of an imminent, severe case of halitosis.

I gave her a reassuring smile. I wasn't afraid of Estrelle.

Much.

The old woman chuckled.

I rolled my eyes and made her drink. I was just sliding the cup across the counter to her when Javier and Redmond came inside the shop. When Redmond saw Estrelle at the counter, he tried to walk back out again, but Javier snagged his arm.

"Good morning," Rose and I said in unison.

Titus let out an impatient sigh and moved over to the recipe board as if completely captivated by the ingredients in Boomy Eldridge's cream cups.

Estrelle also murmured a good morning and was just about to tap her credit card on the reader when Javier held his hand out to stop her.

"That's on us," he said. "As a thank-you. It turns out that flexibility works wonders for fixing broken hearts."

With his face shining with good health, Javier was dressed in nice pressed slacks and a dress shirt and tie, and Redmond was in his new-and-improved upscale athletic wear. They stood close, side by side.

It appeared that the reconciliation everyone had been hoping for had taken place.

"How thoughtful of you," Estrelle said. "Ava, I'd also like a raspberry Danish, if you will."

Redmond's jaw dropped.

Javier only laughed as I pulled a Danish from the bakery case and put it on a plate.

Estrelle's eyes had softened behind her veil, and I thought I caught a hint of a tear as she picked up her drink and the raspberry Danish and carried them to her usual table.

I glanced at Titus, but he still had his back to us, so I smiled at Javier and Redmond. "What can I get for you two?"

Javier said, "An iced mocha with almond milk and a cinnamon . . . muffin."

Redmond said, "I'll try an iced caramel latte today. To go, please."

I was going to have to remember the flexibility advice for the future. It sure seemed to have worked wonders for these two. Both had bent just enough not to break.

Rose and I had their order together in no time flat. As soon as they headed for the door, Titus hotfooted it to the counter before someone else came inside.

I sidestepped once, twice, and grabbed a rag. I hurried around the counter to wipe a table that was already spotlessly clean.

"Good morning, Titus," Rose said, her chin lifted.

"Hello, Rose. Did you have a good trip?"

"It was fruitful despite its unexpected turns. I'm glad to be back. What would you like today?"

Titus scratched his chin. He hemmed, he hawed. Finally, he said, "Today I'll have a black coffee, please."

I'd been absently running a rag across a tabletop and my hand stilled. A black coffee? I threw a look at Estrelle. She had both eyebrows lifted and a smile on her lips.

Rose was moving about behind the counter, working on a drink that was very much *not* a black coffee.

"We're out of drip coffee today," she said, clearly lying, as both machines were nearly full. "Might I offer another recommendation?"

I gave up all pretense of cleaning anything and watched the pair of them.

Titus tipped his head, obviously puzzled. "What do you suggest?"

"Do you like matcha?"

"Y-yes. Do you have matcha?"

"Is this not a well-established coffeehouse? *Of course* we have matcha."

Suddenly catching on to the real reason Rose had gone to Georgia, I smiled so wide my cheeks hurt. She might've visited family while there, yes, but I had no doubt she'd also stopped by a certain boutique coffee shop to learn a special recipe.

"I didn't see it on the menu," Titus said, measuring his words carefully.

"Sometimes we make exceptions. How about lavender? Or chai?" she asked loftily, as if she suggested these options a dozen times a day. "Care for those flavors?"

His lip twitched, and it seemed like he was trying his best to suppress a smile but couldn't stop it from forming. It burst forth, blooming like a delicate flower bud reaching for a shaft of sunlight. "In fact, I do."

"Then I have just the thing for you. Just give me a quick second."

"I have all the time in the world for you."

I just about swooned. I didn't think people could actually swoon. I thought it was simply an old-timey phrase thrown around in historical romances, but no. It's real.

Rose glanced at Titus. For a moment, I was certain they didn't know anyone else existed. It was only the two of them in a magical bubble. I could only imagine the silent promises that crossed between. My heart was full to bursting. They made me believe that there could be happily-ever-afters. That there *were* happily-ever-afters.

A woman came inside and glanced around in the way that told me she'd never been here before, and Rose and Titus both turned toward the door, bursting their romantic bubble. Rose quickly looked down as if she'd been caught doing something she shouldn't have and finished making the drink.

She slid it across the counter, ice cubes bobbing in the milky green liquid. "One iced matcha latte, with a double shot of espresso, chai, and lavender syrup. On the house, since you're such a loyal customer here at Magpie's. Anything else I can do for you today?"

I held my breath. Even the newcomer was watching them carefully, as if instinctively knowing Something Major was happening here. Tension crackled in the air.

Titus said, "Yes, in fact. I'd like it very much if you'd join me for dinner, Rose. Tonight? Tomorrow? Whenever you have time to spare."

I glanced at Estrelle and grinned. Her eyes were dancing as she took in the scene, and it was wonderful to see the joy in her silvery gaze.

Rose lifted her chin. "For you, I have all the time in the world."

He smiled, and she returned it tenfold, absolutely beaming.

"Tonight, then. Six P.M.? I'll pick you up." He lifted his fancy coffee off the counter. "Thank you for this. It means more to me than you'll ever know."

With that, he gave her a nod and headed for the door.

We all watched him leave, and the woman who'd come in said, "I don't suppose he has a single brother?"

Rose smiled. "I'm not sure, but if he does, you best snap him up fast."

I came around the counter to help with the new order, and I glanced at Rose, who had a goofy grin on her face. "What happened to not dating men who iron their jeans?"

She huffed. "Like I said, Ava, sometimes we make exceptions."

I was still laughing when I heard the door open and instantly the room went quiet. All the noise was sucked out into the square, leaving only a heavy silence.

I looked up and my breath caught. My heart squeezed. My head spun.

Because a ghost had just walked in.

My whole body started shaking, and I swayed, lightheaded and woozy, feeling faint. The last thing I remembered before my world went dark was saying Alexander's name.

"I've been waiting for you," a voice said as I blinked against the hospital lighting, slowly waking after a much-needed nap.

Outside, orange streaked the sky as the sun set. Inside, my head ached, my thoughts raced.

I yawned and tried to sit upright. "Good thing you had that large hot chocolate this morning to hold you over."

"I told you it was going to be a long day," Estrelle said.

I winced against the pain pulsing in my head. I'd smacked it but good when I fainted at the coffee shop this morning.

Right after the ghost had walked in and changed my life forever.

From what I'd gathered in bits and pieces since, Rose had called an ambulance and Estrelle had ridden over to the hospital with me. She'd been nearby all day, mostly in the periphery, while I'd been examined in the emergency department, while I'd given a detailed history of my health problems. She'd waited while I'd had tests done. She'd listened as I explained to Maggie and Dez what was wrong with me.

Well. I'd explained some. But not all.

I'd shared most. But not everything.

Not yet.

Some things I was still piecing together.

"You didn't have to wait for me to wake up," I said. "You must be exhausted. You should go home, get some rest."

The hospital staff had wanted to keep me overnight for observation. The hospital was in Foley, well inland, and I already missed the sound of the waves.

Estrelle sat in an armchair next to my bed. Her veil was lifted up, off her face. There was a visitor sticker stuck to her caftan. "I didn't mind waiting until you woke up. I've been waiting for you for *months* now. What's a little more time?"

I rolled slightly to face her better, making sure the IV line didn't get caught up in the bedding. Over my shoulder, monitors kept track of my every breath. "Months?"

"Ever since *I* placed the thimble among Maggie's curiosities."

My eyes widened. "You put the thimble there? But how did Maggie know to give it to me?"

She waved a dismissive hand. "Such is a trifling matter, that.

The more important issue at hand is *why* I put it there. That is the question you should be asking."

I adjusted the hospital blanket and said in a stilted tone, "Estrelle, *why* would you put the thimble there?"

She smiled, a slight quirking of her lips. "Because I need to plan ahead. We all live on borrowed time, and I've borrowed more than my fair share. Don't look so desolate. No one can stay forever."

"But . . . I don't want you to go."

The thought alone filled me with deep, dark sadness. I'd come to care for her greatly in such a short time.

Something soft and glowing filled her eyes. "If you wish, I will try to delay my departure as long as possible."

"I wish."

Oh, how I wished.

She nodded. "Even so, I put the thimble in the Curiosity Corner because I found myself in want of a protégée. Someone who, perchance, would one day inherit my shop. It could not be just anyone. It had to be someone *special*. Unique. Different. Someone with a creative eye. A big heart. Someone who understood the delicate fabric of life and the intricate stitches that hold it together. Someone who would come to love this town, its people, as much as I do."

I listened carefully, trying my hardest to follow along. One thing that jumped out was that for the first time in my life, being called special didn't rankle. It made me feel . . . seen. Loved.

"When I saw you standing outside Magpie's the day you arrived, I knew you were the one I'd been waiting for. Which came as quite a surprise to me, and I shall let you know now, I am not surprised easily."

I used the same stilted tone as earlier as I asked, "Estrelle, why were you surprised?"

She chuckled. "Because, child, I didn't know you were the match for the thimble when I sent for you. I'd known only that you'd *be happy in Driftwood*."

There was something revealing in the way she spoke, her spirited tone, that made me study her more closely.

She lifted an eyebrow, challenging me to make the connection.

I sat up. "It was you? *You* sent me the letter? Why?"

Her eyes flashed. Liquid silver. "In light of your current condition, I thought you would be better suited here with all of us."

With all of us.

Her. Maggie and Dez. Rose. Juniper and Grace. Hannah and Jolly. Norman and Sam.

Sam. His name echoed around my head, making it hurt worse than the concussion I'd suffered.

Estrelle stood up, patted my hand, and placed a gift bag on the bed next to me. The bag itself was designed in Stitchery colors. I had the feeling I knew what was in it.

"But how did you even know of *me*? My condition? I don't understand."

"Questions for another day. The only one that matters now is whether becoming my protégée is of interest to you. These are mighty big shoes you'd need to fill, after all."

I lifted an eyebrow, purposely copying her trait. "I don't actually have to wear those particular shoes, do I?"

She glanced upward, as if seeking advice from her pillbox hat. "Do not sass. It is not becoming."

I smiled. "Estrelle, I'd be honored to learn from you."

She acknowledged my words with only a slight nod.

"I'll let you rest now." She lowered her veil and headed for the door. There, she turned back to me. "I'm most pleased my letter brought you to Driftwood, Ava. I fully believe everyone deserves the chance to fly. Some, like you, deserve that chance more than others."

I swiped at a tear. "Thank you. For everything."

With a nod, she was gone.

I leaned back against the pillows, my mind spinning as I looked at the monitors.

According to the doctors, my epilepsy was still, miraculously, in remission. Earlier, my EEG and MRI had been deemed unremarkable. *Normal.* Only two blood tests had been flagged. One was my iron level—I was anemic.

I opened the gift bag Estrelle had given me, parted the tissue paper, and lifted out a folded square of soft fabric printed with smiling dachshunds. I shook the square loose, letting the fabric fall open, then I hugged it close to my chest. When I saw Estrelle working on this piece in her shop recently, I thought it had been intended as a toddler's shirt or dress. But I'd been wrong. It was a small sleeper sack, the perfect size for a newborn.

The other test out of whack? The elevated level of hCG, a type of hormone, in my blood.

An ultrasound had confirmed the result—I was two months pregnant.

CHAPTER 27

MAGGIE

"A cat-taker?" Ava said, her voice holding a note of disbelief.

"Just hear me out, Sprite. It's like a caretaker, but for *cats*."

I stood just inside the French doors at my father's house, listening to the conversation taking place in the screen room. There was a pile of MoonPies on the table, and seeing them made me smile.

Dad and I had brought Ava home from the hospital early this morning. She'd been advised by the doctors to take it easy for the next week, and so far she seemed to be taking the instructions to heart. Since getting back, she'd been outside, sitting in the shade, sipping from a big glass of water. In between visitors, she'd been quiet, staring out at the water.

She had a lot to think about, what with the baby and all. I'd been in her shoes once, facing single motherhood, taken by surprise, caught completely off guard. I knew how hard it was to deal with all the emotions.

She claimed she'd had absolutely no idea that her health issues lately could be caused by pregnancy. It would've been the last thing I thought of, too, considering all she had going on in her life. What with Alexander's death, moving here, and the health history she'd revealed to us.

It was a complicated situation she was in, to be sure. But she'd been insistent from the moment that she first heard the news that she was keeping the baby, and it had been easy to see her motherly instincts taking root as she wrapped her arms around herself protectively.

I knew those instincts. Knew them well.

My gaze skipped to the water, where two young men were trying to surf in weak swells. Joe Rains and Noah.

I wanted nothing more than to call them out of the water, to see Noah's feet on the beach, away from the dangers of the sea, but instead I took a deep breath, let it out slowly. I fought hard to hear the sound of his laughter—because I could tell by my son's body language that he was having a blast—but the sound was lost to the southerly winds.

I was glad to see him having fun. He'd arrived yesterday for a surprise visit and had been caught up in the whirlwind of what had happened with Ava.

"It's obvious Molly adores you," Dad was saying to her.

That was true. Molly was currently curled up on Ava's lap. I'd never seen her so docile in my whole life and thought perhaps that Ava was some sort of magical cat whisperer.

"As much as I love her," Dad added, "Carmella is highly allergic. I'm going to need someone to care for Molly."

Ava ran her hand over Molly's back.

"You can live here with her until we find you a smaller place. I have a home in mind. A sweet cottage near the church."

"I can't afford—"

"It's a rental of mine. Tenants are planning to move out before Christmas. Rent is reasonable. Landlord is a peach."

She cracked a smile. "Hard to pass up a peach of a landlord."

"This is what I'm trying to say."

"And Molly will come with me?" she asked, her tone hopeful. "If I move to the rental?"

He swallowed hard, and I realized how difficult this was for him, having to choose between two loves. "It would set my mind—and heart—at ease knowing she's with someone who loves her as much as I do."

Ava said, "I'm not sure why it feels like you're doing me the favor rather than the other way around."

"*Pshaw.*" He waved a hand. "It was all simply meant to be."

Puffy white clouds filled the sky, blocking out the sun, keeping temperatures reasonable, in the low eighties. The water was a deep blue green today that reminded me of Donovan's eyes.

He'd come by earlier with sweets from the bakery. Many people had come by, in fact. Bettina and Sienna. Jolly. Gracie and Juniper. Rose and Titus. Each had given Ava a big hug and offers of support, and they brought baby gifts—clothes, toys, a cradle.

Noticeably absent was Sam. It was impossible not to see the hope in Ava's eyes every time the doorbell rang, then the disappointment.

"Now, tell me what you need," Dad said. "A drink? A snack?"

"Actually, all I'd like for now is to talk to Maggie."

"Oh. Well, that's easy enough." He stood up and looked my way, clearly knowing I'd been listening the whole time. "I'm going to leave you two ladies alone and go out and play with the boys. It's been a long time since I hauled these old bones onto a surfboard, and I'm looking forward to it."

Automatically, I said, "Be careful."

His eyes crinkled as he smiled. "Always, Magpie. Always."

As he headed for his bedroom to change, I stepped onto the porch and took his seat. "How's your head?"

"Not terrible," she said. "How's yours?"

"Actually, it's been good ever since the day on the pier. My blood pressure is the lowest it's been in years. I'd been holding a lot in, I guess. I never did thank you—"

"Please don't. I shouldn't have butted in."

"But Ava, if you hadn't, my head might have exploded, and did you really want that on your conscience?"

She laughed. "Well, put that way . . ."

I reached over, took hold of her hand. Molly lifted her head and gave me the evil eye but didn't hiss or take a swipe at me. "Thank you."

Her eyes were full of affection, of friendship. Then they darkened a fraction. "There is something else I need to talk to you about."

Instantly, I went on alert. "Are you all right? Do you feel okay?"

She pulled her hand free of mine and reached for her phone. "Physically, yes. Emotionally, I'll get there. Everyone's been incredible. I never expected to feel like I found a family here."

"You *are* family."

Again, something dark crossed her eyes. "Honorary, yes, but this baby . . . I think this baby has real family here in Driftwood. *Biological* family."

I didn't understand. "What do you mean?"

She looked out at the water. "Yesterday, when I fainted, it was because I thought I saw a ghost walk inside the coffee shop."

"A ghost? Like, a real one? Not Carmella?"

"It wasn't Carmella, and it felt real, but it was only Noah."

I sat up straighter. *"Noah?"*

He'd told me how when he walked in the door of the shop yesterday, Ava had gone pale and started shaking, but I hadn't thought it had anything to do with *him*.

"The moment he pulled open that door, my world started spinning. He's the spitting image of— Hold on." She swiped at her phone and held up a photo. "Do you recognize him?"

My heart started beating faster as I looked at the image of the man on her phone. The wide smile, the curly hair, those blue eyes. I'd know him anywhere. Especially since my son favored him. "Theo Bryant," I breathed.

She said, "I'd only ever seen Noah in old pictures and with a hat on, but seeing him older, in person, with those curls, there was no denying the resemblance." She studied the man in the picture on the phone. "I know this man as *Alexander*," she said. "His full name, as you probably know, was Theodosius Alexander Bryant. He once told me he started going by Alexander in his twenties, and I never really thought much of it, because he was always reinventing himself."

My heart was pounding. "Theo is Alexander?" Realization hit hard, and I gasped. "Your baby . . ."

She watched me carefully with those big green eyes of hers. "Will be Noah's sibling. Half sibling."

Thoughts were coming faster than I could sort them out. Theo was Alex. And he was gone. I watched Noah paddle on the surfboard. Although he'd never yearned to meet his father, I always wondered if he'd change his mind one day. Now he'd never get the chance. Tears stung my eyes.

Ava had told me earlier how Estrelle had been the one who sent the letter, and now I fully understood why she'd done so. "No wonder Estrelle sent for you. Because of Noah, she must've been keeping tabs on Theo through the years. Although she'd never been a fan of Theo's, she loves Noah. She'd want him to know his sibling. And"—I glanced at her—"I suspect she knew she'd come to love you, too."

She nodded, smiling weakly. "I still don't understand how she knows things. I didn't even know I was pregnant, how did she?"

"I have no idea. But I do know she's a softie at heart. She'd want us all together. One big strange family."

She smiled the smile I loved so much. "The strangest."

AVA

Later that night, I reclined in one of the lounge chairs on the back deck, watching the stars, listening to the waves. It had been a long day, full of revelations and surprises, of friendship and *family*.

My eyes had welled with tears when Noah gave me a hug and gifted me with the silver rattle etched with a boat before heading back to school. I didn't know what the future looked like for him and my little one, but I had the feeling they'd be as close as they could be for their age difference.

I had spent a lot of the day trying to come to terms with the fact that my baby would never know Alexander. And I couldn't help wondering if Alexander would've done to our child what he'd done to Noah. Walk away with barely a glance backward.

I was afraid, deep in my heart, I knew the answer.

Alex hadn't wanted to be tied down.

I put a hand on my stomach and closed my eyes, listening intently. Now that I knew what I was hearing, I could pick out the baby's heartbeat, a rapid thump, thump, thump. I wasn't sure why I hadn't heard it before yesterday. Or maybe I had and just chalked it up to something else being *off* within me. But being able to hear it now brought me comfort, helped me to relax.

The porch light spilled muted, sea turtle–friendly orange-red light across the deck, and moths hovered nearby—but no butterflies, for which I was grateful. Dez had offered up an all-natural mosquito repellent when I told him I was going to sit outside for a while, and it felt as though I were sitting in a eucalyptus forest as I listened to the soothing waves hum me a lullaby.

My chest ached, thinking of Sam. He hadn't come by today. I tried not to give his absence too much thought because it hurt just a little too much for me to deal with right now.

"Be right back, Sprite," Dez said from inside the screen room. "You'll be okay while I'm gone?"

"I will." I swung my legs off the lounger to face where he stood in the screen room. He was going to pick up takeout from the Salty Southerner, having insisted upon staying home tonight in case I needed him. Honestly, he'd been more of a caretaker to me today than I'd ever been to him. "Before you go, Dez, can I ask you a strange question?"

"Strange questions are my favorite kind. Hit me with it."

There was one thing about the whole Carmella situation I still didn't understand. "When I first met you, do you remember the seaweed scent we all smelled? And how the air had gone still?"

"How can I forget your ghost? That was something else."

Then he frowned, likely realizing that it hadn't been Alexander with us that day after all, since it had been Estrelle who sent the letter that brought me here.

"Have you smelled that scent since?" I glanced over his shoulder. "In the house?"

He scratched his beard. "Can't say I have. Why? Have you?"

"A couple of times."

"Interesting. Might could be you've got *someone* watching over you after all. How exciting!"

I didn't find the idea as delightful as he did. I found it puzzling.

I was still thinking about it minutes later, after he left to pick up dinner, and only my phone buzzing snapped me out of my thoughts.

> **Mom:** Wilson and I'll be there tomorrow at noon. Anything you need me to bring?

There had been no stopping her once she'd heard—and listened to—everything I'd had to say when I called her earlier. Even though I told her I was fine, she'd insisted she needed to see me with her own eyes, hug me. I had the feeling her hug was going to be a lot like Bettina's and I'd need a pry bar to wiggle loose. I was okay with that. In fact, I found that I looked forward to it.

> **Me:** Not a thing other than you
> **Mom:** See you soon. I love you
> **Me:** I love you too

I put my phone down and stood up. Moonlight created a glittery river of light on the water, and I struggled to tear myself away from its beauty, to go inside to set the table for dinner.

I was still standing there when I heard footsteps on the deck boards and the jingle of dog tags. My breath caught as I turned and saw Norman running toward me along the side porch. I crouched down and opened my arms and he jumped into them. I laughed as he wiggled and licked my face, whining happily.

Sam stepped hesitantly forward, carrying a small package wrapped in tissue paper. "Hope we're not interrupting. On his way out, Dez told us you were back here."

I stood up, keeping Norman in my arms. "Not interrupting at all."

Sam rushed forward. "Should you be lifting him? I can take him."

He'd come so close I could see the warm gold flecks in his eyes. I kept hold of Norman. "He's fine. I'm fine."

I wasn't sure how many times I'd need to say it before anyone believed it. Before I believed it. The worry that my seizures would return was always going to be in the back of my mind, because it would always be a possibility, despite any kind of remission. However, the doctors assured me that even if my disorder did return, epilepsy patients had healthy babies all the time. It had been a relief to hear those words.

"The nurses at the hospital gave me some tips for dealing with morning sickness, so I'm already feeling much better," I added. Might as well get it out in the open. Lay it bare. No doubt he probably knew every detail of my hospital stay by this point.

My heart was beating wildly as I gazed at him, feeling like there was a great distance between us even though we stood only two feet apart.

"I brought you something." He held up the package.

"You didn't have to—"

"I wanted to."

Reluctantly, I put Norman down, and he immediately ran to the screen room, to where Molly sat watching us. The last I'd seen her, she'd been asleep in her pot on the stove. I was going to have to ask Dez if he'd give me that pot, because I didn't think Molly would move in with me otherwise. I opened the door and let Norman inside, and the two of them started bumping noses and rubbing heads.

Sometimes we found friends in the unlikeliest places.

"Come on in, out of the mosquito zone," I said to Sam.

He lunged forward to hold open the door for me, and I brushed past him, picking up his scent, that mix of citrus and hazelnut. I ached with wanting his arms around me, with wanting things that seemed impossibly out of reach now.

I sat in one of the cushioned chairs at the table and he sat in another, and for a moment, we simply watched Norman and Molly tumble and play. Then Sam handed over the package he held.

I took the gift from him and shot him a look as I ran my hands along the shape of it. "What in the world?"

He smiled as I carefully tore the paper, revealing a maraca

with a wooden handle and green egg-shaped head dotted with yellow polka dots.

Sam leaned forward, clasping his hands. "Baby's first instrument."

I smiled as I shook the maraca, listening to the beads or beans or whatever it was inside make a beautiful, soothing sound.

"It's basically a glorified rattle," he added.

I fought tears. I didn't want to cry. I didn't want to make a scene. I didn't want to beg for nothing to change between us. I couldn't. *Everything* had changed. Weakly, I said, "Thank you."

"I debated between that or the tambourine, but the tambourine isn't as baby friendly—the edge on jingles can be sharp sometimes. It's a better gift for an older child, so I'll save that idea. I'm happy to teach him or her any instrument they want to learn, though." He took a breath. "I mean, if you want."

A spark of hope ignited. My heart thumped so loudly I could barely hear his words. I slid him a look. "I want."

"I'm sorry I didn't go to the hospital to see you. I didn't want you to think I was trying to step in and take over your care; though, God's honest truth, I wanted to make sure the doctors were doing a good job. And today, I spent most of the day trying to think of just the right words to say to you. I didn't want to get it wrong."

Not trusting my voice, I simply nodded. I didn't want to get it wrong, either.

"I overthought it, because seeing you was all I needed to find the right words."

He was watching me carefully, now twisting his hands.

I waited for the words, but he stayed silent.

Finally, I said, "Are you keeping the words to yourself?"

He laughed. "You'll hear them soon enough."

Some of the tension eased from my shoulders. "That's rather mysterious."

He hesitated a beat before saying, "I haven't been voted Driftwood's Mr. Mysterious two years running for nothing."

He reached a hand out to me, palm up. I laid my hand in his. His fingers closed around mine and we sat there listening to the night songs and the water's sweet melody until Dez came home with dinner.

Hours later, I turned off the light, more than ready for a good night's sleep. Molly was curled up at the foot of the bed, but when I slid under the covers, she made her way up to my pillow, climbed atop it.

I reached up and scratched her chin, and she let out the shortest purr I'd ever heard, a brief rumble of happiness that I felt deep in my heart.

In the darkness, I smiled. And I waited, listening for what I knew was coming.

It didn't take long.

Sam played the guitar tonight and I focused, wondering what song he would choose in our little game of instrumental *Name That Tune*. The song that would have all the right words.

But as he strummed, I was having trouble placing the song. There was definitely a country vibe to it, with its three-chord pattern. I sat up in bed, tossed the covers off, and walked to the front window. I looked out in the darkness, toward Sam's place, as if being closer would somehow help me identify the tune.

I was surprised to see him sitting on the steps of his house, his head down as he played, his foot lightly tapping on a stair. Norman sat next to him, his tail wagging.

As I listened, I focused on the emotions I heard in the music, feeling the yearning, the anguish, the hope, the plea. It was as if my heart recognized the melody but my mind couldn't find the lyrics to go along with it.

Just when I began to realize that this might be an original song of his, I heard Sam's voice, that slightly raspy, altogether entrancing voice, as he began to sing.

> *Count me out, I'm out of luck*
> *Count me out, I'm out of love*

A broken heart, a quiet life
Until you walked in
Until you walked in

I could barely breathe, caught in the movement of the song, the growing crescendo of that last line. I nearly burst into tears as he sang, his voice cracking and aching—almost crying. Then his voice dropped on the next line, almost to a whisper.

Saying let it ride, let it ride

The crescendo built again, his voice growing stronger, the ache replaced with a sense of wonder.

Count me in, I'm in luck again
Count me in, I found love again
A mended heart that can hear again
Because you walked in
You walked in

He held the last note, letting it drift into the night between us. Then his head lifted, and he looked toward my bedroom window, even though I didn't think he could see me.

"What do you say, Ava? Will you take a chance on me and let what we've been building over the last couple of weeks ride? See where life takes us?"

Tears spilled down my cheeks as what he sang and what he said sank deeply into my soul. It took me a second to gather my senses, then I rushed out of my room, down the stairs, and flung open the front door.

Across the street, he stood and set his guitar on the porch. We stared at each other a moment before I smiled, dashed down the steps, and ran toward him.

He met me in the middle of the street, arms wide, and I threw myself at him, holding him tight.

He smelled of hazelnut and citrus, deep woods and love.

Norman *quabark*ed as he ran around us, and just over Sam's

shoulder, near those pink pylons, I spotted an iridescent butter-fly glowing brightly, like a flash of sunlight. As if it knew I had seen it, it burst into a glittery cloud like a pearly firework, its sparkles slowly giving way to the darkness.

In my head, I heard Dez telling me how butterflies repre-sented new beginnings and transformation. And then I heard Estrelle telling me that until I stopped looking behind me and letting fear hold me back, that the butterfly wouldn't be able to fly free.

And suddenly I knew.

The butterfly represented *me*.

I'd learned to love myself, the old me *and* the new one, too. I'd learned to stop being so scared all the time.

I'd learned to fly.

"Count me in," I said to Sam, my voice breaking. "Count me in."

CHAPTER 28

AVA

No one could've asked for a better day for the Butterfly Fest. Warm but not too warm, with fat white clouds puffed up with charm, their scalloped edges awash in pale golden light. And then there were the butterflies. So many butterflies. Hundreds. Maybe thousands. Their orange wings glowed in the brightness of the day, and they were absolutely captivating as they rested and refueled on delicate milkweed branches.

"Hmm." Sam studied the patchwork animal in his hand, then glanced around the green, his gaze skipping from face to face, tent to tent.

There were many tourists among us, but he was searching for those I knew personally, closely. While I waited for him to finish his perusal, I bent down and patted Norman, who lay in the shade of the table next to my tennis shoes. I'd walked the Butterfly Fest 5K this morning without stopping once for a breather. In fact, I felt better than I ever had now that I was in my second trimester. Norman rolled onto his back, offering up his belly, and I laughed.

The stuffed animal Sam held was a patchwork duck. A crested duck, in fact. It was made of colorful fabric squares, some solid, others printed with clams, snails, shells, sailboats. On its head was a white faux-fur pom-pom.

I'd finished it only last night, one of many patchwork animals I'd worked on in the past month. For every one I made to sell, I made a bear to donate to the local hospital, for the kids who arrived there without a stuffed friend from home to keep them company, bring them comfort. A Junebear of their very own.

Sam laughed. "Is this based on Bettina? Did she see it yet?"

Across the green, the Happy Clams had set up a dunk tank. Five dollars a toss to see a fish, specifically a Bettina Fish, take a swim, with all the proceeds going toward their Mardi Gras float-restoration fund.

Sam had already easily identified the baby goose made of dandelion print that smelled of strawberries as Juniper, the lion that resembled Molly, the dog that favored Norman, the dark ostrich that was a dead ringer for Estrelle, the chicken that had been inspired by Cluck-Cluck, and the feminine octopus that represented Maggie. He'd been stumped only by the seal pup that reminded me of Dez. There were other patchwork animals on the table that didn't represent anyone at all but were simply based on animals I'd noticed around town, like a pelican and a gecko. Then, of course, there were the patchwork butterflies. I hadn't made a white iridescent butterfly yet. I was saving that project to make for my little girl, who was due in springtime, to always remind her to be true to herself, to trust herself, to accept herself just the way she was.

Nodding, I smiled. "Not yet. Do you think she'll see herself in it?"

"Can't see how she wouldn't."

I laughed. The duck was actually one of my favorites that I'd made, playful and quirky but still charming and adorable.

He glanced at his watch. "I should go set up."

"Nervous?"

"A little."

"You're going to be amazing."

"You're just saying that because you love me."

"While that is true, it has nothing to do with your talent."

He'd been back in the studio for a month now, working on new songs, and had decided to test a few of them out here at the festival. It was a surprise performance—no one other than a trusted few even knew he was a singer-songwriter.

He bent down and kissed me. "I'll save you a seat."

As I watched him walk toward the makeshift stage, I thought back to the first day I'd arrived in town. A lot had changed in that time, yet a lot had stayed the same as well.

The church bell still tolled every hour from dawn to dusk. The Mermaids gathered in force after every storm. The Snail Slippers met every Monday, Wednesday, and Friday in the square, with Bettina leading the charge. Estrelle wore all black.

Sienna was now baking at the bakery and hadn't had a single mishap since starting work in the kitchen. In fact, she was flourishing there. Redmond and Javier had added another cockatiel to the family. Marvin. He hadn't escaped once.

Dez had moved in with Carmella and had just closed on the private sale of his house. They were engaged but no wedding date had been set yet. He wanted a beach wedding behind the house they'd bought together but Carmella wanted a church wedding. I had the feeling she was going to win that stand-off. They had taken a lot of guff for going about life the wrong way around, moving in before getting married, but both laughed it off, just glad to be together at all.

Magpie's continued to thrive. Titus had come out of retirement to work alongside Rose at the coffee shop and had convinced Maggie to expand the drinks menu. He was in charge of creating new flavorings, and his first attempt, a brown-sugar-and-cinnamon latte he'd named Sugar Pie, had been an instant hit.

"Estrelle tells me there's an octopus over here with my name on it."

I turned toward an approaching Maggie. She wore a Magpie's T-shirt, denim shorts, and a big smile. All morning she'd been manning a coffee cart not too far from my booth, but currently sixteen-year-old Ambrose Symons stood there in her place, making a hot chocolate for Estrelle, who appeared to be giving him instructions on how to do his job correctly. Poor kid.

Ambrose was another of Magpie's new hires. He'd been an excellent addition to the staff and even managed to keep focus whenever Candi Chitwood came into the shop wearing her crop tops, tank tops, or strappy dresses. A miracle, because Candi was always a sight to behold.

I worked at the coffee shop only once a week now, on Thursdays. The other weekdays I spent at Stitchery, learning anything and everything I could from Estrelle. Word had gotten around that I repaired and restored stuffed animals, and I was already backlogged with the work that had come in. Estrelle and I had cleared a corner of the store for me to have a sewing space of my own. It was a full-time job in and of itself, but I loved every second of piecing back together something so well loved and full of memories.

Maggie dropped down in the seat next to mine and picked up the patchwork octopus on the table, her gaze flicking over the stitches, the fabrics. "Oh my goodness, Ava." Tears filled her eyes as she lifted each of the eight arms carefully, lovingly. One was done in a dinosaur print, another patterned with coffee cups. There were tentacles of orange hearts with the word *Coastie* on them, a nickname for the Coast Guard; flowers; hearts; black Converse sneakers; butterflies; and finally, a penny print.

"I need to buy this."

"No, you don't."

"Yes, I do."

"No," I said. "You don't. It's yours. It's a gift. I wasn't selling it—I was just waiting for a minute to give it to you."

"Really?" She threw her arms around me. "I love it so much. Thank you."

I returned the hug, squeezing her tightly. "You're welcome."

When she pulled away, she leaned back in the chair and looked at the octopus. "This is truly amazing. Have you sold many of the others?"

"I had thirty when we opened this morning." There were only ten or so left.

"You're going to have to turn Stitchery into a stuffed animal shop. You know that, don't you? Repairing, restoring, and creating them."

My heartbeat picked up at the thought of it. "We'll see. Did I hear that you matched a curiosity this morning?"

"Did Estrelle tell you? She saw it all happen. I swear, she's the biggest source of gossip in town." Maggie looked toward the cart, found Estrelle scowling at her, and grinned. "I said what I said."

Estrelle waved a dismissive hand and turned her back on us but not before I'd seen affection shining in her eyes. It was clear to anyone who paid attention just how much she adored Maggie.

I laughed. "What did you match?"

"The hand-carved spoon with the curly handle? It went home with the lawyer from northern Alabama who took over Donovan's lease."

Donovan had recently moved in with Maggie, and it had set tongues wagging about Maggie acting just like her father, living life backward. She took no offense. In fact, she grinned at the comparison.

She had been taking more time off now that she had steady help at the shop, and hadn't joined any new clubs, though she'd been sorely tempted by the scrapbooking club Misty Keith had started in addition to running the book club. I swore Donovan moved in with her just to nip that in the bud and give her something else to focus on.

"Did you find out what he's doing down here, the lawyer?" The man's arrival in Driftwood was the latest town gossip to make the rounds, which had come hot on the heels of Dodge Cunningham and Ernestine Aiken being caught getting *really friendly* on the beach late one night. Much to everyone's disappointment, no garden gnomes had been nearby.

Everything that had happened with me was old news now. Soon, though, I would be the hot topic once again.

"No, but maybe you can get it out of Estrelle. She always seems to have the inside scoop." She glanced over at the coffee cart, saw a line forming, and stood up. "I need to get back. Are you ready for the concert?"

"More than."

She grinned. "Me too. Keeping the secret has been killing me."

She wasn't talking about Sam's music. She was talking about how two weeks ago, a dozen of Sam's and my nearest and dearest had gathered in Gatlinburg to watch us get married in a little chapel in the mountains. Sam was going to share the news with the town today before he started his set.

Life's short, he once said. Too short to be unhappy, living apart, when we knew we were supposed to be together. It felt more like destiny than a whim.

We'd bought our last scratch-off ticket on the day of our wedding. When we hit it big with a hundred-dollar win, we decided that it was time to pass our luck on to someone else. We eventually dropped the ticket in the donation bin at the church on the day we signed the papers to buy Dez's house—Sam finally getting the beachfront property he'd wanted all along. Molly and Norman might be happier living together than we were, and that was saying something.

Maggie gave me another squeeze and took her octopus, hugging it close as she walked away. When she crossed paths with Estrelle, the older woman said, "It's not gossip if it's *true.*"

Maggie laughed and kept on walking.

Estrelle sat down next to me, holding her cup of hot chocolate. "He almost forgot the cinnamon."

I smiled. "He'll learn soon enough."

Norman stirred and I refilled his dish of water and rubbed his ears, which suddenly perked up. He started *quabark*ing as Hannah Smith barreled up to the table. She'd moved on from Cinderella and was now in a *Toy Story* phase. She was dressed like Woody, complete with hat (which covered the part of her head that had needed to be shaved for her surgery), cow-print vest, and cowboy boots. Personally, I missed her light-up sneakers.

"Miz Ava! Miz Ava! Reach for the sky!"

I threw my hands in the air.

She giggled. "Look at my boot!" She lifted her foot, and on the bottom of her boot, someone had written *Andy* in shaky letters.

"I love it!" I said, daring to lower my arms. Behind her, I saw Jolly weaving through the crowd, tracking her energetic granddaughter. Cluck-Cluck was leading the way, straining at her leash.

It had been good news from the hospital. The best news. The tumor had been benign.

"How's Junebear?" I asked.

She looked down at the ground. "Someone got marker on her."

I lifted an eyebrow. "Someone?"

She nodded vigorously. "Might could've been a ghost."

If Dez heard her now, he'd laugh his fool head off. His *ghost* story had taken root in town and now everyone seemed to use it as an excuse for bad behavior.

"Well, bring her to me and I'll get her cleaned up for you, okay?"

She threw her arms around me. "Thank you, Miz Ava! Bye!"

She veered off, running toward the cotton candy machine. Jolly froze, threw a hand in the air, then pivoted to follow. "Lord have mercy, child. Slow down!"

Estrelle took a slow sip of her drink. "That'll be you soon enough, running after your little one."

I put my hand on my stomach, which was still, somehow, flat. The doctor assured me I would round out soon enough. "I'm looking forward to it."

Coming from behind the stage, I picked up the sound of Sam's guitar. He was practicing the opening of "Count Me In," which he'd been tweaking endlessly over the last few weeks. I personally thought the original was faultless, but trusted him when it came to songwriting.

People drifted by the Stitchery tent, picking up, putting down, *ooh*ing, *aah*ing. Most people who stopped bought something. A coaster, a bib, a patchwork animal. Across the way, I heard someone whispering about Estrelle and asking why she always wore black.

Estrelle put her cup down as if ready to stand up and afflict someone with warts.

"Mourning her youth," someone answered.

Estrelle laughed. "That's funny. I'll have to remember that one."

I'd come to realize her hearing was just as good as mine. If not better.

She picked up the ostrich and glanced at me. "The pillbox hat is a nice touch. My hips aren't that wide, however."

I'd named the piece *A Kooky Old Bird*. I smiled. "Artistic license."

She lifted an eyebrow, then pursed her lips. She took a marker from the table and changed the three on the thirty-dollar price tag to an eight, making it eighty dollars. "Don't you dare sell it for a penny less. *It has been said.*"

I laughed, then picked a piece of lint off my shorts as I searched for the right words to start a hard conversation. "Maggie says the curiosity she matched this morning went to the man renting the Pink Peony Cottage. Don't suppose you know anything about him I can pass along?"

"To pass along? No."

"But you know something."

"I know everything."

I rubbed the edge of the table. "About that . . ." I'd wanted to talk to her about this for weeks now but had been waiting for just the right moment. Now that it was here, however, I was suddenly hesitant.

"Spit it out, child."

I shifted in my seat to face her. "I was thinking about how every time I've seen Maggie match a curiosity, you're either in the store or nearby. Maggie also once mentioned her first memory of you was the day her mother disappeared. You were on the beach the day she found the penny in the sand. She's always thought that her mother somehow gifted her with her abilities when she disappeared, but I'm starting to think maybe her abilities came from . . ." I broke off, finding it incredibly difficult to suggest that it had been Estrelle behind the abilities all along. "You," I finished, my heart in my throat.

Estrelle lifted her veil and leveled me with her silvery stare.

The air around us stilled, and I lost myself in the deep, murky gray depths, seeing pain and love and manta rays and pennies and cockatiels and sparkly white butterflies.

Suddenly, I was able to pick up her scent. She smelled of

warm pecans and cocoa, sea breezes and devotion. And sea-weed. The salty scent filled the air and blew around us in a swirl of silvery sparkles.

"Perhaps," she said evenly, "you are both correct."

My breath caught, and my eyes filled with tears, blurring my vision. Suddenly *everything* made a strange sort of sense. Her *knowing*. The butterfly. Junebear's sea-glass nose.

Once, she'd told me we all lived on borrowed time and that she'd borrowed more than her fair share. I hadn't quite realized the enormity of that statement until now.

As the truth sank in, I tried to understand how it was possible she was still here but couldn't quite. Then I realized it didn't matter. All that mattered was that she *was* here, that she'd somehow delayed her departure—and I hoped she'd continue to do so for a long time to come.

Estrelle lowered her veil, lifted her drink. "It's probably best if we keep this conversation to ourselves. Consider it payment in full for that tab I've been keeping."

I glanced at Maggie, laughing with Donovan, who'd come up behind her to give her a hug. I saw Dez, who sat on a blanket on the green, clapping for the jugglers on the stage. Norman started *quabark*ing as Bettina shrieked just before landing in the dunk tank with a loud splash. Somewhere in the crowd, Hannah shouted, "Somebody's poisoned the water hole!" The church bell tolled twice, the sound echoing wide and far. In the distance the waves crashed against the beach. Stunning butterflies colored the sky orange.

It was beautiful chaos.

I reached over and hesitantly took hold of Estrelle's cold hand. After a second, she closed her gnarled fingers over mine. It took me a moment to find my voice. Finally, I said, "To think I ever wanted a normal life."

She laughed, that strange *otherworldly* laugh.

It turned out I hadn't wanted normalcy at all. I'd wanted—and had found—acceptance, for being myself, flaws and all. I was the same person I'd been all along: quirky, creative, loving, curious, different, *special*.

Just like most everyone in this town.

This perfectly enchanting, magical town, where whims were the norm, life existed after death, and love was often in the air, caught on a salty sea breeze.

ACKNOWLEDGMENTS

First and foremost, thank you to generous, talented barista Chris G. for your invaluable help, especially with creating Titus's specialty drinks. Remember, if you ever write a barista tell-all, I'll be the first in line to buy a copy. Needless to say, any barista-type errors are solely mine.

An enormous thank-you goes to editor Kristin Sevick for your help in shaping this book into what it has become. You have an amazing ability to point me in the right direction, for which I'm truly grateful. Thank you, too, to everyone at Forge, who always go above and beyond. Also, a special thank-you to Macmillan Audio and incredible narrators, Stephanie Willis and Hallie Ricardo.

Thank you, Jessica Faust—and the whole BookEnds team. I'm continuously amazed at what you do behind the scenes.

To all the readers, thank you for choosing my books, loving them, and spreading the word about them. If you were as enchanted with Cluck-Cluck as I was, you might enjoy this Facebook page I found during my research: facebook.com/alabamabeachchicken.

A special thank-you to my father, who inspired the electrical fire scene in this story, for the reminder to never plug large appliances into power strips.

And *thank you* doesn't seem quite big enough when it comes to my family, who help me through the hardest days (writing and otherwise) with offers of tea, cookies, smiles, and hugs. Much love.